The Silver Wheel

MARY GILLGANNON

D1737623

To Patrick—because every woman needs a warrior to fight for her.

Acknowledgement

The Silver Wheel would not have been published without the help of my dear writer friends who read and re-read it in its many incarnations and who advised and encouraged me on the long journey to publication. Thank you CAWG members Jeana Byrne, Liz Roadifer and Michael Shay, my sister-of-the heart Jessica Wulf, Joanne Kennedy, Anne Holmberg (who read the first flawed awful manuscript) and a special thanks to Amanda Cabot, the consummate professional and proofreader.

Part 1
Lady of the Moon

Northwest Wales
57 C.E.

Chapter 1

Sirona's heartbeat quickened as she and the two other young women followed the Drui into the darkened forest. The wind murmured in the high branches of the huge oak and beech trees, seeming to whisper of ominous secrets, and the faintly sweet scent rising up from the soft ground beneath her feet seemed to bear the odor of death. She told herself she shouldn't feel so apprehensive. This should be a night of celebration, marking her passage from childhood to womanhood. But she couldn't seem to banish the gnawing anxiety in her stomach.

In the bright moonlight, she began to recognize familiar landmarks: The copse where she'd gathered beechnuts the previous fall. An old gnarled oak, the top blackened by lightning three sunseasons ago. A thicket of blackthorn, the berries just barely beginning to form. All at once, she knew where they were going. They were headed straight for the lake of the dead.

It wasn't much of a lake anymore. Shallow and more marsh than open water. Yet she'd heard it was once deep and clear, teeming with fish. She'd also heard more than a few chilling tales about the fens and the malevolent spirits that dwelled there, the lingering essences of those poor unfortunates who'd died badly and hadn't been able to cross over to the Other Side.

She and her fellow students of the grove, Cruthin and Bryn, scoffing at the stories, had come here several times over the past few sunseasons. But it was always during the day, when the moist air was clouded with insects, and bright copper butterflies fluttered among the bulrushes and water dock. It was different at night, when the mist floated along the ground and everything was reduced to shadows and shapes. Again, Sirona felt a chill of foreboding trace along her spine.

The Drui halted in an open area among the maze of weeds and bushes, close to a pool of water that reflected the glowing silver disc of the moon. Fiach, the head Drui, motioned for the three young women to come forward. With his long arms and tall upright form, he reminded Sirona of a bird of prey. He spoke in his sonorous voice: "We come here this night to welcome Enat, Cailin and Sirona to their new lives as women. We ask the gods to protect them, to make them fertile and to give them long lives. We ask this in the name of Rhiannon, Ceridwen and Arianrhod, protectors of women and givers of life."

1

He made a graceful motion with his hand, then gestured to Cailin. "Give me what you have brought to sacrifice."

Cailin handed him a silver brooch shaped like a deer. Fiach intoned, "She offers this gift that the gods might be pleased and know her as a devoted and faithful woman, one who gives proper reverence to the gods of three realms: the underworld of the deep, the realm of the sky and the realm of this earth." He motioned to indicate the three domains, and then threw the brooch into the water where it landed with a splash.

Fiach repeated the ceremony with Enat, whose offering was an enamel necklace. When it was Sirona's turn, she took off the gold torc, which had come from the chest holding her mother's things at the back of the hut she shared with her grandmother. The torc was fashioned of intertwined snakes, their eyes set with glowing red garnets. It had an eerie, seductive beauty and a part of Sirona didn't want to give up. She quickly quelled the blasphemous thought and handed the piece to Fiach. He cast it into the water and repeated the ceremonial words.

Sirona thought they were finished, but then she looked at Fiach and saw he held a small, curved knife in his hand. He grabbed her wrist and pulled her close to the water. "Sirona, daughter of Banon," he said. "You will die this night."

Her breathing quickened, even though she told herself she was being ridiculous. Fiach wasn't going to kill her.

The head Drui continued, "As a *child*, you will die this night...to be reborn as a woman." He took the knife and carefully nicked her wrist, making a few drops of blood well up. Then he shook her arm so the blood fell into the dark water. "Sirona the child is gone, consigned to the depths of this pool. In her place arises Sirona, the woman." He took a strip of cloth from Cuill and rapidly bound up her wrist.

Fiach repeated the blood-letting with Cailin and Enat, then said to the three of them, "I want each of you to go off by yourself and pray to the gods, asking them for the things you wish for in your life as a woman. Think carefully about these things, for this night you are in the shadowland between two worlds and the gods are close. They will listen and remember."

Sirona dutifully started walking in the direction Fiach had indicated. Her heart was pounding even faster now, but she told herself not to be such a coward. As a student of the grove, she knew the importance of this part of the ritual. She and the other women were being tested, just as the young men of the tribe were tested when they spent the night alone in the forest during their man-making.

She took a deep breath, aware of the throbbing pain in her wrist. Pain, like the pain she would endure during childbirth. Blood, like the blood that had seeped from her body during her first moontime, marking her as a fertile woman. And now she was alone, severed from the safety and protection she'd known as a child. With her training to be a Learned One, she could see the meaning in the ceremony, the pattern it evoked. But for all she told herself she should be pleased and honored to have reached this place, she couldn't shake the sense that something awful was going to happen.

She tried to focus on the gods and her future. What did other young women ask for? Fertility? A long life? That a certain man they favored might ask them to handfast? She wasn't concerned with any of those things. All she desired was to continue to train in the grove. To be one of the Learned Ones and take her place as a valued member of the tribe. But it didn't seem like something she should have to ask the gods for. She was already training in the grove. Although Fiach might not be pleased about it, and some of her fellow students questioned whether a woman should be a Drui, that part of her future seemed assured.

Perhaps she wasn't meant to ask the gods for anything, but to seek out their will for her. Ogimos always said that if a person could quiet their own thoughts and still the wild rush of words and images, the gods' spirit would enter them. *Take deep, even breaths*, he said. *Relax your body, let your limbs grow heavy and your mind become empty and still. Imagine yourself as one of the great oaks, a tree that has stood for generations, alive, but quiet and waiting, enduring as the seasons pass in their endless cycle, the rhythm of life and death.*

An oak. She would be an oak. She felt the sap rise through her solid, inert body, rise and fall as the seasons passed. New leaves, the budding catkins turning into acorns, falling to the ground and sprouting new life beneath her branches. The moon shone down upon her, waxing and waning. Around her, the forest changed, green and lush in summer, gold and copper and brown in the fall, bleak and gray in winter. The creatures of the wood shared her branches, the hollows of her trunk. Birds and squirrels and insects, their lives dependent upon hers. She was part of the forest, all the trees and vines and grasses and ferns and mosses that drew nourishment from the earth.

And in the earth beneath, she could feel the ancient power from which all life sprang. Earth, water, air and sunshine. These were the things that fed her. These were the gods of the oak. And of all creatures.

At last she felt peaceful and content. She opened her eyes, relieved she had been able to make herself reach a state of mind appropriate to this important event. She was a woman now, and must seek to be wise and calm and knowing, like her grandmother Nesta. Like the oak. Someday she would be full Drui and pass on her knowledge and the ancient, sacred cycle could continue.

She glanced around, wondering how long it would be before the three Drui returned and escorted her and the other girls back to the dun. They might not come until morning. She considered sitting down on the grass to wait, but even as she had the thought, a light across the water caught her eye. There was another light…and another. Had the Drui lit torches to show them the way back to the settlement? But why, when they'd traveled here with no more illumination than the moon? Then she saw another glowing point, making four, and knew it couldn't be Fiach and others. But who else would come to the lake of the dead at night?

The lights moved closer. Drawing near to the water's edge, she strained to see. There was a group of people, a surprising number of people. Had the entire tribe come here to watch the woman-making ceremony? But if that were part of the ritual, she would know of it. Besides, the ceremony was over. Perhaps the dun had been attacked. But why not send a messenger? Certainly all these people wouldn't come to fetch them.

Yet there was undeniably a crowd gathered on the other side of the lake. And a lake it was now. There was much more open water here than she'd guessed. Why it had seemed like a small pool previously, she couldn't imagine. She decided to walk around the lake and see what was happening. If she watched where she was going, she would be in no danger of sinking into some hidden morass.

As she began walking, she realized she'd been mistaken. What she'd thought was the other side of the lake was really an island in the middle of it. That's where the people with torches were gathered. She was almost close enough to see the people, but she didn't recognize anyone. It must be the shifting shadows of the torchlight. Then she saw three figures dressed in white crys marked with the sacred colors of red and green. Ah, there were Fiach, Cuill and Flann after all.

Sirona pushed her way through the underbrush, trying to find a better vantage point from which to see. When she looked up again, she froze in place, her mouth open in a silent gasp. The three Drui encircled a young, naked woman, her small breasts clearly visible. The woman's scalp had been shorn, the hair cut so short that her scalp showed through the stubble, and her hands were bound behind her. As Sirona watched, one of the Drui—it must be Fiach—grabbed the woman's head and jerked it back, exposing her throat.

"No!" Sirona cried out. Fiach didn't move, didn't look across the water to see who had shouted. "No!" she screamed again, louder this time. None of the people gathered on the island seemed to hear her. Puzzled, Sirona tried once more. "Fiach!" she yelled at the top of her

4

lungs. "Fiach! Stop!"

There was no response. "In the name of the gods, stop!" Sirona cried. She desperately wanted to prevent the Drui from killing this woman. But there was nothing she could do.

Fiach made a quick motion with the knife and dark blood welled from the young woman's neck. Sirona let out a moan, then stiffened as another Drui stepped forward. He didn't look like Cuill or Flann. There was something in his hand. A small rope or thong. Sirona watched in horror as he wrapped it around the woman's neck and pulled it tight. The woman's body jerked and flailed. The third Drui came forward to grab the woman's hands and hold her still. Sirona closed her eyes. She didn't want to watch. To see this woman die, choking to death.

When she opened her eyes, the first Drui—who she now realized wasn't Fiach—had released the woman, but the other man held her limp body so she didn't fall. Her head lolled to one side and blood flowed freely down her body. The two Drui took hold of the woman's arms and the three men pushed her into the lake. She sank rapidly, so rapidly that Sirona realized they must have weighted her feet with something.

Sirona experienced a sense of panic. She felt as if she'd watched something forbidden. Her heart began to race as she thought about what might happen if she was discovered. She turned and began to run. But the ground was much wetter now and she sank into the mud up to her knees. She knew a moment of dread before she could free herself. After that, she watched where she was going, grimly keeping her gaze fixed on the ground and taking care with every step.

When she finally paused and looked around, she was shocked to realize the edge of the fens was still some distance away. Her distress grew more intense. She didn't want to remain in this place with the spirits of the dead, those who couldn't cross over. The girl who'd been sacrificed was one of them. She'd done something awful and been punished terribly. Now she was trapped here.

Nearly hysterical, Sirona began moving again. Her skin was slick with sweat. She stank of the swamp and her long gown was wet and muddy. The wound on her wrist throbbed and ached. But nothing was as awful as the thought that she might wander aimlessly in the marsh until she eventually collapsed and sank into the muck. Her body might lie there for days, until it was picked clean by birds and water creatures.

In her despair, she grew careless and lost her footing, pitching forward onto her hands and knees. As she caught her breath, she noticed the reflection of the moon in the small pool of water in front of her. Slowly, she raised her gaze to the heavens and stared at the silvery orb. "Arianrhod, Great Goddess, show me the way. Tell me what to do."

A sense of peace came over Sirona and she felt her body relax. She got to her feet and wiped her hands on her gown. Although she was covered with mud, she was unhurt.

She started forward and quickly reached solid ground. Pausing, she glanced back at the marsh. There was really nothing so frightening in this place. The sacrifice she'd seen hadn't been real. It was a dream of some kind. *Or a vision.*

The thought filled her with excitement. During her years in the grove, she'd sought to distinguish herself in some way. But it was difficult. Clever Cruthin always had an answer ready for any question their teachers asked. And for all his whining and complaining, Dichu had an excellent memory and could recite an amazing number of tales. She could easily outshine Math and Miach, but they'd only been training in the grove for a year. And while Bryn was an indifferent student, he was the chieftain's son. Everyone knew he'd be head Drui someday. Now something had happened that suggested she did belong in the grove. Although she didn't know what the vision meant, there was no doubt the gods had spoken to her.

As she left the lake of the dead behind and started back through the forest, Sirona's fear fell away. When she saw Fiach approaching with two warriors, she walked forward with calm dignity.

"Sirona," he demanded, "Where have you been?"

"I've been at the lake of the dead. I stayed there as you told me to."

"You weren't there when I went back to fetch you."

Fiach sounded angry, and Sirona grew uneasy. "You must have missed me. I was there the whole time."

Fiach glared at her. Watching him, Sirona realized it wasn't moonlight illuminating his stern features, but the first glow of the dawn. "You shouldn't have gone wandering alone around the marsh, Sirona," he said. "That was very foolish. You might have lost your way and been sucked down in the fens."

"I…of course," Sirona responded. Although she'd intended to tell Fiach about her vision, now, realizing how angry he was, she decided not to mention it. Perhaps she should discuss it with Old Ogimos first. He was the only one of her Drui teachers she really felt comfortable with.

One of the warriors, Rhodderi, stepped forward. "Your grandmother was very distressed when Fiach returned to the dun without you. She insisted we come and look for you."

Sirona stomach twisted with dismay. "I'm sorry. I never meant to worry anyone. It's only that—"

"You must remember your duty," Fiach snapped. "As a Drui-in-training you have a responsibility to the tribe. Your life is no longer your

6

own. It belongs to the gods!"

"I know, master Drui," Sirona responded, fighting back the sense of resentment she always felt around Fiach. Aye, her life did belong to the gods. And if that were true then the vision she had seen might well have implications for all the Tarisllwyth.

As they walked to the dun in the soft glowing light of dawn, Sirona felt a new sense of purpose. She was a woman now, and also a seeress.

Chapter 2

"Our spirits never die, but go to the Otherworld, from there to be reborn in another body. There is no reason to fear death. We are, all of us, imperishable, our spirits indestructible..."

Although Sirona usually found meaning in whatever Old Ogimos had to say, today as she sat in the grove with the other students, she could hardly keep her eyes open. By the time she'd arrived back at the dun, there'd barely been time to wash and change her clothing before lessons began. Even if she'd wanted to tell Nesta about her vision, there'd been no opportunity. Her grandmother was far too busy scolding her to listen to anything she had to say.

She forced her attention back to Old Ogimos. "The gods are all around us, everywhere," he intoned. "In every tree and stone, in every spring, river and lake. If you seek the quiet center of yourself and listen, the gods will speak to you. But you must be very quiet. You must learn to ignore the distractions of our world..."

It was so hard to be patient, Sirona thought. To wait until their lessons were over so she would have a chance to speak to Old Ogimos in private. She wondered what he would make of her vision, what it could possibly mean. Recalling the grisly sacrifice, she felt a stir of excitement along with her horror. It had seemed so real, as if it were happening at that moment. But now, thinking about it, she felt certain it had taken place long ago in the past, when the lake of the dead was truly a lake.

The main thing was that the vision had come to her, rather than someone else. It meant the gods thought she was worthy of such a gift. *Her*, rather than Cruthin. She shot a surreptitious glance at the lean, dark-haired youth. He looked bored, as if he'd heard everything Old Ogimos was saying many times before and had moved far beyond it. That might be true, but he shouldn't be so arrogant.

"A balance between our realm and the Otherworld must always be maintained," Old Ogimos continued. "Otherwise, the gods will grow angry and bring their wrath down upon us..."

Sirona wondered if the gods were watching even now. Did they know who was paying them proper respect, and who wasn't? She perused the other students. Dichu's narrow face wore a dutiful, serious expression, but that didn't mean he had any appreciation of what their teacher was saying, nor any real devotion to the gods. While Dichu might be gifted at memorizing, he never looked beneath the surface of things.

And Bryn—he was idly tracing the pattern of the great oak's leaves on the ground, his thoughts clearly far away. Sirona couldn't help wondering what the brawny, auburn-haired youth might have done in another life that the gods had cursed him like this. He was clearly meant to be a warrior, yet his father insisted he train in the grove.

She turned her attention back to Old Ogimos as he sighed and spoke in a wistful tone. "You're all so young. Too young to realize how fortunate you are to have been chosen for this destiny. It's a great honor to serve as a Learned One. If you are devoted and dutiful, you will eventually possess all the wisdom and knowledge of our tribe. You will learn the history of our people, the movements of the heavenly bodies in the sky, the stories and legends of our ancestors, the ancient rites by which we communicate with the gods. Knowledge is a powerful thing, more powerful than a warrior's sword arm. It's the only thing that lasts, that doesn't pass away when we die, because it can be carried on with the next generation. I plead with you to take your responsibilities seriously, to learn all you can in your time in the grove."

Sirona's chest squeezed with guilt. She hadn't listened, really listened, this day. She'd been too caught up in her own thoughts.

Old Ogimos used his walking stick to lever himself up. "I'm dismissing you from lessons, but that doesn't mean you're free of your responsibility to the gods. The rest of the day, I want you to think about your duty to Them and what it means for your life."

Sirona got up and waited for her chance. Bryn rushed out of the grove, like an arrow loosed from the bow. The red-haired twins, Math and Miach followed after him, laughing at some secret amusement they shared. Dichu moved off slowly, but Cruthin—curse him—didn't leave, but lingered near their teacher. Sirona couldn't understand why. Cruthin normally had little interest in Old Ogimos's lessons.

As her teacher used his walking stick to limp down the pathway, Sirona called, "Master Drui, wait! I would like to ask you something."

Old Ogimos turned his rheumy blue eyes on her and smiled kindly. Sirona hesitated. Although she wanted to talk to her teacher about her vision, she didn't want to Cruthin to overhear. Sirona shot the youth a resentful glance, but he still didn't move ahead of them.

Ogimos motioned to the pathway with his staff. "Come, Sirona. You can talk to me as we walk back to the dun."

Sirona fell in step beside the elderly Drui, measuring her pace to his plodding gait. "As you know, I had my woman-making last night," she said. "I found the ceremony very meaningful. I felt a real change in myself, as if I was leaving the foolishness of my childhood behind and becoming a woman."

Behind her, Cruthin sniggered. Sirona clenched her jaw and ignored him. "But after Fiach, Cuill and Flann left me, I had a strange experience. Everything in the marsh changed. It seemed there really was a lake, rather than pools of water here and there. In the middle of the lake was an island. I saw people assembling there, so I moved closer, to see what they were doing. In the center of the gathering were three Drui and a young woman. The woman's hair had been shorn and she was naked. The Drui led her to the edge of the water and there..." Sirona stopped walking and took a deep breath. All the feelings she'd experienced during the vision came rushing back. She felt afraid again, and horrified.

"And then what happened?" Cruthin asked from behind her. He sounded genuinely interested now, rather than mocking.

"First, they cut her throat. Then they strangled her. Finally, they pushed her into the lake."

"The triple death," Cruthin murmured. Sirona turned and stared at him. The idea that he had knowledge of this sacred rite irritated her.

"Aye," Old Ogimos said. "The triple death. It's a very powerful ritual."

Encouraged by her teacher's response, Sirona continued: "When I first realized they were going to kill her, I called out to the Drui, to try to get them to stop, but they didn't hear me. I realized then that what I was seeing wasn't real. That it was a vision. I decided it must be something that happened in the past, when there really was a lake in the marsh."

"I'm sure you're right," Old Ogimos agreed. "It's been many generations since a human life has been offered up to the gods."

"Although I feel honored to have experienced such a thing," said Sirona. "I can't help wondering what it means. Was it some sort of sign from the gods?"

Old Ogimos frowned in concentration, causing wrinkles to fan out around his eyes like ripples in a pond. "Visions are always difficult to interpret. It may not be a message from the gods at all."

Sirona tried to quell her sense of disappointment. "What, then? Why did I see what I saw?"

"The young woman you observed being sacrificed," her teacher asked, "Did she appear distraught, or did she go along with the ritual willingly?"

"I'm certain she was terrified," said Sirona. "I could sense her fear, and for awhile afterwards, I couldn't shake my own sense of dread." She was glad no one had been around to see how shamefully she'd behaved immediately after the vision, as she ran around in circles like a frightened child.

"Not a good death then," Old Ogimos said sadly. "Which means the young woman's spirit may not be able to pass peacefully over to the Other Side. Perhaps that's why you experienced what you did. Restless spirits sometimes reach out to the living, as if seeking our aid to help them find their way."

"But why me?" Sirona asked. "Why not one of the other young women? Or, Fiach, or Cuill or Flann?"

"I doubt that Cailin or Enat would ever have such an experience. Having never trained in the grove, they're unlikely to be open to the world of spirits. As for why you, rather than one of your teachers, there are many possible reasons. The unfortunate spirit may think a young woman would be more sympathetic to her fate than a man. There's also the fact that you seem to have a natural affinity for the Drui life. You take your lessons in the grove seriously and are thoughtful and wise beyond your years. Finally, it's possible it might be a warning of some kind."

"A warning?" Sirona asked. "What kind of warning?"

Old Ogimos started walking again. "Perhaps you're meant to realize you must be careful how you live your life, and avoid the mistakes that led to your mother's end."

"My mother?" Sirona knew very little about the woman who'd given birth to her. Whenever she pressed Nesta for information, her grandmother became almost angry. "I don't understand. What did my mother do that led to her death? Was she…" Sirona suppressed a shudder. "…sacrificed?"

"Of course not." Old Ogimos halted and his voice grew gentle. "Her death was an accident. No one intended for her to die."

"And yet, the choices she made led to her end?"

"That's true of most of us. How we live our lives usually influences how we will die."

Old Ogimos was being vague and enigmatic again. Sirona's stomach clenched tighter as her sense of foreboding grew. "*How* did my mother die?" she asked. "What are you trying to tell me?"

"The facts of your heritage should really come from your grandmother. Now that you're a woman, perhaps it's time for you to ask her these things." Old Ogimos gave Sirona a vague smile. "In truth, I don't think you're anything like your mother, except for your beauty. You've always been a dutiful and devoted student, and I'm certain you'll have a bright future ahead of you as a Learned One."

Old Ogimos turned away and started walking again, moving with his slow, awkward gait. Sirona watched him leave, feeling stunned. *What did my mother do? What terrible secret hangs over my life?*

"So, are you going to ask your grandmother about these things?"

Sirona turned in surprise, suddenly remembering Cruthin. He'd been there the whole while, listening.

"Aye, I will. Why do you ask? And why are you lurking around, spying on my private conversation with our teacher?"

Cruthin shrugged, but his dark eyes were intent and serious. "I thought you seemed different this day. At first, I imagined it was because you were now truly a woman in the eyes of the gods. But it seems it's something else. The gods have chosen you. The vision you had makes that clear."

She should be gratified to think that proud, mocking Cruthin was treating her with respect and a hint of awe. But she was far too upset to feel any real satisfaction. "I'm going to go speak to my grandmother now," she said as she left him.

She walked grimly to the dun and entered the small hut she shared with Nesta. Her grandmother was crouched down near the hearth, stirring some sort of disgusting-smelling herbal concoction in the iron cauldron. Nesta was a healer, and the tribe depended upon her for medicines.

Hands on her hips, Sirona faced her grandmother "How did my mother die? I want to know."

Nesta flashed Sirona a wary look, but continued to stir the contents of the cauldron. "What brought about this question? Are you upset because at the feast last night, Tadhg recited the genealogies of the other girls, but said nothing about your family?"

"Nay. It was something Old Ogimos said. He implied my mother made mistakes that led to her death."

Nesta stopped stirring. "What else did he say?"

"He said that perhaps I'm meant to learn from her mistakes. But since I don't know what they are, I don't see how I can possibly do that!" Sirona inwardly winced at the harsh, accusing tone of her voice. Her grandmother loved her. If she'd kept the truth from her, there must be a good reason.

Nesta removed the spoon from the herbal mixture and laid it on a flat rock near the hearth. She rubbed a hand over her face, as if suddenly weary. "Your mother was killed by wild animals one night when she was outside the dun."

This was the information she was supposed to use to shape her life? Sirona couldn't believe it.

"Of course, that's not all of it." Nesta sighed heavily. "She wouldn't have been outside the dun except Tarbelinus had banished her. He'd offered to send an escort with her, but Banon refused. She was always so proud and scornful. Perhaps that's the lesson you're meant to learn from her death." Nesta's pale blue eyes met Sirona's.

"Why did Tarbelinus's banish her?"

Nesta stood. "The real reason was that he wanted to be rid of her. He'd had his pleasure of Banon, yet she failed to give him a son. Rhyell, on the other hand, had done just that." Nesta faced Sirona, her expression grim. "Once Bryn was born, there was no hope for Banon. She might tempt and entice Tarbelinus, but she couldn't give him an heir. The chieftain's pride and arrogance overruled his lust. He had to get rid of her. And Banon, in her foolish rage, gave him the very means."

"What did she do?" Sirona whispered. Her whole body was rigid with expectation.

"She cursed us!" Nesta gestured angrily. "The whole tribe. She said she'd had a vision the Tarisllwyth would vanish from the earth. There was malice in her words. She clearly wanted it to be true. And she said something else...something I won't speak of. Tarbelinus was enraged, of course. He ordered her to leave his sight and never return. Later, he relented and agreed to give her an escort. But Banon had already gone."

Nesta's thin chest heaved. "She took you with her. I was terrified. You were only a babe. I thought I'd never see you again. But when her body was found the next morning, you were beside her, completely untouched. Everyone knew it was a sign that you were different than your mother." Her gaze met Sirona's. "They understood the gods had protected you. After that, it was easy to convince Fiach you should train in the grove."

It was an amazing story. Hearing it made Sirona feel many things. Anger at her mother. Awe that the gods had chosen to let her live. Grief for Nesta that her daughter had been so foolish and had died because of it.

Sirona went to her bedplace and sank down. "About my mother—did she have any other visions? Is there any reason to believe what she predicted might come to pass? Or, was it all a lie?"

Nesta returned to the hearth, picked up the spoon and resumed stirring. "It's hard to say whether it was a lie. Because we carry the blood of the Old Ones, the women of our line sometimes have the gift of sight. Banon might have had some sort of premonition of the future. But even if her knowledge came from a true Seeing, what she did was cruel and irresponsible. Visions don't always come true. From your Drui training, you must know that. But her goal was to frighten and distress us, to punish us. And that was wrong, terribly wrong."

Sirona swallowed hard. "It's a wonder that everyone at Mordarach doesn't hate me after my mother did such an awful thing."

Nesta left the cauldron and came over to where Sirona sat. "They know you're not like her. They also know the gods let you live, which means there must be some special purpose for your life."

Sirona nodded. She was special, chosen by the gods. It was a heady, exhilarating thought. Then she recalled something else. "You said that the women of our line are known to have the Sight, and you mentioned the Old Ones. Who are they?"

"The ancient race of Albion. I know little about them, except they trace their ancestry through the female line rather than the male. They're also said to know magic, but that's probably only a foolish tale."

"What do you mean, they're said to know magic?" Sirona asked.

Nesta shook her head impatiently. "Shapeshifting and that sort of thing, I suppose. As I said, it's probably not true."

"And why do you think we carry their blood?"

"It's obvious in the way we look. While the rest of the Tarisllwyth are tall and robust, those of our line are small of stature and delicately made. The Old Ones also tend to have dusky skin and dark hair and eyes, although that trait has been lost in our family. If you want to know who most resembles the Old Ones, it would be your fellow student Cruthin."

"I thought he was the son of a sheepherder from two valleys over."

"One of his ancestors must have been of the ancient race. Another characteristic of the Old Ones is exceptional beauty. Banon had that trait, as do both you and Cruthin."

Sirona felt uncomfortable. Beauty didn't seem like a particularly desirable quality for a Learned One. She wanted to be wise and respected, not comely.

"Aye. Whether you like it or not, you'll have to deal with the effect your face and form will have on men," her grandmother said. "Your mother reveled in her beauty. She thought her fair face should bring her whatever she wished. When that didn't happen, she turned cruel and selfish."

"This is all so much to take in," Sirona said. "When Old Ogimos told me to ask you about my mother, I never expected this."

"What caused him to mention your mother?"

"It was because of the vision."

"Vision?"

Sirona took a deep breath. "Last night, at my woman-making ceremony at the lake of the dead, I had a vision. Or, at least I thought that's what it was." She got to her feet, restless. "I saw a young woman being sacrificed. Old Ogimos said I might have seen it because the spirit of the woman who died was unable to cross over to the Other Side. He also said it might be some sort of warning from the gods. And then...then he mentioned my mother."

"I would think the old Drui would know better than to bring up such things!" Nesta sounded angry. "He had no right to speak to you that way, to imply what you saw has anything to do with your life, or with your mother's!"

"But it might. Perhaps it's a warning. But never fear, I will heed it," Sirona answered hurriedly. "If I have any other visions, I will be very careful how I speak of them. I won't abuse my power, but ask for guidance from my teachers."

"Nay! You can't do that!" Nesta went to Sirona and seized her arm, her expression desperate. "You mustn't tell anyone you have visions. It might remind people of your mother and what she did." She gave Sirona's arm a little shake. "It might make them think you're like her!"

"But I..." Sirona saw her chance to distinguish herself slipping away. If she couldn't tell anyone about what had happened, her new-found ability was meaningless. "But Old Ogimos already knows," she pointed out. "As does Cruthin."

Nesta sighed. "I doubt Old Ogimos would speak of these things. He knows the story of your mother and understands the implications. As for Cruthin, you must warn him not to tell anyone."

Sirona's insides squeezed with alarm. The surest way to get Cruthin to do something was to tell him not to do it. "I have no control over Cruthin. Perhaps you should speak to him. After all, he does owe you a debt for saving his life when he was attacked by the wolf."

During his man-making trial, Cruthin claimed he called a wolf using magic. He'd ended up killing the wolf, but not before it bit him and caused a grievous wound. Nesta had nursed him back to health using her herbal potions.

Nesta shook his head. "If I speak to him, he'll want to know why I'm warning him of these things. Cruthin always asks questions and tends to keep asking until he gets an answer. And I dare not tell him about your mother. It's bad enough that all the adults of the tribe remember what she did."

"But what should I do? How can I convince Cruthin not to speak of these things?"

"Perhaps you should ask the gods for advice. Perhaps they will help you."

Sirona nodded slowly. Then she went to her bedplace and crawled back to where the large wooden chest was kept.

"What are you doing?" asked Nesta.

"I want to find something to sacrifice. I intend to go to the sacred spring, offer a gift to the gods and ask them what I should do." She undid the latch and opened the chest, then moved aside clothing until she found the soft leather bag. Unfastening the drawstring tie, she spilled the bag's contents onto the thin wool blanket covering her bedplace.

It always amazed her how much jewelry her mother had possessed. Armbands, necklaces, rings, brooches—and all of it fashioned of gold and silver. Much of it was set with gleaming stones. Dark red gems like drops of dried blood, blue or purple jewels like the sky at sunset, creamy pearls and great chunks of amber. It didn't look like the ornaments Hyell, the smith's apprentice made. Everything was foreign-looking and clearly very valuable.

She picked up a silver bracelet, the end pieces fashioned into the heads of wolves with deep red stones for eyes.

Nesta came up beside her. "Is that what you're going to offer?"

"Aye." As Sirona examined the bracelet, she heard her grandmother sigh. "What is it?" she asked.

Nesta shook her head, looking distraught. "It's just that..." She met Sirona's gaze. "Your mother was killed by wolves."

"How do you know?"

Nesta grimaced. "What other creature could have torn out her throat?"

Sirona let out a gasp. She had no memory of her mother, and it seemed Banon had been a less than admirable person. Even so, it was distressing to think she'd endured such a gruesome end.

She quickly put the rest of the pieces away, then tied the bracelet to her belt. After what her grandmother had told her, it seemed ill-fated to put it on.

As she left the hut and walked through the dun, her stomach squeezed with turmoil. She had so many questions: What was the connection between her vision and her mother? Were her visions related to the Old Ones, the strange, mysterious race her grandmother had mentioned? And her mother's vision—had she lied when she predicted the downfall of the Tarisllwyth? Sirona certainly hoped so.

Outside the gate, her distress increased. This valley was her home. The lush summer pastures, the forests teeming with birds, deer, fox and badger, the rolling hills where the goshawks and gyrfalcons hunted, the rushing streams and quiet pools full of trout and salmon and edged with jewel green moss and delicate flowers. This place was part of her spirit, her soul. The Tarisllwyth had lived here for generations upon generations, existing in harmony with the land, honoring the gods and spirits who dwelled here. Her tribe was part of the great circle of life. For them to vanish would be like the creatures of the woods vanishing.

She reached the sacred spring, situated in a stand of trees beyond the fields of barley and wheat and the clearing where the tribe held their ceremonies. Near the spring was a tall rounded stone with a face carved in it. The face gazed back at Sirona now, appearing bored and uncaring. She removed the bracelet from her belt and stared at it. For a moment she saw the image of a live wolf, its fur silver and black, its jaws dripping with blood. With a shiver she tossed the offering into the deep pool at the base of the spring. "Rhiannon, Ceridwen, Arianhrod, great goddesses all. Aid me. Show me what I must do."

The water of the pool was littered with other offerings. Sirona gazed into it, watching the ripples fan out from the place where the bracelet had entered. A tingling began along her spine as the image of a woman formed in the depths of the pool. The woman had red hair, pale skin and blue eyes that burned with a terrible fury. She wore a gleaming gold torc, the sign of a queen. Reflected in the gold of the torc were flickering flames, and as Sirona gazed beyond the woman, she saw a huge building surrounded by fire. Faintly, she could hear the screams of the people trapped inside. She smelled smoke...and something else...the reek of burning flesh.

Breathless with horror, Sirona stared at the vision of the woman. As the red-haired queen's expression changed from hatred to satisfaction, a sense of revulsion rose up inside Sirona. She could tell this woman was pleased that the people inside the building were being cooked alive. Sickened, Sirona drew back from the pool. The hatred she had glimpsed in the woman's eyes terrified her. What did it mean? Did this vision foretell her own destiny? Was she one of the people who would be trapped in the pyre of flame?

She dared to once again look into the depths of the pool. "Please," she whispered. "Show me the way. Tell me what I must do."

She waited, but no more visions came to her. After a time, she rose and started back to the dun.

Near the trackway to the gate, she encountered Cruthin.

"Where have you been?" he asked.

Remembering Nesta's warning, she said, "I was fetching some comfrey for my grandmother."

"Where is it?" asked Cruthin.

"Where is what?"

"The comfrey."

She was a terrible liar. "I didn't find any. I'll have to look again tomorrow."

"I thought perhaps you went to the lake of the dead."

"Why would I do that?"

"To see if you could have another vision."

Sirona froze. Somehow she had to convince Cruthin to forget about her Seeing. She forced a laugh. "Of course I didn't have another vision. Indeed, now that I've had time to think about it, I'm certain what I saw at the lake of the dead wasn't a vision either. I must have fallen asleep and dreamed all of it." She gestured dismissingly. "Fiach said he couldn't find me when he went back. It must have been because I was lying down, sleeping."

"In the marsh?" Cruthin raised his eyebrows in disbelief. Then he studied her, his dark eyes narrowed. "Anyway, it doesn't matter if you were asleep or awake. What you saw still has meaning. Indeed, it reminds me of a dream I had when I was unconscious after I was bitten by the wolf during my man-making trial. You remember that, don't you?"

"It was a very foolish thing you did, Cruthin, trying to call a wolf so you could kill it."

"But it worked, didn't it?" he said, grinning.

"I heard it was an old, mangy beast with not many seasons to live. But aye, you apparently did call a wolf to you and manage to kill it, at some risk to your own life." Sirona started walking.

"Let me tell you about my dream," said Cruthin, falling in step beside her. "I dreamed I was in a great feast hall. Huge timber beams held up the thatched roof, and the beams were carved with the figures of animals and painted bright hues. I was sitting in a place of honor by the central hearth—the place reserved for the chieftain or a warrior who's been chosen as champion of the tribe. The hall was filled with people. They were all smiling and looking at me with admiration. They raised their beautiful enamel and gold cups to toast me."

Sirona resisted the urge to roll her eyes. Cruthin continued, "I saw my parents among the crowd. It was strange to see them, knowing they were dead. Their thin, careworn faces were alight with pleasure, and they were obviously celebrating with everyone else. Perhaps they were smiling because for once there was enough to eat." Cruthin gestured expansively. "Platters of bread, fruit, cheese and honeycakes covered the table in front of me and a roasted haunch of meat lay on a vast wooden plank near the fire pit, oozing with delicious juices. I could tell the celebration was for me. I'd done something wonderful, and the whole tribe was recognizing my achievement."

Of course, Sirona thought, even in his dreams, Cruthin was arrogant and full of himself!

"But the strange thing was," Cruthin continued, "I hardly recognized any of the people gathered in the hall. My parents, of course. But no one else, except you."

"Me?" Sirona exclaimed. "What was I doing there?"

"You were helping serve the food. After awhile, you came over to me, put down the platter you were carrying and beckoned for me to follow you. We entered a large room scented with sweet herbs and flowers. I'd never seen such luxury. Thick furs covered the floor. The walls were adorned with rich fabrics in colors as bright and glistening as a dragonfly's wings. There were cushions to sit upon, also made of fine beautiful materials. You knelt down on one of the cushions. But when you turned around to face me, you become someone else, another woman. One much older, with mead gold hair and gray eyes. Her mouth was deep pink and full-lipped, and she gazed at me with a provocative expression. I leaned down to kiss her, but the coldness of her flesh made me draw back.

Sirona turned to look at Cruthin, who gave a shudder. "She'd turned into a corpse. Empty eye-sockets, a mouth gaping in the frozen scream of death. Strands of dark gold hair clung to her rotting skull and putrid, discolored skin covered most of her body, except for one claw-like, skeletal hand that reached out for me."

"What did you do?" Sirona asked, riveted.

"I watched in horror as the corpse rose to its feet. Then I whirled and rushed back into the main portion of the hall. The place was filled with the dead. Their bodies half-decayed, the wraiths moved and walked about, lifting the beautiful cups to their ruined faces. They gazed at me with ghastly, empty eyeholes, smiling with their lips half rotted or eaten away. I began to run. When I reached the door of the hall, I rushed out. A thick mist was everywhere. I realized it would be foolish to dash blindly into such an impenetrable atmosphere. But revulsion and dread goaded me on.

"I ran and ran. Sometimes the mist would thin and I would see more of the dead. They were everywhere. Their bodies were ravaged, but they were still able to move. They reached out for me as I sped past. Sometimes they called my name. At any moment, I expected to crash into something or fall into empty space. But the mist went on and on. Somewhere along the way I realized I must be on the Other Side, the place where the spirits of the deceased live. I began to wonder if I was dead and they were welcoming me to their realm. But if I was dead, why did I feel so panicked and terrified?

"After a while I stopped walking. I decided that if this was Other Side, then the rules of the world of the living didn't apply. I might run and run and never reach any place other than where I'd started out. I had to find someone and ask them if there was any hope of returning to world of the living. But now that I wanted to find someone to speak to, it seemed I was all alone. I started walking again, a slow, measured pace. I thought perhaps this was what it was like to be dead. No sense of time or place. Only endless mist. Then I saw something. As I neared it, I realized it was a turf wall. The place seemed familiar. Then a sheep bleated and I knew where I was. The place I'd been born and spent my early childhood. I entered the enclosure and saw the small wooden lean-to built against the turf wall. I knew that when I went inside, I would find my mother stooped over the fire, cooking bannocks for the evening meal."

"Is that what happened?" Sirona asked.

Cruthin shook his head. "What happened is…I woke up."

Sirona frowned at him. Parts of the dream sounded like Cruthin might have made them up—like when everyone was toasting him as the hero. But there were other parts that were so strange she didn't think he could have imagined them. Like the part about her turning into another woman, who then turned into a corpse. An unsettling thought came to her. She said, "The woman I turned into, what did you say she looked like?"

"She was beautiful. Her hair was light, but darker than yours…almost the color of mead. Her eyes were gray, and she was very well-formed, yet small and delicate."

Sirona nodded, then turned and started walking up the trackway.

"Where are you going?" Cruthin asked.

"I have to tell Nesta I couldn't find any comfrey."

"What about going to the lake of the dead? Are you afraid?" Cruthin taunted.

"I'm not afraid of spirits," Sirona said in withering tones. Thinking quickly, she added. "I want to think about your dream and try to understand the meaning of it." Maybe if she could get Cruthin to focus on his dream, he would forget about her Seeing.

"Why can't you do that at the lake of the dead?"

"Because I want to be alone. You know how Old Ogimos always says that in order to have the gods speak to you, you must escape the distractions of life."

"Old Ogimos—always so wise and knowing." Cruthin made a face.

"Well, he is. I have the greatest respect for him. And I intend to heed his advice this day."

"Very well." Cruthin gestured angrily. "I'll go to the lake of the dead by myself."

As soon as she was out of sight of Cruthin, Sirona began to run. She raced through the gate, startling Old Dergo, who was standing guard. "Where are you going in such haste?" he called out.

"I need…to speak…to my grandmother," she panted.

She found Nesta in the hut as she'd left her, although now she was grinding some herb between two stones. "I have another question for you, grandmother," Sirona said breathlessly. "You said my mother was beautiful. But what did she look like exactly?"

Nesta frowned. "She had fair hair, but not as light as yours."

"Would you say it was the color of mead?"

"I suppose a bard might. It put me more into mind of oak leaves in autumn."

"And her eyes…what color were they?"

"Gray, like the winter sky."

Sirona slowly let out her breath. Cruthin's dream had been about the dead who are trapped between worlds. And her mother was one of them.

Chapter 3

They were in the grove. As he had the day before, Old Ogimos was giving the lesson. "Let us discuss the purpose of sacrifice, the meaning behind the ritual." He glanced at Sirona and gave a faint nod. "Although death is nothing to fear, it's not something that should be taken lightly either. For every death there must be a reason and proper attention given. When we butcher cattle, either for a feast or when the herd is culled in fall, we offer a part of the animal to Beli, god of the sun, to thank him for blessing us with the light and warmth that makes the grass grow to feed the cattle. When hunters kill the animals of the forest, they leave a portion of the kill to Cernunnos, thanking the god of animals for the meat. When we sacrifice a bullock at Imbolc or Beltaine, we are offering the gift of the animal's life to the gods. As the bullock dies, its spirit floats free, and the balance between this realm and the Otherworld is maintained.

"Everything is about balance. All life flows in an endless circle, from this realm to the other realms and back again. If you seek out a quiet place and concentrate, you can begin to feel that ebb and flow of life, sense your part in it. Understand how everything is connected. Now I want all of you to close your eyes and feel the life force within you, the energy that animates your body. Feel your heart beating. The air flowing in and out of your breast…"

Ogimos continued to speak, but Sirona no longer heard his words. She was focused intently on doing as he said. She could feel the life force within her, how it was linked to everything else. She imagined herself as one of the stars in the heavens, twinkling brightly in the darkness.

A strange tingling began along her spine, and all at once she was looking down at the earth, observing a hillside by the sea. A circle of stones glinted silver and white in the moonlight. Some of the stones were nearly as tall as a man, others only knee high. As she watched, people appeared out of the shadows surrounding the stones. They were naked and had dark markings painted on their skin, swirling shapes, circles and spirals. The people started to dance, weaving back and forth around the edge of stones, but not entering the circle. Bonfires burned all around, turning the hillside into a whorl of shifting light and shadows. As the people danced, it seemed like they were a spindle drawing down the power of the moon and the stars, concentrating it. In the center of the circle, a light began to glow. It grew brighter and brighter. As bright as the sun—

"Visitors! The dun has visitors!"

The hillside vanished as Sirona opened her eyes. Young Avan stood on the pathway to the grove. His freckled face was flushed berry-bright and he panted for breath.

"A whole group of Silures have arrived," he gasped out.

Bryn was the first on his feet. "Do they look like fighting men? Are we at war?"

Avan shook his head. "This is a peaceful envoy. There are warriors among them, but also a Drui."

Old Ogimos used his staff to lever himself up. "Lessons are finished for today. We should all go to the dun. There will be a feast honoring the visitors, so there will be much to do." He began limping down the pathway, following after Bryn, who had dashed off even before Ogimos finished speaking.

Sirona stood up slowly. She felt dazed and weary, as if her spirit had left her body for a time and then returned. The images she'd seen haunted her. What did they mean? Who were the people on the hillside?

"What's wrong with you, Sirona?" Cruthin asked. "Did you have another vision?"

"Vision?" Dichu's voice was scornful.

"I was trying to do what our teacher bade us do," Sirona answered. "To feel the life force within myself. To sense how everything is connected."

Dichu glared at her and then left the grove.

"Tell me the truth," said Cruthin. "Did you see something?"

"Of course not." Sirona started walking toward the dun.

Cruthin fell in step beside her. "Have you come up with any ideas as to what my dream might mean? Or gained more understanding of your vision at the lake of the dead?"

"The night of the ceremony, I drank mead for the first time," Sirona answered. "And then there was the bloodletting during the ceremony. Those things must have affected my thoughts and made me have an especially vivid and frightening dream."

"I don't believe it was a dream," responded Cruthin. "And even if it was, it was surely sent by the gods."

"I don't want to talk about it anymore." Sirona hurried ahead of him. "I must go and see if my grandmother needs any help."

When she reached the dun, she saw Tarbelinus and his warriors gathered near the gate with the visitors. The Silures were shorter and stockier than the Tarisllwyth, and had dark brown, black or deep red hair.

Checked bracco covered their legs and they wore patterned cloaks woven in different colors than the garments of Tarisllwyth, with red and blue predominating. They also wore their hair in a different fashion, tied at the nape of the neck rather than plaited around their faces. One of the warriors had on a cloak banded in six colors, indicating he was of very high status, a chieftain's son or brother. But there was no sign of the visiting Drui.

Sirona continued on to the hut, hoping to speak to Nesta, but her grandmother wasn't there. She must be off helping the other women with the food.

Sirona sat down on her bedplace, closed her eyes and tried to calm her whirling thoughts. The vision of the people dancing on the hillside filled her mind. It seemed to represent some powerful, ancient magic. She was truly blessed to have been given such a vision. But what did it mean? And why had it come to her? Even more unsettling, how would she ever come to understand these things if she couldn't speak of them with anyone?

She agonized for a long while, until she realized quite a bit of time had passed. If she were going get ready to greet visitors, she would have to hurry. She changed rapidly into her nicest gown, fashioned of bright saffron and blue plaid, and quickly combed her hair. Then she left the hut and hurried to the cistern to wash her face. There she encountered Bryn, who was also washing.

"Do you know why the visitors have come?" Bryn asked he dried his hands and face on his crys.

"Are they here to trade?" Sirona asked.

He shook his head. "They've come to ask Tarbelinus to send warriors to fight the Romans. The invaders are pushing west from their strongholds in the sunrise lands. The Silures insist we must join them in stopping the Romans."

"Do you think your father will agree?"

Bryn gestured, his brown eyes flashing. "How can he not? The Romans' greed knows no bounds. They'll keep moving west until they reach us. Then they'll seek to enslave us as they have the eastern Pretani tribes. We must join together with our neighbors to defeat them before it's too late."

"I haven't heard of this Roman threat. Our teachers have said nothing about it."

Bryn's mouth twisted. "That's because they're Drui. They worry about the past rather than thinking about the future."

"The past represents who we are, and defines our connection to the gods," Sirona said. "It's very important."

24

Bryn scowled at her. Then almost immediately, his expression softened. "Of course you would think so. That's your duty as a student of the grove. But a chieftain must think of the future, and boldly take on any challenges to his authority. He can't hang back and see what happens, as Fiach suggests. He must act decisively."

"Fiach's advice seems prudent to me. War should be avoided if possible." Then, realizing she was upsetting Bryn, she added, "So, tell me, where did you learn all this?"

"I listen in when my father meets with his council. After all, I must know about war and strategy if I'm to be chieftain someday."

"How can you ever be chieftain? Your parents insist you train as Drui."

"Old Ogimos told me that there are instances of a Learned One being chosen as chieftain."

"How could that happen? A chieftain must be able to lead warriors into battle. How could a Learned One do that?"

Bryn shot her a conspiratorial look. "He could do it if he was experienced in fighting and war as well in Drui learning." He leaned near and spoke in a low voice. "I've been training nearly every day. I go into the forest early in the morning. I've hidden weapons and a shield there and I practice with them until it's time to go to the grove."

"Do your parents know about this?"

"Of course not." He shrugged. "Usually they don't even wake. The few times my mother has roused, I've told her I'm going to the sacred spring to make a sacrifice."

"And she believes that?" Sirona asked dubiously.

"Why should she not? That's what Drui do, isn't it?"

Sirona shook her head. Poor Bryn. He was so determined to be a warrior. Yet all her instincts told her that no matter what he did, his parents would never relent.

"We should go to the feast hall," she told Bryn.

He nodded, seemingly deep in thought.

As they entered the crowded feast hall, Sirona saw the flash of gold and bronze ornaments and the bright colors of checked and plaid wool clothing everywhere. In honor of the visitors, all the Tarisllwyth had dressed themselves in their finest attire. Sirona was very glad she'd changed her own garments.

She craned her head to see over the tall warriors, searching for the Learned Ones. She finally saw them, seated on skins and mats to one side of the hearth. In the cooking pit a haunch of beef sizzled and steamed, giving off a succulent aroma that mingled with the other delicious smells of freshly prepared food. At this time of year, Sirona guessed the meal would consist of fresh barley bannocks, creamy cheese flavored with garlic and leeks, and honey and nut cakes

Sirona squeezed her way through the crowd. As she did so, she caught several of the visiting warriors staring at her, their blue eyes glittering from the mead being served in bronze drinking cups. She thought about what a relief it would be to finally reach full Drui status. Then she could wear the ceremonial garments of the grove, marking her as different from other women. She sat down next to Old Ogimos. On his other side was the Silure Drui, who was surprisingly young. He had dark red hair and piercing blue eyes.

Smiling at Sirona, he said, "I was just telling the others about the coming gathering on the sacred isle. It will be an opportunity to meet with fellow Drui from all over Albion, and even across the sea in the territory of the Belgae. We'll share knowledge and honor the gods. We'll discuss matters of interest to those of us who guide the spiritual futures of our tribes."

"Forgive me, Kellach," Fiach interjected. "But I'm well aware there's another reason for this gathering. You can't deny you hope to persuade all the Learned Ones to join together in condemning the Romans."

Kellach spread his hands in a placating gesture. "The Romans are certainly among those matters that will be discussed, but it's not the sole purpose for the meeting. There hasn't been a true gathering of Learned Ones for many years. It's time we join together and focus on the real meaning of being a Drui: our duty to preserve the knowledge of the past, to pass on the ancient legends and tales, to revere our ancestors and to convey the will of the gods to our people." He paused and looked around. "Your tribe, in particular, has a great opportunity. The sacred isle lies on the other side of the mountains, only a few days travel away. You should be able to send all of your Learned Ones, as well as those in training."

"You want us to take students to the gathering?" asked Fiach.

Kellach nodded. "At least those who've had a few years of learning. What better chance will they have to be exposed to the knowledge and mysteries of their elders?"

Sirona's heart began to pound in excitement. If she could go to this gathering, she might be able to talk to other Learned Ones about her visions!

"You say the gathering is at the time of the Grain Moon?" Tadhg interjected. "That's less than one cycle of the moon away."

Kellach nodded. "I've already visited the tribes of the sunrise lands. I wanted to give them time to make the journey. In fact, some of those across the eastern sea may have already set out. I travel next to the tribes of the Decangi and then to the Segonti, since they live almost in view of the sacred isle."

"I'm not certain it's appropriate to take students," said Fiach. Sirona tensed with disappointment. *Please let us go*, she thought desperately. *Please.*

"But it's such a wonderful opportunity for them," said Kellach. "This will be their chance to find their place among all the Learned Ones of our people. For a Learned One, being Drui is our first calling. Our primary duty is always to the secrets of the grove, even before the allegiance we owe to our chieftains."

"I understand that," said Fiach. "But I'm still not certain any of our students are ready for this next step."

"Of course, we're ready," Dichu exclaimed. "Or, at least *I* am. I've nearly mastered the telling of nine-times-nine tales required to reach full Drui status. I can name all the constellations and foretell the movement of the moon and sun in the sky almost as well as Cuill. I've worked hard at my lessons. It would be a great injustice if I were left behind!"

"You see?" Kellach said in satisfaction. "This is a great opportunity for your students of the grove. I would advise you to take all of them."

"Perhaps." Fiach's frown grew deeper, and his hazel eyes under the straight auburn brows were dark and ominous. "Although Math and Merin are clearly too young. And Sirona is also questionable."

Sirona's throat went dry. She longed to say something to convince Fiach she should go, but what? Her visions were the only thing that set her apart, yet she dare not speak of them.

"I've heard that many tribes don't even allow women into the grove." Cuill spoke for the first time. "Her presence there might be considered offensive."

"That's not true," Kellach responded. "There are still a number of female Learned Ones among the Pretani. In fact, I have heard it suggested that females might be better suited for some Drui responsibilities than men are. Healing for example. Women seem to have an innate gift for taking care of the sick and wounded." He smiled warmly at Sirona.

"Sirona's no healer," Dichu scoffed.

"They also make good diviners," Kellach added. "Among some of the northern tribes, they have a tradition of soothsaying."

"She's certainly not a seer." Dichu spoke up again, glaring at Sirona.

Sirona wanted to shout that aye, she was a seer! At the same time, she dreaded the thought that Fiach and the other Drui might be reminded of what her mother had done.

"Sirona has always been a very dutiful and hard-working student." It was Old Ogimos who spoke this time, his deep voice ringing out with such resonance that several of the nearby warriors turned around. "I think she shows great promise, and the journey to the sacred isle would help her develop her abilities."

"What abilities are those?" Dichu sneered. Math and Merin giggled.

Old Ogimos's calm dignity never wavered. "Some individuals are born with a special connection to the spiritual realm. I think Sirona is one of those. Over time, she might learn to go into a trance and visit other realms and see glimpses of the future."

Sirona held her breath. Old Ogimos was clearly trying to help her, but did he tread too close to the dangerous truth?

Fiach and Old Ogimos exchanged a look. Then the head Drui's gaze swept over Sirona. His hazel eyes reminded her of a hawk's, cunning, ruthless and observing far too much. He didn't say anything to her, but turned to Kellach and announced, "It's agreed. We'll all go. Except Math and Merin, who are too young, and Ogimos, who feels unable to make the journey."

Sirona let out her breath in relief. A moment later, her tension returned as Fiach spoke in warning tones. "But remember, on this journey I will have complete authority over all of you. If you fail to show proper reverence and respect for the gods, or for Drui wisdom and authority, you will be punished, and punished most severely." As he finished speaking, his eyes met Sirona's. She froze, wondering if he was thinking of her mother.

Chapter 4

Sirona paused on the mountain trackway and gazed around in awe. On either side of her the rocky peaks rose to daunting heights, with the greatest of them all, Yr Wyddfa, filling the horizon to her left. She thought how different a world this was from the one she had grown up in. Instead of rounded hills covered in grass and forest, these hills were bare and rugged, huge slabs of stone thrusting up from the earth.

The mountains reminded her of the massive bodies of sleeping giants, their bulky stomachs and enormous faces forming the peaks, their outstretched legs and arms outlining the slopes of the smaller ridges. This place made her feel small and insignificant, and keenly aware of the power of the earth. She could feel the great heart of Rhiannon, the earth goddess, throbbing in the ground beneath her feet. The gods of the sky were also near: Beli, the sun god, and Arianrhod, Lady of the moon. Their magic seemed to fill the air around her, making it glow with a sharp, pure light.

As Bryn paused beside her, she breathed, "It's magnificent, isn't it?"

"Aye. I suppose so," Bryn responded, his voice devoid of enthusiasm.

Sirona turned to look at him. "You didn't want to come?"

He shook his head. "I'm only here because my father insisted. For me, this whole journey is a waste of time. Although I suppose I should take comfort in the fact that I'm seeing new places and will have an opportunity to meet people from other tribes. Still, they'll all be Drui, so I don't know if I'll learn anything useful."

"But surely it's better than staying home at Mordarach with Math and Merin."

"Maybe. Especially since I'm so angry with my father for refusing to help the Silures that I can barely stand to be around him."

"I thought Tarbelinus said he was going to give the matter more thought before he made his decision."

"That's the same as his saying no. By the time he does decide it will probably be too late."

"Why do you think that?"

"Because by then the Romans will already have taken over. That's what's happened in the sunrise lands. It's only been a generation since the

29

Romans first invaded Albion. Now those lands are completely controlled by the Romans."

Sirona felt a sudden unease. What if Bryn was right? What if the invaders meant to conquer all of Albion? She would have to pay attention and listen to what was said at the gathering.

At that moment, Dichu came dragging up the slope, panting heavily. He paused as he reached them. "I don't see why we have to go so fast." He shot a hostile glance at Sirona. "And I don't see why Fiach allowed *her* to come. Everyone knows females don't belong among the Learned Ones."

"That's stupid," retorted Bryn. "At least half of the gods we worship are female, so there's no reason a woman shouldn't train in the grove. Besides, Sirona's doing much better than you at keeping up, even on the steepest slopes. And she doesn't whine and complain like you do."

Dichu glared at Bryn and then gave Sirona a look of pure hatred. She started to turn away but was stopped by a sudden tingling along her spine. She glanced back at Dichu, and as she looked at him, he abruptly changed. He appeared older, his body taller and much bulkier. No longer was he gazing at her, but staring up at the heavens, his arms outstretched. All at once, his body jerked as if he had been struck. He fell to his knees, although his supplicating posture didn't alter. Another invisible blow hit him and several lines of blood trickled down his forehead. He staggered, then felt backwards and lay still. His blue eyes continued to stare up at the sky, although now they were empty of life.

Sirona closed her eyes and exhaled sharply. When she dared to open her eyes again, Dichu was standing in front of her, appearing completely normal, right down to the disgusted expression on his thin face. "Why are you staring me at like that?" he snapped.

Sirona shook her head, trying to clear it. "It was nothing." Moving past Dichu, she started down the slope. Her heart was pounding and she felt nauseated. This vision had been so real...and terrifying. Although she didn't like Dichu, she didn't want to see him die. She reassured herself with the thought that this Seeing, like the one she'd had in the grove, was clearly of something in the future. The Dichu she'd seen killed was a grown man.

In an effort to escape her distress, Sirona quickened her pace. In a short while, she'd caught up with Cruthin, who was far ahead of the rest of the Learned Ones and students.

When she reached him, he was standing at the top of another ridge. He gestured. "There it is: Yys Mon. The sacred isle."

Sirona looked to where he pointed. The mountains rolled down to a landscape of deep green hills, tan-colored coastal lands and finally, a strip of gray sea. Where sea and sky met, she could barely make out a land mass, a misty apparition floating on the horizon, seemingly at the edge of the world. Sirona felt a prickling sensation along her spine. Although no vision followed, a clear sense of apprehension filled her. "Something's going to happen there," she murmured. "Something...bad."

Cruthin turned to look at her, frowning. "What are you talking about? I thought you wanted to go there."

She struggled to shake off the mood. "Of course I do. It's just..." She took a deep breath. The urge to tell Cruthin about her vision of Dichu was very strong. But she dare not do so.

"I can hardly wait to get to the sacred isle," said Cruthin. "I can feel myself being drawn there like a lodestone to iron." He stretched his arms out expansively. "I know I will find magic there...and knowledge...and power." He started walking again. "The fact is, I've gone as far as I can among the Tarisllwyth. Our Learned Ones have taught me all they're able, which isn't much."

"How can you say that?" Sirona asked, aghast.

"Oh, they've given me a great number of things to memorize," said Cruthin. "Endless genealogies and sagas, laws and ritual handed down for generations. But when it comes to true understanding of the spiritual realm, our teachers are pathetic. Of them all, only Ogimos really has any glimmering of the vast, rich, fantastic world that waits on the Other Side."

"That seems like a very foolish and conceited thing to say. While some of our lessons are tedious, I know I've learned a great deal in the grove."

"Even Ogimos admits his knowledge is limited," Cruthin went on. "He's always saying there are some things that are meant to be mysteries. But I don't believe that. I won't stop searching until I find the answers I seek."

Sirona didn't respond. Cruthin's words only increased her turmoil. She couldn't help feeling his quest for knowledge was going to lead him into danger.

* * *

It took another day to reach the coast. Once there, they all gathered on a cliff overlooking the beach. A large dun was situated on a strip of land almost directly across from the sacred isle. "An impressive fortress," said Tadhg.

Fiach nodded. "The Segonti are a wealthy tribe. The sea is generous, and they're able to grow a great deal of grain on the island. They also have access to a source of copper ore in a place south of here, and between the ore and the grain, they're able to trade for almost any luxury item they desire. I recall Tarbelinus coming here in years past to trade hides and wool for grain during years when our crops didn't prosper."

"I remember that as well." Bryn spoke up. "I begged my father to let me come along, but he refused. I was very young then. I'm not sure I'd even been initiated yet."

"We've been favored with good crops for many years now," said Fiach. "That's because we're so vigilant in honoring the gods."

"I see they have two sets of ramparts." Bryn motioned to the high earthen walls surrounding the settlement. "I wonder what enemy they fear that makes them build such formidable defenses."

"Attack from the sea is their main concern," Fiach responded. "The Scoti, the people who live across the sunset sea, are skilled boatmen. During the sunseason, they come here and ravage undefended Pretani settlements, stealing wealth and metalwork, as well as women and children, who they take back to their own land to enslave."

"What about the people who live there?" Sirona pointed to a small cluster of stone huts set back on the beach, away from the dun. "When the enemy comes, how do they keep from being captured?"

"The fisherfolk have their own ways of surviving. They were here long before our people came. Some say they are related to the Scoti and that's why the sea raiders don't bother them."

Sirona gazed out at the sea, thinking about the Scoti. She could almost see the raiders climbing out of their boats and surging onto the land, brandishing weapons, their expressions fierce and exultant.

Uneasy, she turned away from the coast and looked back the way they'd come. Yr Wyddfa and the other great mountains loomed like dark shadows over the land. Already she missed the highlands, with their complex pattern of ridge and valley, forest and meadow, mist and sky, all woven together like some rich, vibrant fabric. The beach below seemed very flat and barren, and she wondered at the people who lived in a place so exposed.

"So, what's next?" Bryn asked. "Do we go to the dun and ask the Segonti for their help in getting across to the island?"

"If we were going to take the oxen with us, we'd have to ask the Segonti to transport us. Since we're not, it's the fisherfolk in the village who will take us across."

"Why aren't we taking the oxen?" Bryn asked. "What about the cart? Won't we need it on the sacred isle?"

"We can carry our supplies ourselves. There's no need to pay the Segonti to transport the cart and oxen." Fiach gestured to the group of stone huts below. "Although the fisherfolk are a backwards people, they're very skilled when it comes to the sea. They know the tides and the weather even better than the Segonti. We'll be perfectly safe." He turned back to face the group of Learned Ones and students. "Cuill will come with me to try to arrange a crossing before nightfall. We'll meet the rest of you on the beach."

Fiach and Cuill started down the hillside. Everyone else followed more slowly. The wheels of the supply cart kept getting stuck in the soft, sandy soil and they had to push it out. By the time they reached the beach, Fiach and Cuill had already come back from the village. Fiach shook his head as he strode up. "They refuse to take us across today. We'll have to camp here for the night."

"How can they refuse us?" Dichu asked angrily. "Don't they realize as Learned Ones we're favored by the gods?"

"They worship different gods than us," Fiach said. "They follow the faith of the Old Ones."

His reference to the Old Ones immediately caught Sirona's attention. "Are the fisherfolk of the same race as the Old Ones?" she asked.

"How should I know?" Fiach said irritably. "I have little interest in these people. They're crude and primitive and live the same way they have for generations, since even before our people came to these lands. It's said their ancestors built the great cairns and standing stones that dot the coasts and the sacred isle, but I don't believe it. They appear far too ignorant and uneducated for such endeavors."

"If they think they can refuse our request for passage to the island, then they are dense-witted indeed," said Dichu.

"If they're the ones who are skilled in making the journey across the straits, then I'm willing to defer to their decision as to when to cross," commented Tadhg. "I think we're much safer staying here for the night and setting out tomorrow."

Gazing out at the sea, Sirona had to agree with Tadhg. She could sense the great power there, the vast, churning energy of the foaming blue-gray waves. It was terrifying and yet exhilarating.

"There's another group of Drui who are also stuck on this side of the straits." Cuill motioned. "Let's go and greet them."

They went to where the other Learned Ones were camped and discovered they were a branch of the Decangi. While Fiach, Cuill and Tadhg conversed with their head Drui, the Tarisllwyth students set up camp, putting up the leather tents, collecting driftwood for the fire, and helping Ioworth, the youth who had come along to care for the oxen.

They finally finished their duties and gathered around the fire to eat a meal of oat bannocks, dried meat, and berries. The Decangi Learned Ones passed around skins containing a beverage called curmi, which they said was made from fermented barley and herbs. The drink made Sirona sleepy. To shake off the mood, she stood up and walked a short distance from the camp. Although it was almost sunset, she could still make out the settlement of the fisherfolk down the beach. She longed to go there and ask them about the Old Ones. She decided to see if Cruthin would come with her, but when she went looking for him, she couldn't find him. She approached Bryn, who was still eating, and asked, "Have you seen Cruthin?"

He shook his head and continued to gobble down what she guessed was his third or fourth meal cake. After a moment, he shoved the rest of the food into his mouth and stood. "Do you want to go looking for him?"

Sirona suspected Cruthin had already gone to the fishing village on his own. If she wanted to find him, she'd either have to go there by herself or accept Bryn's offer. Given that it would be dark soon, it seemed best to have Bryn accompany her. She nodded.

Bryn got a piece of firewood and daubed it with pitch from the supply wagon to make a torch while Sirona fetched her cloak from her pack.

"Perhaps Cruthin went down by the water," Bryn said when he joined her.

Although she doubted Cruthin had gone this way, Sirona willingly followed Bryn to the shore. The ocean fascinated her, with its sharp, wild scent and mesmerizing rhythm. They moved slowly along the beach, the torch flickering in the breeze. Sirona glanced out at the vast body of water, where the waves stretched out endlessly into the twilight. This was the realm of Manawyddan, the god of the sea. A part of her longed to walk into the water and feel its power. She imagined striding into the waves, then sinking down into the sea's embrace. All at once, she shivered. The sense of foreboding she'd felt earlier had returned. "Let's walk back the other way," she told Bryn.

"Perhaps Cruthin went to the Segonti settlement," he suggested.

"I doubt it."

"I suppose not." Bryn sighed. "Although that's where I wish I could go. I'd love to see the Segonti defenses up close and talk to their warriors. But of course, I can't. They wouldn't speak of such things with a lowly student of the grove." His voice rang with bitterness.

Sirona experienced the familiar pity. It must be difficult for Bryn to have his yearnings thwarted at every turn. "I think Cruthin may have gone to the village of the fisherfolk."

"Why would he do that?"

Should she tell Bryn about the Old Ones? It would only make him ask questions, questions she couldn't answer. "It's merely a thought. A place we could look for him."

"All right. Let's go there."

34

As they started walking, she could sense Bryn watching her. After a time, he said, "I'm very pleased you came on this journey. While I have little interest in Drui matters, I truly admire you, Sirona. Of all the Learned Ones, you're the only one who seems to me to possess any special ability."

She walked a little faster, feeling embarrassed. "That's ridiculous," she told him. "I'm not even full Drui yet. I have years of learning ahead of me."

"But I was speaking of natural ability," he persisted. "Even Ogimos sees it. You seem to understand people and situations better than anyone I know. You always look beneath the surface of things."

"Cruthin does that also."

"Aye, but he is too conceited to make use of his awareness. While you..." He hesitated, then continued, "Sometimes I feel like you see things that aren't there, that you have visions. Is that true?"

She could hardly tell Bryn about her visions; he was Tarbelinus's son. It had been a mistake to go off alone with him. Several times this past spring she'd caught him watching her when they were at lessons in the grove. His interest in her made her uncomfortable.

"Come on," she said, "we're almost there."

Sirona hurried toward the village, which was made up of small round stone huts. They reached the dwellings, but they saw no sign of any people. Then, all at once, two forms loomed out of the darkness. Sirona hurried forward calling, "Stop, please, I would speak with you."

Abruptly, Sirona realized one of the people was Cruthin. He was accompanied by a small, dark-haired woman who wore a plain, roughly woven cloak and a short leather crys, baring her slender legs. "This is Pellan," Cruthin announced. To the young woman he said, "These are my friends, Sirona and Bryn."

"Are you coming back to camp?" Sirona asked.

"Not yet. Pellan and I haven't finished talking."

"You could bring her with you," Bryn suggested. "There's plenty of food."

Cruthin looked at Pellan and smiled. "I don't think Pellan's hungry." He put his hand on her arm in a possessive gesture.

Sirona felt a stab of irritation mingled with disgust. Cruthin wasn't trying to learn about the fisherfolk. He had other things on his mind. "Are there any other villagers around?" she asked. "Perhaps some the elders?"

"They've all gone to bed," said Cruthin.

"Come on." said Bryn. "We should head back."

Sirona nodded reluctantly. If everyone had retired for the night, there was nothing she could do. Perhaps she would get a chance to speak with them in the morning.

She and Bryn started off. Halfway to the Tarisllwyth camp, Bryn said, "How typical of Cruthin, going off on his own with no consideration for anyone else. Of course, it makes no difference to me what he does, but I'm sorry he's upset you."

"I'm not upset."

"You must understand," Bryn continued. "That's how men like Cruthin are. They get their pleasure where they will. Women mean little to them. But not all men are like that, Sirona. Some do not share their bodies freely, but wait for a woman they care about."

Hearing the hunger in his voice, Sirona realized she must get away. "Thank you for going with me," she told him. "I'll talk to you in the morning." She took off running, hoping he wouldn't follow.

She ran all the way back to camp, unable to banish the image of Cruthin with Pellan from her mind. Seeing them together had awakened something inside her, something she hadn't known was there. She couldn't help imagining the two of them going off behind a sand dune and snuggling close...kissing...Cruthin's hand sliding beneath the short, leather crys and touching Pellan's breasts. Although it wasn't a vision, the images came to her clearly and made her feel a strange longing.

As the tents and supply wagon came into view, she sought to push such thoughts from her mind. She didn't have time for such things. As a seer and a soon-to-be Learned One, she had too many responsibilities to be distracted by the yearnings of her body.

* * *

In the morning, the Tarisllwyth placed their heavier supplies on cowhides and dragged them down to where the boats would put out to sea. "I haven't seen Cruthin this morning," Cuill said when they reached the beachhead. "Does anyone know where he went?"

Sirona saw Bryn looking at her. Gazing at him calmly, she said, "I'm sure he'll be here. He was very eager to go to the sacred isle."

Fiach pointed down the beach. "The fisherfolk are coming."

"Shouldn't the Decangi cross before us?" Tadhg asked. "They arrived before we did."

"They're waiting for another group," Fiach said. "They've agreed we should be first."

As the fisherfolk approached, Sirona realized Cruthin was with them. She felt a renewal of her frustration. She wished she could have been the one to meet with the fisherfolk and ask them questions about the Old Ones.

"These men will take us across the straits," Cruthin announced as he strode up. As he smiled, his teeth very white against his tanned skin,

36

Sirona was startled to realize how much he resembled the fisherfolk. He had the same lean, wiry build and dark coloring, although he was taller. If, as her grandmother said, Cruthin carried the blood of the Old Ones, then it seemed likely the fisherfolk were related to them as well.

Fiach gave Cruthin a sharp look, appearing displeased. Then he motioned to one of the fisherfolk. "Show us what boats we'll be taking so we can begin loading. And tell us how many people can be in each boat."

"Four in a boat and one bundle of supplies," their leader answered. His speech had an unfamiliar cadence. It took Sirona a moment to understand his words.

"Cuill and Tadhg, you will come with me in the first boat," Fiach said. "Dichu, Sirona and Bryn in the second." He looked at Cruthin. "You can bring the rest of the supplies with you."

They dragged the hides over to the boats and began loading their supplies. Sirona moved close to Cruthin. "I would like to cross with you. I want to talk to you about the Old Ones."

"Why not?" Cruthin said. "Three in the boat would be better anyway. I'll tell Caw. He's their leader."

Cruthin went to speak to the fisherman. Sirona glanced at Fiach. If the head Drui saw what was happening, he might be angry that she and Cruthin had contradicted his orders. But Fiach appeared too preoccupied to notice. He was directing Cuill and Tadhg as they loaded the first boat.

Bryn noticed, though. Sirona could feel his gaze burning into her. He thought she wanted to be with Cruthin because she desired him. She couldn't tell him the real reason she was seeking out Cruthin was because she wanted to find out if he'd learned anything about the Old Ones.

* * *

"It was wonderful. Pellan told me all about their beliefs," Cruthin said as he and Sirona sat next to each other in the oval, hide-covered boat. She was aware how bright his dark eyes were, how animated he looked. She couldn't help wondering what excited him the most—learning about the Old Ones or being with Pellan. "Their main deity is the Great Mother Goddess," Cruthin continued. "They worship her in all her incarnations. The earth is her body, the sea, her watery womb. In the sky, she shows her face as the moon, exerting her power over the earth and sea. We and all the animals are her children. In some ways it's not much different than what we believe about some of the goddesses. But there's more. These people have learned how to capture the Great Mother's magic."

When Sirona gave him a skeptical look, he nodded. "It's true. The ancestors of these people built the standing stones and the great stone graves. Some of their elders even remember the purpose of those sacred places. Pellan says only a few people are ever initiated into the mysteries.

But those individuals are able to do miraculous things. To change their form into that of an animal. To become one with the Great Mother and visit the Otherworld. Even to travel to the stars." He took a deep breath, obviously entranced.

Sirona was also intrigued. Despite her resentment of how he'd learned these things, Cruthin's words echoed something she'd always felt, that the real power of the gods was in the earth, in the trees and the rocks and water all around them. She'd often experienced a sense of awe when she was walking in the forest, or watching the sunlight reflect on the waterfall at the other end of the valley. It was at those moments she felt closest to the gods, rather than during ceremonies.

"What else did Pellan tell you?" Sirona asked.

"That was mainly what we spoke of, but she *showed* me other things." He smiled a smug, satisfied smile.

Sirona rolled her eyes and turned away. As she gazed across the water at the heavily-forested shores of the sacred isle, the strange sense of foreboding she'd felt in the mountains returned, as strong as ever.

Chapter 5

When they were close enough to see the beach clearly, the fisherman pulled in his oars and climbed out of the boat. He stood in the waist-high surf and gestured for Cruthin to join him. The two of them guided the boat to shore, landing it on the broad beach. Nearby, the other boats had already arrived. Sirona helped Cruthin and the fisherman unload the supplies. Then she retrieved her pack and watched the fisherman guide the vessel back into the water.

Cruthin looked around, his face glowing. "I can't believe we're finally here. Pellan told me there are several sites on the isle that were built by her people. I intend to find one of them."

Although the thought of visiting one of these places excited Sirona, she still resented that Cruthin had been the one to learn these things. "We'll be expected to attend the gathering and take part in ceremonies," she pointed out. "I doubt we'll have time to explore the island."

"There'll be plenty of Drui and students to assist with the ceremonies. No one will notice I'm gone. Or if both of us are, for that matter…if you'd like to go with me."

"I would like to learn more," Sirona said, "but I can't forget Fiach's warning. He said if we failed to show proper respect and reverence to the gods, we would be punished severely."

"Fiach can't watch us every moment. He'll be busy with meeting other high Drui and planning the ceremonies."

Sirona nodded. "I suppose we might have an opportunity to slip away for a short while and look for one of those sites."

Cruthin smiled at her, a dazzling warm smile that immediately made her uneasy. "It's agreed then. I'll come find you when I'm ready."

Dichu and Bryn approached, each dragging one of the loaded hides. Dichu halted, panting. "I can't believe we're expected to transport our own supplies all the way to the gathering. We should have brought Ioworth to help."

"Then who would watch the cart and the oxen?" Sirona asked. "Without them, the return journey would be very difficult."

"The Decangi have slaves to do most of the work," Dichu said. "As do many of the other tribes."

"The bondsmen of our tribe had to stay at Mordarach to begin the harvest," said Bryn, coming up beside Dichu. Sirona noted that his hide was loaded with about twice as much as Dichu's. "Tribes that can afford to send many people on a journey like this are obviously more prosperous than we are."

"Since we don't have slaves, we should force the fisherfolk to help us," grumbled Dichu.

"How would we force them?" Bryn asked. "We're dependent upon them to take us back across the straits,"

"They seem little better than animals to me," said Dichu. "They should be pleased to serve us. We're Learned Ones and far above them in the eyes in the gods."

"They believe in different deities than we do," Sirona said. "Isn't that so, Cruthin?"

"Aye," Cruthin answered. "They have their own religious beliefs. And I hardly think you could say they are inferior to us. In fact, they may possess more power and influence with the gods than we do."

Dichu gave a snort of contempt. "If the gods favor them so much, why do they live in such rude hovels?"

"They choose to live the way they do," Cruthin said. "They could become like the Segonti and live in a walled settlement and herd cattle and till the fields. But they prefer to earn their living from the sea, as their ancestors did before them."

"Why are you stopping here?" Fiach came up, scowling. "It's a long walk to the gathering place, and I would like to arrive before nightfall."

Dichu gave a groan and began pulling his burden along the sand. Cruthin grabbed one of the hides from their boat and started off. Sirona approached the remaining hide. Bryn came up next to her. "I can drag your burden as well as mine."

"I think I should do my part. Otherwise Dichu will say that women are weak and worthless and don't belong among the Learned Ones."

"At least let me carry some of it." Bryn bent down and began transferring the heavy items—skins of mead, cooking pots and two tents—to his hide. They set out after the others. Fiach walked in front, carrying his ceremonial staff and the crimson leather bag that contained the sacred objects of the tribe. Behind him followed Cuill and Tadhg. Tadhg carried his own pack and his harp, Cuill, his pack and Fiach's. The students brought up the rear, each carrying personal items in satchels or leather packs over their shoulders and also dragging a hide full of supplies.

They left the beach and entered the forest, proceeding slowly down a well-worn pathway. As she walked, Sirona's heart raced. All her instincts told her that her visions were somehow connected to this place. But the sense of warning she'd felt before coming to the sacred isle remained. She struggled to push her uneasiness aside and focus on the present. Leaving Bryn behind, she gradually made her way to Cruthin.

"Can you feel them?" Cruthin whispered as she drew near. He jerked his head toward the woods surrounding them. "Ancient spirits dwell here." Sirona glanced around at the gnarled branches of the great oaks and beeches twined with ivy, black bryony and sacred mistletoe. Cruthin continued, "They've watched this pathway over many, many lifetimes. They observe and wait, then whisper what they see to the Great Mother. Their message is carried in the rustle of their leaves and in their seed pods and pollen drifting on the breeze.

"And the Great Mother hears," he continued. "She knows that people pass this way, intruding on her domain. She tolerates us, but feels no connection to us." He turned to look at Sirona. "How arrogant we are in the grove, thinking we can make the gods listen to us. What are we but one small tribe? No more significant than one hill among the highlands, one star among the heavens. Our manner of worship is flawed, too. I can see that now. The Great Mother does not heed boring chants and rituals. She wants fire and light. She wants celebration and music."

Sirona skin tingled with expectation as Cruthin continued, his voice hushed and reverent. "Pellan told me how her people build bonfires on the tops of the hills to celebrate the turn of the seasons. They make no sacrifice, but feast and dance, all the while drinking a special beverage that makes the stars glow brighter and fills their minds with powerful visions and dreams. Pellan was only allowed to go once, and she said she woke up the next morning with an aching head, but also with incredible memories, as if she had visited places far away, other worlds and other times."

Cruthin sighed. "I wish we didn't have to go to the gathering. Nothing important is going to happen there. Most of the Drui are old and ignorant, too caught up in their endless traditions and rituals to understand real power." He made a face, then looked at Sirona. "I'm convinced the Goddess guided me here because she wants me to visit one of these sacred places. She wants me to hold a ceremony there."

"Did Pellan tell you what to do?" Sirona asked. "Do you know how to hold a ceremony honoring the Goddess?"

Cruthin nodded. "I have everything I need. Now I'm merely waiting for the right time."

"Tell me more about the ceremony. What happens? What rituals are involved?"

Cruthin shook his head. "I won't speak of this anymore, not until we have the ceremony. Discipline is required when dealing with the gods. There is a pattern to all things and it must be followed." Cruthin's pupils appeared large and dark in the dim light, as if they had swallowed the irises of his eyes. Gazing into his rapt, fervent face, Sirona knew a thrill. But it was mingled with suspicion. She wondered if he really knew how to hold a ceremony, or if he was just pretending in order to impress her. It seemed very likely the latter was true.

Sirona turned her attention back to her surroundings. Along the pathway, some of the trees were marked with offerings, a piece of cloth or strip of leather, the fur of a squirrel or bright bird feathers. They must be getting close to the gathering place. Thank the gods. Her arms and shoulders ached from dragging the heavy hide. She wondered how Bryn managed to pull twice as much.

The forest thinned, then abruptly opened out into a huge clearing. In the center, dozens of wooden poles supported a great thatched roof covering a structure large enough to shelter all the Tarisllwyth plus two other tribes. The building had no walls, and in the open area around it were scores of people.

Halting at the edge of the clearing with the rest of the Tarisllwyth, Sirona was amazed by how many Learned Ones were there. Some were young and vigorous, but the majority were old, with gray and thinning hair and a certain frailty in the way they carried themselves. Their clothing also varied. Although the full Drui wore crys and cloaks marked with the three sacred colors of red, green and white, the patterns and colors of their bracco ranged from bright saffron to brown, from deep red to blue or green. Many wore their hair pulled back from their faces, while some wore it plaited, like the Tarisllwyth. The majority, especially the older men, had beards.

"I didn't realize there were so many Learned Ones in Albion," she remarked.

"There are even a few women," said Bryn, coming to stand beside her. He glanced pointedly at Dichu.

Fiach said gruffly, "If you don't want to be putting up tents and gathering water and firewood in the dark, you'd best get busy."

"Where should we make camp?" Bryn asked as he surveyed the tents and lean-tos scattered around the clearing.

"I don't have time to decide every little detail," Fiach snapped. "Find a suitable spot and see to your tasks." He hurried off toward the large structure. Cuill and Tadhg dropped their packs on the ground and set off after him.

"Once again, we're left behind to do the unpleasant work," complained Dichu. "I vow, if I'm ever head Drui, I'm going to have a servant who does nothing but wait upon me."

"You'll never be head Drui," said Cruthin.

"Then who will? Certainly not you."

Sirona tensed. She hated this bickering.

Thankfully, Bryn distracted them by saying, "What about making camp over there?" He pointed to an area on the other side of the clearing, near the edge of the woods.

"You would pick a place far away," said Dichu. Despite his complaining words, he grabbed the edge of his hide and began to drag it the direction Bryn indicated. Sirona and the others followed.

When the tents were in place and the supplies unloaded, Sirona offered to fetch fresh drinking water. She hoped to have a chance to speak to one of the female Drui, or perhaps someone who was a seer.

She set out carrying the waterskins. Among one of the larger groups, she saw a tall woman with sandy hair streaked with gray. As Sirona approached, the woman smiled and said, "Welcome. It's good to see a young woman at the gathering. I'm Dysri, of the Cunogwerin, a branch of the Brigantes."

Sirona nodded a greeting. "I'm Sirona of the Tarisllwyth. Can you tell me where I might find fresh water?"

"Aye, there's a stream nearby where the water flows over the rocks and is fresh and clear. Come with me. I'll show you." Dysri started to walk into the woods. Sirona followed, encouraged by the woman's open, friendly manner.

A little way down the path, Dysri glanced back at her. "Did you know that at one time at least a score of female Drui attended the gathering? But fewer and fewer women are allowed to enter the groves these days."

"Why do you think that is?" Sirona asked. "Do you think that there are fewer women Drui because the female deities have lost importance?"

Dysri gave a soft laugh. "Men can be so foolish. The goddesses represent things eternal and profound: the fertility of the earth and all creatures, the streams and rivers and lakes on which all life depends, the Lady of the moon who marks the rhythms of the seasons and guides the wheel of stars across the sky. To suggest that female power is not important shows great ignorance."

They reached a small stream, and Dysri took Sirona to a place where the water spilled over the rocks and tumbled down into a clear, glistening pool. "When there is prosperity and plenty, people often forget about sacred meanings and turn their minds to other concerns," Dysri continued as Sirona began to fill the waterskins. "This is a time of men, of warriors and battles, of struggles for power and dominance between tribes and against the invaders. Because the Great Mother is not believed to directly influence such things, She and Her realm have been deemed unimportant."

Sirona glanced at the older woman. "You speak of the Great Mother. Where did you learn about Her?"

"Among my tribe She is still accorded the highest place of honor among the gods. Is it not so with your people?"

"We worship many goddesses, but none of them are thought to possess the sort of power you speak of." Sirona realized this woman was discussing the same things Pellan had told Cruthin. On a hunch, she asked, "I'm interested in discovering some of the places where the Great Mother was once worshipped. A friend of mine was told there are such sites on the sacred isle. Is that true? Can you tell me how to find one of them?"

Dysri nodded. "But I'll warn you, it's not as simple as seeking out a circle of stones or an ancient mound. The Great Mother shows herself to very few...usually only those who carry the blood of the ancient race of the isle."

Sirona straightened, her excitement growing. "My grandmother says I'm descended from them."

Dysri cocked her head in interest. "Your grandmother? Is she Drui, too?"

"Nay, only a healer."

"Among my people, Drui are often healers as well as training in the grove. Indeed, I'm a healer myself."

Sirona draped the full waterskins over her shoulders and the two women started back. "My grandmother says that my ancestry may also be the reason I have visions." She looked at Dysri shyly. "Do you think that's possible?"

"Aye. Very possible. Tell me, what sort of visions do you have? Do you see the future? Or the past?"

"I don't know. I'm trying to find someone who can help me understand the things I've seen. Do you have any suggestions?"

Dysri grew thoughtful. "If your visions come from the Goddess, I fear you won't get much help from anyone here at the gathering. The Great Mother is not accorded much respect among Learned Ones these days." She glanced at Sirona. "And you're so young. I fear it will be difficult for you convince people of your abilities. Perhaps you should be careful about who you discuss your Seeings with. Drui are really no different than other people. There's as much petty jealousy and competitiveness among those trained in the grove as among any group of warriors." She smiled faintly. "Perhaps that's because most Drui are men, and the male force makes them aggressive and ambitious."

"And the female force—the energy of the Goddess—you think that's different?"

"Aye. Although the Goddess can sometimes be as fierce and ruthless as any male deity. But male and female energy are both necessary for life to exist. There must be a balance between those forces, as in all things."

"I appreciate your advice," Sirona said. "But I would still like to know how to find one of the places sacred to the Great Mother. Can you help me?"

Dysri didn't speak for a time. Then she said, "There's a site not far from here. But I can't tell you how to find it. Your spirit must guide you. If that doesn't happen, then you're not meant to go there."

"Could you at least tell me which direction to begin my search?"

Dysri pointed. "It's that way, toward the sea."

"Thank you," Sirona said.

When they reached the edge of the forest, Dysri said, "Come back to my tent with me. We could share a meal before the gathering."

Although Sirona was intrigued by her conversation with Dysri, she feared being away from the Tarisllwyth camp for so long. "I'll join you in a little while," she said.

"My tent is over there." Dysri gestured. "Come and join me as soon as you can."

Sirona carried the waterskins back to their camp. Bryn was sitting on one of the hides, eating. "Have some food," he said. He motioned for her to hand him one of the waterskins. He took it and drank rapidly.

She sat down beside him, then wondered if she should do so. Recalling the way he'd acted the night before, she grew uneasy. Getting to her feet, she said, "Where's Cruthin?"

"Oh, he's around somewhere. Sit down and eat. I traded some of our mead for freshly cooked bannocks and cheese. It's delicious."

"But we brought food with us."

"Not as good as this." He held out a fresh bannock, which smelled wonderful. Sirona's stomach growled, but she forced her hunger aside. "I should find Cruthin."

Bryn scowled at her. "I'll eat it all if you don't join me now."

Sirona started to walk away. Bryn called out, "Don't go far. Fiach says everyone's going to the meeting hall." He jerked his head in the direction of the huge timber structure. "I'm fairly certain they're going to discuss the Romans."

"I'll return shortly," Sirona told him.

She searched the open area and finally found Cruthin coming out of the forest with a load of firewood. "I've met someone you should talk to," she said excitedly. "Her name is Dysri and she told me more about the sacred sites of the Old Ones. She said one of the places isn't far from here. Perhaps this would be a good time to look for it, while all the Learned Ones are busy."

Cruthin shook his head. "Tomorrow the moon will be full. It'll be better to go then."

"But tomorrow there will be ceremonies. It will be difficult to get away."

"I'm not ready yet," Cruthin said. "I still have some things to prepare."

"Such as?"

He shook his head. "I can't tell you."

Again she wondered if he really had a plan. "Don't you want to meet Dysri? She told us to come and eat with her."

"Did she tell you anything of the mysteries? Did she explain what rites and rituals the Old Ones used?"

"Nay, but we'd barely met. You can't expect her to share such knowledge with someone who's almost a stranger."

"It's likely she doesn't really know very much. Pellan told me to be wary of the Learned Ones. She said that years ago, they tried to steal her tribe's magic. They tortured some of her people, trying to get them to reveal their secrets. She says you can't trust the Learned Ones, at least in matters like this."

Sirona could hardly imagine Dysri torturing anyone. "Perhaps Pellan doesn't know very much about the mysteries either," she said coolly. "Perhaps she warned you away from the Learned Ones so you wouldn't talk to other people and find out she's lying."

Cruthin's mouth quirked. "Perhaps you wish it was you who was alone with me by the sand dune last night."

"Don't be ridiculous!" Sirona responded, feeling embarrassed and angry. "I have no interest in engaging in loveplay with you! I have no time for such things!"

Cruthin cocked his head and regarded her with heavy-lidded eyes. "Sex magic is often part of ceremonies honoring the Goddess."

"Who told you that? Pellan, I suppose."

"Nay. She *showed* me. Sex magic is very powerful. If you give me a chance, I'll share what I learned with you."

Sirona turned away. She suspected Cruthin was manipulating her, trying to get her to lie with him to satisfy his own needs. But what if his assertion was true? "I'm going to find Dysri," she said. "I'm going to ask *her* if sex magic is part of the Old Ones' rituals."

"You're never going to discover the mysteries if you're not willing to take any risks," taunted Cruthin.

Sirona hurried to Dysri's camp. She was very disappointed to find the place deserted, except for a servant tending the fire. "Where's Dysri?" she asked.

The man answered with an accent so rough and harsh, it took a moment for her to understand his words. "She's gone into the meeting place with the rest of them." He pointed to a wooden platter of mealcakes on a rock by the fire. "You should eat. There's plenty." Sirona's stomach had been growling ever since she smelled Bryn's food. She sat down on a cowhide by the fire and began to eat.

The man brought her a skin containing a slightly bitter beverage that reminded her of the curmi the Decangi had brought. He also offered her a basket of berries and a small white cheese. "Thank you. You're very generous," she told him.

It seemed odd that a servant should treat her so cordially, but perhaps Dysri had mentioned her and said she would be coming back. She scrutinized the man. He was fairly old, and moved with a limp, but his dark, wavy hair was untouched by gray. His fair skin was sprinkled with small brown freckles and he had light eyes, perhaps gray or pale blue, although she couldn't tell by firelight. He seemed to possess a mixture of the characteristics of her own race and the darker coloring and smaller stature of the fisherfolk.

"What's the name of your tribe?" she asked him.

"I serve the Brigantes," he said. "They're from the north."

Serve. So, he was a slave. Remembering Cruthin's words, she couldn't help asking, "Have you ever heard of the Old Ones?"

The man smiled. "I am one of the Old Ones."

Sirona stared at him a moment. Then a thought came to her. "Why are you a slave? How do they make you serve them?"

"I've chosen this," the man answered. He pointed to his leg. "When I was young, I was chasing a great stag and fell among some rocks and broke my leg. It was a very bad injury. My people took me to a woman healer. She straightened the bones in my leg and gave me medicine. She healed me, and now I owe her my life."

"Was it Dysri?" Sirona asked.

The man nodded.

"But why do you owe her your life? Your injury was not so bad that it would have killed you."

The man shook his head. "My people are hunters, and a hunter with a wounded leg is worthless. Life is harsh for my people. It wouldn't have been fair to ask them to provide me with food for the rest of my life because I couldn't hunt."

"They would have let you die?"

The man nodded again.

"And so you serve Dysri now."

The man smiled. "It's not an unpleasant life."

"What's your name?"

"Lovarn. It means 'wolf'. Hard to believe that I was once as fierce and strong as one of those beasts." His smile widened.

"I'm Sirona. I thank you for your generosity. Do you think Dysri will be back soon?"

"I don't know. She's eager to meet with the other healers. But you could wait for her," Lovarn suggested.

Sirona nodded. "For a while. In the meantime, tell me about the Old Ones."

"What do you wish to know?"

"I've heard your people possess magic."

"Some of us do."

"And that you worship a female deity called the Great Mother."

"My people live simply. We don't need many gods. If the earth should grow barren, the animals would die and we would die as well. The earth is our mother. She is more important than anything."

"Is it true your people built the great stone cairns and raised the standing stones?"

"Aye. But that was a long time ago. We no longer possess the magic used to create those things."

"It's been lost?"

"Some of it lingers, but it is rare to find anyone who can use it. Most of my people no longer try. Why should we bother? The magic didn't save us from your people. They conquered us and enslaved us and pushed us into the wild and barren lands. Our children went hungry and our numbers declined. Now there are few of us and many of your people."

"My people? What does that mean? Anyone who is not one of the Old Ones?"

Lovarn nodded. "The Pretani. And the Scoti, from across the sea."

"But if you had magic, how did they defeat you? And if the Great Mother is such a powerful deity, why did she allow you to be defeated?'

"The Great Mother represents the power of the earth. The actions of men aren't important to her, for they don't affect the things that are eternal: The rivers and streams. The trees and plants. The animals. All the things of this realm. She doesn't care for one kind of animal over another, so why should she care for us more than other men?"

"Because you petition her. You sacrifice to her."

Lovarn shook his head. "That's not our way. In our rites we try to reach out to the Great Mother, to become one with Her. But we don't bargain with Her as you do with your deities. We don't believe She will save us. Why should She? If we're meant to die out, then it will be so."

"But that is sad! So much has been lost. The magic has dwindled and almost disappeared."

"You don't understand. Magic can be used for evil as well as good. And it's dangerous. Those who wield magic must always pay the price." Lovarn's expression grew hard. "To use magic is to change things. There are few people who are wise enough to do that. We're all part of the pattern, and if one piece of it is altered, then the whole pattern changes. It's like a stone dropped into a lake. The ripples fan out, out and out, until the whole lake is affected.

"Magic is power and very few people can wield power without destroying a part of themselves. You must be very strong to do so. And the selfish desires that have a hold on our hearts make us weak and vulnerable. Unless you can say that you do not have such desires, then you shouldn't use magic."

Although she couldn't explain why, Sirona had the sense that Lovarn was speaking of Cruthin. He was so determined to seek out knowledge, no matter the cost. In his arrogant quest to know the mysteries, he might well be risking his life. The thought aroused the familiar sense of foreboding. Sirona suddenly felt an urgent need to find Cruthin and make certain he was well.

She rose from her place by the hearth. "Thank you for the food. And for talking to me." Despite his age and the fact that he was a slave, Sirona felt strangely drawn to Lovarn. She smiled at him one last time, then started off.

The meeting of Drui was finished and everyone had returned to their camps. Two dozen fires glowed here and there in the clearing. Sirona saw a group of bards near one fire, practicing with their instruments. She heard the lilting melody from a pipe, like the voice of a small runlet. Then the drums joined in, loud as thunder, yet rhythmic like the sound of mighty footsteps. Soon after, harp music rippled through the air, glistening and bright. The melody tore at her heart, as if the strings being plucked were inside her.

She walked through the clearing and observed Fiach and Dichu with some Learned Ones she didn't recognize. Continuing her search, she saw Bryn with some other young Drui. She approached the group. A young man wearing the garments of a full Drui was speaking. "Strategy is for the chieftains to worry about," he said. "*Our* responsibility as Drui is to earn the favor of the gods. We must increase the number of our sacrifices, and be scrupulous in carrying out every detail of the rites of those sacrifices. We must also consider whether we haven't grown meager and grudging in our offerings. Once we spilled human blood in our rites. Then we decided that the practice was wasteful. But what if human blood is what the gods desire? It could be that the reason that the gods have turned away from us and allowed the Romans to gain power is because *we* have turned away from the old ways and become stingy in our offerings."

The man's words caused a choking dread to rise up inside Sirona. She remembered her first Seeing and the terrifying images of the young woman being killed. She quickly moved away from the young Drui, not wanting to hear any more.

A dozen fires lit the area with a soft glow, and from all directions came the murmur of voices. There were so many people gathered here. How would she ever find Cruthin? She decided to head back to Dysri's camp. Even if the Brigante woman hadn't returned, Lovarn would be there.

But when she reached the camp, there was no sign of Lovarn or Dysri. Sirona decided to wait and sat down by the hearth. The beverage skin Lovarn had offered her was still there. She drank some more of the bitter liquid and it made her sleepy. Sleepy enough that she curled up in her cloak and closed her eyes.

* * *

"Sirona. Little one."

She woke to see Dysri leaning over her. Sirona sat up stiffly, trying to remember where she was.

"I wouldn't have left if I'd known you would come back," Dysri said. "There's still plenty of food if you're hungry."

"I ate already. Lovarn said there was plenty."

"Lovarn?"

Sirona tried to collect her thoughts. How could Dysri not know who Lovarn was? "You know, the man whose leg you mended, and so to repay you, he now acts as your servant." When Dysri didn't respond, Sirona realized something was wrong. "Why are you staring at me? Why don't you answer?"

Dysri released a long slow breath. "The man named Lovarn is dead. He died a long time ago."

"Nay. That can't be! I sat here and spoke with him. It was just before nightfall."

Dysri sank down beside Sirona. "May the Great Mother keep us," she murmured.

Sirona felt cold. It must have been a vision. But this one had been so real. She could remember every detail.

After a long while, Dysri said, "I did once treat a man named Lovarn. He had a terrible leg injury. The broken bones were poking through the skin and the wound had begun to putrefy. I told him that to save his life we must cut off his leg. He refused. He said he would rather die. And so, after a few days, he did."

"But you...you must have been kind to him. You must have tried to heal him and that's why he remembers you. And perhaps his spirit does serve and protect you, even if his body is no more."

"Perhaps," Dysri said. "Tell me, what did he look like?"

Sirona described Lovarn.

Dysri nodded. "Aye," she said. "I remember him. It seemed such a waste that a vital, handsome man should have to die. But the Old Ones don't fear death. They understand as well as any Drui that life and death are simply different faces of the same thing."

"He told me about the Old Ones. And about magic and the gods. He seemed to be warning me." The chill inside Sirona deepened.

"Has anything like this ever happened to you before?" Dysri asked.

Sirona shook her head. "There was no hint that Lovarn wasn't real, even though we spoke at length. Other times when I've had visions, it has felt as if I were watching from a distance. But Lovarn was right there, close enough to touch. As real as you seem to me now."

The more she talked about it, the more it bothered her. She'd had a long conversation with a spirit. And the things he had told her. Hints of danger. Insinuations that she was seeking something she could never possess.

Suddenly Sirona didn't want to talk about the Old Ones. She wished she had never brought up the subject. "I thank you for your concern and generosity, but I think it's time for me to go back to my tribe's camp."

"There's no need for that," Dysri protested. "You could sleep here. Almost everyone will be talking long into the night. I doubt you'll be missed."

"If my friend comes back to our camp, I want to be there." That was not the real reason Sirona had decided to leave. She wanted to be away from Dysri's camp, to forget about meeting Lovarn.

"As you wish," Dysri said. "But if you should ever want to talk, feel free to search me out. You appear to possess extraordinary gifts for someone so young. I would hate for those gifts to be wasted, or for you to be hurt trying to wield a power that's too great for you."

Lovarn had also spoken of power and the perils in using it. Everywhere she looked, there seemed to be a premonition of danger.

She thanked Dysri once more, then returned to the Tarisllwyth camp. Bryn had built a fire and was staring into it with a gloomy expression on his face. Despite her worries about encouraging his interest, Sirona sat down beside him.

"They'll never do anything," Bryn muttered. It sounded like he was gritting his teeth. "They'll never agree to fight the Romans." He picked up a piece of wood and poked angrily at the fire. "I went to the gathering. At first I was full of hope. One of the men who spoke was Cangerix, the chieftain of the Durotriges. He told how the Romans have overrun his lands, built fortresses and demanded tribute. He even said they had banished the Learned Ones from his territories. Cangerix asked for the aid of the Learned Ones in petitioning the gods to favor his cause. He also asked them to go back to the leaders of their tribes and urge their chieftains to make war against the menace that threatens all of us. Then Elidyr, the head Drui of the Durotriges, spoke. He warned that if the Romans aren't stopped, someday all of the Learned Ones would vanish and with them all the knowledge our people have nurtured and honored since the land first rose out of the sea. He made it sound like a call to war. I was ready to shout out a battle cry and offer to lend my sword arm to the cause."

Bryn let out a groan. "But then everything went awry. Another group of Learned Ones began insisting the Romans are *not* a threat. That as long as our people pay them tribute, the enemy will allow us to honor our gods and continue our traditions. The meeting went on and on, with one group arguing for fighting the Romans and another group arguing against it. After a while, I could tell it was hopeless. These stupid fools are never going to do anything. They'll talk and talk, debating and arguing, and in the end, nothing will happen." He shook his head, obviously distraught. "By Beli, I wish I'd never come!"

"I'm sorry," Sirona said. She wondered what he thought of the young Drui's suggestion that they return to the practice of sacrificing human victims. But she wasn't about to bring up the matter.

Bryn looked at her, face flushed, eyes bright in the firelight. "You understand, don't you? You realize the Romans must be defeated, that if we don't drive them out of Albion, they'll eventually enslave us all?"

"I don't know what to think," Sirona answered. "I've only really heard about the Romans this sunseason. What you say makes sense, and yet..." She tried to make her voice soothing. "War frightens me. It seems like such a waste of life. What if you go into battle with the Romans and ended up being killed? You're so young, your whole life ahead of you. Think how your parents would feel. You're their only child, the only real legacy they leave behind."

Bryn stared at her a long while. Sirona grew uncomfortable and wondered if he was angry with her. Although she sometimes grew tired of Bryn's attentions, she still valued his friendship.

At last he said, "As a female, you must think the way you do. Women are the keepers of life, so it is natural for them to be cautious. I won't condemn you for your reluctance to engage the enemy. But I do blame the men who think like you, especially the Drui. For it's clear to me that if the Romans prevail, all that we are taught in the grove will eventually perish."

His words made Sirona feel cold inside. *It's true*, a voice whispered. *As the Pretani defeated the Old Ones and drove them to the margins of the land, so the Romans will do to us. Someday we will be only a memory, a dream of glory and greatness that is no more.*

Chapter 6

"Sirona, get up. It's nearly time to leave." Bryn poked his head in the entrance of Sirona's tent.

"Leave? Where are we going?" she asked sleepily.

"To a place called the lake of sacrifice for a special ceremony. Fiach told us about it last night, although I guess you weren't around."

"How far away is this lake?"

"Quite a long walk. Nearly on the other side of the island."

Which meant they would be traveling *away* from the sacred place of the Old Ones. "Do we all have to go?" she asked.

"Aye. Fiach will insist."

Sirona got up and began to search her pack for a change of clothing. Bryn was right. There was no way she could refuse to make the journey.

She dressed and plaited her hair, splashed her face with water, then joined Bryn and the other Tarisllwyth. Dichu was going on and on about how exciting it was to be around Learned Ones who possessed so much knowledge. He had spent the night with a group of Drui whose main responsibility was to keep track of the laws and traditions of their tribes, and he was obviously enthralled by the idea of having such influence. "These men, called brehons, make certain the laws apply equally to both kings and to cattle herders," he asserted. "When it comes to the settlement of disputes and making certain the proper punishment is meted out to wrongdoers, they have more power than even the chieftain or the head Drui. Our tribe has never had a brehon. Perhaps it is time we do," he added with a small smile.

"Oh, I'm certain you would like that," Bryn answered. "As long as you're the one chosen."

Dichu's expression grew serious once more. "Obviously, I'm not ready for such responsibility. I have much to learn when it comes to these matters. In fact, I'm going to ask Fiach if instead of returning to Mordarach, I can live with a tribe called the Trinovantes for a time, so I could train with their brehon. I think I could do more good for my people by pursuing such a path, rather than staying at Mordarach and continuing my studies there. I don't feel I can learn much more from Ogimos and Fiach. And Cuill's and Tadhg's knowledge lies in other areas." He nodded to the two younger Drui, clearly hoping to gain support from them for his plan.

Bryn gave a contemptuous snort. "Good luck persuading Fiach. If you do succeed at going off on your own, I can't say we'll miss you much." He shot a look at Sirona, as if seeking her agreement. The thought came to her that it probably didn't matter what Dichu did with his life. If her vision were true, he didn't have many years left.

The memory of her vision of Dichu reminded her of her conversation with Lovarn and her plan to tell Cruthin about it. As she was looking around for Cruthin, Fiach returned. "It's time to leave," he said. "Cuill and Tadhg will carry our offering. As for the rest of you," he glared at the students, "Remember, this is an important rite. I expect you to behave with dignity and restraint. As we walk, you should keep your thoughts on the gods and the sacred ritual we are about to perform. No talking, except in quiet, respectful tones."

The Tarisllwyth took a place near the middle of the procession of Learned Ones. Many of the other tribes carried bundles wrapped in red cloths. Others transported their offerings in carts pulled by slaves or oxen. One tribe had brought a two-wheeled vehicle pulled by two sleek tawny-brown horses. Sirona had only seen horses a few times before, when traders came to Mordarach. "The chariot belongs to a tribe called the Iceni," Fiach told them. "They intend to offer the vehicle as their gift to the gods."

Sirona couldn't help staring at the chariot, which was driven by a stocky, fair-haired man. Something about the vehicle and the horses seemed familiar, although she couldn't imagine what it was.

Bryn also appeared intrigued by the vehicle...but aggravated as well. "What a waste," he told Sirona. "They would be much better off using the chariot in battle to defeat the Romans."

Fiach must have heard him, for the head Drui's expression grew tight with irritation. "Without the gods' favor, we are nothing," he admonished Bryn. "Remember that, and remember your place as a student, as I have told you before."

Bryn's face flushed as bright as a cranesbill blossom, but he said nothing further. Only later, when Fiach had moved off to speak with someone from the Decangi tribe, did Bryn mutter, "Fiach's a fool. They all are. The gods won't save us. We must use our weapons for fighting, not squander them as offerings."

Sirona was surprised at the tension between Bryn and Fiach, but didn't give it much thought. What she really wanted was for Cruthin to show up so she could talk to him about the man-spirit called Lovarn.

The procession started off, following a pathway that looked as though it hadn't been used for some years. They made their way slowly through the oak and elm forest, their progress limited by the number of people in the procession and the feebleness of the older Drui. Sirona was glad for the sluggishness with which they progressed. Cruthin would have plenty of opportunity to catch up.

After a while, they reached an open area of cultivated fields. The grain had already been harvested, leaving behind golden stubble where crows and chaff finches searched for fallen grain. Sirona was impressed with the size of the fields and the obvious richness of the land. No wonder the Segonti were such a prosperous and powerful tribe.

They walked along the edge of the grainfields, then once more entered thick forest. Sirona realized she could smell the sea. The coast must be nearby.

The procession continued on, winding through woodlands that showed hints of summer's passing. The blackberries and elderberries were almost ripe and there was a slight tinge of brown to the fern and bracken along the pathway.

Well past midday they reached their destination. The lake of sacrifice was a large, open stretch of water surrounded by willow, sedge and flowering rushes. A pair of swans floated on the calm surface of the lake. Overhead, an osprey searched for prey. Everyone gathered in an open area near the lake, grouping together by tribe. Sirona, Bryn and the other Tarisllwyth ate mealcakes and dried meat from their packs and passed around a waterskin while Fiach conferred with the other head Drui.

When Fiach returned, they joined the rest of Learned Ones at the edge of the lake. A man named Elidyr—who had seemingly been appointed the leader of all the Drui—stood on the shore and began to speak in his ringing voice. He called down the gods, evoking them in triads so their power would balance each other: Beli, Llew and Gwyn Ap Nuad; Bran, Gwyddion and Govannon; Cernunnos, Arawn, and Manawyddan; Ceridwen, Rhiannon and Arianrhod.

As he spoke, the pair of swans took flight and an ominous sense came over Sirona. As a tingling began along her spine, she tensed. Her last few visions had been so distressing; she wasn't certain she wanted to experience another one. In an effort to halt the vision, she sought to focus on the details of the ceremony before her: the sound of Elidyr's voice as he evoked the gods, the expressions on the faces of the members of each tribe as they solemnly presented their gifts. The beauty of the objects offered: the curving lines and elegant shape of a ceremonial bronze shield. The sleek, bold form of a sword as it was flung into the air and tumbled end over end until landing in the water. The glitter of jewels on a dagger hilt. The sheen of polished metal and bright colors.

She thought about the days of craftsmanship that had gone into fashioning these weapons. As each item splashed into the water, she imagined the offerings drifting to the bottom of the lake, past fish and reeds and seaweed. Down to the place where the spirits dwelled, where the forces of life and death lurked. Down into the realm of Ceridwen, the dark mother of pools and lakes. With each tribe's offering, her sense of foreboding increased.

The chariot was brought forward. The fair-haired man no longer drove it but led the team of horses, guiding them by the harness. As the vehicle neared the edge of the lake, Sirona saw the image of a man lashed to the inside of the chariot. His head lolled around and his body jerked as the vehicle moved over the uneven ground. When she blinked, the image of the man vanished. She dug her nails into her palms, her body rigid.

The chariot halted at the water and two Drui came forward. They spoke the name of their tribe, the Iceni, and the name of their clan's special deity, Epona. The tingling along Sirona's spine started again and before her eyes, the one chariot became many. They were arrayed in a long line. Warriors stood on the platforms of the vehicles, their long hair and mustaches riffling in the soft breeze. Their bare torsos flashed with bright gold and bronze neck and armpieces. Their checkered war cloaks— thrown back over their shoulders—bore the colors of a dozen tribes. Woad blue and saffron yellow plaid, crimson and deep green check, purple madder, yellow and rust brown, sloe black, scarlet and bleached white. A multitude of hues against the green landscape.

Behind the chariots stretched an army. Pretani men with swords, staves, axes and daggers raised for battle. The fire of determination glowed in the warriors' eyes. Gazing upon their ferocity, their exultant battle lust, Sirona was filled with a terrible dread. *They're going to die. All of them are going to die.* She closed her eyes, trying to banish the vision and fight off the sense of horror. It's not real, she told herself. *It's not real.*

She opened her eyes when she heard someone cry out. It was Bryn. His face was a mask of fury and Fiach had a fierce grip on his arm, restraining him. Sirona looked to where Bryn's attention was focused. The chariot and horses were in the water. The horses were trying to swim, but the chariot had been weighted and the vehicle was dragging the horses down. They whinnied and struggled, their eyes wild. All around, the Drui watched, their faces impassive.

Sirona felt sick. No wonder Bryn had cried out in protest. She'd assumed they would unharness the horses before they pushed the chariot into the water, rather than drowning the poor beasts. A shiver of revulsion traveled through her. Between her Seeing and watching the doomed horses, she felt overwhelmed with death and despair.

"Turn me loose!" Bryn spoke in a low, dangerous voice as he tried to jerk from Fiach's grasp.

"You will not shame us," Fiach warned in a whisper. "If you do, I'll—"

"Nay, I'll not shame you," Bryn answered harshly, "But turn me loose this moment!"

Fiach did so, and Sirona experienced a sense of relief. But it didn't last long. One of the horses whinnied frantically, and her stomach twisted with distress. Her anguish wasn't merely over the animals. The lingering dread her vision had aroused wouldn't leave her. Why had she seen the chariots and warriors? And why did she feel certain that everyone in her vision was going to die?

She gazed steadily at the alder and willow bushes on the other side of the lake, trying to dispel the terrible feeling of loss. When she finally dared look out at the water, the surface of the lake was patterned with a skein of shimmering ripples, but there was no sign of the horses. They had sunk into the dark depths. She shuddered violently at the thought.

"Sirona?" Bryn spoke beside her. "Are you all right?"

She turned to him, but the man standing next to her was not the Bryn she knew. This was a warrior. He had a worn war cloak flung back over his shoulders and a metal and leather garment covered his chest. Muscles bulged in his ruddy, weathered arms as he held a round wooden shield in one hand and a huge sword in the other. His face seemed harsh and manly. A bristly auburn mustache hid his mouth, and his brown eyes were so fierce and bright, it took her breath away. She swallowed hard, willing the image away.

"Sirona." He gave her a little shake. Two heartbeats passed and Bryn was himself again. Sirona forced herself to appear calm, but she still felt sick.

Now that the ceremony was over, people began to congregate in small groups. There would be a period of relaxation and rest before the final rite of the gathering, which was the traditional sacrifice of Llewnasa, the seasonal rite giving thanks for the harvest. It seemed early for such a ceremony, but Fiach had mentioned that many of the Learned Ones were anxious to return to their tribes before the autumn rains began. Some of them had to travel a very long distance, clear across Albion, and in some cases, across the sunrise sea as well.

Sirona followed the other members of her tribe to a sheltered area under the trees. Her thoughts on her visions, she took little note when Fiach shouted, "Where have you been? How dare you neglect to take part in the sacred rites?"

"I didn't miss the ceremony," a familiar voice answered. "I watched from the forest. I can tell you every object that was sacrificed."

Sirona's head snapped up at the sound of Cruthin's voice. He looked very pleased with himself, which made Sirona wonder if he'd discovered one of the sacred places. She hurried toward him, eager to find out what he'd learned.

Fiach continued to berate Cruthin. "It was most irresponsible of you to wander off. All the Learned Ones and students are needed at every ritual. The more of us there are, the more influence we have with the gods. Tonight, I expect to you to be part of the sacred circle." The head Drui fixed Cruthin with a severe look, then walked off.

"Where were you?" Sirona asked Cruthin.

Cruthin smiled. "I was with the Great Mother Goddess."

Bryn, who had also joined them, snorted. "Rather than a goddess, I think it more likely you went back to the mainland and spent the night with your friend Pellan."

Sirona was startled. "Is that what you did?"

"Of course not. I told you, I went into the forest to prepare for tonight." He stared at her, his expression dark and mysterious.

Bryn looked from one of them to the other. "What are you planning?"

"Nothing," said Cruthin. He glanced at Bryn. "Aren't there some people here discussing the war with the Romans? Don't you want to go talk to them?"

"Nay," Bryn answered. "I'm staying here with the two of you." He gestured to Sirona. "Sirona looked unwell during the ceremony. I want to make certain she's all right."

"It was nothing," she responded. "I haven't eaten much the last few days. Then, when I saw the horses drowning, I started to feel sick."

"Horses?" Cruthin asked.

"Aye." Bryn's voice was scathing. "The stupid fools sent a whole chariot and team to the bottom of the lake. A hideous waste, and cruel besides. Those poor beasts were terrified." He turned to Sirona. "It was very upsetting, I agree. But it still doesn't explain the way you looked a few moments ago. You were as white as bleached wool."

Sirona made her voice coaxing. "Would it be possible for you to get me something to eat? I think that would help. Not traveling food, but something like what you brought back to camp last night?"

Bryn frowned. "If I fetch you some fresh food, will you promise to stay here?"

Sirona nodded. "I promise."

Bryn shot Cruthin a narrow-eyed glance, then turned back to her. "I'll find you something."

As he walked off with long, rapid strides, Sirona breathed a sigh of relief, although it was mingled with guilt. "Bless Bryn for his soft heart." She turned to Cruthin. "So, what happened? Did you find one of the sacred places?"

"Not yet, but I will." He smiled at her. "Tonight I'll show you all the secrets."

"Tonight? You mean, after the ceremony?"

Cruthin shook his head. "If we wait until the sacrifice is finished, it'll be too late. We must leave before it's over. We still have to find one of the sacred places. That might take awhile."

"You heard what Fiach said. He expects us to attend the ceremony."

"As long as we're part of the circle at the beginning of the ceremony, that's all that matters. There will be so many people there—how can Fiach keep track of us? We'll stay on the outer edge of the gathering, then slip away when no one is watching. The Great Mother Goddess will aid us. We're meant to do this, I know it. Come with me now," he urged. "We'll hide in the woods until the rite is about to begin, then find a place where it will be easy to slip away."

"I promised Bryn I would remain here."

Cruthin shrugged. "Do what you will." He turned and started to walk off.

"Wait!" She ran to catch up with him. "Aren't you going to tell me what happened? You say you were with the Goddess—what does that mean?"

"I can't explain it," he said. "You'll have to experience it for yourself." He turned once more to leave her.

"Wait," she cried again. "Don't you want to hear what happened to *me* last night?"

He shrugged.

Rapidly, she explained about going back to look for Dysri, about meeting Lovarn and their conversation, then coming back later and finding out that Lovarn was a spirit. "Isn't it amazing?" she asked. "What do you think it means? I felt like Lovarn was warning me about something, but I don't know exactly what it was."

Cruthin cocked his head and gazed at her intently. "Are you still going to deny that you have visions?"

Sirona stiffened as she realized she was doing exactly what her grandmother had warned her not to do. But pretending she didn't have visions had begun to feel futile, at least with Cruthin. She would have to trust him to keep quiet. "Aye, I do have visions," she answered. "But please don't tell Fiach, or any of the other Learned Ones."

Cruthin nodded. "They wouldn't be pleased that one of their students had such power, especially a female."

"And there's something else," Sirona said. "Another reason no one from our tribe must know about my visions. My mother made a terrible prediction about the future when I was a baby. It was so awful that Tarbelinus sent her away. If any of the tribe who were adults back then learn I have Seeings, they might think I'm going to do something like my mother did."

"What did your mother predict?" asked Cruthin.

Sirona hesitated, loathe to repeat the awful prophecy. Finally, she said, "My mother predicted the Tarisllwyth would be destroyed. That we would disappear from the earth."

Remembering all the things Bryn had told her about the Romans, Sirona experienced a sudden chill. What if her mother's Seeing was a true one...and the Romans were the reason for her tribe's downfall? She recalled her vision during the sacrifice: The vast number of warriors lined up for a battle. Her terrible sense that they were all going to die.

She met Cruthin's gaze. "What do you think? Do you believe what my mother predicted might actually come to pass?"

"How should I know?" Cruthin responded. "Anyway, it isn't important. I don't really care what happens to the Tarisllwyth. I'm concerned with the mysteries and our connection to the gods and the Otherworld."

Cruthin's attitude shocked Sirona. But she probably could have guessed he would react that way. He always seemed to have utter contempt for anything he wasn't interested in. His cold attitude disturbed her, and make her worry she'd made a mistake in confiding in him. "You won't tell anyone about my Seeings, will you?" she asked anxiously.

"Of course not," he answered. "Fiach's a fool. He knows nothing about the things that truly matter." He made a sound of disgust. "All those years of training in the grove, and no one even mentioned the Great Mother Goddess. She's the one we must honor, the one we must worship." His gaze met Sirona's. "That's what you and I will do this night."

Although a part of her agreed with him, she still had doubts. "I don't see why we can't wait until after the ceremony to search for one of the sacred places. It's going to be very awkward to leave in the middle of the rites."

"Nay, it won't. Everyone will be focused on the ceremony. They won't pay any attention to us."

"But shouldn't we be focused on the ceremony as well? Won't the gods be angry with us for leaving in the middle of it?"

Cruthin shook his head. "I told you, the other gods are nothing compared to the Goddess. She is the one we must honor."

Cruthin walked off. Sirona watched him go, feeling torn. A part of her believed she was meant to go to this sacred place. That there she would find answers to the questions troubling her. But another part of her was afraid. When she'd first beheld the sacred isle, she'd experienced an overpowering sense of dread. Did she dare ignore that warning?

* * *

The sky was dark, the Grain Moon beginning to rise. Its pale golden shape was barely visible through the trees surrounding the clearing where the Learned One gathered, some carrying torches. The participants began to form a circle, surrounding the large altar stone set in the center of the clearing. Sirona watched from behind a massive oak, waiting for the rest of the Drui to find their places. She'd managed to get away from Bryn by giving him the excuse of needing to go into the woods to relieve herself. Bryn obviously suspected she and Cruthin were planning something.

Bryn was probably right to worry. If she and Cruthin were caught slipping away, Fiach would certainly punish them. Sirona suppressed a shudder and tried to decide what to do.

She'd thought several times of seeking out Dysri and asking her about Cruthin's plan, but the few times she caught sight of the Brigante woman, she was always surrounded by other people. Sirona would have to wait until tonight and look for some sign from the gods—or the Goddess—advising her what to do.

Of course, maybe Cruthin wouldn't come, and she wouldn't have to decide. The circle was almost complete, and he still hadn't appeared. The thought that he might have gone without her filled her with frustration.

Elidyr and two other high Drui entered the clearing carrying torches. Behind them, led by slaves, were two white bullocks. As people stepped back to allow the Drui and sacrificial animals to enter the center of the circle, Sirona hurried to find a place among the ring of participants.

The bullocks were led to the altar and the head Drui of all the tribes positioned themselves around them. Elidyr gestured for silence. At the same time, Sirona felt someone touch her arm. She turned and saw Cruthin standing behind her. Exhaling in mingled relief and aggravation, she focused her attention on the center of the circle.

Elidyr evoked the gods, and all the Learned Ones began to chant, a low, ringing sound that echoed off the huge ancient oaks surrounding them. As a soft wind blew through the clearing, the hair on the back of Sirona's neck stood up. It was as if the gods had come, and she could feel them moving around her. A huge owl flew across the clearing, directly over the two bullocks in the center of the circle. In the moonlight, the bird's feathers flashed white, then it was gone. A murmur of wonder went through the crowd.

Sirona's body tightened with expectation. The owl's appearance seemed to be a message from the Goddess. Was this a sign she should follow the bird?

The Learned Ones began to chant more fervently. Elidyr spoke again, extolling the gift they were about to offer, not one but two sacred bulls, proof that they were a dutiful and reverent people who honored the gods with the best they had.

Sirona observed the bullocks in the center of the clearing. Most sacrificial animals had a white patch on their hide, marking them as sacred, but these beasts were almost completely white. They were also mature, well-muscled animals, not the young beasts that usually fell before the knife. Some tribe had carefully raised these animals, preparing them for years for this special sacrifice.

As the two other Drui came forward with the red leather bag carrying the special knife used to cut the animals' throats, Sirona felt a gentle touch on her hand. She turned to see Cruthin motioning with his head, indicating they should leave. She was torn. This was no ordinary sacrifice, but a powerful ritual such as had not been held for many years. All the Learned Ones gathered here believed the shedding the blood of these two special animals represented an act of devotion so profound that the gods could not help but listen to their pleas.

She closed her eyes, searching for some sign indicating what she should do. Abruptly, she remembered her vision of the circle of stones on the cliff above the sea and the people dancing around them. The smell of the ocean. Throbbing, surging music, guiding the dancers as they looped and swirled. The moon, high in the sky above the stone circle and the people. The stars whirling in the heavens above the dancers, gathering light, drawing it down to the people, filling the air around them. She could feel the light, like a caress against her skin. A whisper of breath passed over her.

When Cruthin touched her hand again, Sirona jerked back to awareness and opened her eyes. All at once, she knew she had to go with him. Arianrhod, lady of the silver wheel, goddess of time and destiny, was calling to her.

Cruthin moved off into the shadows. Sirona waited a few heartbeats, then followed.

* * *

They walked a long while in the pitch dark woods. The moon had gone under a cloud, but Cruthin insisted they keep moving. At last he stopped, and she pulled up beside him. "Do you know where we're going?"

"Of course."

Sirona suspected he was lying, that he had no idea which direction to go. "We can't keep on like this, wandering around blindly. We'll get lost and never find the sacred place."

"What do you suggest?"

"Perhaps if we tried asking the Great Mother to show us the way, She would answer."

"You mean, if *you* tried...if you had some sort of vision." There was an edge of derision to his voice.

"Not a vision, exactly," Sirona said. "But if we opened our minds, the Goddess might communicate with us. That's what happened at the ceremony. I wouldn't have left with you if I didn't have a clear sense that the Goddess wanted me to go."

Cruthin shrugged. "Do what you will. Otherwise, we're stuck here, waiting for the moon to reappear."

Sirona took a deep breath and closed her eyes. She tried to think of the Mother Goddess. Instead, the image of Lovarn filled her mind. He gazed at her intently, and all at once, she knew exactly which direction the sacred mound lay. She could see it in her mind. She opened her eyes and pointed. "This way."

"Perhaps the Goddess speaks to you because you're a woman," Cruthin said irritably. "Perhaps she favors you because of that."

She turned to start walking, but Cruthin grasped her arm. He pulled her around so they faced each other. "This night, you will *become* the Goddess." Abruptly, he leaned over and kissed her.

As his mouth met hers, Sirona was startled, but her surprise soon turned to pleasure. She savored the feeling of Cruthin's body against hers, hard and male. His mouth on hers, subtle, caressing. His smell, like an animal's, wild, dark and musky. He deepened the kiss, urging her mouth open. She tasted him and the world whirled around her. The blood rushed through her body, making her breasts and groin throb.

As abruptly as he'd grabbed her, Cruthin released her and stepped back. "Mmmm," he muttered. "Sex magic with you will be most potent. But first, we must find the Goddess's place. Show me which way we should go."

Stunned, Sirona didn't move for a time. Then she started walking, focusing on the inner sense guiding her.

As they walked, the clouds shifted and a shaft of moonlight flickered down through the trees, illuminating their way. But Sirona didn't need the moon to show the path. She walked on steadily and confidently, sensing the pull of the sacred place. As Cruthin followed after her, she recalled the kiss. It had felt wonderful...and somehow *right*. As if they were meant to be together.

She realized she'd always been attracted to Cruthin, to his dazzling dark looks and lithe body. At this moment she ached to have Cruthin hold her in his arms, to press her beneath his body, to feel his bare skin next to hers. The very thought of it made her shiver with expectation.

Chapter 7

The forest thinned and finally ended. In the open area was a mound. Too round and perfect to be a hill, it rose up abruptly from the level terrain all around. There was a ditch around it and stones arranged in a ring at the base. As they drew near, Sirona saw an opening on the side of the mound. Breathless with excitement, she made her way through the ring of stones to the opening. Boulders blocked what appeared to be an entrance into the mound, with dressed stones marking the top and sides. The moon shone down, making the pale gray rocks glisten.

She examined the stones. On them were markings, spirals, dots and lines, weathered but still visible. Tingling with awe, she stroked her hand over the markings, wondering what they meant.

"What is it?" Cruthin called.

"There's a grave here, an ancient one." She returned to the ring of stones at the base of the mound. Laying her palm on the rough surface of one of the stones, she closed her eyes and concentrated. All at once, she was falling. She could see stars above her. Below was endless, empty space.

Astounded, she drew her hand away. Cruthin was standing nearby. "What do you think?" he asked. "Is there magic here?"

She nodded, then glanced around and tried to shake off the dizziness the brief vision had aroused.

"What's wrong?"

"This isn't what I expected. There's power here. The stones hum with energy. But what it means..." She shook her head.

Cruthin approached her. "Come with me."

She followed him to a grassy area a short distance away. He spread out his wolf pelt cloak—made from the animal he'd killed during his man-making trial a year before—then began to take things out of his pack. A waterskin. Leather bag. A small gold knife. The weapon looked like no weapon Sirona had ever seen before.

"Where did you get that?" she asked.

"Pellan. She said it was something passed down through her family. Her people believe gold has special powers. Don't be afraid. It's not a weapon, but a kind of amulet. Now, eat with me. Drink."

"Pellan gave you all those things? Why?"

"She recognized I had a special connection to the gods. When she discovered I wanted to hold a ceremony honoring the Goddess, she agreed to help me."

"That was very generous of her," Sirona said skeptically.

"She said no man could ever get as close to the Goddess as a woman could. That's why it's important you are here."

It seemed as if Cruthin was using her. Yet, she wanted to be part of this. The idea of worshiping the Great Mother Goddess and feeling Her power enthralled her.

Cruthin held out the skin. Sirona accepted it and took a swallow. She'd expected mead, but this beverage didn't taste sweet and fiery, but cool and dark, like the earth. "What is it?" she asked.

"Magic," Cruthin said. "It will give you enchanted dreams."

Sirona drank a little more, then handed back the skin. Cruthin opened the leather pouch and took out a mealcake. "Take a bite," he urged.

Sirona did so, then watched as he gulped down the rest of the contents of the skin and finished off the mealcake. "What's next?" she asked.

Cruthin smiled lazily. "Next, I evoke the Goddess."

He drew away from her, then lifted his arms to the heavens and began to sing:

> *"Arianhrod, Ceridwen, Rhiannon,*
> *Blodeuwedd, Modran, Don,*
> *Branwen, Cyhiraeth, Morrigan.*
> *I invoke you—maiden, mother, crone*
> *Lady of the moon,*
> *Keeper of the cauldron,*
> *Great queen,*
> *Maiden of summer,*
> *Lifegiver,*
> *Grain goddess,*
> *Lady of love and desire,*
> *Keeper of pools and springs,*
> *Raven of death.*
> *Enfold me in your warm, soft flesh.*
> *Fill me with your light.*
> *Quench my thirst with your gleaming rivers and streams.*
> *Feed me from your supple breasts.*
> *Make me strong.*

Make me powerful.
Make me invincible."

Sirona had never heard Cruthin sing before. He had a bard's voice, beguiling and honey sweet, yet edged with power. For the first time she saw him not as the fellow student she'd known nearly all her life, but as a Drui. Listening to him evoking the magic of the night sky sent a thrill down her body.

If he seemed changed, then she was as well. She felt keenly alive, her senses heightened. When Cruthin came to where she stood and said, "Take off your clothing," she didn't hesitate. She reached down, grasped the skirt of her gown and pulled it over her head.

Cruthin's gaze moved over her. She could feel it lingering on her breasts, making her nipples tighten, then moving down to her groin. Never before had she felt so acutely aware of her own flesh. Of the softness and fragility of her skin. Of the heat of her blood flowing through her veins. The weight of her breasts, as if they pulled her toward the earth. Of the hidden opening between her thighs. Of her womb, small and empty inside her, and yet ready to grow and swell and burst with life. All that was needed was a man's seed.

Cruthin drew near. He put his hands on her shoulders, then cupped her breasts. She gasped at the pressure of his callused palms against her nipples. He kissed her, then nuzzled aside her hair and nibbled on her neck. She sighed with pleasure. His soft breath tantalized her skin. His mouth enflamed her flesh. Swirling, dark energy.

Her limbs went limp, and she leaned against him, grabbing his shoulders to keep from falling. With a swift, easy movement he picked her up and carried her over to the mound. She heard his harsh breathing as he labored up the slope. At the very top, he lay her down upon the soft grass. "Wait here," he said.

As if in a trance, she watched him climb down. The stars swirled overhead. The moon shone down upon her body. She was cold. She was on fire.

He returned in moments. Very carefully, very deliberately, he laid the small gold knife between her breasts, with the blade pointing downward. She wanted to ask what it meant, but she couldn't speak. He stood over her and began to undress. She drank in the vision he made. The long, sinewy grace of his torso. His strong neck and proud features. The way his dark hair brushed his shoulders. His narrow hips and lean, tanned legs. And rising up between them, his phallus. Bold and alive, it thrust out like a weapon. She stared at it in amazement, wondering how it could possibly fit inside her. He saw the direction of her gaze and smiled. "I will please you."

He came over to her and straddled her hips, looking down at her. "Take me, Sirona. Become the Goddess and mate with me."

She was overwhelmed by desire. A hunger she had not fathomed. It welled up inside her, making her body ache with need. The need to be joined with this man, to feel their bodies fit together. Her flesh a sheath for his living, pulsing dagger.

"Aye," she whispered. "Aye."

He knelt between her thighs and used his hand to guide himself into her. There was pressure, then pain. She closed her eyes and gritted her teeth against the searing, stretching sensation. As her flesh yielded, she gasped with relief and desire. Then she looked up at him.

It wasn't Cruthin who leaned over her, but some creature with the torso of a man and the head of a stag. And it wasn't a stag's eyes that met hers, but the ferocious golden-eyed gaze of a predator. Sirona screamed and began to struggle. The beast held her down. She fought harder, flailing her arms, clawing and writhing with all her strength.

At last, somehow, she threw the creature off. She lay there panting, afraid to look. Afraid the beast meant attack her again. Dreading that she would once more have to gaze into those cold, yellow eyes. Finally, trembling, she dared to turn her head. Cruthin lay beside her, his face and torso livid with deep, bloody scratches. "Why did you do that?" he asked.

Sirona felt numb with shock. "I'm sorry," she said. "It wasn't you who I was fighting. It was…some creature. Part man. Part stag. Part…wolf, I think. I thought it was going to…devour me." She shuddered.

Cruthin sat up. "Cernunnos," he said. "You saw Cernunnos?" His voice was taut with excitement. "Of course. Arianrhod, the Lady of the moon, the goddess of the silver wheel, she is the consort of the Horned One. I made you a goddess. And you, in turn, conjured a god. But why…" He looked at her quizzically. "Why did you fight Cernunnos? Why didn't you accept him—accept me—into your body?"

"I couldn't help it," she said. "I was afraid. The creature I saw was monstrous."

"A pity. If you weren't such a coward, you could be my consort. Together we could make great magic."

Cruthin stood and climbed down the mound. Sirona watched him in dismay and confusion, then began to dress. When she finished, she made her way down as well. Looking around for Cruthin, she saw him dancing in the open meadow nearby. His movements were wild and unrestrained. Flailing arms. Twirling body. Jumps and leaps. Pure, instinctive movements. As if he heard music. All at once, Sirona heard it, too. A wild, keening melody, sad and lovely.

She watched Cruthin, in awe of the beauty of his movements. He reminded her of an otter cavorting beside a stream. A salmon leaping the rapids. A deer bounding through the forest. Lithe and graceful. The moonlight flashed over his spinning body, black, then silver, then black again. Light and shadow. Life and death.

As he jumped and twirled in the tall grass among the bracken and heather, people came out of the shadows to join him. Slender and naked, they danced around him, moving in a slow, rhythmic pattern. They began to chant in a language Sirona had never heard before. And yet, it seemed familiar, as if the meaning of the words was buried in her mind somewhere.

When she returned her gaze to Cruthin, he had turned into Cernunnos again. On his head were the antlers of a stag, while his body remained that of a man. She couldn't see his face. But she knew now that he was the god of the animals, of the hunt, of death. This time she was not afraid. She was watching from a distance, not feeling the hot breath of the beast looming over her. Faster and faster he whirled, until he was a blur. The moonlight shone down, turning him into a vivid, bright light. The light grew in intensity, blazing, brilliant, the brightest thing she had ever seen. Then it vanished.

She blinked in shock. No matter how she strained her eyes, she could see nothing in the place where Cruthin and the other dancers had been. "Cruthin," she cried. "Cruthin, where are you?"

She moved forward, her gaze sweeping the area. A cloud had covered the moon, and everything was cloaked in darkness. Gradually, her eyes adjusted, and she caught sight of Cruthin lying nearby. She ran to him. He didn't move when she touched his face, and she had the horrifying thought that he was dead. She put her hand to his throat and cried out in relief when she felt his pulse.

She rushed back to where they had left their supplies and grabbed up the wolfskin and their other clothing. Returning to where Cruthin lay, she balled up his bracco and put them under his head, then covered him with his crys. She put on her gown and stretched out next to him, then dragged the wolfskin over them both. Cruthin seemed to be in either a trance or deeply asleep. She was also exhausted. She couldn't keep her eyes open...

* * *

When Sirona awoke, the sun was already up and shining hotly on her face. She sat up slowly, and memories of the night before filled her mind. She recalled the desire she'd felt. Then the terrifying sight of the monster looming over her. Yet, it hadn't been a monster, but Cruthin.

Cruthin had turned into Cernunnos. He'd called down the Goddess and She had transformed him. She had also brought the people who danced in the circle of light.

Sirona shook her head. It must have been a dream, or some sort of Seeing caused by the potent brew they'd drunk. A dream…and yet…here they were, far from the rest of the Learned Ones. All at once, panic engulfed her. They'd left a sacred ceremony. Now it was morning and too late to go back and pretend they'd been there all along!

She leaned over and grabbed Cruthin's shoulder and shook him. "Wake up! It's morning. We must go back." She shook him again. When he didn't respond, she jostled him more vigorously.

"Uhhh," he moaned, rolling away from her.

"Come on, Cruthin. Get up."

He mumbled something but didn't rise.

"Please, Cruthin. Please." She shook him again, roughly this time. After several attempts, she was able to rouse him. He was sleepy and disoriented, and she had to help him dress. Seeing the marks of dried blood on his chest and face made everything seem more real. She hadn't dreamed it. Cruthin had turned into Cernunnos. It was incredible. Astounding. And yet, in the cold light of day, she wondered if even such an amazing experience could compensate for what they now faced. To leave an important sacrifice, a ceremony meant to honor the gods…. Her breath caught as she wondered what their punishment would be.

She finally got Cruthin walking, although he still acted as if he were half-asleep. As they made their way across the clearing toward the forest, she glanced back at the mound and remembered the small gold knife. She went back to look for it, climbing on top of the mound. By daylight, the sense of power had all but vanished. And so had the knife. She couldn't find it anywhere.

She returned to where she'd left Cruthin. He'd lain down again and she had to rouse him. Eventually, she got him moving again. She decided they should go back to the gathering place, rather than returning to the lake of sacrifice. That way they could say they had returned there on their own after the ceremony.

She was able to find the pathway between the gathering place and the lake of sacrifice and they started walking. Cruthin didn't speak. He still seemed to be in some sort of trance. She wondered what he remembered from the night before.

She recalled the people who had appeared and danced around Cruthin. Were they spirits, visitors from another time? Were they the Old Ones? She tried to remember what they had looked like. Dark-skinned, small-statured men and women, like the fisherfolk. Their naked bodies had been painted with strange symbols, some of which reminded her of the markings on the stones at the entrance to the mound. They reminded her of the people she'd seen in her first vision.

She wondered if the events of the night before were that Seeing come to life. But there were differences. Her vision had been of a hillside by the sea. There had been no mound there and the circle of stones was much larger. And something told her that the time of her vision was still in the future.

When they drew close to the gathering place, Sirona slowed her pace. If they didn't rejoin the others, they would be left behind on the sacred isle. Would that be such an awful fate? But neither she nor Cruthin knew much about surviving on their own. To even attempt such a thing would be foolish. Then she heard voices, and the decision seemed to have been made for her. They walked into the clearing, which was full of Learned Ones.

Someone said, "There they are." In moments, they were surrounded by Drui.

* * *

"These young people have failed in their duty and damaged our relationship to the gods. What does it matter how many bulls we sacrifice if some of our number have no regard for the sacred rituals?" Elidyr paused for breath, then continued, "I'm not certain what punishment is appropriate here. Nothing like this has ever happened at a gathering. For that matter, I know of no incidence of such disrespect among my own tribe, or any other. If these two were children and just learning their responsibilities as Learned Ones, it would be one thing. But they have been through their man-making and woman-making rituals. As adults, they must be held accountable."

"I agree," Fiach answered. "In fact, this is not the first time that Cruthin..." He pointed, "that this young man has shown disregard for our rules. I warned him that if he went off again on his own, I would see him expelled from the grove."

Sirona stood rigid. It was as bad as she had feared. They were in trouble, grave trouble.

"Of course, he must be expelled," another man spoke. "But is that enough? He has trained for years to learn the mysteries, the secrets of the grove. Can we let him walk away with that kind of knowledge when he clearly has no respect for it? What will the gods think of us if we allow the sacred wisdom to be tainted and betrayed in such a manner?"

"What of the woman?" someone asked. "Is she to be held accountable the same as the man?"

"Her failing sheds doubt upon all female Learned Ones," said another Learned One. Sirona recognized him as the young man who'd was talking about making human sacrifices to the gods. He was young, with black hair and strange pale eyes. "I say we should expel all females from the grove!"

"That's nonsense." It was a woman who spoke now. An ancient-looking crone Sirona had only seen only once or twice during the gathering. "If you reason thus, then men are not fit for the honor of the grove either, since one of your number has broken the sacred law as well." The woman motioned to Sirona and Cruthin. "I, for one, would like to know why these two young people left the ceremony. Perhaps they had good reason for doing so."

Should she speak? Sirona wondered. Should she tell them about the incredible things she'd seen at the mound?

She opened her mouth, but before she could utter a word, she heard Cruthin's harsh whisper. "Tell them nothing. They're too stupid to understand."

Inclining her head to him, she whispered back, "What if they decide to kill us? Will you advise silence then?"

"They won't," he said. "The Great Mother Goddess won't allow it."

"If you would speak, then share your words with all of us!" Elidyr thundered. He took a step toward them, his face a rictus of harsh lines. "Tell us the reason for your blasphemy!"

Cruthin's expression was calm, almost disdainful. "What happened to us last night is beyond your understanding."

"Your defiance is matched only by your arrogance." Elidyr turned away. "Such willful disobedience must be punished severely!"

"I will speak! I know why they left the ceremony." Sirona saw Bryn making his way through the crowd. "They wished to go to a place of the Old Ones," he said breathlessly.

Sirona stared at Bryn in astonishment. There was no way he could know such a thing, unless Dysri had told him.

"Come forward." Elidyr urged Bryn nearer, and Bryn obeyed. He was taller than most of the Learned Ones, his bearing, proud and bold, like a warrior. Guilt squeezed Sirona. She had lied to Bryn more than once and not always treated him kindly. What if he was punished for defending her?

"Tell us why you believe they had some purpose other than making a mockery of the ceremony," Elidyr said.

"I heard them talking about their plans to find a place of the Old Ones. That woman." Bryn pointed to Dysri. "She will tell you it's true."

Dysri stepped forward, her voice calm and assured. "It is indeed true. The young woman came to me for advice, asking me to help her find a place sacred to the ancient race. She seemed very serious and respectful. I don't think she meant to offend the gods by her actions."

"It matters not why they left the ceremony, only that they did so." The young man spoke again, his voice harsh and impatient. "The council of high Drui must decide on an appropriate punishment. I would argue for death myself. Send their spirits to the Otherworld, to apologize for what they've done."

"You can't do that!" Bryn cried. He moved closer to Sirona. "This woman is a seer. The gods speak to her. If you kill her, they will be angry. Are you willing to risk that?"

Everyone looked at Sirona. She wanted desperately to speak, to tell them what she'd experienced. But she felt Cruthin behind her, his eyes boring into her. Was he right? Would speaking about what had happened to them taint the sacred nature of what they'd experienced?

Elidyr turned to Fiach. "This woman is of your tribe. Do you have any reason to believe she's a seer?"

Fiach stared at Sirona, eyes narrowed.

"Has she told you she has visions?" Elidyr asked.

"Nay," Fiach answered.

"This is absurd," interjected the young, dark-haired Drui. "If those of her own tribe don't know of her visions, I don't think—"

"It's true!" Dysri moved to stand between Sirona and Elidyr and the other Drui. "Sirona has exceptional gifts. During the gathering, she came to my tribe's camp to find me. I wasn't there, so she spoke with a man who appeared to be guarding the camp. She conversed at length with this man, named Lovarn. When I came back to the camp, she told me of the incident, and I told her that the person she had spoken to had been dead for a dozen years."

There was murmuring among the gathering. Then the young Drui said, "She might have made that up. She could have learned of this Lovarn from someone else and created this tale to make you think she talks to spirits."

"Nay," Dysri said. "No one else here knows about Lovarn. What she experienced was indeed a glimpse into the other realm. These things come to her unwilled. She doesn't seek them out. Perhaps it's true the gods wanted her to leave the ceremony. Perhaps they had some other purpose in mind for her last night."

"And what of the man? Does he also see visions? Is he also 'gifted'?" The young Drui's lips curled in disgust.

"Aye." Sirona stepped forward, unable to remain silent any longer. Her voice came out strong and bold. "Cruthin is more than gifted. He doesn't merely see visions, he becomes one with the gods. Last night, I saw him turn into Cernunnos. I saw the antlers upon his head. His face became that of a beast...with yellow eyes and a cruel mouth. And there was more. I saw people dancing in a circle, drawing down the magic of the night sky. I—"

"Silence!" Elidyr cut her off. "You can make up whatever tales you wish, but it doesn't change what you've done." He made a slashing motion. "The council will discuss this matter in private and decide your fate. For now, you'll both be confined to your tribe's camp." He nodded to Fiach. "They must be guarded at all times."

"Of course," Fiach answered.

Chapter 8

"Take them to our camp." Fiach ordered. Cuill and Tadhg moved to obey.

As Sirona and Cruthin were led away, she heard Bryn imploring Fiach, "Tell the other Learned Ones that Sirona is a seer and they won't punish her so harshly. As for Cruthin, if you can make them believe Sirona convinced him that the gods were speaking to her, telling her to leave the ceremony, they may be lenient with him as well."

"They broke the sacred laws and shamed our tribe," Fiach retorted. "Why should I help them?"

"Because if you don't, I'll go back and tell my father you did nothing to prevent the deaths of two members of our tribe. He won't be pleased. By rights, their lives belong to him, not to you!"

"Their lives belong to the gods," Fiach said coldly.

Sirona's heart sank. Bryn had tried his best, but it seemed unlikely his words would sway Fiach.

She walked numbly back to the camp, where Cuill ordered her and Cruthin to go into their tents. Inside the hide shelter, Sirona tried to quell the queasiness in her belly. Would she come to the same awful fate as the young woman in her vision? It was not so much the thought of dying that troubled her, but the idea that if she were sacrificed, her spirit would never be at peace. It horrified her to think of ending up like that young woman, doomed to wander endlessly in the twilight realm between worlds. A sob welled up inside her. She pressed her fist into her mouth to stifle it. *Please, Great Mother, help me!*

She recalled what she had experienced at the mound and the circle of stones—the light from the sky, the people who appeared out of nowhere, the image of Cruthin as Cernunnos. She'd known great magic. But was one night of dazzling wonder worth losing her life?

Some time later, she heard Fiach's voice outside the tent. She moved near the entrance, hoping to learn what their fate would be. A moment later, there was a strangled sound. "He's gone," Fiach cried. "Sirona!" Fiach thrust himself into her tent and dragged her out. "Where is he?" Fiach demanded, looming over her. "Where is he?"

Sirona shook her head, too startled and stunned to answer.

Bryn, who was standing nearby, seized Fiach's cloak and tried to pull him away. "Leave her alone!" he shouted.

"How dare you assault me!" Fiach cried, twisting from Bryn's grasp.

"Leave her alone," Bryn repeated. He wrenched his eating knife from his belt and brandished it.

"Your father will hear of this," Fiach muttered. "He won't be pleased." To Sirona, he said. "Get up. Get up and tell me what you know of Cruthin's disappearance."

She stood. "I know nothing."

Fiach's gaze swept over her and a cruel smile touched his lips. "How does it feel to know your lover has abandoned you? You are cursed, as your mother was." His mouth twitched, then he turned back to the others. "Tell no one about this," he said. "We'll leave for Mordarach tonight, before anyone can discover our prisoner has escaped. We won't speak of Cruthin ever again. It will be as if he never existed. If you should see him in this realm, I want you to fetch as many warriors as you can and order them to kill him."

Sirona didn't know whether to be relieved or despairing. If they were going back to Mordarach, then it was unlikely she would be sacrificed. But she would still be punished. Perhaps banished as her mother had been. The thought made her feel sick inside.

Fiach turned back to Sirona. "Take down your tent and pack up your supplies. Quickly."

As soon as Fiach left, Bryn approached Sirona. "Come on," he said. "I'll help you get ready to leave."

* * *

Sirona paused on one of the high peaks and surveyed the vast landscape around her. The mountain vistas that had seemed so exhilarating on the journey to the sacred isle now struck her as desolate and lonely. She watched an eagle circle, floating effortlessly on the wind currents. All she could think about was the bird's ruthless search for prey, and that when it spied a hare or a vole or other small animal, it would swoop down and impale the helpless creature with its huge claws and sharp beak.

The next moment, she thought of Cruthin, and her distress turned to anger. He had left her, and without a thought for what might happen to her after he was gone. She tried to tell herself he'd had no choice, that there was no way the two of them could have slipped away without notice. He had chosen to save himself, that's all. But she knew she would never have abandoned *him*.

"It's a spectacular view, isn't it?" Bryn came up behind her. "We've been very fortunate it's been clear both times we've crossed the mountains. I'm certain it's often stormy and blustery, or the sky is heavy with rain clouds. From here, doesn't it seem you can see to the end of the world?"

Sirona nodded, but without conviction. Beautiful scenery did little to lift her mood. Before leaving for the sacred isle, she'd promised her grandmother she wouldn't get into trouble on this journey. How miserably she had failed.

"Don't worry," Bryn said softly. "Once we get back to Mordarach, Fiach will have to defer to my father's wishes, and Tarbelinus won't allow the punishment to be too severe."

Sirona looked at him. No matter how much Bryn wanted to protect her, her fate was beyond his control. "I appreciate all you've done for me," she said. "You've been a loyal friend."

He moved nearer, his brown eyes hot and intent. "I would like to be more than your friend, Sirona."

She searched her mind for something to say, a means of discouraging him. But after all he'd done for her, every response she thought of seemed too harsh. "Please, I don't want to speak of these things." She walked away, retreating once again into the anguish of her thoughts.

* * *

When they arrived at Mordarach, everyone came out to welcome them. As soon as she saw Nesta, Sirona stiffened. She could hardly bear to look at her grandmother.

Nesta started to make her way over to Sirona. Before she reached her, someone asked, "Where's Cruthin?"

Fiach, who had been quietly talking to Tarbelinus, jerked around. His powerful voice rang out. "The young man called Cruthin has betrayed our tribe and offended the gods. We'll speak of him no more. He is expelled from the grove, and from our tribe. If he's ever seen near Mordarach, he'll be put to death."

Everyone stared at Fiach in stunned silence. Then Tarbelinus said, "Come with me, Fiach." To the rest of the tribe, the chieftain announced, "Later, when the travelers have washed and rested, we'll celebrate their return."

Nesta finally reached Sirona. Her blue eyes were dark with concern. "What happened, Sirona?"

Sirona shook her head, fighting back tears. The sense of shame and failure overwhelmed her.

Nesta grasped Sirona's shoulder. "What is it, granddaughter? Why are you so distraught? Is it because Cruthin's been banished?"

"I'm sorry," Sirona whispered. "I thought...I truly believed we were being guided by the gods." She turned away.

Nesta let out a cry. "Whatever Cruthin did, you were involved as well?"

Sirona nodded.

"Let's walk back to the hut. We can speak of this there."

When they reached the dwelling, Sirona sank down on her bedplace. The familiar scents—herbs and cooking—both soothed and tormented her. She might be on the verge of losing everything she cared about.

"Sirona," Nesta said sharply. "Tell me what happened."

She shook her head. "Not now, grandmother, I'm…I'm too tired."

Nesta let out her breath in a long sigh. "Very well. I'll make you some broth. You should eat something after your long journey."

* * *

She was being pursued by wild beasts. When she looked back, their yellow eyes glowed in the mist. She could see the glint of their vicious fangs. Their huge, gaping mouths. A voice told her to surrender, to stop running and let them kill her. But she could not. She did not want to die like that, torn into bloody pieces. Alone in the darkness.

"Sirona." She woke to find Nesta gently shaking her. She clutched Nesta's hand and sat up on the bedplace, trembling.

"Sirona." Nesta's voice sounded strained. A moment later, Sirona turned and saw Tarbelinus sitting near the hearth. The chieftain seemed much too large for the small space. With his masses of tawny gold hair and big, muscular body, he reminded Sirona of a cat waiting to pounce on its prey. It was as if the terrors of her dream had followed her into the waking world.

Tarbelinus spoke in his deep voice. "Sirona, you must leave Mordarach. I'm sending you north. Your father is a warrior there, with one of the Brigante tribes. Perhaps you can find him."

She was being sent away. It was as bad as she feared.

"I'll send an escort with you," Tarbelinus said. "You'll be safe, guarded at all times." His expression softened. "It will be better this way. There's nothing for you here."

Nesta made a choked sound. Sirona looked at her, feeling empty.

"The chieftain wants to make certain nothing happens to you," Nesta said. "Is that not kind of him?" Her voice dripped sarcasm.

Sirona looked from her grandmother to the chieftain and back again. "Before I go, I want to hear the truth about Banon."

Something changed in Tarbelinus's eyes. Sirona could sense hostility…and a kind of fear. "Nay," he said.

"Aye," said Nesta. "She has a right to know."

Tarbelinus took a deep breath. "I'm responsible for your mother's death. She didn't deserve to die…like that anyway." He paused. "But that's not to say I'm sorry." He gestured angrily. "She made my life miserable. She threatened my family. Terrorized Rhyell. I had to send her away. I promised Banon an escort, but…we parted in anger. I should have sent someone after her. But I didn't. I must live with that."

He shifted his weight. Sirona could tell he longed to stand up and move about, but the hut was too small. He continued, "Before she left, Banon threatened us. Cursed us. Said the dun would be destroyed. That I would be led away in shackles. She said that Bryn…" He paused again, as if afraid to utter the words. "She said my son would be killed in the first battle he fought in. That's why I've never allowed him to become a warrior."

So, that was the secret Nesta wouldn't share with her. The reason Tarbelinus had made his son's life miserable all these years—insisting he train to be a Learned One when he had no calling for it. Thinking about the unhappiness Bryn had experienced because of his father's decision, Sirona grew angry. "You had no right to try to change Bryn's destiny," she said. "If the gods will it, then he will die in battle. His life until then should be of his choosing. Not yours!"

"I have every right," Tarbelinus said. "I'm not merely his father, but also his chieftain. I make use of the abilities of any man of the Tarisllwyth as I see fit."

"You will fail," Sirona said. The memory came to her swiftly. "I've seen a vision of Bryn in battle attire. He's meant to be a warrior."

Tarbelinus's blue eyes flashed fire, and he struck her across the face. She fell back.

Nesta knelt beside Sirona. "How dare you!" she cried.

An image flashed into Sirona's mind. A lovely woman with dark gold hair and deep gray eyes stood before Tarbelinus, hands on hips, taunting the chieftain. Her sneering gaze was cold and empty, heartless. Sirona realized she couldn't blame Tarbelinus. Her mother had been cruel and selfish. She hadn't cared who she hurt.

And her blood runs in your veins. You are cursed as well. As the thought filled Sirona's mind, she felt cold and sick.

Nesta released Sirona. Straightening, head held high, Nesta faced Tarbelinus. "Leave us. I must prepare my granddaughter for her journey."

As soon as Tarbelinus had gone, Sirona turned a pleading look to Nesta, "Grandmother, come with me."

Nesta shook her head. "I would never survive the hardships of the journey."

Sirona felt tears spill down her cheeks. Nesta came to soothe her. "You possess the same sort of power your mother did, although you can choose to use it for good rather than ill. I'm convinced the gods have a purpose for you, and they will protect you."

"Are you very certain, Grandmother?"

Nesta nodded. "Beyond my faith in the gods, I've insisted Tarbelinus give you a proper escort and furnish you with supplies and household goods. With that and the wealth you have from your mother— along with your fair face and youth—some northern warrior will be eager to handfast with you."

"But what about…being a Learned One?"

"I'm afraid that path is closed to you now. It would have been difficult enough here, among your own people. But to go to another tribe and expect them to accept you as Drui…." Nesta smiled, although the expression looked forced. "Perhaps it's better this way. You'll be able to have the life of a normal woman, instead of enduring the rigid discipline of the grove. You'll have children and enjoy the pleasures of a family."

"But I know nothing about running a household… or being a wife!"

Nesta placed a hand on her arm. "Our lives don't always turn out as we expect, and most of us experience sorrow and disappointment. But sometimes joy comes from unexpected things. While Banon was always a trial to me, she gave birth to you. And raising you has been the greatest satisfaction of my life."

Sirona began to weep. She felt as if her life was over. For as long she could remember, all her energies were focused on being a Drui. Now that could never be.

Nesta embraced her, holding Sirona against her frail, bony body.

After a time, Nesta gently drew away. "There's something else I must tell you. Something that Tarbelinus requires in exchange for your escort. It's a small thing, and one that—out of kindness—you should be willing to do."

Sirona gazed at her grandmother warily. "What does Tarbelinus want?"

"He wants you to tell Bryn that you don't return his affections."

Sirona gave a quick, bitter laugh. "Why should that matter? I'm sure Tarbelinus has made it very clear to his son that he can have no future with me."

"That's true. But Tarbelinus would prefer it if you told Bryn these things yourself. The chieftain has only recently discovered Bryn's…fondness for you, and I think it reminds him of his own unreasoning passion for Banon all those years ago. He realizes Bryn won't give up easily, and he thinks the best way to end his son's hopes is for you to make it clear you don't love him." Nesta paused and her forehead furrowed. "That's true, isn't it? You don't return Bryn's feelings?"

Sirona considered carefully. She'd grown up with Bryn, and until recently thought of him as a brother. But now, facing the prospect of losing him, she could see how much she'd come to depend him...and care for him. Those feelings might have turned into love if given the chance. But that could never happen now.

"Sirona?" Nesta prompted.

She met her grandmother's gaze, "What would it matter if I said I loved Bryn? Tarbelinus would never allow us to be together."

"That's true," Nesta agreed. "And given that fact, no matter what you feel, it would be kindest if you told Bryn that you don't care for him the way he does you. There's no point making him yearn for something that can never come to pass."

The aching sense of loss inside Sirona deepened. There was no chance she and Bryn could ever be together. It would be cruel to make him continue to hope for such a thing. She nodded slowly. "Very well. I will do as Tarbelinus asks."

Nesta looked relieved. "You must speak to him soon. Tarbelinus is much more likely to be generous in the supplies he sends with you if he knows you have fulfilled your part of the bargain. As a matter of fact, I'll fetch Bryn now."

While she waited, Sirona felt the bitterness build inside her. She was sick of Tarbelinus and his belief that he could control the lives of those around him. He'd manipulated Bryn all his life, and now he sought to command even his son's heart.

A moment later, Bryn pushed his way into the hut. "You wanted to see me." Warm brown eyes met hers. Seeing the longing and despair in their depths, Sirona's heart twisted. *Poor Bryn, forced into a life he despised, and all because of Banon's prediction.*

She cleared her throat. "As you know, I'm going north."

"You mean, my father's *sending* you north." His voice was edged with fury.

She shrugged. "The fact is, I'll be far away from here. It's likely I'll never return."

"I could go with you." Hope sprang into Bryn's eyes.

"Your father would never allow it."

His fierce gaze met hers. "I could follow you. I'm a man now. My father doesn't control me."

If only Bryn could come with her. It would make all the difference. Her other losses would be almost bearable. But then reason returned and she shook her head. "Your father would pursue us, and when he found us, he would have his warriors drag you back to Mordarach. As for me...it's likely he would have me killed."

Bryn stared at her. Then he nodded. "I could come and find you later."

Sirona remembered Nesta's words. It wasn't fair to allow Bryn to plan his whole life around her. She must force him to face the finality of the situation. "My grandmother...she implied that in order to be accepted into another tribe, I will have to handfast with one of their warriors."

"Why not handfast with me?" Bryn implored.

Sirona winced, knowing the pain her words would cause. "Because you're not a warrior, and except in your father's tribe, you have no hearth to call your home."

Bryn looked as if he had been dealt a brutal blow. "It's true," he finally said in a ravaged voice. "But only because I haven't been given a choice."

Sirona ached for him. There must be some way to ease his despair. All at once, it came to her. "You were right, Bryn. I do have visions of the future. In fact, I've had one of you. In it, you were dressed in battle attire. You appeared to me as a warrior."

His face lit up. "A warrior? What do you think it means?"

"Perhaps it's time for you to leave Mordarach, find a place in another tribe and train as a warrior with them. I don't think any chieftain would turn away an able-bodied young man who vowed to serve him."

"Perhaps a tribe in the north?" Bryn said hopefully.

"Nay. If you travel the same direction as I do, Tarbelinus would surely find you and bring you back. You must set out east or west or south, so your father doesn't realize where you've gone until you're far away."

Bryn nodded. "It's a good plan." He smiled at her faintly. "And since it was given to me by a seeress, I know it's what I must do. I'll find another tribe to train with. When I'm a blooded warrior and have a place in a tribe, I'll come and find you."

His brown eyes burned into Sirona's. The love she saw there both warmed her heart and tore it to pieces. It seemed to her that few people in life ever realized their dreams. If Bryn got his chance to be a warrior, he must be content with that.

But what if her mother's prediction for Bryn came true? What if by encouraging him to pursue his dream, she ended up sending Bryn to his death? She must tell him of her mother's prophecy and let him decide for himself. "There's one more thing, Bryn...the reason your father has refused to allow you to train as a fighting man. When you were a baby, it was predicted..." She could not bring herself to mention her mother, "if you became a warrior, you would die in the first battle you fought in." She held her breath, waiting for Bryn's reaction.

He stared at her, eyes bright with emotion. "If I die, I die. But at least I will die knowing I have fulfilled my destiny. All the years training in the grove have taught me not to fear death. But I do fear not fully living my life while I remain in this realm."

Sirona nodded. She felt certain she was doing the right thing in freeing Bryn from the crippling control of his father. Only by leaving Mordarach could he ever have a chance for happiness. That happiness might be fleeting, but at least he would know it for a time.

But what of her? She was losing everything, and all because she'd followed what she thought was the Goddess's plan for her. That night at the mound and circle of stones had been magical, but not enough to make up for what she now faced. And even that experience was flawed. Because of her fear, she had rejected Cruthin and lost the opportunity to know sex magic. Her failure gnawed at her, despite her anger at Cruthin for leaving her.

Bryn interrupted her thoughts. "Sirona, in your vision, did you see any sign or symbol on my shield that might tell me what tribe I will fight for?"

She frowned in concentration, trying to remember. "You were older...with the long mustache of a warrior. You wore a kind of leather garment on your chest. I didn't really take note of the colors you wore. But there was..." Her gaze snapped up to meet his. "...there was the outline of a white horse on your shield."

"A white horse?"

She nodded.

"I've never heard of a tribe that used such a symbol," he said, his eyes wide in wonder.

"Then perhaps you'll have to search for them."

"I wish you would have told me this when we were still at the gathering. I could have asked around to find out which tribe uses the white horse as a battle emblem."

Sirona touched his arm. "Don't let what I have told you guide your life too completely. So far, none of the things I've seen have come to pass. Instead, follow what is in your heart, what you sense the gods are telling you to do."

Bryn smiled sadly. "It's true that I have a long way to go before I'm worthy of handfasting with you. But someday, Sirona, I will be a warrior. Someday when you need protection, I'll be there. I won't fail you."

As Bryn turned and left her—ducking awkwardly under the low porch of the hut as his father had before him—Sirona felt the tears begin to fall. She wasn't certain what she wept most for: her own loss, or Bryn's heartbreaking innocence of the cruelties of life.

* * *

Her circumstances were so luxurious as to be almost embarrassing, Sirona thought as they left Mordarach. Tarbelinus had provided a cart for her to ride in and two warriors to guard her. He'd also offered to send a bondswoman to wait upon her, but Sirona had refused. She didn't see why some other young woman's life should be disrupted along with hers.

Sitting back in the cart, which was filled with sheepskins, blankets, cooking utensils and her new garments, she contemplated how different her "banishment" was from her mother's. Her mother had left on foot, carrying few supplies, while Sirona was well provided for. Yet despite her comfortable circumstances, she felt a yawning emptiness.

The idea of going to live with a northern tribe seemed like a tale told about someone else. She couldn't imagine it, this new life among a people she'd never met. Although she tried to see some vision of her future, nothing came to her. As they traveled farther and farther away from Mordarach, her sense of despair deepened. She was leaving everything she'd ever known. Her grandmother, whom she'd never truly appreciated. The world of the grove, which had filled her days and shaped her thoughts. It seemed like she was dying, as surely as Banon had died. To the people of Mordarach, she would be dead. Like Cruthin, she would cease to exist to them.

Cruthin. She wondered where he was. Had he returned to the mound on the sacred isle? Gone back to the mainland? She tried to see him in her mind, to catch some glimpse and reassure herself that he yet lived. But she saw nothing. She cursed silently. What was the point of having visions if they wouldn't come when she needed them most?

Her anguish deepened, and tears blurred her eyes as she watched the scenery pass. She became aware of a change in the landscape and realized they were leaving the highlands. The hills weren't as steep here, the contours of the land a little softer, the grass a lusher green. They were traveling into the territory of the Cornovii.

With each step the oxen took, the pain built inside her. Finally, overcome, she called out to the two men. "Please, stop. I need to…" She searched her mind for some excuse to go off into the woods and spend her grief in private. "I need to relieve myself," she finished.

They halted the oxen. Sirona grabbed her pack and climbed down from the cart. As she started off into the woods, the tears welled up in earnest. By the time she reached deep forest, she was sobbing.

She staggered forward, half blinded. Gradually she realized that if she went too far, she might get lost, and her fear of being left alone in strange territory caused her to halt. She slid to the ground and rubbed at her swollen eyes. Gazing up bleakly at the sky, she wished it were night time, so that she could see the moon. Arianrhod's silver light would comfort her.

She sighed, then, looking around, noticed several fluffy white blooms of a flower Nesta used in some of her medicines. The blossoms were formed of many tiny white flowers clustered together with one tiny purple flower in the center. As a child, Sirona had pretended that a wish made upon the secret purple center would travel directly to the ears of the gods and be granted. Now, she picked one of the flowers and inhaled the bloom's perfume, then touched the purple center. "Please, Arianrhod," she whispered. "Lady of the moon, who guides the silver wheel of the heavens, tell me what to do."

She sat there, waiting for an answer. After a time, she realized she must go back. Culhwch and Einion would worry if she stayed away too long.

She started back to the cart, and had gone a little distance when she heard men shouting. At first she thought it was Culhwch and Einion calling for her. Then she realized the language was unfamiliar. She took a few more steps, and suddenly knew that Culhwch and Einion were in trouble.

As she moved toward the voices, the sounds grew quieter. When she reached the edge of the trees, she understood why. Culhwch and Einion's bodies lay on the ground by the cart. They had been no match for the warriors milling around the area.

The enemy men were dressed very strangely, in short crys that bared their legs. They also wore metal helmets. Observing their foreign attire, Sirona decided they must be Romans. Bryn had been right. They *had* come this far west.

She counted ten, twenty. Several explored the cart, digging among the supplies meant to equip Sirona's household when she arrived in the north. Finding a waterskin, one man put it to his lips and drank. He made a face and dumped it back in the cart. She wondered what he expected it to contain.

As the man continued to paw through the supplies, she worried they would find the jewelry in the bottom of the cart. Then she realized it didn't matter. They were going to take the whole vehicle. As she watched, one of the men used a stick to prod the oxen forward. The other enemy warriors followed behind.

Sirona closed her eyes. She had the faint hope that what she was seeing was a vision, a glimpse of something which might take place but had not yet actually happened. But when she opened her eyes, the sight of her tribesmen's bodies told the horrifying truth. This was real. She was wracked by tremors, and her stomach threatened to heave itself up. For a time, she was afraid to move. The dread that the men might come back paralyzed her.

She waited in the trees until almost twilight, then cautiously approached the place where the cart had been. Culhwch had a huge gash in his chest. The blood from the wound had soaked his crys like a dark lake spreading out over the fabric. He appeared so young. Sirona tried to remember how many years it had been since he'd had his man-making. Not more than five, she thought.

A few paces away Einion lay face down. She thought of turning him over, but decided she couldn't bear to. Einion had a wife and two small boys back at Mordarach. If she looked upon his face, knowing his family would never see him again, she would start weeping.

And she must not weep. Must not mourn these men who would never have been in this place except for her. She had a task to complete before she gave in to her grief.

She surveyed the area and began to gather up rocks, the largest she could carry. She piled them on top of the two dead men, hoping to protect their bodies from wild animals. A poor burial, but the best she could manage. She worked steadily, moving farther and farther away to gather the rocks. Her legs trembled with fatigue. Her back ached. But she kept at her task. When the moon appeared over the horizon, she knew it was Arianrhod offering her blessing.

She guessed that near half the night was over when she finally decided the two mounds of stones were large enough. A determined animal could still dig its way in, but this time of year, with plenty of game around, perhaps the scavengers would find easier pickings elsewhere.

She straightened, one hand on her aching back. "Culhwch and Einion, brave warriors both, I ask Arianrhod, Lady of the moon, to carry your spirits on her fine pure light and set them gently down in the Otherworld. There may you live in happiness and plenty, fighting battles where no man is injured or suffers, and there is feasting and celebration for eternity."

Tears slipped down her cheek as she said the words. Then she gestured as she'd seen Fiach do and stepped back, away from the two rock cairns, waiting for the dead men's spirits to be released and float free.

Her task over, she staggered back to the forest and burrowed into a pile of leaves under a great oak tree. She fell into a dreamless sleep.

When she woke it was twilight. She decided she must have slept the rest of the night and the day following. Although nothing had bothered her as she lay among the leaves, now that she was awake, she realized how vulnerable she was. This was exactly how her mother had died, alone in the forest, attacked by predators.

The thought made her get to her feet and start walking. She left the woods and moved out into the open, finding the ruts made by the cart and following them back the way they had come. Her heart thudded with dread. Each breath she took seemed to catch in her throat. She had gone only a short distance when she realized her worst fear had come to pass. Glancing back at the moonlight-bleached landscape, she caught a glimpse of movement. Something was stalking her.

She moved more rapidly, her panic building. Now she could hear the beast's footfalls as it pursued her. She kept her gaze straight ahead and quickened her pace, although she didn't run, fearing that as soon as she did so, the animal would pounce.

Then gradually her mind began to function again. She reminded herself that she'd been trained for years not to fear death. And if she must die, she wanted it to be a good death, not this—being brought down like helpless, hunted prey. Determination filled her, and she made up her mind to stop and confront the predator. She slowed her pace and fumbled in her pack for her eating knife. A puny defense, but after all, Cruthin had killed a wolf with just such a weapon.

As soon as she found the knife, she whirled and faced her pursuer. Twenty paces away was a huge wolf. In the moonlight, its fur seemed tipped with liquid silver. Sirona waited, breathless with tension. Then her fear ebbed away as the beast sat down on its haunches.

She could feel the animal watching her, not with the fierce, feral yellow gaze of a predator, but with eyes that were dark, solemn and somehow wise. She was stunned. Death had seemed so close, and yet it had passed her by again. The gods surely must have a hand in this.

She slipped the knife back in her pack and began to walk away. The wolf followed, moving closer. It circled around to block her pathway. "Not this way," it seemed to be saying.

Its dark eyes probed her, reaching out, as if trying to make her understand. All at once, she realized what the animal wanted. The wolf was trying to get her to follow it. "Did Arianrhod send you?" she whispered.

The wolf watched her with its patient gaze. When she started toward it, it got up and loped off. She followed, wondering if she had gone mad.

Chapter 9

Bryn drew his oiled leather cape more tightly around himself and glanced up at the sky. His face was immediately pelted with cold raindrops. He grimaced in frustration. In this weather, it was impossible to tell what time of day it was, let alone what direction he was headed. He must follow his instincts and hope he didn't end up walking in circles. The only other alternative was to find a place to wait out the rain.

But a rain like this could last for several days, and he had to keep moving. His father would certainly send someone after him. Tarbelinus would assume he was following Sirona, but that didn't mean he was safe from pursuit. Sirona and her escort would also have headed east for the first few days of their journey.

At least he had a day's head start. That had been a stroke of luck. Another Ordovice tribe had come visiting, seeking news about the gathering on the sacred isle. Tarbelinus had taken their guests hunting, and while all the warriors were gone from Mordarach, Bryn had set out. Of course, that meant he hadn't been able take his favorite hound, Cadarn, since the dog was with the hunters. But that might be better anyway. Having the dog with him would make him easier to track.

He tried to decide who his father would send after him and whether those men were be sympathetic to his plight. Some of the warriors had told Bryn they thought Tarbelinus was a fool for insisting he train to be a Learned One. If those men were the ones sent in pursuit, Bryn didn't think they would follow too aggressively. As he walked along, trying to travel in a straight pathway, he felt excited and pleased with himself, although occasional thoughts of Sirona dampened his mood. Almost a sennight had passed since she'd left Mordarach. By now, she should have reached the territory of the northern peoples. He hoped they would appreciate her and care for her. Perhaps she could even locate Dysri's tribe. The Drui woman seemed to have a fondness for Sirona.

But it wasn't enough to know she was safe. He wanted to be with her. With effort, he struggled to suppress the yearning. It wasn't time for them to be together. Before he made Sirona his wife, he must prove himself as a man and a warrior.

A twinge of anxiety prodded his stomach. It wasn't going to be easy to walk into the fortress of another tribe and gain acceptance. He might be tall and strong, but he was also young and inexperienced. He'd never fought a man in real combat. Never wielded a spear except against hunting prey. Other young men his age were so much farther ahead in their training.

At the thought, he cursed. So much time wasted. And what had he learned? The names of the gods and how to honor them. The way the sky changed over the seasons. Lists of ancestors. Laws and legends. Useless things. He cursed again. It galled him to be so far behind. Irritation made him quicken his pace. The sooner he came upon another tribe, the sooner he could begin to make up for all the years he'd lost, learning endless nonsense in the grove.

* * *

Bryn felt a rush of excitement as he heard the bellow of hunting horns in the distance. If he could meet up with members of another tribe soon after they'd made a kill, they would be in fine moods and more likely to welcome him to their dun. He listened until he heard the baying of hounds, then took off.

He circled around the area where he thought the prey must be, stopping every little while to gauge the location of the dogs by the sound of their frenzied bellowing. Although he was breathless and sweating from sprinting with his heavy pack, he relished the exertion. It was almost like he was one of the hunters, experiencing the excitement of the chase, the expectation of the kill. This why he had left Mordarach, so he could be one of the men who tested their endurance and cunning against the beasts of the forest...or against other men.

Hearing the sound of something moving through the woods, he pushed his way through the thick underbrush. He reached a game path and a few seconds later, jerked to a halt as he saw a man coming towards him. Their eyes met for a heartbeat. Then Bryn whirled and ran as fast as he could.

Even as his legs pumped and his lungs frantically sucked in air, his mind registered what had sent him on this desperate flight. One look at the man's dark, cropped hair and his strange garments told Bryn he was face-to-face with a Roman…a Roman carrying a wicked looking hunting spear. Running away seemed like his only option.

He ran and ran. Only as the muscles in his legs started to cramp with exertion and his breath come in great heaving gasps did he slow. At last he paused, doubled over, too spent to continue. He listened for pursuit, but the blood was pounding in his head so loudly, he couldn't hear anything else. Gradually that subsided, and he glanced around. The only noise was the trill of birdsong. All at once, a sense of shame came over him. Why hadn't he pulled out his short sword and confronted the man?

Why had he immediately assumed the Roman would best him? A hunting spear was dangerous, but difficult to wield in the cramped space of a forest pathway. If he'd had time to get out his weapon, he could have defeated and killed the other man.

The next moment he told himself he'd done the sensible thing. Where there was one Roman, there would be others. He might have run into a whole troop of the enemy, and found himself facing impossible odds. Flight was his only hope. It would be foolish to throw his life away in a confrontation. He was hardly ready for combat against experienced warriors. That was why he was making this journey, so he could find a place to train, so that someday, he *would* be ready.

He let a breath out like a sob, suddenly overwhelmed with frustration and fatigue. Three days he'd been traveling east. Now, he'd have to turn back, or change direction. What if he went south? As far as he knew, the tribes there hadn't been overrun by the Romans.

He cursed aloud, then started forward. The first thing he must do was find a stream where he could drink his fill and replenish his waterskin. And from now on he would have to proceed with more caution.

He glanced up at the sky, trying to gauge direction. Aye, he would go south. It seemed the wisest thing to do. For a brief moment, he considered that the sighting of the Roman might have been a sign from the gods. Maybe they were trying to tell him that his destiny lay elsewhere. Or, he might be imagining things because he was so drained by his panicked run. "I wish you were here, Sirona," he said aloud. "I could sorely use your insight and wisdom."

The only response was the sweet, bright cry of a lark.

* * *

Someone was following him.

Bryn halted and glanced back into the gold green blur of the thick elm and oak forest. Or, maybe it was some *thing*, he thought uneasily. Whatever it was, man or beast, it had been pursuing him since he set out that morning. When he'd first heard the tell-tale crack of branches and rustle of dried leaves, he'd assumed it was some sort of game. Getting out his bow and an arrow, he'd slipped behind a large tree trunk to wait. When no deer or boar appeared, he'd decided the animal had caught his scent and left the area. He'd started walking once again, but soon experienced the unmistakable feeling he was being stalked. Remembering his encounter with the Roman, he decided to put away the bow and arrow and get out his short sword.

Now he paused, listening, gripping the wire-wrapped wooden hilt of the weapon tightly in his sweaty palm. His heart raced. Why would a wolf pursue him when there was so much other prey around? If it were a man, then why didn't he confront Bryn and be done with it? Why stealthily follow after him?

He took a deep breath and tried to decide what his father or one of his warriors would do. They wouldn't wait for their pursuer to strike, but would boldly seek out whoever or whatever was following them. The only trouble was, it seemed as soon as he halted, the being tracking him also halted, so he had no clear sense of exactly where his pursuer was. How could he confront an enemy he couldn't see? Somehow, he must set a trap for his pursuer.

He increased his pace until he was going as fast as he could without tripping. Then, all at once, he whirled and started back the other direction, his eyes scanning the forest, searching for a blur of movement. He thought he saw something and headed straight towards it. As he passed a large tree, something flashed to his left. He jerked to a halt and stared hard in that direction. Although he saw nothing he could identify as anything other than a natural feature of the woods, he started toward the place where the hint of movement had been. He held his sword at the ready, his whole body thrumming with tension. As he passed several hawthorn bushes large enough to conceal a man, his breathless dread increased. Now he was certain his pursuer was human. No animal would behave like this.

He searched the bushes but found nothing. Frustrated, he halted his quest and looked around. He knew, simply knew, there was someone out there. Why didn't he show himself? He began to slash at the bushes around him, swearing oaths, "Coward! Dog! Come out and show yourself!"

As he raised his arm for another go at the hapless vegetation, he felt something sharp dig into his back. "Here I am," a male voice said from behind him.

Bryn could feel the weapon piercing his crys. As several heartbeats passed, he considered that at least the man had spoken in the Pretani tongue. He wasn't facing a Roman this time, but one of his own people.

"Who are you?" the man finally asked. "And what are you doing slinking around in the territory of the Dobunni?"

"I wasn't slinking around," Bryn said. "I was merely traveling through. If I'd encountered a settlement or farmstead, I would have stopped and announced myself."

"Oh, really?" the man sneered. "I saw you pass right by a cattle bothy, creeping through the trees so you wouldn't be seen."

Bryn experienced a twinge of shame at being caught in a lie. The fact was, he'd decided not to approach any settlement or dwelling until he'd had a chance to observe the inhabitants. He'd fixed upon this plan after encountering a dead man among the trees. The body showed several sword wounds, now covered with maggots. The discovery had sent a chill of horror down Bryn's spine. Bad enough to think he might be set upon and killed while he was alone and far away from his family, but the idea of having his body left to rot truly sickened him.

"You can't blame me for being cautious," he said. "I'm a stranger here and don't know how I might be greeted by your tribe. What I don't understand is why you didn't approach me."

Bryn felt the point of the sword or knife point dig more deeply into his flesh. "I'm approaching you now," the man said. "So, what are you doing here?"

"I'm seeking a place in the warband of some chieftain. I've left my own tribe, for reasons I don't wish to reveal. I would serve another man, if he be valiant and honorable. And, most of all, I wish to fight the Romans."

All at once, the pricking pain in Bryn's back eased, and his captor let out a guffaw. "You want to serve a chieftain who is honorable and valiant, and you've come to the territory of the Dobunni? That's a fine jest. My father knows nothing of honor, although he is brave enough." He gave another hearty laugh.

Bryn turned to stare at the man, who was now red-faced with mirth. He was young, perhaps a year or two older than Bryn, short and stocky, with wild, wavy black hair and dazzling blue eyes. He wore leather bracco beneath a crys of plain, undyed wool, with a strip of crimson-dyed leather for a belt.

While Bryn gazed at him, puzzling over his words, the man's expression turned wary. He looked Bryn up and down, sizing him up. "Are you skilled with weapons?"

"Some," Bryn hedged.

The man held up his sword. "We'll fight. If you win, I'll take you to my father and you can swear yourself to him, if you wish."

"And if I lose?" Bryn asked, his stomach sinking.

The young man grinned wolfishly. "Perhaps I'll spare your life. Perhaps not."

"Please," Bryn said. "Before we fight. Let us introduce ourselves. If I'm going to die, then I want to know the name of the man who kills me. I am Bryn ap Tarbelinus of the Tarisllwyth branch of the Ordovice."

"And I am Cadwalon ap Cadwyl of the Dobunni," the man said. Then he lunged.

Bryn only narrowly avoided the blade. He backed up and tried to recall all the advice he'd heard about swordplay. *Watch the man's eyes.*

Rest your weight on the balls of your feet. Keep your sword up.

As they engaged in earnest, Bryn found he could barely keep out of harm's way. His opponent moved with lightning quickness, and it was only Bryn's desperate panic that enabled him to avoid being stabbed. As he was steadily driven backwards, Bryn realized he'd soon get pinned against a tree and be unable to maneuver. Then he would die.

He tried to feint, to throw the other man off balance. It was no use. His opponent was too experienced, too wily and quick. *Llew, save me,* Bryn thought desperately. *Cernunnos, lord of the forest, come to my aid!* He didn't want to die here, alone, unmourned. Sirona's face flashed into his mind. He wondered if he'd ever see her again.

He tried to go on the offensive, driving forward. By the time he reached the place where the other man had stood, Cadwalon was gone, and Bryn's weapon slashed thin air. He let out a yell of rage and began to flail wildly with his blade. Cadwalon repeatedly moved out of reach at the last moment. Then, when Bryn grew winded, his opponent began to press him once more. Bryn tried to meet each blow and deflect it. Finally, a second too late, he lost his grip on his sword and it went spinning off into the bushes.

"Aha!" Cadwalon cried in triumph. He backed Bryn into a tree, his sword blade digging into Bryn's throat. Bryn waited, breathless and terrified. He wanted to beg for his life. Digging his nails into his palms, he fought the cowardly urge. He would die a man. Perhaps his spirit would someday return to the living and he would have another chance to prove himself as a warrior.

He saw his opponent's mouth quirk and one of his dark brows went up, reflecting surprise and, it seemed, amusement. All at once, Cadwalon drew back. He nodded, looking pleased. "I like you, Bryn ap Tarbelinus. I would offer you a place in my warband." Bryn opened his mouth to answer that he would be delighted to fight beside someone so skilled. But before he could speak, Cadwalon continued, "But the fact is, I have no warband. I'm still forced to fight for my father. It won't always be this way, I promise you. Someday *I'll* be chieftain."

Bryn let out his breath in a sigh of relief. He wasn't going to die after all. Had his prayers to the gods been answered, or was it simply his destiny to live a while longer? He remembered Cruthin saying after the wolf almost killed him that it clearly wasn't his time to die yet. At this moment, Bryn felt the same. Yet his future was far from settled. Remembering Cadwalon's words, he said, "You told me your father is not an honorable man. What does that mean?"

Cadwalon shrugged. "I could give you many instances of my father's defiance of the law. Which tale would you like to hear?" When

Bryn shook his head, not knowing how to answer, Cadwalon continued, "After my father had his face slashed in battle and his eye put out, the Drui said he could no longer be king because he was flawed and therefore, unacceptable to the gods. So he killed all the Drui and left their bodies to rot." Cadwalon smiled broadly. "Or, perhaps you would like to hear of how when he couldn't get Oswael and his warband to stop raiding our cattle, he invited the chieftain to come to our hall for one of the festivals. After the meal was over and Oswael and his men were very drunk, my father had his warriors fall upon the visitors and kill them."

Bryn gaped. The things that this man, Cadwyl, had done were terrible, horrifying violations of the sacred laws of their people. He shook his head in disbelief and said, "Doesn't Cadwyl fear the gods will punish him?"

Cadwalon threw back his head and laughed. "My father fear the gods? Nay! Cadwyl fears nothing. Not in this realm or the next. Ask him, he will tell you it is so!"

Bryn experienced an abrupt letdown. He'd finally found a tribe that might accept him. But how could he serve a man who flaunted the sacred laws and dared the gods to punish him for his defiance?

Cadwyl saw his expression and said, "What's wrong? Has our little skirmish changed your mind about being a warrior? I wasn't going to kill you. Truly. It wouldn't be right." He raised his chin proudly. "Unlike my father, I do have some honor. Without honor, you can gain men's fear, but not their respect. When I am chieftain, men will serve me and fight for me because they recognize me as a strong and brave leader, not because they fear I will kill them if they don't do my will."

"But, as you said, you're not chieftain yet," Bryn pointed out. "If I'm to be accepted by your tribe, I must serve your father. And I don't know if I could give my loyalty to such a man."

Cadwyl cocked his head. "You're an odd fellow, Bryn ap Tarbelinus. You look big and brawny, but you have little experience with weapons. You say you wish to find a place in some chieftain's warband, yet you don't wish to serve a man such as my father. What makes you so arrogant that you would refuse the offer of a place in his hall?"

"I'm not arrogant," Bryn said. "It's only that..." He'd hoped to leave that part of his life completely behind. But it seemed he could not. "I trained in the grove for a time. I was supposed to become a Drui. I have no desire for that life, but...I can't say those years didn't influence me."

"And so when I tell you that my father killed the Drui, you're shocked? You think he must be some sort of monster?"

Bryn nodded.

"Well, he is a monster," Cadwalon said. "But he's also the most powerful, ruthless man you'll ever meet. The thing is with Cadwyl, you either give in to him, or you die. Or, in your case, you could turn around and go back home." Cadwalon gazed at him questioningly.

Bryn considered this, then shook his head. "I can't go home. That would be worse than anything."

"Well, then, you must learn to think as I do. Cadwyl can't live forever. And he's made many enemies, including both of my brothers. Perhaps one of them will finally kill him."

"Then, what will you do? Serve them?"

"Nay, of course not. Then I will fight my brothers for the kingship. They are no more honorable than Cadwyl, and weaker and less canny besides. Cadwyl used to favor them, but when they rose up against him, he declared them outlaw and made me his heir. Of course, who knows if he truly means to see me be king after him. Cadwyl is a canny old wolf, playing all of his sons against each other."

"What does your mother think of all this? Whom does she favor?" Bryn asked, curious about this family that sounded so different from his own.

"My mother?" Cadwalon cocked his head in surprise. "What does she have to do with it?"

"Well, does she take your side, or that of your brothers?"

"My side, of course." He smirked. "You must consider that each of us was birthed by a different woman. My father has no loyalty when it comes to his consorts either."

Bryn was shocked. He'd heard of chieftains who had more than one wife, but, thinking of his mother Rhyell and her temper, it didn't sound like a good idea.

Cadwalon cocked his head. "I've told you something of my people. What of yours? Why are you here, so far from your home dun? Did you do something to disgrace yourself?"

"Nay, of course not. My father and I simply didn't see eye-to-eye about my future. He wanted me to continue to train the grove. I was determined to become a warrior."

"And so you left and traveled all the way here?" Cadwalon gave him an incredulous look. "Surely you could have found another tribe closer to your homeland. What about the Silures or the Cornovii?"

Bryn didn't really want to explain about how he'd turned south when he'd encountered the Roman. Now that he was far away from the potential danger, his decision seemed cowardly. "I decided to travel this direction so I might see more of the countryside."

"Huh," Cadwalon responded. "Well, I think your father is a fool to want you to be a Drui. You'll need a lot of training, but you're certainly big enough and quick enough to make a fine warrior." He smiled. "Perhaps by the time I'm chieftain, you might serve in my warband."

Cadwalon's words thrilled Bryn. At last someone saw his potential. But then he remembered that for the immediate future, he would be serving Cadwalon's father. Could he overlook the terrible things this Dobunni chieftain had done? He reminded himself that he'd had no other offers. And however cursed and wicked Cadwyl might be, the chieftain was successful and powerful and had undoubtedly surrounded himself with skilled warriors. By spending time among them, Bryn would be able to learn a great deal. When he was finally ready to go off and fight the Romans, the fact that he need feel no loyalty to a man like Cadwyl might make leaving easier.

He nodded. "Take me to your father and I will swear to him. If he will have me, that is."

"No need for that. Cadwyl doesn't take oaths from his men. He simply offers them the choicest war booty and a life of ease and idleness when they aren't engaged in combat. That is why his dun is crammed with skilled fighting men."

Bryn wondered what Cadwalon meant. Everyone knew that warriors were served first and given the choicest portions. They enjoyed a life of ease and comfort when there was no threat against their people. But even those things wouldn't be enough for the warriors of Bryn's tribe to give their loyalty to a man like Cadwyl. He found he was very curious to meet this strange southern chieftain—this man who defied the will of the gods and the rules of men.

* * *

As soon as Bryn saw Cadwyl's dun, he was struck by the fact that the Dobunni settlement had clearly been attacked on more than one occasion. The earthworks showed evidence of being rebuilt several times and the palisade walls were badly scarred by fire on two sides. But it appeared the inhabitants of the fortress had not only withstood the assault but eventually gotten the better of their attackers. Arranged on poles around the entrance to the palisade were nearly a dozen rotting human heads. "That's where my father will put the heads of my brothers, Awmlaad and Hueil, after he kills them," Cadwalon said, his face split wide with a grin.

Bryn had heard of trophy heads, but never seen one. From his Drui training, he understood the significance of the practice. The spirit resided within the skull, which meant that if a man's head was detached from his body, he couldn't return as a whole being from the Otherworld to seek revenge. Still, as he passed by the empty-eyed, gruesome visages, Bryn felt a little sick. He wouldn't like to think of his own head being stuck on a pole and left out for the birds and insects to feast on. As they entered the dun, he once again wondered what he'd gotten himself into.

The inside of the hillfort reeked of charcoal fires, rotting meat, dung and animals. Bryn thought of Mordarach and the way the workshops, stables and midden were located away from the dwelling places and hall. But here, everything seemed to be mingled together. The smith was near the entrance, which wasn't far from where the butchering was apparently done, which was only a little way from what appeared to be the kitchen. The smells of all those activities blended together to form a thick, odiferous haze over the whole fortress. By the time they reached the chieftain's hall, Bryn was almost gagging.

The inside of the hall was no better. It was dark and smoky, and a foul stench seemed to waft up from the rushes covering the floor. The place was crowded with fighting men. Most were dark like Cadwalon, although a few had red hair. Their necks and arms glinted with gold and enamelwork jewelry, but their hair and beards were long and matted and their crys and mantles torn and dirty. Looking at them, Bryn could almost see why the Romans were said to consider his people savages.

And yet these coarse warriors looked utterly formidable. They were brawny and thickly-muscled, although many of them weren't as tall as Bryn was. He told himself that if he trained with these men, he would learn the skills he needed to defeat the hated enemy.

Cadwalon continued to push his way through the mass of warriors. Bryn followed behind him, trying to quell the nervousness in his belly and appear assured and confident.

All at once, Cadwalon leaned close and said, "That's him. That's Cadwyl."

Bryn squinted in the dim light and saw what looked like a bear seated on a stool near the hearth. A tangled mass of head hair and great, bushy beard obscured the man's face and spilled over his shoulders, mingling with the thick black pelt he wore as a mantle. As Bryn drew near, he decided part of the reason Cadwyl had such an unkempt appearance was to make himself appear more formidable. He wasn't a large man. He was wider than his son, but no taller. And much, much uglier. Cadwyl's features were blunt and thick, his skin weathered and leathery. And then there was the hideous wound that cut through the place where his left eye should be. It was a face to give anyone nightmares.

As Bryn approached, he felt Cadwyl's good eye upon him, shrewd and calculating. Although he strove to appear calm, he was drenched with sweat, and his heart raced. He didn't doubt that if Cadwyl disliked anything about him, the chieftain was capable of ordering him put to death and adding his head to the gory trophies guarding the gate of the dun. To make things worse, Bryn could sense that Cadwalon wasn't altogether at ease either. They stopped a few paces away from Cadwyl. "This is Bryn ap Tarbelinus," Cadwalon announced. "A man in search of a chieftain to fight for."

Cadwyl grinned. Then he jerked a great knife from his belt, the hilt decorated with gold wire and red and purple enamel and the blade fouled with dried blood. He held the knife as if he meant to lunge at Bryn and stab him in the chest. Then, abruptly, he turned to the carcass of a pig sitting on the table beside him and chopped off a hunk of meat. Skewering the meat on the tip of the knife blade, he held it out to Bryn.

Bryn reached out and took the greasy chunk and put it in his mouth. As he chewed the rich, succulent meat, he realized that for better or worse, he was now Cadwyl's man.

Chapter 10

Sirona sat down on a rock and opened her pack. She took everything out and searched the bottom, hoping to find some crumb or particle of food she'd overlooked. Finding nothing, she sighed. A short distance away, the wolf waited, lying down like a hound before the fire.

They'd been traveling like this for four days. The wolf would set off and she would follow. When she grew tired or hungry, she would stop and the wolf would come back and wait for her. Once she'd left out food, but the wolf hadn't approached the dried meat. She'd understood then. It was a spirit, not a real animal. Which was why she continued to follow it. She believed the gods must be speaking through the wolf and it was leading her where she was meant to go.

But there were times when doubts overwhelmed her. She had no idea where the wolf was taking her, and she was haunted by what she'd left behind, the loss of everything she cared about. At those moments she felt like giving up. Lying down and surrendering to her fatigue and hunger. The dried meat and barley bannocks in her pack were gone and, despite the verdant green forest, there was little to eat but a few berries here and there. She hoped the wolf realized they must reach their destination soon or she would collapse from starvation.

Sirona took a drink from her waterskin. Maybe quenching her thirst would revive her. That morning they'd entered a thick forest of oak, pine and yew, so dense and impenetrable that without the wolf, she wouldn't have been able to travel a stone's throw without getting hopelessly lost. She glanced at the animal, and the wolf raised its head expectantly. It was a beautiful creature. Much darker than the wolf Cruthin had killed for his man-making, so many cycles of the moon ago. This wolf had black fur tipped with silver. Its face was silvery gray, with dark eyes. They weren't wolf's eyes, but seemed human.

She wondered if the wolf was Lovarn. He'd told her his name meant wolf. She had tried talking to the animal, asking it to appear to her in human form. It continued to gaze at her with those strange, compelling eyes. She decided it didn't matter who or what the wolf was, only that the animal had been sent to guide her.

But guide her *where*? She knew they were traveling north. If she encountered another tribe, what would she tell them? How could she explain how she came to be there? And why should any tribe take her in? Her hair was disheveled, her clothing dirty. She'd lost the bronze comb Rhyell had sent with her, and she had only one change of clothing, and that gown was nearly as old and soiled as the one she wore. All the jewelry from her mother was gone. Except for what was in her pack, all her possessions had been stolen by the Romans.

Thinking of these things, she grew even more discouraged. For all she knew, she was going to die here, lost in these endless woods. Forgotten. Alone. Cursed. Tears welled up in her eyes. She was so tired. She'd been walking for days, with no clear destination ahead. Now she was out of food. What was the point of going on? Why not stay here until death came?

She slumped over, head in her hands. Then she heard a sound. The wolf. It began to circle her, growling. Not threateningly, but as a sign of impatience. "Go away," she whispered. "Leave me alone."

But the animal wouldn't relent. It circled ever closer, finally darting in to nip at her clothing. Sirona sat up and watched the wolf stop a few paces away. "What do you want?" she asked. "Why won't you leave me in peace?"

The wolf again moved in a circle, whining. Obviously, it wanted her to get up and follow. She groaned, but didn't rise.

The animal rushed toward her, grazing her body. Even this close, it had no odor. The awareness reminded her that this was no natural creature. It was one thing to defy an animal. Another to ignore a messenger of the gods. She stood up wearily and began to follow the wolf.

The forest was a blur of green, endless, oppressive. If she kept on like this, she would eventually collapse and die. Her body would rot away and she would become part of the earth again. Her flesh and bones would feed the animals and nourish the soil. Her spirit would return to the warmth and safety of the great mother's womb, from there to be born again into a new life, a new body. The idea soothed her. It wasn't such a terrible fate. Perhaps in her next life she would be more fortunate.

A short while later the forest ended, and Sirona halted, staring. Pink campion, blue harebells and mauve heather grew in profusion around a mound like the one on the sacred isle. The wolf ran to the mound and disappeared behind it.

Sirona followed, her despair replaced by wonder. On the other side of the mound was a small doorway, much like the one in the mound on the sacred isle, except there was no stone blocking the entrance. Seeing no sign of the wolf, she decided the animal must have gone inside. She dropped her pack on the ground, then ducked down and stuck her head inside the passageway leading into the mound. It smelled earthy and pungent, like a fox's den. She felt a hint of fear, wondering what sort of animal might wait within. Then she decided the wolf wouldn't have gone in if she weren't meant to follow.

She crawled inside, where light filtering down through an opening in the top revealed a cozy dwelling space but no sign of the wolf. Sirona was puzzled. After guiding her for days, why would it simply vanish?

Unless this was her destination. She glanced around. There was a small hearth, with animal skins and large, flat rocks for seating arranged around it. Numerous baskets and jars were pushed back against the sloping sides of the stone wall of the chamber. She went to one of the baskets and opened it. Inside was some ground-up meal. She dipped her finger in the powdery substance and licked it. The meal tasted like hazelnuts. Another of the baskets was full of dried berries. She picked up one of the jars, removed the beeswax seal and sniffed. Then she brought the jar to her lips and drank. It contained a strong, vaguely sweet beverage. She drank some more. The drink made her dizzy, but also revived her.

She explored further. The baskets and jars and other objects in the chamber were tidily arranged, but there was a layer of dust over everything. Someone had been here, but a long time ago. She puzzled over why the wolf had guided her to this place. Was she supposed to rest here and eat the food? What if the people who had stored it away came back and were angry she'd dared to help herself to their hoard?

But she was too hungry and exhausted to agonize over these matters for long. She pulled the baskets and the beverage jars over to the hearth and began to eat. The nutmeal was rich and nourishing, but difficult to consume by licking her fingers. She wondered if she added water if she could make a kind of mealcake over the fire. If she had a fire. She took several deep draughts of the beverage. It made her sleepy. She decided to go out and get her pack, so she could wrap up in her cloak.

It was getting dark, and there was no sign of the wolf. Now she was completely alone. Then Sirona saw the faint outline of the moon, gleaming through the trees at the edge of the clearing. The increasing moon, when the lighted half circle resembled a pregnant belly. She felt certain she'd been guided to this place for a reason. Although that purpose hadn't yet been revealed, she must trust that the Goddess had a reason for bringing her here.

Turning back to the mound, she noted that it was also shaped like a pregnant belly. She would be safe inside the earth mother's womb.

* * *

Sirona woke to find the underground chamber filled with fire. She jerked upright, terrified. The flames danced before her eyes, gleaming and bright. Then they died back, and she realized she was looking into an ordinary hearth fire. She blinked in amazement, trying to understand what had happened. Then she saw someone seated on the other side of the fire. A woman, small-boned and gracefully built, with long, thick dark hair and a beautiful haughty face. She gazed at Sirona with a patient expression.

Sirona immediately had the sense of being in the presence of someone incredibly strong and powerful. For a moment, she wondered if she were seeing a vision of the Great Goddess herself. Then, even as she had the thought, the woman changed. Her hair turned white. Her face became as thin and hollow as a skull. Her body grew stooped and wizened. Sirona took a deep breath. "Who are you?" she whispered. "Are you the Great Mother?"

The woman gave a cackling laugh. "If I were, you would have been burned to nothingness. The power of the Great Mother is awesome. To come in contact with even a tiny portion of it is to risk annihilation."

"Then, who are you? *What* are you?"

The old woman laughed once more. "I am Itzurra. I have come to claim you."

Claim her? The implication of her words chilled Sirona. "Why?" she asked. "What have I done?" She looked around. "I didn't mean to eat your food...but I was so hungry. And I didn't mean to intrude upon this place either." She thought about mentioning the wolf guiding her there but wasn't sure the woman would believe her.

"It's not what you have done, but who you are. It's time for you to face your destiny."

"My destiny? What is that?" Sirona's heart was pounding. Her whole body went rigid as the woman moved nearer.

"You are the one who will carry the past into the future," Itzurra said. She grasped Sirona's arm in her claw-like hand. "The blood of the Old Ones runs in your veins. You have it from both your mother, Banon, and from your father."

"My father? What do you know of him?"

"He was a warrior of one of the Brigante tribes. He's dead now, because he couldn't endure the legacy of his mixed blood. Many people can't. They want to be from one world or the other, and can't survive in the twilight space between. But do we not all live our lives in the doorway between two worlds?"

"You mean, this world and the Other Side?"

Itzurra smiled. Despite her great age, she had all her teeth. "Although much of what the Learned Ones teach is nonsense, some of it is true. I suspect it won't be difficult to instruct you. You will understand some things because of your Drui training, and the rest will come easily because it's already in here." Itzurra touched her chest.

"You're going to teach me magic?" Sirona asked excitedly.

Itzurra's smile wavered. "I wish I had more to offer you. But much of the power has been lost."

"What about my visions?" Sirona asked. "Will you tell me what they mean?"

"Your visions aren't from our world, but the other. I can't help you with those."

"What other world?"

Itzurra's expression grew grim. "The world of men, of warriors." The old woman shook her head. "It's the mixture of your blood that torments you. You can never truly belong to one realm. This conflict led to your parents' deaths, but I think you are stronger. I think you will be able to learn to balance the two kinds of power and use them wisely."

Sirona nodded. This was why the wolf had led her to this place. So she would finally learn the secrets of the Old Ones. She thought of Cruthin. If she ever saw him again, she would be able to tell him she'd finally discovered what they'd sought.

"Sit by the fire," Itzurra said. "Let me tell you the story of the Old Ones from the beginning." Sirona settled herself on the animal pelts. Itzurra began, "Long, long ago, the gods came down from the sky. They taught us all about the realms of thought and being. They taught us magic. For a time, our people prospered. Then we began to fight among ourselves, to use the sacred knowledge and power to hurt each other. The gods grew angry and went away. All except one god named Dyeus. He'd fallen in love with a woman named Ane. He mated with her, and they had children. Their children had not only the knowledge of the gods, but some of their blood. Their female children were especially gifted and could do great magic.

"When Ane died, her children buried her in a great mound of earth. Dyeus came and took her with him, back to the sky. Their descendants are the Old Ones. At first, their descendants had great power and knew how to do great things. But gradually their magic dwindled. They became desperate to entice the gods back. They erected the standing stones and monuments, trying to convince them to return. When one of their number died, they buried them in mounds of earth, hoping that Dyeus would come and take the deceased back to the heavens, as he had Ane."

Itzurra raised her head and looked at Sirona sadly. "The fact is, the descendants of Dyeus and Ane became so obsessed with the realm of the gods, they squandered their magic. That's how most of it was lost. But the things they built still possess a little of their power. That's why this mound remains green and fertile even in the dead of winter. For someone like you, who possesses some of Dyeus's blood, these places call to you. You feel the power there. But like all who possess the blood of the Old Ones, the part of you that belongs to the gods is always yearning, longing to return to the stars. Always you are in turmoil. Your flesh is drawn by the earth, which represents Ane's blood. Your spirit, by the stars and the realm of Dyeus. And you also have the blood of the newcomers, those who call themselves the Pretani."

"No wonder I feel so confused, so torn in different directions," Sirona said.

Itzurra nodded. "It's the blood of the Pretani that makes you afraid. While the Pretani raise their children not to fear death or pain, they are still uneasy with the realm of the Other Side."

"I have another fear," Sirona said. "I fear I will end up like my mother. That I will have a horrible death and be trapped in the lonely realm of spirits who are unable to pass over to the Other Side."

"Your mother was nothing like you. She refused the training we tried to offer her and became caught up in the world of men. She never learned how to use the power she possessed. She was like a child who hurts itself as it unwisely struggles to have its own way."

"You knew my mother?"

"Aye."

"What was she like? I have only the tiniest memory of her and..." Sirona grimaced. "...what I've seen in my visions."

"She was beautiful, like you. But she didn't have your wisdom or your spirit. Her spirit was weak, and so, in her confusion, she sought out the power of the Pretani world rather than that of the Old Ones. She used her gifts to meddle in the world of men, of politics and power, and she died because of it. You won't make the same mistake. Already you know what true power is. It's not possessing great herds of sheep and cattle, or, in your mother's case, jewels and fine garments. It has nothing to do with how many people defer to you or heed your will. Power comes from your connection to the earth and the sky. To all life. To the energy of everything around us. To all we can see and all that we cannot see."

Sirona nodded. Old Ogimos had said these same things. She felt in her heart that it was true. "I understand," she said.

Itzurra smiled. She reached under her crys, which was made of some sort of animal fur, brown and soft and amazingly thick, and pulled out a narrow strip of leather with a large blue-green attached. Pulling the necklace over her head, she handed it to Sirona. "Put it on."

"What is it?"

"Something passed down through the women of our line. Although this is not the same one, it's said that Ane possessed an amulet made of this special stone. It's also said Dyeus gave it to her, and it came from the stars."

Carefully, reverently, Sirona looped the thong over her neck. When she touched the stone, cradling it in her fingers, it felt warm and alive.

"Ah," Itzurra said. "It knows you. Recognizes Ane's blood. Perhaps it would have done the same with your mother, but she refused it. She favored gold and silver, and shiny stones that caught the light."

Sirona looked up. "I can't imagine refusing such a gift."

"You would not. And because you know this stone and it knows you, it will protect you and aid you. As long as you wear it, you will be safe from the dangers of the world of men. You must never take it off. Or, if you do—perhaps to put on a new thong to carry it—you must still hold it close to your heart all the while."

Sirona nodded. "Thank you. It's a wonderful gift." She gazed at Itzurra. "How can I repay you for...all of this?"

"Merely to see you smile is repayment enough. I have waited many, many years to find someone to whom I might pass on my Goddess stone. Now, I can die content."

Itzurra's words alarmed Sirona. "Die? What do you mean? I thought you were going to teach me the magic of the Old Ones?"

Itzurra lay back on the animal pelts. Her breath seemed to come harsh and shallow. "You already know nearly as much as I do. And the rest, the rest you must learn for yourself."

"By the Goddess, what's happening?" Sirona knelt beside Itzurra. "You can't die now. We've barely met! I've only begun to learn."

"It's time." Itzurra's voice was barely audible. "One last thing, I ask you."

"What? Anything! I will do whatever you wish! Only...please don't die..." Sirona's words ended in a gasp of despair.

"Lean closer," Itzurra whispered. "Aye, like that. Please leave my body here, in this place. Perhaps..." Her voice grew fainter. "Perhaps Dyeus will come for me."

The fire, which had started to flicker, suddenly went out. Sirona was left in pitch black darkness. Even the smokehole in the top of the mound let in not the faintest light.

"Oh, no," Sirona moaned. "How can this be?" She clutched her head in her hands, wondering if it were all a dream. Then she touched the amulet. The feel of the warm stone provided some reassurance, but she still felt empty and despairing. "How could you leave me?" she whispered. She sniffed loudly, feeling the tears course down her cheeks. "But I must be strong. Itzurra said that as long as I wore the amulet, I would be safe." The words didn't alter her sense of loss. Sighing, she lay down next to Itzurra. The old woman's corpse felt tiny and frail, her bones like a bird's. Already her flesh was growing cold. Sirona moved her hand so she was touching Itzurra's garment. She kneaded her fingers in the soft luxuriance of the fur. It seemed warm and alive, as if the essence of the creature it had come from still lingered there.

* * *

She was woken by sunlight filtering down through the smokehole in the top of the mound. Looking around, she was startled to realize that Itzurra was gone. As she had the night before, Sirona reached for the amulet. It still hung between her breasts. That meant Itzurra had existed, that it wasn't all a dream. But where was the old woman now?

Sirona glanced around and was startled to find a gold necklace lying on the fur next to her. It was made up of disks of gold etched with strange symbols. She puzzled over it, wondering what it meant. Had Dyeus come and taken Itzurra away, leaving the necklace behind? She stroked the gold lovingly. If this was all that was left of Itzurra, then it was fitting it should remain here. But for her, it was time to leave. The sense that her destiny lay elsewhere was very strong. When she touched the amulet once more, it seemed that it spoke, telling her to go.

She thought of taking some of the food and a few jars of the tart beverage, then decided against it. Those things were meant to remain here, for the next traveler in need. After one last glance at the necklace, gleaming brilliantly in a shaft of sunlight filtering down through the opening in the top of the mound, she crawled out of the entrance. Outside, the wolf was waiting for her.

"Hello, wolf," she said, smiling. "Where will you lead me today?" She'd come to this place feeling overwhelmed and hopeless, but now that dark weight was gone, and her mood was expectant, almost joyful.

Chapter 11

The wolf continued to lead her through the forest. They reached open pastureland, where there was a herd of cattle, tended by two youths with dark brown hair. She waved to them and approached. As she neared the youths, she decided they must be brothers. Their features were very similar and they both had freckles covering their faces and exposed skin.

"I am Sirona from the Tarisllwyth tribe. Can you give me directions to the dun where your people live?"

The youths stared at her. Then one of them said, "The settlement is that way." He pointed. "Down that ridge and over the hill."

"Thank you." Sirona looked back for the wolf, but the animal was gone. She made a gesture of farewell. "Thank you, wolf," she said. Then she started off the direction the boy had indicated.

A short while later, Sirona climbed to the top of the hill and looked down at the settlement below. There was no palisade or other defenses, only several dozen round dwellings made out of hides stretched over timber supports, and some sheds for storage. A few plots of land nearby had been recently harvested, with only brown stubble remaining.

She started down into the valley and soon met a group of women and young children coming back from berrying, their baskets overflowing with dark red and purple fruit. The women and children all had reddish or brown hair and were dressed in clothing with a dark green and crimson checked pattern. They stopped when they saw her, regarding her warily.

Sirona greeted them. "I am Sirona, a traveler from the sunset lands."

The tallest of the women responded, "I am Ciorstan, of the Cunogwerin branch of the Brigante tribe." The woman's speech had a different cadence than that of the southern tribes, a certain roughness around the edges of the words.

"In the name of the Great Mother Goddess, I greet you, Ciorstan," Sirona said, then hesitated. How did she proceed from here? The tribe name, the Cunogwerin, sounded familiar to her, but she couldn't remember where she'd heard it. Dare she ask these people for food and shelter, at least for a night or two? After a moment, she said, "Is there a Learned One or Drui among your tribe?"

"Aye, we have a healer who has much knowledge of Drui lore."

"Could I speak with them? I also trained in the grove for many years."

Ciorstan nodded. "Come with us."

Sirona followed the Cunogwerin as they made their way back to the settlement. The women talked quietly among themselves while the children shot her curious glances. Sirona felt apprehensive. Why should she expect this tribe, or any other tribe, to take her in? What did she have to offer? She reminded herself that she had been guided to this place by the wolf, who was surely a messenger of the gods. There must be some purpose for her being here. She had to trust that it was so.

As soon as they entered the camp, they were immediately greeted by a pack of enormous hounds, long-legged hairy beasts with pelts from gray to black. The racket the dogs made was earsplitting. The pack singled her out and surrounded her, sniffing eagerly. Sirona couldn't help laughing. Cunogwerin meant "dogfolk". It was obviously a fitting name. She patted the head of one animal and was soon besieged by the others, also begging for attention. As she struggled to satisfy them all, she looked up and saw Ciorstan watching her intently.

"They clearly approve of you," the woman said. "Usually I must give some sign indicating that a visitor is accepted before they will stop barking. But they behave as if they know you already."

Sirona wondered what Ciorstan would think if she told the woman that her closest companion for the past sennight had been a wolf.

Ciorstan finally shooed the dogs away and led Sirona into the settlement. While the women and children who had accompanied her drifted off, other people stopped to watch Sirona pass. In the center of the encampment they reached a large structure, which Sirona presumed was the chieftain's hall. A little further on, Ciorstan paused before a dwelling. Leaning near to the hide doorway, she called, "Dysri, there's someone here who wishes to speak with you."

At the mention of her friend from the sacred isle, a smile spread across Sirona's face. That's why she recalled the name of this tribe. The gods had indeed guided her to this place.

Dysri came out of the hut. As soon as she saw Sirona, she embraced her. "Ah, little one, it's so good to see you," she exclaimed. "I've been worried about you ever since the gathering."

"It's been an interesting journey here," Sirona answered. She couldn't stop smiling. It felt so good to see a familiar face, to realize she was in the company of someone who might understand what she'd been through.

"Come in, come in," Dysri said. "We've much to talk about."

"Perhaps I should wash first." Sirona indicated her soiled appearance.

"Aye," said Dysri, laughing. "You do look a bit worse for wear."

The older woman took Sirona to a cistern near the center of the camp. To Sirona's surprise, the cistern was made of stone. "I wouldn't have thought you would have a permanent water-collection system here," she said. "This appears to be only a temporary settlement."

"We come here every summer. There's plenty of good pasture and land for growing crops."

"But then you move to another location as the weather changes?"

Dysri nodded as she filled a pottery basin from the cistern. "By the time the Acorn Moon has waxed and waned, we'll be gone."

"Where will you go?"

"Farther north where the forests are denser. There's forage for the herds and plenty of game to see us through the winter."

"I notice you have no wall or earthworks," Sirona said as she splashed water from a basin onto her face and neck. "Does that mean you don't fear other tribes making war on you?"

"Sometimes there are cattle raids, but not often. We've been fortunate to know several years of peace."

"Is there an overking of all the Brigante tribes?" Sirona asked.

"Not a king, but a queen. Her name is Cartimandua."

Sirona gazed at Dysri in surprise. "And all of the tribes of the Brigantes accept her as their leader?"

Dysri nodded.

"Is it because of her that your people are at peace?"

"In a way. She has allied herself with the Romans, and with their support, she's been able to keep the various chieftains from making war against each other."

Sirona shook her head, remembering what had happened to Einion and Culhwch, as well as Bryn's warnings. "I don't trust the Romans. I think they are using Cartimandua, and she will someday regret this alliance."

"Perhaps. But for now, it's good not to have tribe set against tribe. To be able to travel from our summer lands to our winter ones and not worry about attack." As they started back to the hut, Dysri said, "But that's enough talk of politics and war. Tell me what has happened since we last saw each other on the sacred isle. How do you come to be here, arriving with no escort and few supplies?" She motioned to Sirona's pack, hanging limply from her shoulder.

"It's a tale such as the bards tell," Sirona answered. "Full of twists and turns, secrets and…" She smiled. "…even a little magic."

"You must tell me everything."

They went inside the hut and sat down by the hearth. Sirona told

Dysri what had happened after she returned to Mordarach from the sacred isle. She recounted the first part of her journey north and the attack by Romans. Finally, she mentioned the wolf who had led her on the journey, and her experience in the burial mound with Itzurra. Dysri's hazel eyes grew wide, her expression more and more wondering.

"...and so, I left the mound and journeyed north until I arrived here," Sirona finished.

For a time, Dysri said nothing. Then she rose and fetched Sirona some milk from the stone container at the back of the dwelling. There was a small opening on the side of the hide structure. Through it, Sirona observed the light was beginning to fade. It had taken a long time to tell everything that had happened to her in the past fortnight.

When Dysri brought her the milk in a pottery cup, Sirona asked, "So, what do you think of my tale?"

Dysri sat down next to Sirona. Her face appeared distant and intent. "When I first met you, I thought were special. I believed you would have great influence on the future."

"And now?"

"And now..." Dysri smiled. "Now I am certain of it."

"But what am I supposed to *do*?" Sirona asked. "There are times when I feel the hand of the gods upon me, guiding me. But then when I reach the place I've been led to, I discover more mysteries. Questions rather than answers. On the sacred isle, I knew I must go to the mound with Cruthin. I felt something important was going to happen there. But, looking back, I'm not certain what any of it meant. Our actions brought down the wrath of the Learned Ones upon us, and I've come to think that my being banished from my tribe was meant to be. And now I've been guided here, but I still don't know why."

"I wish I could advise you, but you've already moved far past me."

"But you must have some thoughts on why I'm here."

"You must be patient. You've barely even had your woman-making. Give yourself time to mature. Time to get used to having visions. Perhaps you've been guided here because I'm a healer and you need a respite from your burdens. For now, if you can, stop seeking answers. Forget the future, and the past. Feel your heart beating at this moment. Savor the rhythms of life. The change of day to night. The turn of the seasons."

"It's true. I am weary. So much has happened since the golden wheel of summer first filled the sky."

"For now, my advice is to do nothing," Dysri said. "Let your spirit rest. Soon the plants will begin to die back, and the earth turn to the darkness. In the bellies of ewes and cattle and deer, the spark of life will be sown. As the winter winds blow and the world turns cold and harsh and gloomy, that life will grow and swell. Come spring, it will burst forth, restless and eager. This is the winter of your spirit, for as long as you need it to be. Rest as the fallow earth rests. Wait, as the beasts do, sluggish and slow, for the sun to return and make the grass green."

Sirona nodded. There was wisdom in what Dysri told her. Not magic, but quiet truth. "Your tribe will accept me?"

"I'll tell them that you are some kin of mine come to serve as my apprentice."

"I fear I have no gift for healing."

"It won't matter," said Dysri. "No one will question my choice." She rose. "Now I must make you known to the chieftain, Ruadan, and to the rest of the elders. They'll be in the hall waiting for us."

* * *

Beneath Sirona's feet the bracken and cane brake was a dull bronze, and as she passed a blackthorn bush, she saw that the plant's bluish fruits were almost gone, picked clean by birds and squirrels. Above her, only a few lonely leaves fluttered from the branches of the oak boughs. She bent down and began to scoop up acorns, filling another basket. Tedious work, and yet she was pleased to be able to contribute to the Cunogwerin's winter foodstores. As Dysri promised, the tribe had taken her in, offering a place to spend the snowseason, or longer if she needed it.

As soon as the hazelnuts and acorns began to fall and gold and copper leaves covered the ground, the Cunogwerin had headed north, packing up their hide and timber dwellings and other possessions and loading them on carts drawn by sturdy black oxen. It was a long, slow journey with the carts, but Sirona had enjoyed observing the gradual changes in the landscape. As the deep green of pine trees replaced the brighter foliage of oak and elm, it struck her that the midnight lands were a darker and more somber world. The mists, creeping over the valleys, felt heavier and more chilling. They encountered still, mirror-like lakes and dark, murky boglands, rather than the swift streams, runlets and waterfalls of her home territory. This was an ancient place, where the spirits were wise and solemn, rather than fierce and wild.

When her gathering basket was full, Sirona sought out Dysri. The older woman helped Sirona place a stick over her shoulders to carry her two full baskets, then devised a similar arrangement for herself. Then they started back to the tribe's winter camp.

"What will you do with all these acorns?" Sirona asked. "Our tribe never gathered them. Instead, we turned the pigs out to forage among the mast."

"It's possible to make a kind of flour out of ground acorns," Dysri told her. "If we are fortunate, our stores of oats and barley will last all winter, and we won't need to resort to acorn meal. But it's good to be prepared. If the snows are too deep for the men to hunt, we'll have to survive on the food in our storage pits."

Sirona nodded. The Cunogwerin had culled their herds only a few days ago, butchering all but the main breeding stock, and salting and smoking the meat. They stored the meat, along with grain, dried berries, beans, and some roots and tubers, in stone pits in the ground at the edge of their camp.

"What about the Old Ones?" Sirona asked. "If it's a difficult winter, how do they survive?"

Dysri shook her head. "No one knows how the Croenglas manage." Croenglas, which meant "blue-skinned", was what the Brigante tribe called the Old Ones. "Perhaps they go into some secret underground place and sleep away the winter like bears," Dysri said, smiling. "Although I think it more likely that they move to areas along the coast and survive by fishing."

"So, you think it's unlikely I'll encounter any of them until spring?"

Dysri shrugged. "And maybe not even then." Her smile faded. "I'm sorry to disappoint you. But you must understand that the relationship between the Croenglas and our people is an uneasy one. In times past, there have been strange incidents involving them. Some tribes claim that when the Croenglas are around, their livestock fall ill, and there have been tales of children and babies who sickened and died after the Old Ones were seen in the area. Magic often inspires fear as well as awe. It is thus with my people and the Croenglas. The two races usually avoid each other."

"What about Lovarn?" Sirona asked. "That was an incident where an individual of their race approached one of your people."

Dysri nodded, her eyes far away with memory. "I was alone that day, out gathering herbs in the forest. There was no sound or warning and then, suddenly, two men were in the clearing, with Lovarn on a kind of sledge between them. I went over to see to Lovarn, who was obviously wounded. When I looked up, the two men were gone." Dysri shuddered. "I still feel strange when I think about it."

"And you told Lovarn that the only way you could save his leg was to cut it off?"

Dysri nodded. "It was a grave wound, down to the bone and already rank with poison."

"And then what happened?"

"He told me that if that if he must lose his leg to save his life, he would die. Then he thanked me. A while later, the two men came back and carried him off, dragging the sledge between them. They returned two days later, when I was in the forest, and told me he was dead."

"And that's the only contact you've ever had with the Croenglas?"

Dysri nodded.

Sirona felt the familiar frustration. She'd hoped that here in the north she might find answers, about the Old Ones, about her visions, about the purpose and meaning of her life. Over a cycle of the moon had passed and she hadn't yet discovered any of the things she sought.

A loud bellow sounded in the distance. A few heartbeats later, there was an answering bugle. Both women halted a moment to listen. "Ah," Dysri said. "The stags are in rut. Soon the hunters will bring home fresh meat. This is the best time of year to track the forest king, when he is distracted by the does in season."

The image of a great antlered stag reminded Sirona of what had happened at the mound on the sacred isle. A pang of grief went through her. She'd had a chance to mate with the lord of the forest, the stag king, Cernunnos. And like a yearling doe, she'd reacted with dread and fear. *Cruthin, where are you? Will I ever see you again?*

She started walking again, tears stinging her eyes. Dysri observed her distress. "Don't grieve so," she said, catching up to her. "Here in the north, you have a chance for a new beginning."

Sirona nodded. She must be patient and wait for the gods to reveal her pathway. Still, she couldn't help mourning the world of her childhood she'd left behind. She thought of her grandmother, imagining Nesta in the autumn woods, collecting herbs for her medicines, small and frail, her skin and hair near as pale as silver, like the mist flowing along the forest floor. And like the mist, the image of Nesta gradually faded, until she was no more than a breeze riffling the leaves, a white owl floating silently overhead.

The ache inside Sirona deepened. She told herself she was being foolish. Although she might never again see Nesta alive, her living, breathing fleshly form, her grandmother's spirit would always be with her. And it was that spirit, the essence of a loved one, that mattered.

* * *

The next night, Sirona pushed aside the hide door of the dwelling she shared with Dysri and went out into the cold stillness. She moved quickly through the camp, stopping only to pat one of the hounds, stretched out, guarding the doorway of a dwelling. She rubbed the huge, fawn-colored animal behind its ears, and it gave a shuddering sigh. After giving the dog a final pat, she straightened and moved on.

She walked to the edge of the settlement and sought out a herding path that led up into the hills. The ground crunched with frost as she walked, and overhead the stars hung in the blue black sky like sparkling ice crystals. On the western horizon, the crescent moon gleamed like the blade of a curved ceremonial knife. The going was rough, the trackway rocky and edged with furze. As she picked her way along, a wolf howled in the distance. But her heart didn't race, nor did she tense with dread. It was a wolf that had led her to this place of sanctuary.

The brisk air pierced her clothing. She pulled her mantle more tightly around her body and quickened her pace. The pathway crossed two hills, gleaming faintly in the moonlight, then led down into a ravine thick with thorn and bramble bushes.

She pushed her way through the brush and dodged the stones littering the pathway. At last she came to a clearing where a handful of knee-high, lichen-splashed boulders were arranged in a circle. She took a deep breath and then entered the circle. After pausing a moment to gather her thoughts, she lifted her hands to the sky. "Arianrhod, Lady of the moon, the face of the Goddess who rules the sky and shines her bright light upon the land, show me the way. Tell me what I must do."

She waited, but heard nothing except a faint whisper of breeze stirring the leaves of the nearby bushes. A sigh escaped her lips. She understood that she was meant to go to the sacred isle, to share what she'd shared with Cruthin, even if their mating had fallen short of completion. She was meant to be banished from her tribe and to travel north. But after that, her destiny, her purpose, grew blurry and vague. Bits and pieces of knowledge had come to her, but so much else eluded her. It seemed the answers lay in the future, a future that she could not see, no matter how hard she tried.

Please, Great Mother, she begged silently, *give me a sign.* Once again, she raised her arms to the heavens and repeated her exhortation. But no tingling started along her spine and her inner vision remained empty. Above her the stars shone, cold and brilliant, and the face of the Lady gazed down upon her with silence.

She sighed again, thinking she should return to the settlement. There were no answers here.

She thought then of Old Ogimos, the ancient, solemn Drui who hadn't lectured on the movement of the stars, nor made them recite endless tales and genealogies, or demanded that they learn the proper way of performing a ceremony. Instead, Ogimos had taught them things of the spirit, awakening in them a sense of the pattern all around, the way everything was connected. Now his words came back to her. *You must not be impatient with the gods, but let them reveal their purpose for you in their own time. You must remain quiet and still and listen. Listen with your heart and your spirit. The answers will come to you on the whispering wind, or the voice of a stream splashing over the rocks.*

Secrets await you in the dark shadows of the woods, in the perfection of a flower hidden among the fallen leaves and dried grass. The flower waits for the right moment to bloom, to come forth in all its glory. And so, someday, the answers will be revealed to you and you will understand at last.

His words made her look down at the ground. Her gaze fell upon the dried bracken at her feet, the curling mosses that would be green in summer, but which now looked dead and brown. The earth and most of the plants and trees would sleep through the coming season of cold and snow. They would reawaken in the spring, but for now they were dormant. Perhaps that was what she was meant to do also, here in the land of the north. Perhaps as Dysri had suggested, she wasn't supposed to take action or to pursue her destiny. Perhaps, like the brown, lifeless vegetation all around her, she was meant to enter a time of waiting, to draw close within herself and absorb the life force all around, to gather it in, so when the time came to act, she could be strong...and powerful...like the Goddess.

The thought made her impatient. She didn't want to wait. She wanted knowledge and answers. And yet, the earth told her that this was the way of all things. The rhythm of life, of the seasons, couldn't be rushed. Her own body told her this as well. She was still very young. Her moontimes had begun only a turn of the seasons ago. She had scarcely crossed the threshold of womanhood. Perhaps that was why things had gone wrong with Cruthin. They were both too immature, too unfinished, to complete the ceremony as it should be completed. More children playing a game than adults performing a sacred rite.

But someday... She thought of her first vision. That time would come. She knew it, could feel it with every breath she took. But first she would be tested, tested cruelly.

Even as she had the thought, the visions came. She began to shiver violently as her mind was filled with images: Nesta lying dead on the ground. A terrified woman fleeing a warrior with a sword. The red-haired queen, her face a mask of triumphant cruelty. Chariots and warriors. Fire and blood. Death and destruction. She gasped and slumped to her knees, covering her face with her hands.

If this was what was to come, then she had no desire to hurry to meet the future. She was not ready yet. Not ready...

The images vanished and Sirona got slowly to her feet. The Goddess had answered after all, telling her that she should enjoy this time of quiet and peace, this season—or seasons—of her spirit lying fallow.

She gazed up again at the sky, silently thanking the lady of the moon for her soft, beneficent light.

Part 2
The Raven of Death

61 C.E.

Chapter 12

The settlement was crowded with many wooden buildings, although they didn't look like the round dwellings of a Pretani settlement. The air was full of the haze of smoke. Ahead of her, Sirona saw a woman with long, reddish gold braids. The woman moved cautiously, a bundle clutched her to her chest. Her eyes darted around, wide with fear and dread.

The tall form of a man loomed out of the murk. He wore a long warrior's mustache and carried a club and a round shield. With his club, he knocked the woman down. The woman struggled to rise, but her attacker swung the club once more, striking her on the side of the head. As the woman fell, the bundle she carried went flying. The babe inside the wrapping tumbled out and lay squalling on the ground.

The warrior crouched over the woman, as if to make certain she was dead, then straightened. He started to move on, and then spied the baby lying there, screaming, tiny fists flailing. With a swift kick, he sent the infant sailing into the wall of a nearby building.

Sirona awoke, pulse pounding, stomach churning. She sat up and took a deep breath as she sought to shake off the horror of the dream. Dysri, lying nearby in the leather-walled shelter, also roused. "Sirona, what is it?"

"A Seeing, I think." Sirona swallowed, struggling against a wave of nausea. "This one was awful."

"Do you want me to brew some mint and thyme to help calm you?"

Sirona touched the blue-green stone hanging between her breasts, seeking comfort from the warmth of the object. "I'll be all right. I didn't mean to disturb you."

Dysri sat up on her bedplace. "You've had several troubling dreams lately. What do you think it means?"

Sirona shook her head, unwilling to discuss the matter. "Go back to sleep, and I'll try to do the same."

Long after Dysri's breathing had grown deep and even, Sirona lay there, wide awake. She kept seeing the dream in her mind. Both the woman and the warrior had appeared to be Pretani. So, why had the man killed her? And why did these visions come to her now, when she had lived in the north for four untroubled years?

Her sense of foreboding grew until it felt like a rock lodged in her belly. She could feel her destiny reaching out for her... a claw-like hand groping in the darkness. Shuddering, she once more shifted position on the bedplace.

* * *

"Sirona, wake up." Dysri nudged her. "There's a visitor in camp."

Sirona's stomach still felt unsettled from the vision of the night before, and her eyes were gritty from lack of sleep. But once awake, she hurried to dress and comb her hair. She felt certain this visitor and her visions were connected.

Although he appeared fairly young, the man talking to Ruadan in the chieftain's hall wore the garb of a Learned One. As soon as he saw her, the man's blue eyes widened. Gradually, she recognized him. It was the young Drui who had come to Mordarach the spring before the gathering on the sacred isle.

He smiled and beckoned her near. "It's a pleasure to find another Learned One here in the north. I am Kellach of the Silure tribe."

Sirona cleared her throat and responded, "And I am—"

"Sirona of the Tarisllwyth," he finished for her. "I remember you from when I visited your home dun."

Sirona stared at him, not knowing what to say. Kellach's blue eyes focused on her keenly. "I recently went back to Mordarach. When I asked about you, I was told you were dead. They said you went north to find your father's tribe. When your escort didn't return, they sent out a search party but found nothing. They thought all of you had been killed by Romans."

"I wasn't there when the Romans attacked," Sirona explained. "I had gone off to fetch some water and when I came back, my escort was dead. I attempted to bury the two men, then wandered on my own for days until I made my way here. Tell me, how did Tarbelinus's search party know we were attacked by Romans?"

"Of course it was Romans," Kellach responded. He glanced at Ruadan. "Who else would have done such a thing?" He looked back at Sirona. "Apparently, you haven't been in contact with Tarisllwyth these past years. It would seem I have much news to share with you."

Ruadan, a florid-faced, burly man who got his name from his bright red hair, gestured broadly. "Let us seat ourselves before the fire and you can share your tale with all of us."

Once settled on some furs with a cup of heather beer in his hand, Kellach began, "This is the story of Sirona's home tribe. Three years ago, Romans came to their settlement. At first, they demanded tribute and their chieftain, Tarbelinus, gave it to them. But he eventually grew angered by the contempt they showed his people and plotted his revenge. This previous sunseason, when a Roman envoy came to collect the tribute, Tarbelinus had them killed. That brought the wrath of the Romans down upon them. A large force was sent to the settlement." He shook his sadly. "They tried to fight, but they were easily defeated. There were simply too many of the enemy. The Romans took Tarbelinus away in chains. Later it was reported that he died on the journey across the sea."

Sirona felt sick to her stomach. Her mother had predicted this. Thank the gods Nesta had not been alive to see it happen.

Then Sirona thought of Bryn. Her mother had also said he would die in the first battle he fought in. Had that prophecy also come true? The thought deepened her turmoil. Had she made a mistake when she encouraged him to go off and become a warrior? "What about Tarbelinus's son?" she asked Kellach breathlessly. "Have you heard anything of him?"

"As I understand it, he left the settlement many years ago, soon after you did. No one knows where he is."

Sirona's mind raced. Bryn might still be alive… but his father was dead. She could scarce believe it. Tarbelinus had always seemed as strong and enduring as the timber walls of Mordarach itself. She raised her gaze to Kellach's, dreading his response. "When the Romans attacked Mordarach and took Tarbelinus prisoner, what happened to the rest of the tribe?"

"The Romans didn't kill them, but made them a subject people. That way they can continue to produce wealth for the Romans to steal."

"What of the Tarisllwyth Learned Ones?" she asked.

Kellach shrugged. "Fiach and the others were allowed to remain with the tribe. But it's not the same. The tribe's connection to the gods has clearly been disrupted."

Kellach turned to Ruadan and began to detail more of the abuses of the enemy. Gradually, through her own grief and shock, Sirona started to understand. This man had come here to convince the Cunogwerin chieftain to join in the fight against the Romans. He was using the tale of what had happened to her people as a warning of what might happen to the northern tribes if they didn't take action.

Sirona felt a touch on her hand and turned to look into Dysri's sympathetic gaze. Sirona nodded, feeling very glum. When her mother predicted Tarbelinus's fate, she'd said the Tarisllwyth would be destroyed. At least that part of the prophecy hadn't come true… yet.

She turned her attention back to what Kellach was saying.

"I'm traveling the whole width and breadth of Albion, warning our people that the time to stop the Romans is now. If we all band together, we can defeat them and drive them out of our territories. An uprising is being planned by Boudica, queen of the Iceni. She intends to attack the Roman settlements in the eastern territories. She's asking all the Pretani tribes to send warriors to aid her." Kellach's voice grew imploring. "What say you, Ruadan? Will you send men to fight the Romans? Will you consider joining this uprising?"

"Life is difficult here in the north," Ruadan said. "I can't commit warriors to fighting an enemy we haven't even seen."

"But you *will* see them, I vow it! The highland peoples thought the same as you, that there was safety in their isolation. But they were wrong, and now they are paying for their blindness." Kellach shot a fierce glance at Sirona, as if asking her to confirm his words.

After a moment, she nodded, and Kellach continued, his voice taut with conviction. "We *must* fight the Romans, all of us, everyone who bears a drop of Pretani blood. If we don't, there will be no future for our people."

Ruadan still appeared dubious. "I can't believe the Romans would ever come this far north. If they did, what would they steal from us? Our cattle? By the time they drove the animals into their territories, the beasts would be naught but skin and bones, worthless except for their hides." He shook his head. "There's nothing for the Romans here. They won't trouble us."

Kellach made a sound of disgust. Then he seemed to realize such an attitude wouldn't help sway Ruadan. He turned to Sirona. "What of you? Your home has been destroyed by the Romans. Your people killed or subjugated. Doesn't that distress you? Have you no desire to seek vengeance against the enemy?"

Sirona had to admit she hated the Romans. She would never forget what they had done to Enion and Culhwch. But what did Kellach expect her to do? She wasn't a warrior.

Kellach rose abruptly. "I hope you will think on these things, Ruadan. Perhaps talk to your warriors about what I've said." He motioned to Sirona. "Come, Sirona, walk with me."

She got to her feet. As they left the chieftain's hut and moved through the settlement, she felt as if she were in a daze, her mind struggling to take in all that Kellach had told her.

"Ruadan's stubborn." Kellach's voice was bitter. "Like so many chieftains. They won't listen until it's too late." He turned to Sirona. "Will you help me? Will you try to convince him to send warriors to fight the Romans?"

"I have no influence with Ruadan."

"But these people respect you. No one questioned that you should be included in the discussion."

"The Learned Ones here don't perform the same functions as the Drui of the southern tribes. When there is a ceremony to mark one of the important events in the wheel of the seasons, it's led by Ruadan, not Dysri or myself. Life for these people is harsh and demanding, and their religious rites have become simpler and more straight-forward. And yet, they are very devout," she added, hoping she hadn't given Kellach the wrong idea. "For every aspect of their lives, they give thanks to the gods, offering a sacrifice each time they slaughter one of the herd or kill a wild animal. They will not pass a spring or pool without whispering a blessing to the spirit that dwells there. In the ceremonies, they mostly honor Cernunnos, and Bran, a war god."

Kellach grunted. "If I were you, I would be angry not to be accorded more authority."

"I may not have much authority, but I've been treated very well. I'm not charged with the responsibilities most Brigante women have. I'm not required to spin or weave, to grind grain or work in the fields in the summer."

"And no man has asked to handfast with you, has he?" Kellach asked, his blue eyes shrewd.

"Nay. But there's no man here I desire."

They walked in silence for a time, then Kellach said, "Then there's nothing keeping you here. No reason you couldn't leave." He stopped and turned to look at her. "Do you still have visions, Sirona?"

She hesitated, uneasy.

His gaze continued to pierce her. "I remember what you did on the sacred isle. It doesn't trouble me, but makes me think that my first impression of you was right—you're very gifted." Kellach drew nearer, his eyes seeming to burn with blue light. "Tell me. What do you see for our people? Will we defeat the Romans?"

"I don't know," she said. "Things come to me only in glimpses."

Kellach started walking again. Sirona followed. His questions haunted her, reminding her how little she knew about her abilities and what she was meant to do with them. They reached the edge of the Brigante camp. Ahead of them stretched hills covered with the reddish glow of blooming bell heather and edged with dark forests. "Come with me," Kellach said.

"When you travel north?"

He shook his head. "I've decided to turn back. There's no point going deeper into the midnight lands. If I can't convince Ruadan of the Roman threat, I'll fare no better with the other Brigante chieftains. I'll go west instead. The people of your homeland are not so stupid and stubborn. They will realize we must join together against this common threat."

"But why do you want me to go with you?" she asked. "If you think the Silure and Ordovice chieftains will heed you, why do you need me to come with you?"

"Because you're trained as a Learned One."

"But my training is incomplete," she pointed out.

"Yet it's better than nothing." Kellach gestured. "Why shouldn't you leave here? This isn't your tribe, your people. They accept you, but you're not really one of them. You spoke of Bryn, Tarbelinus's son. Perhaps if you came with me, you might find him. Or, the young man with whom you got into trouble on the sacred isle."

Kellach was clever. Astute enough to realize she might be convinced to go with him in order to search for the companions of her youth. Reluctantly, she thought of Cruthin and the magic they had shared at the mound on the sacred isle. Then she pushed the memory away. "Tell me about this Iceni queen," she said.

Kellach's mouth quirked, as if he were amused she'd changed the subject. "Her name is Boudica. She and her family suffered terribly at the hands of the Romans, and she's vowed revenge. She plans to lead a large army—as many men as I can bring to her cause—and attack the enemy's eastern settlements."

Sirona thought of the red-haired, regal woman in one of her first visions. The look of cruel satisfaction on the woman's face was burned into her mind. "Have you met this woman, Boudica? Can you describe her?"

Kellach's expression grew intent. "Why do you ask? Have you seen a vision involving her?"

"Perhaps."

"Tell me, in your vision, does it appear that Boudica and her forces are victorious?" Kellach's voice was tense and breathless. His blue eyes bored into her as if he could will the Seeing from her mind to his own.

"In my vision, I saw a tall, strong-looking red-haired woman. There was smoke and fire behind her, and I could hear the screams of the dying."

Kellach smiled. "So, it's truly going to happen. This time we will prevail over the Romans."

Remembering her recent dream, Sirona wasn't so certain. A destiny of death and destruction awaited someone, but she didn't know if it was the Romans or the Pretani.

Kellach seemed to sense her unease. "Consider this, Sirona. Even if the Tarisllwyth banished you, you still have a duty to your tribe. Now that Tarbelinus is dead, his son, Bryn, is needed at Mordarach. You also have responsibilities as a Learned One. The Romans are a threat to all we stand for. Surely you must see that now."

"I'm no longer a Learned One," she repeated.

"And yet, you continue to look at the world as a Learned One would. That's something that's sorely needed."

Kellach was giving her another chance. He knew what had happened on the sacred isle, yet didn't reject her because of it. She thought about the sense of isolation and loneliness that had gnawed at her since coming north. At one time she'd believed this was where she would find the answers she sought, but it hadn't happened.

Kellach continued his coaxing. "You could be a great help to me, Sirona. The number of Learned Ones has dwindled greatly. Your knowledge and insight are desperately needed. And then there is the fact that you're a seer. I believe you've meant to use your visions to alter the future. Our future. The destiny of our people."

Kellach's words tantalized her. To imagine there was a purpose behind the awful images. To believe that she might use her Seeings to help those she cared about. And yet she remembered Itzurra saying that involvement in the realm of men was what had destroyed her mother. How could she prevent the same thing from happening to her?

"I'll have to think on it," she told Kellach. "When are you leaving?"

"Tomorrow. Now that I know Ruadan won't listen, I'm impatient to leave."

Nearly four turns of the seasons she had dwelled in the north, and nothing much happened. Now, in the span of a day, everything in her life seemed to have changed.

"We should return to the settlement," she told Kellach. "Ruadan may not listen to your pleas to join in fighting the Romans, but he will still hold a feast in your honor. The traditions of hospitality are strong here."

Kellach smiled at her. "I must admit I grow weary of traveling food. That's one of the difficulties of the life I've chosen. But there are many rewards. I've met many different people on my journeys, and learned a great deal, more than I would have if I had stayed with my tribe. I sense you are also searching for knowledge, Sirona. Which is another reason you should come with me."

Sirona didn't answer, but started walking back to the Brigante camp. Kellach's arguments were compelling. There were times in the last few seasons she felt as if she was merely existing, like a tree that appears black and barren in the midst of winter. Now the sap again ran in her veins.

* * *

"You're going out?" Dysri mumbled sleepily from her bedplace next to Sirona's.

"Aye, I have some thinking to do."

"That man who came—Kellach—I'm not certain I like him."

"What do you mean?" Sirona paused at the hide door of the dwelling.

"There's something sly about him. Sly and… dangerous."

"In what way?"

"It's only a feeling. I can say no more than that."

"He's offering me a chance to resume my life as a Learned One. It's what my grandmother always wanted for me." A wave of sadness went through Sirona. It had been nearly three years since Nesta's death had come to her in a vision. She'd seen her grandmother walking in the woods, collecting herbs. Then Nesta had fallen and lay still, her blue eyes gazing up sightlessly at the sky. The memory still caused a tightness in Sirona's chest. How strange that she had seen her grandmother's death, but had no inkling of the other things that had happened at Mordarach.

Dysri spoke again. "And what of you? What do you desire for your life?"

"To be different than my mother," Sirona said resolutely. "To use my abilities for good. To live up to the expectations the Goddess has for me."

"The Goddess wouldn't have chosen you if you were not strong enough to become what she wishes."

"I hope that's true."

"It is." Dysri rose from the bedplace and embraced her. "But I can't help being afraid for you."

Sirona gently disengaged herself from the other woman. "I must go out for a time, to be alone with my thoughts."

"Aye, I know." Dysri said sadly.

As she left the dwelling, Sirona realized the other woman was weeping. The thought brought tears to her own eyes. If she decided to go with Kellach, this leave-taking would be difficult. Perhaps more so than when she was banished from Mordarach. She had felt safe here in the north, watched over and protected by Dysri.

It wasn't yet dawn, but hints of pink and gold colored the horizon as she walked swiftly through the settlement. The faint crescent of a waxing moon still hung in the sky. Soon it would be Beltaine, the night that marked the true beginning of the sunseason. The Cunogwerin would build bonfires on the tops of the hills and hold a sacrifice in honor of Olwen, the goddess of the golden wheel of summer, and Blodeuwedd, the maiden of flowers and growing things. Afterwards, the young men and women, wearing circlets of hawthorn blossoms, would dance and drink the heather-brewed curmi that the Brigantes favored. As the night grew late and everyone became merry and high-spirited, couples would pair off and disappear into the darkness together. Babes conceived at Beltaine were believed to be especially blessed.

But Sirona knew she would conceive no babe, for no Cunogwerin man would grab her hand and pull her laughing into the shadows. All the people here seemed to view her with awe and a little fear, and the men especially so.

It filled her with loneliness to think of these things and made her yearn to be back among the Tarisllwyth. Perhaps that was the Goddess's plan for her, that she should return to her own tribe in their time of need.

She felt a stir of excitement at the thought of going back to her homeland. There were things left to do there, things unfinished. She thought of what she had shared with Cruthin on the sacred isle and her first vision of the people dancing near the circle of stones by the sea. One moment was in the past, the other, the future, but both took place in the sunset lands.

She left the settlement and took a herding path into the hills. The sky was brightening, while the morning mists rose. Wreaths of vapor floated along beside her, obscuring the heather and yellow furze at her feet. The ground was wet with dew, soaking her leather shoes. She startled a hare, and farther on, saw a vixen carrying a mouse in its mouth, an early meal for its kits. The fox ignored her as it trotted back to its den, and she wondered if the animal remembered seeing her here before and knew she was no threat. She had come to this place several times since the Cunogwerin first chose this valley for their early summer camp three years ago.

Climbing a ridge, she sighted her goal. Not a circle of stones, but three craggy, weathered boulders standing tall in a grassy meadow. She approached slowly, absorbing the beauty of everything around her. The sky, radiant with the pale hues of dawn. The delicate mountain avens and primrose budding among the grass. The stones themselves, darkened and weathered and covered with lichens, until they seemed to blend into the grass and the bracken and become a part of the land itself.

Reaching the standing stones, she turned to look back the way she had come. Then she glanced up at the sky and sighted a goshawk swooping low as it began its morning hunt. She watched the bird for a moment, in awe of its grace and power. When she turned back to the boulders, there were three men standing there, their upright forms echoing the arrangement of the boulders. Their dark hair, blue-patterned skin and rough leather garments marked them clearly as Croenglas. They faced her, their elegantly beautiful faces expressionless.

She'd encountered the Croenglas several times since coming to the midnight lands. They always greeted her with solemnity and respect, but when she sought to speak to them, they told her only that the Goddess had sent them to watch over her.

Seeing them, Sirona's heart began to pound. She felt certain they had come to say goodbye. Could there be any clearer sign that she was meant to go with Kellach?

She made the hand to the forehead salute. "Greetings. May the Goddess send the sun to warm your back and bless your spirit."

They responded with the same gesture. One of the men approached her and held out a small knife. "It's made of metal from the stars," he said. "It will protect you."

"I have the goddess stone to keep me safe," she answered. Reaching beneath her mantle and gown, she drew out the amulet and cupped it in her fingers.

"Where you are going, the things you will face, even a star stone may not be strong enough."

His words chilled her. The pathway ahead must be treacherous indeed.

He made the forehead gesture and then stepped back. All three men turned and walked off, disappearing into the bushes.

Sirona shivered. A part of her yearned to stay here with the Brigantes and live her life that was half a life. But she knew she couldn't do that. The visions were her destiny. Perhaps if she went with Kellach, she would finally discover the answers she sought.

Sirona left the standing stones and started back to camp.

Chapter 13

The smell of the fens filled his nostrils and gnats circled around Bryn's head. He swiped at them with his free hand and turned to look for Cadwalon, crouched in the willow bushes on the other side of the marshy meadow. After catching a brief glimpse of his companion, Bryn adjusted his grip on his ash wood spear. How many times had they done this, waiting in ambush as days and nights passed by? Sometimes they were pelted by wind and sleet, or shivered in a cold rain. This day they were being tortured by heat and insects.

A faint sound reached Bryn's ears, barely distinguishable from the buzz of the gnats and the call of the marsh tits. Again, he searched out Cadwalon and spied him across the ragged expanse of the fens. The youth Bryn had met years earlier had grown into a stocky, muscular man, with shoulders that seemed too wide for his short frame. The seasons spent outdoors had weathered Cadwalon's skin and bleached strands of his wavy black hair and beard. Except for his vivid blue eyes and his strong white teeth, everything about Cadwalon was brown, a coloration that allowed him to seemingly disappear into his surroundings.

A useful trait for men like them, Bryn thought, men who lived on the fringes of a powerful chieftain's territory. For two years, ever since Cadwalon had broken with his father Cadwyl over his alliance with the Romans, they had been harrying Cadwyl's warriors and ambushing his trading parties. They'd had many successes, enough to entice some of Cadwyl's younger warriors to join them. But none of those men were with them this day. The rest of Cadwalon's warband remained at their summer camp, hidden on an island in the fens. This was meant to be a hunting trip only, a foray into the forest edging the marsh to track down the boar that foraged there.

They had anticipated no need for their swords, and so were armed only with the long, clumsy boar spears and the well-used, functional knives they carried on their belts. Then Cadwalon's sharp ears had discerned they were not alone in the woods, and he signaled to Bryn that they should make their way back. To their surprise, the person they were trying to avoid decided to follow them. Bryn could hear the sound of someone struggling through the fens—a small splash now and then, the swish of reeds and rushes as the intruder moved along.

An older man came in sight. He had gray hair braided away from his bearded face, but he moved briskly, his back straight and his movements vigorous as he groped his way from dry spot to dry spot in the treacherous morass of mud and reeds. A few heartbeats later, Bryn caught a glimpse of the pattern of red, green and white edging the neck and sleeves of the man's crys and realized their pursuer was a Learned One. The idea of a Drui venturing into this place startled him so much he forgot about Cadwalon. By the time he thought to indicate to his companion that they shouldn't attack, it was too late. Cadwalon had charged with his spear raised.

Bryn ran after his companion as Cadwalon rapidly closed the distance between himself and his target. "Stop!" Bryn yelled. "Stop!"

The Drui didn't flinch as Cadwalon bore down on him, but stood still and rigid as if resigned to his fate. At the last moment, Cadwalon turned the spear aside. A few paces later, he stopped, panting, then whirled and glared at the man. "What do you want?" he bellowed. "Why are you following us?"

The man smiled. "Ah," he said. "You must be Cadwalon, son of Cadwyl. I've been looking for you.'"

Cadwalon's face went slack as he stared at the Drui.

Bryn rushed up, almost faint with relief that Cadwalon hadn't attacked the man. "He's a Learned One," he panted. "See? He wears the sacred colors."

The Drui turned to look at Bryn. The freckled skin around his eyes crinkled as he smiled. "You're right. I am Moren, a Learned One of the Trinovante tribe. I have come here seeking warriors who bear a grudge against the Romans. Men who would be willing to take part in an uprising in the east, to finally drive the hated invaders back into the sea."

Bryn's heart seemed to leap into his chest. These were the words he had waited years to hear. "Then you have found what you seek," he answered. "I would gladly join any army that had such a noble goal."

The man nodded and turned to Cadwalon, eyebrows raised. "And what of you, my feisty young fellow? Would you also join in this war? Or would you rather stay here and gnaw away at your father's power? Perhaps in ten or twenty years, you might finally claim the kingship."

Cadwalon's face flushed mightily and Bryn again knew fear for the bold-spoken Drui. "It's forbidden to harm a Learned One," Bryn said, stepping between the two men. "They're protected by the gods."

Cadwalon glared at him. Then he glanced back at Moren and gave him a wintry smile. "It's fortunate for you that my companion once trained in the grove and knows the laws of your kind."

Moren raised his brows and looked at Bryn. "Is that true? Did you train as Drui?"

For a moment, Bryn's resentment and frustration came rushing back as he recalled the wasted years training as Drui when he could have been honing his warrior skills. Tarbelinus's stubborn insistence he become a Learned One had ultimately driven him from his home, his tribe, his birthright. And yet, those years in the grove were part of what he was. He could not deny them. "Aye," he answered.

"Then you understand more than most men what a threat the Romans are," Moren said. "If they aren't stopped and banished from our territories, they will destroy us."

"There's no need to convince me," Bryn said. "I've been eager to take up my sword against the invaders since before I had my man-making. I've merely been waiting for the right opportunity."

"Then your wait is over. The queen of the Iceni, a woman named Boudica, has raised a large army. She intends to attack the Roman settlements in the sunrise lands. These places aren't well-defended, and they will fall easily. That will draw the main force of the Roman troops from their positions in the north and east. When they arrive to defend their settlements, we'll wipe them out."

"A bold plan," Bryn said. "But are you certain this Boudica has sufficient warriors to defeat the army of Rome?"

Moren smiled. "She may not yet, but she will before the sunseason is finished. I and other Drui are traveling the length and breadth of Albion, seeking out men like the two of you. Men who have not yet allied themselves with the enemy. Men who have everything to gain if the invaders are defeated." He turned to look at Cadwalon. "If the Romans were expelled from Dobunni lands, would that not aid you in overthrowing your father?"

"Perhaps," Cadwalon said grudgingly.

"Ah," Moren said. "I see you need more convincing. I would be delighted to talk with you about these matters, if only we could do so under more comfortable circumstances. At this moment, I'm standing ankle deep in muddy water as the flies and midges consume my flesh. I've been told you have some sort of camp or settlement nearby. Could we not go there to discuss these things?"

Cadwalon's eyes narrowed. "If we take you there, what's to keep you from revealing our hiding place to our enemies?"

Moren laughed easily. "Having traveled this far into the marsh, I can assure you that even if you showed me the way a dozen times, I'd never be able to find it again. But if you are still concerned, I vow upon my honor as a Drui never to reveal the location of your stronghold."

"That's the most powerful vow a Drui can make," Bryn affirmed. "If he should break it, the gods are supposed to strike him down dead."

Cadwalon still looked suspicious. He glanced at Bryn. "Do you trust this man?"

"Aye, I do," Bryn said. "Not all Drui are honorable, but I sense this man is."

Cadwalon grunted, then said, "We'll take you to our camp." He set off. Bryn and Moren followed after him.

They moved from hillock to hillock, from clump of willows to clump of willows, picking their way across the subtle pattern of the fens. Bryn wanted to ask the visitor more questions about Boudica and her plan, but he hesitated to distract their guest while the footing was so treacherous. Besides, Cadwalon was really the one who needed to hear these things. Bryn had already made up his mind that he would join the uprising.

For Cadwalon it would be a much more difficult decision. He was fighting to gain control of the territory of his birth, for the chance to take his father's place as king of the Dobunni. Why shouldn't he remain here and see what happened? If the Romans were defeated, he would be able to use that to his advantage. If the uprising failed, he would have lost nothing.

The thought of leaving his friend behind distressed Bryn, but not enough to alter his decision. He was no longer beholden to the Dobunni man. Any debt he might have owed Cadwalon for sparing his life when they first met had long since been repaid in the years he'd spent fighting at his side.

Bryn glanced back to meet Moren's gaze. The Drui gave him a shrewd look that seemed to say, *Don't worry. I'll convince him.*

When they reached the island camp, they were greeted by a young warrior standing guard. "This is Moren, a Drui," Cadwalon told the youth tersely. "Go and tell everyone to gather around the cooking hearth, that we might hear what this man has to say."

The sentry dashed off. Bryn, Cadwalon and Moren followed more leisurely. As they walked, Moren slapped at his arms to drive away the midges. "How do you bear it here? I feel like I'm being eaten alive."

"The old woman, Gwladus, makes an oil out of plants that we smear on our skin to keep the insects away," Cadwalon

"You have women here?" Moren looked surprised.

"Only old Gwladus and her granddaughter. The girl is still young enough to consider this an adventure, while Gwladus has been with us almost from the beginning of our struggle against Cadwyl. She hates him and would do anything to see him defeated. Gwladus and the girl help with the cooking, prepare medicines and treat wounds."

They had reached the main cooking hearth. Moren looked around, observing the casks of Roman wine and amphorae of oil stacked nearby. He nodded. "You've done well in your raiding."

"We also have baskets of grain piled near to the ceiling in the storehouse." Cadwalon pointed to a nearby structure. "Along with metalwork, linen and woolen cloth. I would say that of every three supply wagons that cross my father's territory, only one makes it to his fortress. As for the cattle we've stolen, they're kept elsewhere."

Moren turned to look at Cadwalon, his gray eyes keen. "Despite all your successes against Cadwyl, can you truly say you are close to defeating him?"

Cadwalon scowled at Moren, and Bryn grew uneasy once more. Cadwalon could be hot-tempered and impulsive and Moren's words probed a sore point.

"To defeat my father, I would have to kill him," Cadwalon said. "And since he spends all his time in his fortress surrounded by Roman traders and Roman lackeys, as well as a strong force of fighting men, I've not had an opportunity to do such a thing." He spat on the ground, his eyes flashing.

"Then why not turn your attentions elsewhere?" Moren suggested in a coaxing voice. "If the Romans are routed in the east, it might change things here in the summer lands."

Cadwalon grunted in a way that indicated neither agreement nor disagreement.

The men began to gather around. They were dressed as Bryn and Cadwalon were, in deerskin bracco stout shoes and little else. In the heat of the sunseason, many shaved except for their mustaches. Their hair was braided away from their faces or pulled back and fastened with leather thongs. Behind them came Gwladus and the girl, Eurolwyn. The two females possessed the striking blue eyes and dusky skin of the Dobunni, but while Gwladus's hair was streaked with gray, her body bent and twisted, Eurolwyn's black tresses fell away from her face like the glossy feathers of a raven and her posture was as graceful and upright as a spear.

Seeing the girl like this, as a stranger would, Bryn was surprised to realize that Eurolwyn was growing into a very attractive young woman. In another turn of the seasons, it would not be safe for her to live in a camp of rough fighting men.

Moren greeted the men and explained why he had come. As he told about the eastern queen, Boudica, and her plan to attack Roman settlements, Bryn saw a few wary looks exchanged. He speculated that some of the men were uncomfortable with the idea of being led by a woman. Or maybe they couldn't imagine that events taking place so far away would have any meaning for their own lives. Bryn grew frustrated. If Cadwalon's warband refused to go and fight the Romans, it was unlikely Cadwalon would agree. It didn't matter, Bryn told himself. Whether Cadwalon went or not, he'd made up his mind to join Boudica's army.

"There have been campaigns against the Romans in the past," said Dirmyg, an older man. "Why should we believe that this time there is a chance of success?"

"Several reasons," Moren answered. "First of all, never before have several tribes combined their forces against the enemy. Although there are many more of us than there are of the Romans, up to now we haven't used our numbers to our advantage. Second, this is not a direct assault on the Roman forces, but on their settlements. These places, called coloniae, are not well defended and will fall easily. And finally… " Moren glanced around the gathering, meeting the gaze of everyone there with his keen gray eyes. "… even as the attacks are taking place, all the Drui in Albion will gather on the sacred isle. We will use our power to call down the gods and bring their wrath against the Romans. In the past, the Learned Ones couldn't agree to make a stand against the Romans. This time, we are resolved that the enemy must be destroyed."

Cadwalon made an angry motion. "It's easy for the Learned Ones to make such vows. They're not the ones who will meet the Romans on the battlefield." Several of his men nodded in agreement.

Moren's voice became even more insistent. "This won't be like any ceremony held in the past. It won't be a bullock that is sent to the gods as a sacrifice, but one of our own. Aye," he said, glancing around. "A Drui will be sent to the realm of the Otherworld to speak to the gods on our behalf."

"You think this will sway the gods to your cause?" Dirmyg asked.

"Of course," Moren answered. "What could be a more powerful offering than the life of a Drui?"

"What if it is *you* who is chosen to give your life?" Cadwalon asked with a sly look.

"I would consider it an honor," Moren answered. "Although, it's doubtful that it would be someone like me. Whoever is sent will be someone important, someone who has a special connection to the gods."

Ah, Bryn thought, *that's what all of them will tell themselves. The lowlier Drui will imagine they are not important enough for such an "honor", while the more powerful ones will assume they have enough influence with the gods to avoid such a fate.*

"The purpose of sacrifice is balance," Moren continued. "If we wish something of the gods, we must offer them something equal to their gift.

And so, we offer the life of one of our own to save the lives of our people. The Romans have changed us. They have caused our people to turn away from the gods of our sires and grandsires. We must do something to make the gods understand that they are still important in our lives. We must restore the balance between ourselves and the Otherworld."

Moren's talk of the Otherworld reminded Bryn of Cruthin. He could easily imagine his former companion of the grove offering to go to the gods and speak to them. Of course, that would never happen now, since Cruthin had been expelled from the grove. He wondered if Cruthin was even alive. The foolish youth had never bothered to learn any survival skills. How had he managed after being banished?

Thoughts of Cruthin reminded Bryn of Sirona. Beautiful, magical Sirona. He hoped she was safe somewhere in the north.

Moren was talking now about the atrocities the Romans had committed. "There was a chieftain in the highlands who had paid tribute for years. Finally, he sent his warriors against the Romans. They were defeated and the chieftain taken captive. Instead of offering him a noble death, the enemy took the chieftain to Rome and paraded him through the streets so their people could taunt and humiliate him. The man later died, his spirit broken."

The words "highland chieftain" made Bryn's heart pound. "What was the chieftain's name?" he demanded. "What tribe was he from?"

"I know not. Perhaps Decangi. It doesn't matter." Moren motioned dismissively. "What happened to this chieftain could happen to any of us. The Romans hate the Pretani. They consider us like animals, to use as they see fit. Since coming to Albion, they've enslaved many of our people, taken them away from their homelands and forced them into a vile life of servitude. Freemen and warriors like you and even chieftains such as this man I mentioned."

Decangi. That was a relief, Bryn thought. For a moment, he'd worried his father might be the chieftain who had been defeated and humiliated by the enemy. But that was unlikely. Tarbelinus didn't have the courage to lead a rebellion against the yoke of Rome. Last Bryn had heard, his father had made peace with the enemy and was paying them tribute. The thought that the wild, beautiful hills of his homeland now belonged to the Romans made him furious.

More than once he had considered returning to Mordarach. After his first year in Cadwyl's warband, having killed two men in fair combat and earned the respect of his fellow warriors, he'd made plans to go back and show his father how wrong he had been. But then he heard that his homeland had fallen under Roman control and his father was reduced to paying tribute to the enemy. Cadwalon persuaded him that if he went back, he would end up doing something witless and getting himself killed. Bryn knew it was true. Never could he bear seeing his people subjugated.

And so he had stayed and honed his fighting skills. When Cadwalon broke with his father, it had seemed natural to join his friend. Together they would defeat the Dobunni chieftain and restore Cadwalon's birthright. In return, Cadwalon would someday lend Bryn men to return to the highlands and recapture Mordarach and free his own people. They would pronounce him chieftain and he would at last assume the life he was born to. Then he would seek out Sirona. She would be awed by his accomplishments and finally realize they were meant to be together.

A magnificent dream. The problem was that now, four years later, he was no closer to his goal than he had been when he left Mordarach. He'd become a warrior, but that was all he'd accomplished. It was time to move on, and this uprising in the east promised the opportunity to fulfill one of his other goals. If the hated Romans were driven out of Albion, it would be that much easier to regain control of Mordarach and convince Sirona that he was worthy of her love.

Moren was still talking about all the evil acts the Romans had committed. Bryn glanced at Cadwalon, wondering at his friend's thoughts. This decision wouldn't be easy for him. Cadwalon had made progress toward his own goal. The constant attacks and raids had caused Cadwyl to hide away in his hillfort. Since traders and merchants were no longer willing to go there, Cadwyl had been forced to send out supply carts guarded by his warriors. Lately, the supply carts had been accompanied by Roman soldiers. They had stout armor and good weapons. They were disciplined and controlled and not so easy to scare off. Bryn decided that maybe he could convince Cadwalon that as long as his father had the Romans as his allies, Cadwyl might hold out indefinitely. He made up his mind to tell his friend these things as soon as he got Cadwalon alone.

Cadwalon announced that it was time to eat. Eurolwyn had finished making meal cakes and Gwladus brought out a caldron of leftover venison stew she had been keeping in the cool waters of the little spring on the island. Once heated, the stew offered a hearty mixture to dip the mealcakes in. As they ate they talked about the Romans and how much they despised them. But Bryn knew this sort of talk meant little. Hatred did not always result in action.

When the meal was finished and the marsh glowed with the golden light of sunset, Bryn saw an opportunity to speak privately to Cadwalon. He followed the other man as he went to the midden heap to relieve himself. Standing there as the rays of the red gold disc lit up the pools and channels of the fens and turned them into a blaze of light, Bryn finally said the things on his mind. "I'm going east. I have to. I made a vow to fight the Romans long ago."

"Aye." Cadwalon finished and began to refasten the belt of his bracco. "I well know your dreams. I've heard them often enough. First, the Romans. Then when they are safely driven from Albion, you mean to find your little seeress, take her back to Mordarach and found your own dynasty." He eyed Bryn. "What do you think of this queen, Boudica? Do you really believe she means to lead an army into battle?"

Bryn was surprised... and encouraged. Cadwalon appeared to be considering Moren's call to arms. He answered, "From tales in the grove I know that at one time Pretani women trained as warriors. And among the northern tribes, women still hold positions of power. For myself, I would eagerly follow a woman into battle, as long as it's against the Romans. For that matter, the fact that Boudica has managed to get the Iceni and the Trinovantes to work together is an impressive accomplishment. What man has ever been able to forge such an alliance?" When Cadwalon nodded, Bryn continued, "And if her envoys, like Moren, succeed in attracting warriors from other tribes to join the battle, her army will swell even larger."

"Do you think many men will be swayed to her cause?"

"It's hard to say." Although he hoped to persuade his friend to join him, Bryn felt he must be truthful. "The Silures will, for certain. They've been fighting the Romans for years. It's more difficult to know about the other highland tribes: the Dematae, the Decangi and the Ordovices. There will probably be some chieftains, like my father, who worry that if they leave their home territories, their neighbors will raid them. As for the eastern tribes, Moren mentioned that some of the Coritini had been won over, and it's really only the Catuvellauni and the Cantium who are so in bed with the Romans that they're certain to remain their allies."

"Do you believe there's a chance this uprising will succeed?" Cadwalon asked.

"Aye, I do. As Moren pointed out, we have the advantage of numbers. If Boudica's army is large enough, how can we be beaten?"

He must have faith they would prevail, Bryn thought. Otherwise the future was too grim and hopeless to contemplate. He went on: "I know you would be risking a great deal to leave your homeland to fight the Romans. You must feel you are close to defeating Cadwyl and realizing your dream."

Cadwalon snorted derisively. "The old bear could hold out for years. It's satisfying to have these successes, to admire the booty we've stolen, to notch our belts for the men we've killed. But this isn't a life any man would want to live forever. My warriors are young, but soon enough they will yearn to wait out the snowseason in a snug, secure dun. To have a woman in their beds. To beget children, so that their seed will be carried on into the future." He gave a short bark of laughter. "The fact is, I've begun to yearn for those things myself."

"So, you would consider traveling east to fight the Romans?"

"Aye, I would." Cadwalon turned to look at him. The golden splendor of the sunset had turned to a rosy orange glow and Bryn could clearly make out his friend's features. "The difficult part will be telling my men. I worry they'll be disappointed, that they'll think I've given up."

Bryn nodded. He could imagine the weight Cadwalon felt on his shoulders. Things were different when you were the leader and responsible for others' lives. "Perhaps some of them will want to come with us," he suggested.

"I would rather they stayed here and guard what we have won. But if they want to come along, I won't stop them."

"When will you tell them your decision?"

"Tonight. I see no reason to wait."

"While you're doing that, I'll make plans with Moren."

Cadwalon nodded and the two men started back to the hearth. When they reached it, Bryn went to stand by Moren. "Cadwalon wants to speak to his men in private." The Drui gave him a startled look, then rose and went with Bryn.

Bryn led Moren off into the willow and alder bushes. "I must admit I'm surprised he decided so quickly," Moren said when they were out of earshot of the others. "Most men like to think turn things over in their mind for a while."

"Cadwalon has always acted boldly. I also think he was influenced by my decision."

Moren nodded. "What are the two of you to each other? Not brothers surely—I can that tell by looking at you. But something close."

"We've been battle companions for years now." Bryn said. "Ever since I left my home tribe in the highlands."

"Why did you leave?"

"My father was the chieftain and we could never agree on my future. Even though I should have trained to succeed him, he insisted that I spend my days in the grove, learning to be a Drui."

"An unusual decision on the part of your father. And one that obviously didn't bear fruit."

Bryn nodded. "I never enjoyed my training. All I could think about while my teachers droned on about the principles of Drui wisdom was that I would rather be out hunting or practicing swordplay."

"And so, one day you decided to leave? I'm curious," Moren said.

"What brought you to that decision?"

Bryn stopped walking and stared off into the growing darkness, filled with the twitter of birds and the swelling chorus of frogs. "I went to a Drui gathering on the sacred isle. Seeing the inability of the Learned Ones to make a decision, I became overwhelmed with frustration. I realized then that I must pursue my dream of being a warrior or I would go mad."

"And that was four years ago?" Moren asked.

"Aye."

Moren nodded. "I have heard of that gathering, although I didn't attend. As I recall, a troubling incident occurred there. Two young people, not yet full Drui, left the ceremony of sacrifice. Some say that it was their blasphemy that angered the gods and that's why we have had continued trouble with the Romans."

Bryn snorted in disgust. "Blaming our troubles with the Romans on the gods is foolish... but typical of the Learned Ones. No wonder I have no regrets at leaving the grove."

Moren shrugged. "I agree that Drui are often slow to respond, but at least they are finally taking action."

Bryn nodded. "It's about time. I've wanted to fight the Romans since before I was a man."

They walked back to the hearth. To Bryn's surprise, Cadwalon was alone, except for Gwladus and Eurolwyth squatting near the fire, cleaning up the remnants of the meal.

"I told them I was going to join Boudica's army," Cadwalon said. "Some of them were angry. They think I'm giving up. But your words are sound, Moren. The Romans are a threat to all of us. As long as my father has them to hide behind, I'll never be able to defeat him."

"Are any of your men going with you?" Moren asked. "You should take your whole warband, as many as possible."

"Nay, I don't want them to come. At least if my men stay here, I won't lose all the ground I've gained. They'll guard my herds and the trade goods I've stolen. I've appointed Dirmyg as leader while I'm gone."

"Surely not all of them need remain here," Moren argued. "How many men does it take to guard this place? It's very well hidden."

Cadwalon gestured curtly. "I've made up my mind. Only Bryn and I are going."

Moren didn't speak for a time. Then he said, "The territory east of here is held by chieftains who sympathize with the Romans. It might be risky for the two of you to travel without an escort. As warriors, you'll arouse suspicion. Other tribes might wonder what you're doing in their lands. If they find out your plan is to join an uprising against their allies, they might feel compelled to prevent you from reaching your destination. It's possible you could be imprisoned or even killed."

Bryn guessed why Moren was saying these things. He hoped to persuade Cadwalon to bring some of his men along. But Cadwalon appeared unconvinced. "If it's so dangerous to travel across these lands, how did you manage it? You are Drui and carry no weapons."

"That's exactly the reason I've been left alone. Even those tribes who have turned away from Pretani ways are reluctant to harm a Drui. As a Learned One, I'm not considered a threat. But the two of you, stout warriors carrying weapons... " He shook his head. "I suggest that you take some of your men for protection."

Cadwalon's face had grown hard and stubborn, a look Bryn well recognized. Abruptly, Cadwalon said, "Perhaps the answer to is for us to travel as Learned Ones. Bryn used to be one, so it will be easy for him to take on the trappings of the life. And he can show me how to do the same."

Bryn felt his jaw drop. Instantly, he protested, "If we travel as Learned Ones, how will we carry our swords and shields? We could never hide them in our packs."

"What good are swords and shields if we're hopelessly outnumbered?" Cadwalon asked. "Besides, I'm certain that once we reach Boudica's stronghold, we can purchase new ones."

"What about garments? If we're to be Drui, we must look the part. Where will we get crys or cloaks that bear the sacred colors?"

Cadwalon looked at Moren. "You must carry some extra garments. We'll buy them from you."

Frowning, Moren glanced from one man to the other. "What if some chieftain asks you to perform a ceremony, or consults you on a matter of law or has a question about the gods?"

"Bryn can manage those things," Cadwalon said. "Can't you?"

Bryn glared at his friend. He didn't like this idea at all. But if it was the only way to get Cadwalon to go with him, he would have to agree. "I suppose I could deceive someone who wasn't too familiar with Drui learning, if it were necessary."

Moren didn't look pleased. "What about the Romans?" he asked. "If you encounter Romans while pretending to be a Learned One, they might kill you."

"You've survived, haven't you?" Cadwalon pointed out. "Besides, you told us that most of the Romans troops are in the north and west. Those Romans we encounter are likely to be traders and merchants, and unlikely to attack anyone unless they fear for their own safety."

Moren was silent. Bryn guessed the Drui was trying to think of another argument against Cadwalon's scheme. But he must realize that convincing two skilled warriors to join the cause was better than nothing. "Very well," Moren said finally. "I will aid you in this deception. In the morning, we'll make our final plans."

Cadwalon told Eurolwyth to take Moren to his own dwelling and make certain he had everything he needed. The girl rose and led the Drui away. As they vanished into the darkness, Cadwalon said, "Eurolwyth's grown up, hasn't she? I've never noticed before how comely she is."

"Aye," Bryn said. "It won't be long before you have to send her away. Otherwise she will cause trouble among the men."

"Or, I could handfast with her myself." When Bryn looked at him, Cadwalon shrugged. "Why not? I will need a wife some day and she's as loyal as any woman can be."

Bryn thought again of Sirona. Had she handfasted with a northern warrior as Nesta suggested? He would not think about that.

He forced himself to focus on the upcoming journey. "Are you determined we will travel as Learned Ones?"

"You said yourself that people believe Learned Ones are under the protection of the gods. No one will question us too closely if we pretend to be Drui."

"But without our weapons, I'll feel naked, completely helpless."

"We'll have our eating knives. And we can conceal a short sword in our packs."

"But I won't give up my mustache," Bryn said. "It's the mark of who I am."

Cadwalon shrugged. "If we dress as Drui and carry no weapons, I doubt anyone will question the rest of our appearance."

Bryn shook his head. What had he gotten himself into?

Chapter 14

Sirona watched as Kellach got up and walked away from the grove of elms where they had made camp for the night. Although reluctant to confront her traveling companion, she could not keep quiet any longer. She rose from her place by the fire and went to where Kellach stood looking up at the stars. Her gaze took in the blue-black expanse of the heavens, seeking out familiar constellations. Aye, she thought as she spied the arrangement of stars called The Hunter. They were definitely traveling east.

She cleared her throat and said, "When were you going to tell me you decided not travel to the sunset lands?"

Kellach continued to gaze up at the stars for a while. Finally he turned to face her. "There isn't time to go west. The uprising will take place before mid-summer. It would take too long to go all the way to the highlands, then back to Iceni territory. By then it might be too late to meet up with the rebel forces."

Sirona felt her resentment well up. "You could have told me your plans had changed."

Kellach's voice was soothing. "I'm sorry, Sirona. I didn't want to upset you. You must understand that there's no point going back. The people of the highlands are broken and beaten. Those who haven't given up and accepted Roman rule have already fled north, or made the same journey we're about to make, traveling east to join up with the Iceni. When we arrive, you'll see that the finest of the Pretani forces have gathered there."

"But surely there are some people left in the highlands who don't know about the uprising. They might be willing to join in if they were aware of what was planned."

Kellach put his hand on her arm. "You're thinking of your friends, Cruthin and Bryn. But you haven't seen either of them in four years. If there's been no news of Cruthin for that long, how can he possibly be alive? As for Bryn, you've said he hates the Romans and his whole ambition in life is to fight them. If he's still living, he's probably already heard of the uprising and is on his way there now."

"It's not only Cruthin and Bryn I worry for. What about the rest of the Tarisllwyth? I should go back to Mordarach and see how they fare."

"Do you really want to see your home overrun by Romans? Observe your people reduced to slaves and servants?"

"But they might need me."

Kellach moved away. "Suppose you are right, and life continues on at Mordarach as you remember it. Although there must be a new chieftain, it's likely Fiach's still head Drui. If you went back, how do you think he would react?"

Fiach. The thought of facing him made her stomach clench. She repressed a sigh, wondering why she had left her safe, comfortable life in the north. And what in the world had compelled her to leave with Kellach? It seemed like a mistake, all the more so as she glanced his way and saw the expression on his face, faintly illuminated by moonlight. As Dysri had warned, there was cunning in his eyes, and something else, something she could not quite put a name to.

He drew near and his warm breath wafted over her face. "I'm sorry you're disappointed we won't be returning to your homeland. I know you must still have feelings for those people. But it's better this way, I assure you."

Her jaw clenched. He had deliberately misled her.

Kellach touched her arm again. "You don't need Cruthin or Bryn," he said. "They are but boys, even now. What you need is a man."

His words puzzled her at first, because she hadn't been thinking about either Cruthin or Bryn. Then she realized what he meant. He was trying to coax her into lying with him. She sought to draw away, but he grasped her wrist and held her close. She resisted him, saying, "When you offered me a chance to be a Learned One, I didn't realize the price would be sharing your blanket."

He maintained his grip and used his other hand to gently stroke her face. "I would please you. Make you happy. I've had many women, and I know how to pleasure a female, especially a sweet, lovely innocent like you."

He could force her if he wanted to. But she didn't think he had a taste for rape. She might be able to reason with him. Recalling his mention of her innocence, she said, "I'm not a maiden any longer. I was with Cruthin on the sacred isle."

She could tell this angered him, but his voice when he spoke was still gentle and coaxing, "He was merely a boy then. What pleasure could he have shown you?"

Sirona recalled watching Cruthin turn into a beast, and her violent, desperate reaction. But she also remembered the delight of his kisses and the breathless desire his touch had aroused. She knew it would not be like that with Kellach. "I'm sorry. I don't want to lie with you."

"Why not? Is my form displeasing? I promise you, underneath my crys, my body is as hard and strong as a warrior's." He took her hand and placed it on his chest, so she could feel his muscles.

She drew her hand away. "I must obey what my inner spirit tells me to do, and it tells me this isn't meant to be."

"That's only your natural shyness. You're uneasy because this is strange and different for you."

Every fiber of her body grew tense. Instinctively she reached for the goddess stone. She clutched it in her fingers, feeling its comforting hardness. Kellach saw the movement and asked, "What are you doing?"

"Touching my goddess stone, so I might know what She desires me to do."

"Let me see."

Sirona withdrew the amulet from beneath her garment and held it out.

"A serpent's egg," he said. "Where did you come by that?"

"One of the Old Ones gave it to me. The Croenglas, the Brigante call them."

"The Croenglas are savages. Crude and stupid people. If they possessed something like this, they must have stolen it."

"You're wrong," Sirona said. "The woman who gave it to me was magic. She appeared first as a young woman, then an old crone. Then she vanished."

"That's impossible," Kellach said derisively. "You found this stone somewhere and made up this story."

"Whatever you wish to think." Sirona made her voice as hard and as scornful as his. The goddess stone had grown warm, as if it were lending her some of its power. She knew what she must do. As Kellach examined the stone, she used her free hand to search for the knife the Croenglas man had given her. She freed it from the little pouch where she kept it fastened on her belt and held the weapon in her palm.

"Take off the amulet so I can see it more closely." Kellach said.

"I will not."

As Kellach grabbed the thong holding the stone, Sirona reached up and pressed the knife against his throat. He made a hissing sound. "I won't lie with you, Kellach," she told him.

Silence hung between them, heavy and dark. At last, he responded. "I never meant to force you." He released the thong and backed away from her.

As she watched him turn and walk off into the shadows, Sirona drew a deep breath and tried to slow her pounding heart. If Kellach left her, she would have great difficulty finding her way back north, or to Mordarach either.

She put the knife away and slipped the amulet back underneath her gown. Then she went off under the trees and made a bed of leaves. Wrapping up in her cloak, she lay down to sleep. A shiver of dread went through her as she considered that Kellach could easily assault her while she slept. She reached once more for the knife, clutching its cold hardness with her fingers. She thought of the Croenglas giving her the weapon and wondered if this was the reason. Was Kellach's unwanted attention the only danger she would face on her journey? Or would there be other threats?

* * *

In the morning, Kellach said nothing about the events of the night before. In fact, he didn't speak at all as he dismantled their camp, kicking dirt over their burnt-out fire and rolling up the sheepskin he had slept on and stowing it away in his pack. Sirona ate some dried meat and berries from the bag of supplies Dysri had sent with her. Then she told Kellach she was going to the nearby stream to wash. As she relieved herself among the bushes on the way to the stream, she realized he could easily leave and take all their supplies. She took a deep breath and reminded herself that whatever happened, the Goddess would show her the way to safety, just as the wolf once had.

When she returned to their camp, Kellach was still there. "We should go," he said tersely. "It's a long way to Iceni territory."

Sirona nodded and set out, walking beside him, but not too close. Before, Kellach had talked freely while they traveled, telling her of the adventures he'd experienced on his journeys, about the beliefs and Drui practices of other tribes and many other things. Now he was silent.

Sirona concentrated on the landscape around them, trying to memorize details in case she had to return this way on her own. This land was less rugged than Brigante territory, the hills gentle and sloping. Much of it had been cleared at one time, so that there were patches of forest— oak and elm and birch—then areas of open space. Good grazing land, Sirona thought, although they'd seen no cattle or sheep.

They came upon an abandoned cattle bothy. The earthen walls were overgrown with weeds and tumbling down, while the remnants of the wooden dwelling were scattered and rotted. Nearby, the furrows of a plowed field were still visible through the grass and weeds.

"Where did the people go?" Sirona wondered aloud. "Did the Romans come and kill them?"

Kellach shook his head. "More likely, they moved on for some other reason. It's not the Roman way to slaughter farmers. They have no desire to leave our lands wasted and empty. If we don't prosper, they can't bleed us for our wealth."

They fell silent again, walking steadily through a long patch of forest. The trees were in full leaf and the air was alive with the calls of thrush, sparrow, wren and bunting. When they reached more open ground, there were flowers everywhere—red campion, yellow iris, purple foxglove and pink dog roses. Even early summer was not this lush in the highlands, Sirona thought, or in the north either. This was a rich, fertile land. So why was it deserted?

There was a low, ominous sound in the distance. Sirona halted and looked at Kellach. He frowned and pursed his lips. The sound grew louder. Sirona glanced at the sky. It was overcast, but the silvery gray clouds gave no hint of a storm. If not thunder, what was it?

The next moment, Sirona realized they were hearing the steady thud of footsteps. "We must hide." Kellach pointed to a small stand of hawthorn bushes back the way they had come. "Hurry," he said. "When you reach the thicket, crouch down and cover yourself with your cloak."

She ran toward the bushes. When she reached them, she tore off her cloak and draped it over herself, leaving an opening so she could see. Kellach crouched beside her. She could hear his harsh breathing. Her own heart seemed to pound in her ears like a drum. Her stomach churned and sweat broke out on her skin.

"Thank the gods that our cloaks are worn and faded and blend into the underbrush," Kellach muttered.

There were voices, the rhythmic, throbbing sound of the Roman language. Recalling the sight of Einion and Culhwch's bloody bodies, she went utterly still. The Romans crested the hill. There was a whole army, or so it seemed. Row upon row of warriors, treading steadily forward. Except for the men in front carrying banners, they all looked alike. The same leather garment upon their breasts. The same metal helmets on their heads. The same reddish mantles thrown over their shoulders. They carried spears and shields, and other weapons hung from their belts.

It was like a herd of animals, she thought. All looking so much alike that it was difficult for a predator to pick one out. And yet, these were not prey animals, but predators. A shiver of horror swept through her as the Romans moved past, so close she could see the shoes they wore, fashioned of strips of leather, and their hairy calves.

As the army continued to march by, Sirona's skin began to tingle and the scene before her eyes altered so that she was looking out over a vast valley. There were still Romans there, but many, many more of them, as many as ants in an anthill. They marched forward to meet another huge army, this one marked by the vivid colors, shaggy hair and gleaming metalwork of her people. Her vantage point was of a goshawk flying high above the valley, and she could see that although there were many more Pretani than Romans, not all of them were warriors. There were women and children in wains and carts at the rear of the army. If the battle went against the Pretani, they wouldn't be able to flee.

She heard horns blowing, a terrifying bellow, and the Pretani charged, the mingled cries of the warriors making a dull roar even louder than the horns. As they neared the enemy's lines, the Romans let loose with their javelins. Hundreds of the deadly missiles flew through the air and Pretani warriors began to fall. The dead and wounded blocked the pathway of those behind them. The men driving chariots struggled to maneuver, but there was no place to go. The noise grew louder and more terrible: the screams of the wounded, the whinnying of the horses, the clash of weapons as the Romans moved forward, wielding their short swords. The Romans cut steadily through the Pretani ranks like a scythe through grain. All at once, Sirona knew how it would end. Observing the devastation, she gave a low moan of anguish.

Kellach grabbed her cloak and pushed her closer to the ground. "Silence!" he hissed.

When she became aware again, the sounds of the battle had faded away and the only noise was the dull tread of the Roman army's footsteps receding in the distance.

"In the name of Bran, that was close," Kellach breathed after several heartbeats had passed. He stood and brushed off his cloak.

Sirona lay with her face pressed to the cool earth. She felt dizzy and sick. The sense of impending disaster, of utter ruin, wouldn't leave her.

"What's wrong?" Kellach asked.

She got unsteadily to her feet. "I... saw... how it's going to end." Tears filled her eyes. "The Romans are going to defeat us," she whispered. "Annihilate us."

Kellach stared at her. She could see the how the hairs of his beard were not all red, but some were blond or brown. The freckles that dotted his fair skin were the color of rust. And the look in his blue eyes was one of pure hatred.

"You're wrong," he said. "That wasn't a vision, but your own fear clouding your mind. We will prevail." He turned his fine-boned, handsome face away from her, his jaw working. "Come on. We have a long way to go."

* * *

Sirona walked steadily, putting one foot in front of the other. The horror brought by her Seeing seemed to dwell inside her body. She couldn't escape it. Although she hadn't envisioned the very end of the battle, she knew what was going to happen. She could sense it, as intense as if she were there, smelling the blood and the stench of death, seeing the piles of bodies lying in the grass and mud.

Was it a true Seeing? Or only one possibility of the future? She thought of her mother's visions. Banon had predicted Bryn would die in if he became a warrior. Yet Sirona didn't believe Bryn was dead, even though he must have fought in a battle by now. That prediction had been false. This one might be also.

But why had it come to her? She couldn't shake the sense she was being sent these Seeings for some purpose. What was it? When would the reason be revealed? And when it was, would she be strong enough to do what the Goddess commanded her to do?

She glanced at Kellach. Now he despised her more than ever. But perhaps that was for the best. He wouldn't wish to lie with her now. But it was going to be a very uncomfortable journey. And yet, she now realized she was meant to travel east—east to meet Boudica. Over the past day, she'd come to believe that the fiery queen of her visions was connected with her vision of the battle with the Romans.

Sirona's thoughts were interrupted by the low of a cow. A moment later, there was another bellow. They crested a hill and saw a pasture full of fat black cattle. There were a great number of them, making Sirona think that a chieftain of some wealth lived nearby. Looking farther down the valley, she saw a wooden palisade, enclosing a number of square buildings. Except for one large structure on one end, all the other buildings were arranged around the edges of the palisade. The very neatness and order of the complex struck Sirona as strange. This didn't look like a place where her people lived.

"Do you think the enemy dwells here?" she asked Kellach, her body tight with apprehension.

Kellach was also regarding the settlement intently. "Even if the inhabitants are Roman, I see no sign of any warriors who would be a threat to us." He started forward.

Sirona followed uneasily. "Do you intend to stop here?"

"Why not? We need more supplies, and this place looks as if they might have a surplus of food to sell."

"But what if they're Romans? I thought you hated them."

"That doesn't mean I refuse to have any dealings with the enemy. Besides, some of the people here are probably Pretani. This far east, both races often live side-by-side."

Sirona didn't want to go to this place. She sensed darkness and suffering here. But she could think of no argument that would convince Kellach. She reassured herself he wouldn't knowingly lead them into danger.

They started down the hill. As they neared the settlement, Sirona grew more and more uneasy. A dog began to bark inside the palisade. It kept barking as they approached. When they reached the gate, they saw a small opening in the center covered by a piece of wood. The wood was moved aside and a sharp-eyed, older man gazed out at them. He asked them a question in the tongue of the Romans.

Kellach answered, "We're Pretani, not Roman. Does anyone here speak our language?"

"Some," the man said in Pretani.

"Who's the chieftain of this place?"

"There's no chieftain. Calpurnius Ostorius holds this property."

"Tell your master that we're willing to pay Roman coin if he will offer us a warm meal and a place to spend the night."

The man went away. "Do you really intend to stay the night here?" Sirona asked, her voice full of anxiety.

Kellach narrowed his eyes at her. "Why shouldn't we spend the night in comfort? I'm tired of sleeping on the ground."

The man returned a short while later and opened the gate. After they entered, he closed the gate behind them and then guided them toward the large, sprawling building. A huge tan dog with black markings ran up. It barked once, then greeted Sirona, its tail wagging happily. She felt reassured, until she remembered the Romans were said have a great passion for hunting dogs, offering rich goods in trade for them.

Kellach followed the sentry and Sirona hurried after him. She told herself she would eventually be forced into contact with the enemy. In this part of Albion, it would be impossible to avoid all Romans.

The servant led them to an enclosed area planted with flowers and herbs. Many of the plants Sirona had never seen before, and she gazed at them with curiosity. The trees and other vegetation were arranged in neat, straight rows, similar to the rest of the settlement.

The man took them inside one of the buildings. The room was very large. Flat, smooth stones made up the floor, while three of the walls were covered with a gleaming white substance and a fourth painted with the images of birds and animals. There were benches and a table, but no hearth. To Sirona, it seemed very bare and empty.

A middle-aged man got up from where he sat on one of the benches. He looked like a Pretani, with fair, thinning hair and ruddy skin. But he was dressed in an odd-looking white wool garment that was wrapped around his body many times. His hair was cut short and his face clean-shaven, without even a mustache. He regarded them with narrowed blue eyes. Then he snapped his fingers. A slave appeared, a sullen-looking boy with bright yellow hair. The man, who Sirona assumed was Calpurnius, spoke to the boy in the rhythmic Roman tongue.

The boy ran off. Calpurnius gestured to the benches. "Sit down," he said in Pretani. They placed their traveling packs on the floor and were seated. "I don't get much news in this place," Calpurnius said. "Tell me where you are going and where you've been. I would be delighted to hear any sort of tale you would share with me."

"We've been in the north, in the land of the Brigantes," Kellach answered. "We're traveling east."

"What's the purpose of your journey?" Calpurnius asked.

"It's a trading expedition," Kellach responded. "In the east, we can obtain wine, oil, guara, all sorts of essential goods."

Calpurnius shot a puzzled glance at Sirona, making her uncomfortable. She worried their host wouldn't believe Kellach's story. They obviously had no means of transporting anything back to their home territory, which made the tale of them being traders unlikely. And she could tell from Calpurnius's expression that he was mystified as to why a woman would be included on a trading expedition.

Calpurnius grunted. His blue eyes bored into Sirona, making her want to run away. "Is this your wife?" he asked Kellach.

"Nay. She's my slave."

Sirona was stunned. She opened her mouth to protest, then closed it again. If she contradicted Kellach, Calpurnius might become suspicious.

Kellach said, "Perhaps one of your servants could take Sirona somewhere she could wash off the traveling dust before the evening meal."

Calpurnius snapped his fingers to summon a servant.

Chapter 15

Sirona followed the female servant down a hallway. She didn't understand what was going on. Kellach had said she was a slave, so why was she being offered an opportunity to bathe? And what about this preposterous story of being traders?

The servant stopped at a doorway and indicated Sirona should enter. Inside the small room, she saw a pool of water filling a deep depression in the stone floor. When the servant left, Sirona dropped her pack on the floor and approached the pool. She knelt down and put her hand in the water, expecting it to be cold. Instead, it was pleasantly warm. The stones around the edge of the pool were heated, as if there were a fire underneath the floor. On the floor by the pool was a jar of scented oil she decided was meant to anoint the skin and a drying cloth of finely woven linen.

Sirona took off her mantle, shoes and gown and stepped into the water. It reached to her waist and she sank down, submersing herself. It felt very comfortable, very soothing. She dunked her head and doused her hair, then came up and swished her body around to wash off all the grime. She immersed her head again and ran her hands through her hair. It had been a long time since she'd been able to bathe like this. The streams and lakes of the midnight lands were cold, even in summer, and not conducive to bathing or swimming.

She soaked for awhile, then climbed out and used the drying cloth. Now that she was clean, it seemed foolish to put her soiled garment back on, so she searched in her pack for her spare traveling gown. As she was hunting for it, she came upon the garment Dysri had given her when she first went north. The fabric's crossbar pattern of dark green, crimson and white reminded her keenly of the Cunogwerin tribe, and she felt a sudden longing for the safe, uneventful life she had left behind.

Her turmoil increased as she took out her bone comb and began to untangle her wet tresses. She wanted to grab up her things and flee. But if she did that, she might endanger both her own life and Kellach's. Restless, she finished her hair and began to pace. When time passed and no one appeared, she began to wonder if something had happened to Kellach. What was to prevent Calpurnius from taking Kellach's possessions and killing him? But if that's what Calpurnius intended, why had she been sent to bathe? To get her out of the way?

151

More time passed. Finally, she decided she had no choice but to try to find Kellach. Grabbing her pack, she left the room.

After the warmth of the bathing chamber, the corridor leading back to the main part of the dwelling felt drafty and chilly. Sirona soon reached another passageway and followed it. In this hallway, oil lamps shed their light from niches cut into the wall, illuminating her way. She passed several closed doors, then halted. Her mind was filled with the image of a young woman lying on a raised bed. The woman was dark-haired, her features delicate and lissome. But she was very thin, and deep shadows encircled her huge brown eyes. She appeared to be wasting away. Some sickness was eating up her flesh.

Sirona sensed the woman was behind this door, in this room. Even more intensely, she felt the woman needed her help. She opened the door and slipped inside. At first, she could see next to nothing. Then her eyes adjusted to the dim light filtering in from the hallway. She could make out a bed with a purple coverlet was pulled smooth over the top. There was also a chest in the room and a table with a box on top. Sirona approached the box, made of pieces of light and dark wood cunningly fitted together. She opened it. Inside was a jumble of jewelry, heavy and elaborate. On the very top of the pile of valuables was a necklace made up of thick gold squares with purple stones in the center of each square. The necklace looked like no ornament Sirona had ever seen.

She picked it up and knew instantly that it had belonged to the woman of her vision. But the woman had no use for the necklace any longer. She was dead. She had died in this room. Calpurnius had built this place for this woman. He'd brought the flowers and herbs here so she could look upon the bright blossoms and smell the sweet scent of the growing things. Designed the bathing room so she could wash in warm, soothing water. Planted the fruit trees so she could enjoy juicy plums and apples in the sunseason. Purchased the jewels that had once adorned her and that now filled this beautifully made wooden box.

The young woman was his daughter. This awareness surprised Sirona, who had assumed at first the woman was Calpurnius's wife or concubine. But no, his love for her was purer, and more desperate. A father's desire to protect the rare lovely flower he had sired.

Sirona held the necklace a while longer, then carefully put it away and left the bedchamber. In the corridor she met the female slave who'd taken her to the bathing room. She was accompanied by a strong, well-muscled young man, with sandy colored hair. Neither of the servants spoke to Sirona, but gestured she should follow them. Something in their manner filled her with foreboding. She wanted to run, to dash down the narrow corridor and find out a way out of this place.

She told herself she was being witless. These servants had probably been sent to fetch her for the meal. There was nothing to fear. In a few moments they would take her to where Calpurnius and Kellach waited.

After going down yet another corridor, the servants stopped in front of a doorway and motioned that Sirona should enter. This room was similar to the bedchamber of the young woman, although larger and more lavishly furnished. Several benches were arranged around the room, and the bedplace was covered with a shiny blue fabric trimmed in gold. Enticing smells wafted from a table on the far side of the room. But there was no sign of either of the men.

The manservant indicated to Sirona that she should make herself comfortable. Then he left the room, closing the door behind him. Sirona went over to the table, where a repast as extravagant as any she had ever seen was laid out on dark red pottery dishes. There was roast fowl, its skin a crisp, golden brown, cheese, a thick, puffy bannock large enough to feed several people, a bowl of oil with herbs, two other bowls full of nuts and large black berries. She stared at the food. Should she wait for the men?

After a while, she gave in to temptation and began to eat, breaking off pieces of the fowl, the cheese and the chewy bannock and eagerly consuming them. She tried the black berries. They weren't sweet, but rich and oily.

She soon grew thirsty and picked up the large bronze ewer left near the food. There were two bronze cups placed nearby. Sirona paused. Two cups. Did this mean she was intended to share this bedchamber with Kellach? That would be awkward. One of them would have to sleep on a bench while the other took the bed. She poured some of the contents of the ewer into a cup. The dark red beverage tasted like fermented berry juice, sweeter and mellower than beer, but with a similar kind of tang. The beverage went down easily, warming and relaxing her. In no time at all, she drank the whole cup.

Afterwards, she wiped her hands on the linen cloth that appeared to have been left for that purpose. Then she went to sit on one of the benches. Nearby was a metal log-shaped object on legs. Through the slits in the top of it, Sirona could see glowing coals. No wonder the room felt so warm and comfortable.

Between the drink and the cozy glow of the coals, she grew sleepy. She considered lying down on the bed, then decided she should wait and see if Kellach came. Her gaze strayed to the table of food. She wished the servants would return and cover it or take it away so it wouldn't be wasted. It amazed her to see this amount of food and so few people to eat it. Did anyone live here besides Calpurnius and his servants? To Sirona, who had always lived in large, noisy duns, the emptiness of this place seemed desolate and forbidding. Why would anyone choose to dwell like this?

Thinking of the young woman dying there all alone, Sirona repressed a shudder. A darkness hovered over the settlement, a pall of suffering. All the beautiful things couldn't banish the feeling of despair and desolation that lingered here.

She looked around the room once more, thinking of the many chambers in this sprawling structure, like cells in a beehive. She thought of the stout roof overhead, the supports, walls and floors made of stone rather than timber. They were meant to keep out the elements and provide a snug dwelling place. But didn't they also keep out the gods, the spirits of the air and earth and growing things? In this safe, enclosed world, the powerful life forces of nature seemed absent. She touched the goddess amulet under her clothing. It felt neither cold nor hot, but empty. Perhaps its power didn't reach to this place.

She wanted desperately to go outside and breathe the night air, to look at the sky and to feel Arianrhod's light upon her. She got to her feet, thinking that if she encountered anyone, she would say she'd grown tired of waiting.

As she was putting on her mantle, the door opened and Calpurnius entered. Sirona immediately became uneasy. "Thank you for the food and the chance to refresh myself," she told him, fidgeting with the pin fastening her mantle. It seemed rude to announce she was leaving, but the urge had become overwhelming. Looking at his face, her alarm increased. She saw calculation in his eyes and her heart began to pound. "Where's Kellach?" she demanded.

"Kellach has gone." He smiled as if it pained him to tell her this.

Sirona took a step back, certain Calpurnius's distress was feigned. "Gone?" she asked. "Gone, where?"

Calpurnius waved his hand. "Wherever he was headed on his journey."

What of me? Sirona screamed silently. But she feared she knew the answer. "I must also leave."

Calpurnius smiled again, a false expression. "That won't be possible. I have purchased you."

"Purchased me?"

Calpurnius nodded. "Kellach offered you to me as a slave."

Sirona was stunned. This couldn't be happening. "I know Kellach said I was a slave, but it's not true. I'm a free woman. I trained for years as a Learned One."

"It doesn't matter what you were in the past. Now I own you."

His words appalled her. Kellach had left her to the mercy of this man. She glanced at the doorway, thinking how difficult it would be to escape this place with its maze of corridors, stout walls and grim, dutiful servants. She must reason with Calpurnius. "I would make a poor slave," she argued. "I have no womanly skills. I can't spin or weave, grind grain, plant crops or do any of the other things most girls learn when they're small. As a Learned One, I was instructed in many kinds of knowledge, but nothing that would be of use in running a household."

"You won't be a kitchen slave," Calpurnius said. "But a bed slave."

She flashed a glance at the bed. "Nay," she said. "I wouldn't do that."

Calpurnius smiled his feral, dangerous smile once more. "Kellach warned that you might not be agreeable. But you'll learn soon enough." He gestured to the table spread with food. "I don't doubt that hunger will eventually cause you to see things my way."

"You would starve me, unless I become your concubine?" Sirona gazed at him in horror. To be trapped here, held at the whim of this man, this half-Roman monster. She shook her head. "Then I will starve to death, and whatever coin you've paid Kellach will be wasted. I won't lie with you. If you force yourself upon me, my body will be all you possess, for my spirit will have fled. I'm not the helpless female Kellach has implied. The power of the Goddess flows through me." Her anger rose, replacing her fear. "If you dare to touch me, you will pay, I vow it."

Calpurnius took a step toward her. Sirona was on the verge of calling on the Goddess to strike him down. Then another thought came to her.

She waited, motionless. As he reached out and touched her cheek, she let her mind fill with an image, holding it in her thoughts until it was bright and vivid. Then she willed the image to enter his mind.

He gasped and withdrew his hand. He shook his head, his eyes wild. "Risa, nay, I didn't mean it. I'm sorry." He covered his face with his hands and began to weep.

Sirona held onto her rage, though pity threatened to sweep it away. "Aye, your daughter sees you and knows you for what you are, lustful and cruel. Her spirit is everywhere in this place. She weeps for you, to see what you've become, locked away with your bitterness and despair, letting it fester and grow until it consumes the man you once were, the man she loved as her father."

Calpurnius sank to the floor, sobbing. Sirona continued, "You did all this for her, created this place of beauty and luxury. But she died anyway, wasting away before your eyes."

"Why?" Calpurnius moaned. "Why did she die?"

"Perhaps it was your punishment for turning your face away from the gods," Sirona said. Then, softening, she added. "Or, perhaps there's no reason for it. Life is harsh and pitiless, and death is everywhere."

"I did pray to the gods," he cried. "I did! Look on the other side of the courtyard, near the garden. You will see the shrine I built to Minerva. I made offerings daily, did all I could to ask for the goddess's aid. But in the end, everything was useless. Useless! Risa died before my eyes!"

The man who threatened her only moments before was now slumped on the floor, weeping. Sirona couldn't hold on to her outrage. The same awareness that allowed her to sense Risa's spirit also caused her to sympathize with this man's abject suffering.

"Hush, now," she said, as if speaking to a child. "You've mourned long enough. You did all you could for her when she was alive. You must go on with your life. It's time to leave this place and go back to your homeland." Sirona tried to imagine this man returning to Rome. Then she realized he was from another place. He had spent much of his life in the lands directly on the other side of the narrow eastern sea. That's why he spoke her language so well. "Go back to your homeland," she repeated. "This place is not for you. If you stay here, your grief will never leave you."

Calpurnius looked up. His face was red and swollen. "What about my villa? My servants and slaves?"

"You'll never find peace here," she said. "Which do you prefer—to possess wealth and fine possessions? Or to rid yourself of your grief and despair?"

Calpurnius got slowly to his feet. He stared at her, his expression altogether different than a short while before. There was awe in his eyes. And fear. "Who are you? Are you Minerva?" He shook his head. "I should have known when I saw you. I should have guessed you weren't merely a comely slave girl."

"I'm not Minerva," Sirona said. "But perhaps she speaks through me."

Calpurnius nodded. "I beg pardon for… what I was about to do. But I am so lonely."

"Aye. That's why you should return to where you once lived. You don't belong here. None of your people do. A few will leave their blood behind, mingling with the blood of my people. But someday all that will be left here of Rome will be the buildings and structures. The stones will be your legacy. But the rest of this island—the forests and meadows, the highlands and wetlands and moors and lakes and streams—all those places will be untouched by you. They belong to the gods, and to the Old Ones."

Calpurnius let out his breath in a sigh. "I will go. I've never been happy here. This place was cursed from the beginning. The cold and damp is what made my Risa sicken. And now, she is gone... and I have nothing."

"You have your memories of her," Sirona said gently.

Calpurnius nodded. He stood there, staring into space, his expression empty and sad. Sirona decided it was time to leave. She picked up her pack and started toward the door. A part of her worried he would change his mind. That his cruel nature would reassert itself and he would try to stop her. But he made no movement as she left the room. Indeed, he no longer seemed aware of her.

Outside the bedchamber, Sirona followed one corridor to another. She'd almost started to panic when she finally spied an open doorway leading out into the area planted in flowers. Taking only a moment to catch her breath in the cool, fresh air, she raced toward the gate. To her relief, there was no guard on duty.

Sirona found the gate latch and opened it. The gate was heavy and cumbersome and she could barely manage to squeeze through. But at last she was on the other side of the high wooden walls. She took off at a run. What would have happened if the Goddess hadn't given her the inspiration to use his daughter's memory as a means to distract Calpurnius? If she hadn't been able to manipulate his thoughts? She imagined herself crushed beneath Calpurnius's weight. Would her spirit have managed to escape her body as she had told him?

She wouldn't think about that. The important thing was that she was free. She must get as far from this place as possible. But first she must figure out which way to go. She stopped and stared up at the sky. Thick clouds obscured the stars and moon. She glanced back at the villa, illuminated by torches lit around the outbuildings. That was the way they'd come. This way must be east.

She started walking, trying to move in a straight line. She passed rows of trees full of green apples, then followed the edge of a newly planted field. After a time, she turned to look back. She could no longer see the lights of the villa, nor any other landmarks. With nothing to guide her, she could easily end up walking in circles. Better to wait until morning. As soon as it grew light, she would start off again and travel toward the dawn. Toward Iceni territory.

A chill of fear swept through her as she realized she would be heading the same direction as Kellach. But what choice did she have? She had to find Boudica, the red-haired woman of her vision.

Seeking a place to spend the night, she came upon a grove of trees. She drew nearer and recognized the thick trunks and spreading branches of a stand of old oaks. An aching familiarity throbbed through her. She'd found a Drui grove. At some time in the past, a group of Learned Ones had trained and worshiped here.

She sought out a mossy spot beneath one of the oaks and took out her leather rain cape and spread it on the ground. After wrapping herself in her mantle, she stretched out. She closed her eyes and listened to the night sounds all around her. The rustle of leaves and branches. The slow flap of wings as some night bird swept by overhead. The soft footfalls of animals moving along the forest floor. She imagined a vixen or she-cat at returning from the hunt, a hare or vole dangling from the animal's mouth. Off in the distance was another sound. A wolf, singing its wild, lonesome night music, calling to its mate or the other members of its pack.

The sounds soothed her. She felt safe here among the animals. They would not betray her or seek to imprison her.

* * *

Kellach woke with a start. He was covered in sweat, chilling him in the brisk morning air. Sitting up, he glanced around. It was barely dawn, and the world was gray and indistinct. So, this was where he had finally stopped, too weary and uncertain of his direction to risk continuing. He got to his feet and brushed the leaves and twigs off his mantle. His belly felt queasy and he couldn't shake a feeling of dread. Grimacing, he spoke aloud. "She deserved it. She was going to arouse doubts in everyone she met. I had to stop her."

The words echoed emptily back to him. He told himself he believed them. But deep down, he knew part of the reason he'd sold Sirona as a slave was because she had rejected him. He, a powerful, respected Drui. A man many women had eagerly taken to their beds. He'd had chieftains' wives and daughters. Why should he care what a puny little mouse like that thought of him? She really wasn't so attractive. He preferred his women tall and voluptuous. Sirona was too serious, small and plain. He could hardly believe he'd considered bedding her.

He threw back his mantle, pulled down his bracco and relieved himself. Good riddance, he thought as his urine flowed out, steaming in the morning air. Good riddance to that quarrelsome, difficult seeress. He didn't regret leaving her behind. The bag of coins Calpurnius had paid him would come in handy when he reached the eastern territories. He might despise the Romans, but he had no dislike of their silver.

After rearranging his clothing, Kellach set out. He walked slowly at first, trying to get his bearings. It was cloudy, and would probably rain later, but he could see a lighter tinge to the sky on the far horizon. That way must be east. His surroundings looked unfamiliar, which relieved him. He'd worried that in his haste to leave he had gone the wrong direction. It would be most aggravating if he found himself back where he started.

His thoughts turned to the night before and the desperation with which he'd fled. He could have sworn that as soon as he was out the gate some creature had begun to track him. It had been too dark to see, but even though he never caught sight of anything, his fear and urgency had grown stronger with every step he took. It was as if he could feel the beast's hot breath upon him, hear its rapid footfalls, sense the animal preparing for the kill. He had run on blindly, hoping he wouldn't lose his footing and fall into a ravine or crash into a tree.

Kellach smiled to himself, realizing what a fool he'd been. The darkness and his sense of guilt had caused him to imagine things. Guilt, aye, he felt a little of that, no matter how hard he tried to squelch it. Bad enough that Sirona should end up a slave, but a bed slave. What an indignity for a woman who'd been educated in the grove.

But he'd had no choice. He couldn't let his personal feelings interfere with what was best for his people. After dedicating his life to expelling the Romans from Albion, he could not have some misguided seeress planting doubts wherever she went. Sirona could be very convincing. When she spoke of her Seeings, her blue eyes shone and her face seemed to glow. For a time, she'd almost made him believe she possessed real power. If she could dupe him, then there was no telling what she might accomplish among the untrained. Crude warriors would be drawn to her appealing combination of innocence and wisdom. Even Boudica, proud Boudica, might make the mistake of listening to Sirona's ridiculous fears.

There was no room for doubt. They must act decisively, boldly, every tribe committed. They must attack the Romans and destroy them. It could be done. His every sense told him that this was what he had been born for. To defeat the Romans and drive them from these lands.

A satisfied smile played upon Kellach's lips as he pushed his way through a thicket. Then, all at once, he gave a cry of delight. There was a sacred spring here, an ancient place of worship. He approached eagerly, seeing the tell-tale, if rather aged, signs of veneration. Tattered pieces of fabric still clung to the nearby trees and the pool below the spring was filled with rusted and corroded offerings. Kellach gazed down into the still waters of the pool, feeling an immense satisfaction.

Then a wind blew through the forest, sending ripples across the formerly calm pool. Kellach bent down, squinting to make out what appeared to be an image floating on the surface of the water. Was it a vision, his very first Seeing? He held his breath, staring at the shape that began to form there, gradually growing clearer. A wolf. A huge dark gray wolf. Kellach frowned at the apparition, wondering why he should see such a thing. Then he heard the deep growl behind him and his blood ran cold. He turned slowly, barely breathing. His gaze met the dark-eyed, savage visage of the animal. It lunged. Fangs as big and sharp as daggers sank into his throat. Blood filled his gullet and choked him. The world grew gray and distant. His pulse thundered in his head, then slowed and stopped.

Chapter 16

This was it, Sirona thought as she gazed down at the valley: The stronghold of the Iceni queen. The gathering place of the Pretani tribes who would soon march into battle against the Romans. She could make out the many tents, wooden huts, animal pens, cookfires and supply carts dotting the area where the warriors had made a temporary settlement to accommodate their families. Recalling the women and children in her vision of the battle with the Romans, her stomach clenched in dread.

On the other side of the settlement were paddocks filled with horses—horses that would be used to pull chariots. She recalled her Seeing at the lake of sacrifice, how the chariots had become mired in the mud, trapping the Pretani warriors so they were cut down by the Romans. Did the eerie similarity between the details of this scene and those in her visions mean the events of her Seeings were inevitable? Were her people doomed to destruction?

Nay, she wouldn't accept that. She must try to change the course of events, to alter the future.

In the center of the army camp was a group of buildings enclosed by a stone wall, the dwelling place of Queen Boudica. Sirona knew she must go there and convince Boudica that disaster loomed ahead.

A daunting prospect. The Iceni queen must be a formidable woman, to have won the respect of all those warriors gathered in the valley below. These men were willing to follow her into battle, to kill and to die for the cause she represented. Someone as obviously strong-willed and determined as Boudica would not be easily influenced. If Sirona had a chance to speak with her, what would she say? How could she convince her to listen?

Sirona touched the goddess stone beneath her clothing. She must believe the right words would come. Had not the Great Mother shown her the way many times before? Sending the wolf to guide her to safety in the north. Saving her from rape by Kellach. Giving her the means to escape Calpurnius.

The Goddess had also aided her on her journey here. There were many times on her way that she'd feared she was hopelessly lost. The terrain was difficult, marshy and treacherous. It rained much of the time, and the sky was so dark and heavy with clouds it was impossible to be certain of the path of the sun in the sky.

But always some sign had appeared telling her which way to go. Once the bright plumage of a kingfisher had caught her eye. Following the progress of the bird as it searched for prey in the wetlands, she'd found a pathway through what appeared to be a nearly impenetrable stretch of marsh. Later, when she reached a place where the river branched off in three directions, she had seen a group of otters playing by the middle stream. She'd drawn closer to watch them slide down the muddy bank into the water. All at once, laughing at their antics, a weight upon her had lifted and she'd known this branch of the river would lead her to her destination.

The same waterway now shimmered in the distance, like a silver thread woven through the swathe of vivid green vegetation on either side. Compared to the ugly sprawl of the warriors' camp, the river and the area surrounding it seemed like a refuge, a blessed, magical place.

Sirona started down the ridge, but instead of approaching the army camp, she veered toward the river. There would be time enough to speak with Boudica. For now, she needed to refresh her spirit and regain her connection to the Goddess.

She followed the waterway, which was bordered by patches of willow, alder and hazel, to a place where a small stream split off from the main river. Several women were fetching water from the stream, but they took little note of her as they talked and filled their water skins. Their gowns were patterned in yellow and crimson with a little green mixed in, and their hair was light red or golden. Sirona wondered what tribe they were from, but didn't ask. It seemed to her that there were too many people here. They'd made a muddy mess on the stream bank and begun to foul the area with their slops and cooking refuse.

She walked on toward the forest, hoping to find a grove where she could sit under the ancient trees and listen to the voices of the spirits that dwelt there. She was soon surrounded by stands of birch and oak. The ground was covered with fern, bracken and ivy, the treetops alive with birdcalls. She inhaled deeply, filling her lungs with the scent of life.

Hidden among the trees was a small, square stone building. The structure looked foreign, and she couldn't imagine why it been built here, away from the main settlement. There were tall, round supports on either side of the doorway, and the lintel over the entrance was decorated with a complex design of curving lines entwined with the images of plants and animals.

The open doorway seemed to beckon her to enter, and she ducked under the lintel and went in. Lamps set in recesses in the wall lit the interior, which was empty except for an altar of finely dressed stone. On the altar were offerings of food and drink. On the wall behind the altar was the image of three women in long flowing gowns. Sirona drew closer and saw that the image had been formed by tiny colored bits of stone pressed into the wall.

A female voice called out, "Who's here?" A moment later a woman entered the temple through a doorway at the side. The woman had the white hair of a crone, worn long and loose, but her face was unlined and her posture erect and youthful. Her slender form was garbed in white. "I'm Plancina," she said. "I serve the Three Mothers."

Sirona stared, unsure what to say. "I'm Sirona," she finally answered. She gestured to the image on the wall. "Are those the Three Mothers?"

Plancina smiled and pointed. "Ancamna, Damona and Nantosuelta."

"But why do you worship them here?" Sirona asked. "In this building where the sky is hidden?"

"Come," Plancina said. Sirona followed the woman behind the altar and out the side door. There was a separate chamber at the back of the larger building. Inside, a spring flowed into a large basin formed of stone, then gently trickled out, like a tiny waterfall pouring over the lip of the basin and soaking into the ground around it.

"A sacred spring," Sirona said.

Plancina nodded. "The spring has been here for a very long time. The temple was built around it."

"But why not let the spring be as it was, flowing freely onto the earth?"

"It's the way of our people," Plancina said. "We have always built temples."

"Are you Roman?"

"Not Roman, but Belgae. Our people live in the land across the eastern sea."

"And who built this temple? Was it Boudica?"

"Nay. A Belgae nobleman built this place. He married a local woman and settled here to raise horses. They had a farm, although all evidence of it is gone now. A sickness befell the family and they all died. The place was abandoned until Boudica came here after being turned out of her home. She had her men use the tumbled down buildings of the farm to build her palace."

"And what of you? Have you been here all the while, serving the Three Mothers?"

"Nay, I used to live with Boudica and her family at their old palace farther south. There was a shrine there as well, although that one was dedicated to Apollo, who your people call Llew or Beli. Then Prasutagus,

Boudica's husband, died and she was cast out by the Romans. When she settled here, I came with her. But she soon grew angry with me, saying I was a fraud and the gods don't listen to me. She banished me from her household and I took refuge here. I survive because people bring offerings, especially women. If Boudica is successful in getting her revenge against the Romans, someday there will be a great settlement here, a city like those in my homeland. This shrine might become a very important one."

"If Boudica is successful… " Sirona said grimly, feeling a chill. "I fear she won't be successful."

"Why?" Plancina asked.

Sirona hesitated, trying to decide whether to trust this woman. The aura of calm that surrounded Plancina reminded Sirona of Dysri. "I'm a seeress. I've had visions of what will happen in this conflict between my people and the Romans. Indeed," she continued. "I've come here to warn Queen Boudica about my Seeings. If the battle in my vision takes place, it will be the end for the Pretani."

Plancina observed her sorrowfully. "I wouldn't want to carry such knowledge of the future as a weight upon my heart."

"I have tried for many years to deny my visions, to ignore them, but always they return. I realize it's my destiny to share what I have seen."

"And so, you will go to the queen and tell her she must not make war against the Romans?" Plancina's dark eyes were pitying. "She won't listen. The woman is consumed with hatred. She will have her revenge. It's all she lives for."

"I understand what it is to hate the Romans. It's certainly not my plan to urge Boudica to make peace with them. But I must warn her about this battle. If it takes place... " She shook her head.

"Boudica won't listen. Any suggestion that her army won't prevail will throw her into a rage. You must be very careful or your life could be in danger."

Sirona's insides clenched with warning. Every instinct told her she must do this thing, whatever the risk. "Tell me how I should approach Boudica. Advise me on what to say to her."

"Don't go to the gate and tell them you wish to see the queen. You will be turned away. Find some other reason to enter the palace."

"What reason?" Sirona asked.

Plancina smiled. "You're a seeress. I'm certain something will come to you."

Sirona nodded. The Goddess had guided her thus far on this journey. She must continue to trust in Her.

"Come to my dwelling and share a meal with me." Plancina gestured toward a pathway leading away from the spring.

"What are your duties in serving the Three Mothers?" Sirona asked as she followed Plancina through the forest.

"I keep the oil lamps lit and burn herbs so it smells pleasant in the temple. I talk to the people who come to the shrine and listen to their requests, then tell them what sort of offering they should make to please the Three Mothers."

"Why don't the people speak to the gods themselves and ask them directly for their aid?"

"Many people don't know what to say to the gods."

Sirona nodded. It was similar to the role of the Learned Ones among her people. They performed the rituals, spoke the sacred words and made certain things were carried out in a way that satisfied the gods.

"What of you?" Plancina asked. "What gods do you serve? How do you worship them?"

This was not an easy question to answer, Sirona realized. Once she would have named all the gods the Tarisllwyth honored, listing them in threes and mentioning the forces or attributes they were connected with. But her contact with Itzurra, with the Old Ones and Dysri, had altered her beliefs and made them more complicated.

"Most of all I believe in a female force, the Great Mother. She is the earth and all its aspects: water, land, plants and animals, the wind and the rain. She is also connected to the moon and the heavens. She is everywhere, in every goddess my people believe in: Arianrhod, Lady of the moon and the heavens; Ceridwen, goddess of the earth, of wisdom and fertility, Rhiannon, queen of the other realms, of dreams and enchantments. Cyhiraeth, goddess of streams and water. Olwen of the golden wheel of summer. Morrigan, the goddess of death and battle. Modren, as my people call the Great Mother... " Sirona shook her head. "There are so many names, and yet, somehow, I believe they are all part of the same force."

"You've named only female deities," Plancina said. "Don't you believe in male gods?"

"Of course. The female force must be balanced by a male one. I honor Cernunnos, lord of the animals, Beli, god of the sun, and Manawydan, god of the sea. And yet, when I call out for aid, it's the goddesses who seem to hear my plea. Their power seems more real to me and more meaningful. But there's another thing," Sirona continued, "There are times when I feel as if the great force of the Goddess is inside of me... and in everyone... and everything. As if the fire of life that burns in all of us is the same as all the forces of the heavens and the earth. As if everything is connected. One spirit flowing through all of us. One force.

One energy. It's only that our minds are too weak and foolish to grasp this idea, and so we make up the names of the gods, trying to define their aspects, to count and control that which we don't understand."

Plancina nodded. "There's wisdom in what you say. It's complicated, dealing with the gods. Like trying to hold water in your hands. It slips away just when you think you've grasped it. We can use only words to speak of these things, and yet, it's beyond words. It's feeling and energy, the spirit that moves inside us."

Sirona smiled. It was odd to meet someone so different, yet who saw things much as she did. She was glad she'd accepted Plancina's offer to come to her dwelling.

* * *

They talked late into the night. In the morning, Sirona bid farewell to Plancina and went to the river to wash. Afterwards, she sat on a rock along the grassy bank, listening to the laughing voice of the river as it flowed by. She smelled the scent of earth and growing things, an odor ancient and soothing. Around her feet, dewdrops and wood orchids grew like stars among the vivid green vegetation.

She released her breath in a sigh of satisfaction. This was a place more sacred than any temple. All the aspects of the Great Mother were here—water, plants, earth. She touched the goddess amulet, feeling its connection to the life force. "Make me strong," she whispered. "Make me wise. Help me understand what I must do." The stone's energy seemed to radiate through her body. A tingling, soothing force, as if it were driving away her doubts and fears and healing her spirit.

Healing, aye, that was it! She sat up sharply, struck by her inspiration. When she went to the fortress gate, she would tell the guard the amulet was a healing stone and she was a healer. That would be a way into the palace. Plancina had suggested a pathway would be revealed to her, and so it had.

She left the river and started back to the world of men. Circling the noise and squalor of the warriors' camp, she headed up the trackway to the gate of the stone enclosure. Her confidence was high. The amulet stone swung between her breasts as she walked. Meeting Plancina was exactly what she'd needed. Through the other woman, she had reaffirmed her understanding of the forces around her and her own connection to the Goddess.

At the gate she was met by a fierce-looking sentry dressed in a heavy leather crys. His fair hair was braided away from his face and his body bristled with weapons. Perusing her with bright blue eyes, he asked, "What's your business here?"

"I'm a healer. I have heard the queen has need of one. I would aid her, if possible." Sirona's heart pounded as the guard regarded her intently. "See, this is my healing stone." She pulled the amulet from beneath her gown and held it out.

He examined the stone and then nodded. "The queen's chambers lie in the center of the complex."

Sirona stepped through the gate, exhilarated. How easily her plan had succeeded. The Goddess clearly had a hand in this.

The outer area of the palace stronghold was crowded and noisy and reeked with the odors of metalworking—charcoal fires, steam and the smell of hot iron cooling. Sirona passed several workshops where men with leather aprons worked, red-faced and soaked with sweat. Slaves ran to and fro carrying firewood and water. Outside one of the shops she observed the crude image of a bearded man carved on a wooden plank. She guessed the image must represent Govannon, the god of metal and craftwork. Nearby stood a half-finished chariot. She took a deep breath, remembering her vision of the destruction of the Pretani war chariots, and hurried past the bustling workshop area.

The queen's dwelling was a sprawling structure. It had dressed stone walls and a red tile roof like Calpurnius's house, but it was much larger, the largest building Sirona had ever seen.

Her doubts resurfaced. The guard had been easy to fool, but the servants and sentries here would be more wary. They would know if the queen needed a healer. Yet the Goddess had put the words into her mouth, so there must be a reason for it. She approached the doorway of the dwelling and told the guard, "I'm a healer. I've heard Boudica has need of one."

The man, who was of middle age with graying hair and eyes as dark as sloe berries, stared at her. Sirona thought he meant to turn her away. Then he said, "How did you know to come? Last I heard, the queen had not yet decided to send for a healer."

"I'm also a seer," Sirona said boldly.

The man nodded and motioned for her to follow him into the dwelling.

Inside, they passed through a large room with walls painted with designs and pictures. On the floor, tiny bits of stone had been arranged to form the likenesses of plants, birds and fish. They entered a corridor lit with oil lamps along the walls. Glancing in the other rooms they passed, Sirona saw life-sized stone figures and furniture decorated with gold and enamelwork.

Finally the servant halted outside a doorway and motioned for Sirona to enter. The small chamber was poorly lit compared to the rest of the dwelling. Cloth hangings blocked light from the window and a single lamp barely illuminated the rest of the room. A young woman lay on a raised bedplace. An older woman, clearly a servant, sat nearby. "This is a healer," the man told the servant. "She's come to help Julia."

The man left. Sirona took a step nearer, wondering what she should do now. She didn't know what was wrong with Julia.

The servant stood and approached Sirona. "You're a healer?"

Sirona nodded.

"You look very young for such things."

"My abilities are a gift from the Great Goddess," Sirona answered. She touched the amulet. Then she motioned to the young woman. "What troubles her?"

"You don't know? The Goddess didn't tell you?" the woman asked scornfully.

Sirona stared at the bedplace, waiting for the words to come. All at once she was filled with feelings and sensations, as if the young woman's thoughts had seeped inside her mind. "She's in great pain," she said, almost gasping at the intensity of the experience. "Not an ailment of the body, but of the spirit. She's given up. She wants to die."

The servant nodded. "You do have power, despite your youth. Julia won't eat, nor leave this chamber, nor speak to anyone, not even her mother." The servant shook her head. "It's because of what the Romans did to her. She feels shamed, degraded. She can't overcome the grief that afflicts her."

Sirona pushed aside her awareness of Julia's pain and tried to understand what had caused it. She recalled what Kellach had told her, that after her husband died, Boudica been turned out of her home by Romans. When she protested their treatment, the queen had been flogged by the Romans and her daughters raped. This must be one of those unfortunate young women. "There's another daughter," she said. "Is she like this as well?"

"Nay, Sybilla has vowed vengeance. Even now, she trains with the men, learning how to throw a javelin and wield a sword, so she might ride into battle and kill the brutal monsters who raped her."

Sirona approached the bedplace, trying to find a balance between experiencing the misery of the young woman and maintaining enough detachment to help her. "Why didn't Boudica send for a healer long before this?" Sirona asked.

"Perhaps she didn't think it would do any good. Or perhaps she's ashamed to see her own daughter behave like this. She thinks Julia should train to fight like her sister."

Sirona felt a fierce anger toward Boudica. How could a mother be so arrogant and selfish that she would let her daughter waste away rather than seek aid?

Moving nearer, Sirona reached out and touched the young woman's arm. Julia flinched violently. "Shhh," Sirona whispered. "It's all right. I won't harm you. I serve the Goddess, the Great Mother." Again, she touched the woman, feeling the dry, loose skin of her arm. "The Mother is with you," she said. "She wants to heal you, to bring you back from that place of darkness."

Julia whimpered, then began to cry quietly. Sirona's insides twisted in sympathy. How could she ease this woman's suffering? How did one heal a wound of the spirit?

She closed her eyes and concentrated. *Someone held her down. Clothes tearing. Rough hands. A heavy weight crushing her. Sharp pain. Why won't someone help me? Please, help! Please...*

Sirona shuddered and opened her eyes. Instead of aiding Julia, she was being sucked down into the woman's terrible memories.

She tried again, seeking to find the essence of Julia's spirit before she was hurt. The scene changed to a lovely garden. Julia was in an apple tree, peering down through the branches. Beneath the tree was a young woman who must be her sister... and a small black and brown dog. Sybilla was scolding the dog, calling him Hector and telling him to be quiet. Julia plucked an apple and took aim. As the apple struck her, Sybilla cried out in surprise. Hector continued to bark.

The images faded. Sirona went to the maidservant. "Where's Hector?" she asked.

The woman gaped at her. "The dog? Hector was injured when Julia was attacked. One of the men kicked it in the head. The poor beast has been blind ever since. We've kept this from her." The servant motioned to the still form on the bed. "We feared if she learned what had happened to Hector, she'd fall into even deeper despair."

"But the dog still lives?"

"Aye. The queen told someone to drown it, so she wouldn't have to endure its whimpering as it cried for Julia, but one of the slave boys took pity on the beast and took it to live in the kitchen, where Boudica never goes."

"Fetch it now," Sirona said.

"What do you mean to do?"

"Julia needs something to live for, something outside herself."

"But when she learns that the animal is blind because of what those awful men did... "

"That the animal is damaged serves my purpose even better. I can argue that the dog needs her, that she must eat and gain strength for the sake of the dog."

The old woman frowned at her. "What sort of healing is this? Why didn't you use your amulet? Why didn't you lay hands on her and draw out the ill humors from her body?"

"I may yet do those things, but first I need the dog. It's a reminder of the past, of the life she knew before she was hurt. She needs to find her way back to that life."

The servant left. Taut with resolve, Sirona went to the bed. She could do this. The Great Mother would guide her. She took Julia's hand in hers. The goddess stone burned on her breast, filling her mind with the words she must use. "It's time to return to the world of the living, Julia," she said sternly. "You can't drown in your grief any longer." Julia moaned. "Listen to me," Sirona said, "You are needed in this world. Hector needs you. Your dog was injured trying to defend you. You owe him a debt. You must try to overcome your suffering, for his sake. "

"Nay, nay," Julia moaned. "I can't."

"Aye, you can. You *must*."

Julia opened her eyes and looked at Sirona. Then she closed them again, moaning. "Why should I listen to you? You're only a girl. You look even younger than me."

Sirona fought off the doubts Julia's words aroused. *The Goddess wouldn't have given you this task if you didn't have the power to accomplish it.* "I've had years of training in matters of the spirit," she said resolutely. "I was a student of the Learned Ones. I see visions. I saw you in the apple tree. And I saw Hector. He's small and brown and black. One of his ears droops a little."

"Someone must have told you what he looks like. Probably my sister. She also told you about the apple tree." Julia's voice was petulant. Sirona could feel the battle going on inside the young woman. It was easier to give up, to return to that dark hopeless place.

As Sirona struggled with what to say next, the servant returned with a small dog on a leash. It walked in slowly, sniffing the floor. When it was released from the leash, it ran toward the bedplace, barking excitedly.

"Hector?" Julia whispered.

"Aye, Hector is here." Sirona lifted the dog onto the bed, where it began to sniff and lick Julia.

The young woman moaned again. "Nay, Hector. You can't help me. No one can help me." Julia began to cry softly. The dog snuggled next to her, whimpering. "Let us both die together," she whispered. "Let us both die and then we'll be safe. We will travel to the Otherworld together."

"You won't be welcomed in the Otherworld," Sirona said. "The gods don't condone cowardice."

"I'm no coward," Julia retorted. "I couldn't stop them. I tried, but I couldn't..." Her words ended in an agonized gasp.

Sirona went to the bed and sat down beside Julia. "I didn't mean you were a coward because you couldn't stop the attack. That wasn't your fault. But you *can* stop what is happening to you now. You can fight *now*. Fight for your life. Fight to reclaim that which has been taken from you. Although those men abused your body, your spirit is intact. It still belongs to you, and only you can control what happens to it."

"I can't bear to live! I want to die!"

"Dying will accomplish nothing. If you starve yourself to death, the gods will be disgusted with you. They'll probably send you back in another body and force you to deal with your weakness in another life. You can't escape the path that's ahead of you. If you don't struggle with it and learn from it now, you'll have to do so in another time and place. This is a test your spirit must endure."

"It's so dark here. So terrible. They hold me down... hurt me..."

"Nay, don't think of that. Think of your life before the attack." Sirona took Julia's hand and guided it to Hector. She moved her hand so that Julia was stroking the dog. "The gods left Hector behind to comfort you, to see you through the darkness. Although he's blind, he can see what's on the other side of your pain. He will lead you to the light, to life and hope."

Julia sighed heavily but continued to pet the dog. Sirona got up and approached the servant, who waited in the shadows. "Bring food, something easy to eat, broth or pottage."

The servant nodded and left the room. Sirona went to one of the windows and removed the cloth covering. "Nay!" Julia cried as daylight streamed into the room.

"The time for grieving is over. You must go on with your life." Sirona returned to the bed and gently pulled Julia's hands away from her face. "You're a lovely young woman, Julia. You shouldn't hide such a comely face."

"But no man will want me now... now that... " She broke off, sobbing.

"That's not true," Sirona said. "I'm a seeress, and I believe you will marry and have children someday." Even as she spoke, she felt a certainty that someday there would be a man who would love Julia. Who would admire her for her courage and character as well as her fine features.

For Julia was a beauty, despite her gaunt body and hollow eyes. She had the bold coloring of the woman in Sirona's visions, but tempered with a softness and delicacy that had nothing to do with the fierce-eyed queen. Julia's fragility and tender nature had nearly cost her life, but if she survived this incident, it would draw men to her like bees to clover.

The servant returned with the food, and Sirona carried the tray to the bed. "You must eat," she told Julia.

Julia drank some of the broth. Then she began to cry. "I don't want men to look at me. I don't want to get married, ever. I hate men. I hate them for what they did to me!"

"Shhh, shhh," Sirona soothed, stroking Julia's arm. "Not all men are like that. Indeed, most men are not like that. The kind who would hurt a woman are worse than beasts. Don't even think about them. Banish them from your thoughts."

Julia took a gulping breath and resumed eating. Sirona went to the servant and spoke quietly. "The battle isn't over. She'll need to be reassured again and again. But I think she has begun to take the first steps back on the pathway of life."

The old woman smiled at her, eyes glittering with tears. "Thank you. You've done what I thought no one could. I feared the little one was lost to us."

"Have you been with the family many years?"

"Since before the girls were born. Julia has always been my favorite. Such a gentle disposition."

"You must try to protect her from any further ordeals." Sirona paused, remembering her vision of the great battle and the masses of carts full of women and children, families of the warriors, who waited at the edge of it… waiting to celebrate a victory that would never come.

She said, "If Boudica should try to take Julia away from here in the next few months, you must argue against it. If she leaves, she might be caught up in events that would threaten not only her fragile spirit, but her very life. Promise me. Promise me you will insist Julia remain here."

"But if her mother decides to take her away, what can I do? I'm only a servant. And the queen is a force to be reckoned with."

As if conjured there by those words, a tall woman with vivid red hair strode into the room. She fixed Sirona with gaze of blue fire and said, "What are you doing here? I sent for no healer." She motioned to the two warriors flanking her. "Seize her, the wretched little spy!"

Chapter 17

As the warriors grabbed Sirona's arms, she cried out, "I'm not a spy! I'm Pretani. The Romans are my enemies. Why would I spy for them?"

Boudica strode toward Sirona. "Then what are you doing here—in my daughter's bedchamber?"

Julia sat up and called out. "Mama, she's a seer. She can see the future."

Boudica stared at her daughter, obviously startled to hear her speak. Her gaze jerked back to Sirona. As the queen gazed at her threateningly, Sirona struggled to find her voice. Finally, she said, "Aye, I'm a seer. I have seen visions of you, Queen Boudica."

Boudica took a step nearer. "What have you seen?"

Sirona swallowed hard as she remembered Plancina's warning words. *If you tell her she will be defeated, she will have you killed.*

"I have seen you triumph over your enemies. I have smelled the reek of Roman bodies burning. I have seen Roman blood staining the paving stones of their settlements."

Boudica smiled in satisfaction.

Sirona began to tremble as she continued, "But I have also seen a great battle where the Pretani are overwhelmed by the enemy. I have come here to warn you… if a time comes for you to meet the Romans with all your forces, you must not do so. You must find some other way to fight them. If the battle I've seen takes place, our people will be vanquished."

Boudica's gaze pierced Sirona like blue lightning. "How dare you come to me and predict my defeat!"

"I'm not predicting your defeat," Sirona said quickly. "I'm warning you about one battle. If you avoid that conflict, you may yet prevail against the enemy." Even as she said the words, Sirona wondered if there was any hope of triumphing over the Romans. But she dared not reveal her doubts to Boudica.

She recalled something Bryn had told her many years before, soon after the Silures came to ask Tarbelinus to aid them in fighting the Romans: *The way to defeat the Romans is to wear them down,* he had said. *Attack them as they patrol. Raid in small groups, steal their livestock, destroy their crops, disrupt their supply routes.* She repeated these things to Boudica and added, "You must strike where they're weakest and make their lives miserable. Grind them down until they begin to wonder if Albion is worth their trouble. All is not well in the Romans' homeland. If you could make it seem that it will be too difficult for them to conquer and hold Albion, the powerful men of Rome might decide to take their armies elsewhere."

"But what about the Romans already here?" Boudica demanded. "They won't leave on their own. They're a plague upon the land, a stench in our nostrils!"

"If the Roman soldiers left this place, then the people in their settlements would no longer feel safe, and they would either come to accept Pretani ways or leave."

Boudica stared at her. Then she said in a contemptuous voice, "The Pretani have never been afraid to meet our enemies in battle. We've always avenged ourselves against our rivals. You've obviously never trained in combat, never learned the code of the warrior. I've been wronged, and I intend to make the Romans pay for what they have done... to me, to my family and household."

She took another step nearer. Her breath was hot on Sirona's face. "I don't care what visions you've had. I don't care what nonsense you speak, pretending it's the voice of the gods. I've had enough of visions and seers, of priests and priestesses telling me what I should do. I don't need the gods' favor to triumph over the Romans. For that, I need only warriors and chariots, spears and swords!"

Julia let out a gasp. "Mother, you shouldn't say such things! It's blasphemy!"

"That's what they would have you think, the puling cowards who call themselves Learned Ones," Boudica told her daughter. Turning back to Sirona, she demanded, "If the gods have power, why didn't they unleash it upon the Romans when they raided my home and humiliated me and my daughters? I've made many offerings to the gods, honored them faithfully, but they betrayed me. They let the Romans attack and rob me!"

Sirona took a deep breath, trying to find an explanation. All at once, she recalled Lovarn's words. Gently, she said, "I don't know if the gods even concern themselves with such things. Perhaps they are beyond the petty conflicts of our kind."

Boudica's eyes filled with hatred. "Petty? You think my sufferings are petty? I should have you killed for speaking so disrespectfully." She motioned to the guards. "Take her away."

Julia sat up again. "Nay! Don't hurt her! Please! I beg you. She's helped me. Made me want to live again. You owe her for that, don't you,

Mother?"

Boudica turned to her daughter. "Do you swear you'll eat? Resume your life?"

"I… I'll try," Julia said, her voice thin and weak. "But only if you agree not to hurt this woman." With great effort, she stood and walked to Sirona, her whole body trembling. "Please, Mother, listen to me. The Goddess speaks through her. You'll be cursed if you cause her harm."

Boudica's nostrils flared as her cold gaze again fixed on Sirona. "I won't have her killed. But neither will I permit her to spread these lies. This woman will remain here, in this bedchamber. No one will be allowed to have contact with her except you and the servants." She nodded to Julia. "I'll spare her life, but only for your sake."

To Sirona, she said, "You'll stay here until my army marches out to destroy the Romans. Once we're gone, you'll be allowed to leave. Until then, you'll have no contact with anyone but Julia." She moved closer, looming over Sirona. "Don't think for a moment that your prediction of my defeat worries me. I know I'll prevail in the end. But I can't afford for any hint of your prophecy to reach the ears of my warriors. Whispers of failure can spread like a poison and taint the resolve of the men who hear them. I won't allow such a thing to happen." She stalked out of the room, the two guards following.

"It's settled then," Julia said. "You'll remain here as my companion and friend." She smiled winsomely.

Sirona took a deep, steadying breath, wondering how she would endure being trapped in this place, away from the forest and the river and the other gifts of the Goddess. But if she was compelled to stay in this place, it must be part of the Goddess's plan. She must not despair.

* * *

"Which way to Iceni territory?" Cadwalon asked Bryn when they came to a place where the river they'd been following divided into three branches. Bryn looked up at the sky, observing the location of the sun and calculating the place on the horizon where it had risen. "The middle one seems to lead east."

"Do you think we're close?" Cadwalon asked.

"The Iceni are said to be herders and we've seen much grazing land."

"And few settlements," Cadwalon added.

"Thank the gods." Since leaving Dobunni territory, they'd tried to avoid any dwelling places. At first it had been difficult, as the Catuvellauni territories were dotted with the Roman-style farms that Moren had called villas. But for the last day, they'd seen only a few shepherds and cattle herders. They'd felt relatively safe, confident that none of the common folk would bother them, especially in their guise of Drui.

As they followed the middle river, the land grew marshy and they saw many water birds: grebes, terns, herons and osprey. But they had to backtrack and change their course several times to avoid the wetter areas. To make things even more uncomfortable, it began to rain, a steady downpour that seemed to find its way through their oiled rain capes and soak them to the skin.

"No Romans here," Cadwalon commented as they slogged through a swampy patch of chest-high reeds and rushes.

Bryn grunted in agreement. "Too wet."

A short while later, they came upon the remains of a hillfort almost hidden by an overgrowth of alder and willow. It had obviously been abandoned many seasons ago. From the half-rotted remnants of the palisade and dwellings, they could see it had once been a Pretani dun. "I wonder what happened here?" Bryn asked. "Maybe the course of the river changed and they had to move to drier land."

"Or, the Romans overran this place and killed them," Cadwalon responded.

They continued past the ruins. Bryn stopped and exclaimed, "Look here! This must have been their sacred grove! See, the altar stone?" He glanced around. "All these old oaks. They're dying now. The soil's too wet. But once they must have been magnificent."

"I don't understand what's so important about a bunch of trees," Cadwalon said.

Bryn shrugged. "I spent many days of my life in a grove like this one. At the time, I hated it. I wanted to be out running in the woods, chasing after the hounds, hunting or training to be a warrior. But now I can't help feeling a kind of power here. There's a reason this place was once used for ceremonies." He looked at his companion. "Don't you ever sense the gods are close by?"

"Never," Cadwalon said emphatically.

"I suppose it's my Drui training." Bryn started walking again. "I never thought I would say this, but there are times when I'm almost glad of those years." Cadwalon turned to look at him, eyebrows raised beneath the hood of his rain cape. Bryn met his gaze with a rueful smile. "I did learn a few things. Not much that's useful in everyday life, but I do have a kind of understanding of how everything fits together. I don't believe the gods control my destiny, but there does seem to be something guiding it."

"That sort of thinking is too complicated for me," Cadwalon said. "It makes my head ache merely to talk about it."

Bryn shrugged. "I used to say the same thing. I wonder what

happened."

"Perhaps wearing the sacred crys on this journey has aroused old memories of your years in the grove and caused you to reconsider your beliefs."

Bryn nodded. As they traveled, he'd thought a lot about his early Drui training, recalling all the time he'd spent with Sirona and Cruthin. In some strange way, he couldn't help feeling the destinies of the three of them were entwined. That he should feel this way about Sirona made sense, but not Cruthin. He hadn't seen the youth for years. Indeed, Cruthin wouldn't be a youth any longer, that is if he'd found a way to survive after being banished.

He shrugged off the thought, telling himself he was just feeling wistful about the past because he was so far from his homeland. But someday he would return... if, the gods willing, he survived the confrontation with the Romans.

At the thought of what lay ahead, he quickened his pace. Cadwalon caught up with him and asked, "Is there a reason why you're suddenly in a hurry?"

"It's nearly time for the Hay Moon. If Boudica is planning a long campaign this sunseason, she must lead her warriors into battle before too long. I don't want to miss any part of it."

* * *

The next day they left the marshlands and the rain behind and the terrain changed to open country. "Good pastureland," Bryn said.

"Aye," Cadwalon agreed. "And see, over there, those must be the famed horses of the Iceni."

Bryn squinted and made out brown, black and tan specks dotting the vivid green pasture. A thrill of excitement swept down his body. He remembered Sirona's Seeing, how she'd said he would fight with the symbol of a white horse on his shield.

They crossed the low valley. Passing the herds, Bryn counted nearly three score horses. They were beautiful creatures, graceful and powerful. "I wonder what it would be like to drive a chariot pulled by those beasts," he mused.

"I have no desire to find out," Cadwalon answered. "I'd prefer to march into battle on my own two feet."

They crested a hill. On the other side was a long valley with a vast settlement spread out on one end.

"Ah," Cadwalon said in satisfaction. "Moren didn't lie. There's indeed a vast army here. The question is, are there enough men to overwhelm our enemies?"

"Only time will tell," Bryn said. "Let's change back into our normal attire. We want to arrive here as warriors, not Learned Ones."

After they changed their garments, they started down the ridge. The army camp reminded Bryn of an ants' nest. The whole place bustled with activity. Many of the warriors had brought their families with them. Children and dogs played in small groups while women tended cookfires. Warriors sat on the ground, polishing or repairing weapons and armor, fletching arrows and repairing shields. Other men were engaged in making new weapons. The smell of charcoal and hot metal was strong, almost overpowering the odors of cooking food, rotting refuse and dung.

Bryn stopped a warrior leaving the camp. "Where can we find the chieftain who leads this army?"

The man, who was garbed in a faded green crys and russet and green-checked bracco, pointed to the walled complex. "Queen Boudica herself will lead us into battle when the time comes." The man hesitated. Then he added, "But if you'd rather talk to a man, there's a warrior here who takes care of the chariots and horses. He's called Gwynceffyl, 'the white horse'."

"Where can we find this Gwynceffyl?" Bryn felt another surge of excitement. Everything was coming to pass exactly as Sirona had predicted.

"Over there." The man pointed. "That's where they exercise the horses."

Bryn and Cadwalon headed in the direction the man had indicated. On the other side of the encampment there were rows and rows of chariots. The beautiful wicker vehicles reminded Bryn of graceful water birds. Pulled by the horses they had glimpsed earlier, the vehicles would be nearly as fast as a plover taking flight.

They stopped and examined the chariots, admiring their elegant shape and lavish decoration. Some were ornamented with bronze and enamel fixtures on the wheels and hand-holds. Others were painted with swirling shapes or the forms of animals.

"They look rather flimsy," Cadwalon remarked. "It wouldn't take much to tip one over or crush it altogether. For that matter, what if the wheels got stuck in the mud? You'd be helpless, utterly trapped."

"If that happened, you could turn the vehicle on its side and fight from behind it, using the body of it like a shield."

"Not me." Cadwalon shook his head. "I wouldn't mind racing one of them for the fun of it, but when I go into battle, I want to be able to maneuver swiftly. All I need is a shield and a sword. Let other men carry spears, or a quiver of arrows. Arrows are fine until the enemy is in your face."

Bryn understood the sense of Cadwalon's words, yet that didn't alter his yearning to drive one of these impressive vehicles.

Moving past the chariots, they came to the paddocks where the horses were kept. Seeing the animals up close, Bryn was even more entranced. There was such nobility and pride in the way the beasts held their heads. Such grace in their sleek lines. Such beauty in their burnished bronze, tan and black hides and their dark intelligent eyes.

"Come on," Cadwalon said. "You can't spend all day here admiring the horses. We've a war to prepare for."

Bryn nodded, although it was an effort to move on.

"Your friend likes horses, does he?"

Bryn turned to see a fair-haired stocky man of middle age approaching.

"Aye," Cadwalon answered. "He's been mooning over them like a lovesick fool."

The man laughed, strong white teeth flashing beneath his heavy, dark gold mustache. "Many men have been struck down with a passion for Epona, the horse goddess." He approached Bryn. "I am Gwynceffyl. What are you called, young warrior?"

"I'm Bryn ap Tarbelinus. And my companion is Cadwalon ap Cadwyl. We've come to join Boudica's army."

"What tribe do you hail from?"

"From the Dobunni," Cadwalon responded. Bryn thought of mentioning that he was originally from the Tarisllwyth, but decided that here in the sunset lands his tribe would not be known.

Gwynceffyl nodded. "You've come a long distance. We're pleased to have you with us."

"We're pleased to be here," Cadwalon responded. "There's only one difficulty. We have no swords or shields. But we do have Roman coin, if you can tell us where we can purchase such things."

"What happened to your weapons?"

Bryn wondered if this man would think them cowards because they'd pretended to be Learned Ones while they traveled. Cadwalon apparently didn't have this concern, for he answered, "On our journey here we posed as Learned Ones. We thought that if people believed we were Drui, no one would bother us. In fact, that turned out to be true. But since Drui don't carry weapons, we had to leave our swords and shields back in our home territory."

Gwynceffyl grinned. "That was clever. I have to wonder if you would have made it here so easily if you looked like warriors. I can certainly get you weapons. There's no need for you to purchase them. The queen has vowed to provide weaponry to any man who vows to fight the Romans."

"That's very generous of her," Bryn said.

Gwynceffyl's smile faded. "'Generous' is not a word I think of when it comes to the queen. She has a goal and she'll do whatever is necessary to achieve it. If having her metalsmiths work night and day making broadswords, helmets and spear tips is what it takes to defeat the Romans, then she'll make certain it happens." He regarded them with shrewd blue eyes. Then he said, "Come with me to the feast hall of the Iceni. We'll share a cup of wine and discuss the weapons you'll need."

Gwynceffyl took them to a camp on the other side of the palace. In the center was a large, crudely-made timber shelter. Inside, men gathered around a hearth, polishing weapons and armor, playing games with carved wooden boards and bone counters and drinking from red pottery cups. A number of women were there also, weaving, sewing and waiting on the men. In a corner, a half dozen children played with a leather ball.

"This is where my tribe has gathered," Gwynceffyl said.

"Are all these people Iceni?" Bryn asked.

"For the most part. Although we do sometimes invite other warriors to join us." He gestured that they should seat themselves on sheepskins near the hearth. As soon as they sat down, a woman appeared carrying a tray with cups of wine. Bryn took one of the cups and said. "Does Boudica also supply the wine?"

Gwynceffyl nodded. "As for the grain and meat, that's tribute from the farmers of the Iceni. We're fortunate to be close to the lands of our people. The other tribes here have to make do with the game they can take and the food they've brought with them."

Bryn took a drink of the wine. It was even richer tasting than the wine they'd stolen from Cadwyl. "Queen Boudica must be very wealthy," Bryn said. "Yet I'd heard the Romans turned her out of her home and took all her possessions. Where does she get the coin to purchase wine for all these men?"

"Boudica traveled all over this territory, telling everyone how she and her daughters were humiliated and abused. Many people were outraged and offered her gifts. Even some of the chieftains who were so entangled with the Romans that they couldn't come out openly against them still supplied her with foodstuffs, wine and other goods to help her set up another household. She's used much of that wealth to equip the men who've come to join her cause.

"In addition," Gwynceffyl continued, "her husband, Prasutagus, had two other dwelling places besides his main palace. Faced by the outcry over what they had done to Boudica and her daughters, the Romans wisely decided to leave her other properties alone. The fact is, Boudica has many resources, and she's made the most of them. But we'll have to march soon or we risk running out of supplies. And the warriors, out of patience. I told the queen that only the other day."

"And what did she say?" Bryn asked.

"She said she would know when the time was right. I hope she doesn't delay long. The army assembled here ripens like grain in the sun. If she doesn't harvest her 'crop' soon, some of it will fall to the ground and be lost or, even worse, a storm might come and set the mold and rot to growing and ruin the whole harvest." Gwynceffyl raised his dark gold eyebrows expressively.

Bryn nodded. He could easily imagine Pretani turning against Pretani and the opportunity to defeat the Romans being lost forever. "What do you think Boudica's waiting for?" he asked.

"I don't know," Gwynceffyl answered. "I wonder sometimes if she isn't afraid, for all her ruthless talk. Cowardice doesn't fit what I've seen of her, but then, I don't really know her well. In the meantime, we build more chariots. Although at this point, we've run out of men trained to drive them."

Bryn drew a deep breath. This might be the opportunity he had hoped for. "I would like to learn to drive a chariot. It seems like a bold and wonderful way to ride into battle."

Gwynceffyl grinned. "It is that. But there are also dangers. If you fall, you could be dragged by your team and killed."

"I'm certain there are risks," Bryn said. "Even so, I would like to try it."

"What of you?" Gwynceffyl turned to Cadwalon. "Would you also like to learn to drive a chariot?"

Cadwalon shook his head. "Not me. I prefer to fight while standing on the solid ground."

"It's not for everyone," Gwynceffyl agreed. "And Boudica needs archers and swordsmen in her army as much as chariot drivers." He looked at Bryn. "But since you're interested, we'll begin your training tomorrow. Normally, it takes a whole season for a man to learn to maneuver a chariot with enough adeptness to ride into battle, but you strike me as a man who catches on quickly. There may be enough time to get you ready, especially if the queen continues to delay."

Bryn took another sip of the wine. He felt elated and yet apprehensive at the same time. To learn to drive a chariot seemed like the glorious fulfillment of a dream.

That thought reminded him of Sirona. As always, he wondered how she was faring. At least she was far away from all the upcoming conflict and danger. It bothered him that so many of the warriors had brought their families to this place. If they attacked the Romans and failed to defeat them decisively, the enemy would undoubtedly retaliate, and the women, children and slaves gathered here made a very vulnerable target.

Chapter 18

"Use your legs to brace yourself," Gwynceffyl called from the side of the track. "Now ease up on the reins. Gently. Gently. That's it."

Bryn stood on the wooden platform of the chariot, sweat dripping down his face and body as the horses gained speed in the straightaway. He'd had no idea driving a chariot would be so difficult. The horses were barely even trotting and he still struggled to maintain his balance. Seeing the curve in the track ahead, he pulled on the reins to slow the team. As they rounded the bend, he felt on the verge of losing control at any moment. He imagined the chariot toppling over and then being dragged through the mud. But neither disaster occurred and he breathed a prayer of thanks to Epona, goddess of horses.

As they turned again onto the straightaway, he began to relax and enjoy the thrill of moving so quickly. The ground sped by. The bronze fittings on the horses' harnesses jangled merrily. The wind whipped his face, cooling his sweaty brow. Then, all at once, the next curve was ahead. He pulled on the reins, trying to slow the team. The chariot tilted as they went into the turn. Bryn held his breath and adjusted his stance, fighting for balance.

They made it! Once again, the fear ebbed away, replaced by exhilaration. Before he knew it, he was back on the straightaway.

"Not bad," Gwynceffyl called as Bryn swept past him. "A few more days practice, and you'll have mastered it."

Bryn pulled the team to a halt and dismounted. After handing the reins to a slave, he went to speak to the horses, stroking their sleek necks and thanking them for the glorious ride they'd given him. As Gwynceffyl and Cadwalon approached, he knew he must be grinning like a small boy. He felt buoyantly alive, as happy and excited as he'd ever been in his life.

"You did very well," Gwynceffyl said. He motioned to Cadwalon. "Are you certain you don't want to try it?"

Cadwalon shook his head. "I don't want to be at the mercy of two animals."

"It's not that difficult," Bryn said. "If you spent time with the horses, you would come to understand their spirits and learn how to talk to them."

Cadwalon shook his head again. "It's your Drui training that makes you think you can speak to dumb beasts."

"Drui training?" Gwynceffyl looked at Bryn in surprise. "You said you posed as a Learned One on your journey here. Is there more to it than that?"

Bryn shrugged and Cadwalon said, "Aye, my friend here trained in the grove for nearly ten years."

Gwynceffyl gaped openly.

"Aye, it's true," Bryn admitted. "Although I never mastered the necessary skills to become full Drui."

"Still, you must have learned a lot of the mysteries, the strange things only bards and brehons and seers know." Gwynceffyl sounded wary, but also respectful.

"I suppose that's true." Bryn wanted this conversation to be over. He preferred talking about horses and chariot fittings. "Let's go back to camp," he suggested. "I think I've practiced enough for this day. And the horses need a rest."

Gwynceffyl nodded. The slave took the team away and the three men started toward the Iceni camp. Gwynceffyl and Cadwalon discussed the feasibility of a charioteer carrying a spear as he drove. While the two talked, Bryn thought about how easily the Iceni horsemaster had accepted them, and how fortunate they were to have found a place among this rabble of fighting men. He also thought about Sirona's prediction that someday he would fight under the symbol of a white horse. Sirona was gifted, he had never doubted it. Yet it still amazed him she could predict the future so accurately. Gwynceffyl was having shields made for both him and Cadwalon featuring a design of a white horse.

The Iceni camp had a large cistern to collect rainwater. After washing there, the three men headed to the feast hall. The women were cooking stew in a huge iron cauldron simmering over the hearth. It was a way to stretch the meat from the steer that had been butchered the day before. Even with the large herd in a nearby pasture to draw from, it was becoming more and more difficult to keep everyone in the Iceni camp fed. Most of the other tribes had already killed and eaten all their livestock, and were reduced to hunting for game or bartering for goods with the Iceni. He worried once again that Boudica was waiting too long to give the order to march into battle. Already a Catuvellauni man had been killed during a squabble in the main camp and two Cortani warriors were banished for fighting. A few more days, he thought. By then he would be able to handle the chariot well enough to ride into battle.

As they sat down at the hearth, a woman came over with cups of wine. When she reached him, Bryn waved her away. Ever since he learned that Boudica bought her stores from Romans traders, he'd refused to drink the wine served in the Iceni camp. Instead, he filled his waterskin from the cistern and carried it with him everywhere. Cadwalon told him he was a fool to be so stubborn. Bryn didn't care. He had no desire to drink wine that was bought, rather than stolen, from the enemy.

Another woman brought the three men pottery bowls filled with stew and some warm bannocks. Bryn accepted the food eagerly. A fine Pretani steer had gone into making this stew and he wouldn't waste it.

Soon after they finished eating, a man dressed in the coarse brown crys of a slave approached Gwynceffyl. Despite his attire, the man appeared well-fed and wore sturdy shoes, making Bryn think he must be of higher status than most slaves. The man bowed to the Iceni leader. "The queen wishes to know if there are any Drui in the camp."

"Drui?" Gwynceffyl asked in surprise. He looked at Bryn before turning back to the servant. "What does the queen want with a Learned One?"

"Apparently there's a seeress at the palace, and the queen wishes to discredit her. I have been ordered to find a Drui and take them to the queen so they might prove that this woman is a fraud."

"A seeress?" Bryn got to his feet and stared at the man. "What does she look like? What tribe is she from?" His heart seemed to leap in his chest. He'd been thinking about Sirona only a short while before.

"They say she's young and comely," man answered. "Although I haven't seen her myself. They also say the only reason she's alive is because Julia, the queen's youngest daughter, begged Boudica to spare her."

Young and comely. Bryn took a sharp breath. How many young, comely seeresses could there be? And this woman had made some sort of prediction that angered the queen, which sounded very much like Sirona. "I trained as a Drui for ten years," he said abruptly. "I will go and see this seeress."

The servant looked him up and down. "Do you know how to read the auguries and perform ceremonies to determine the will of the gods?"

"I do," he answered.

The servant nodded, then gestured that Bryn should follow him.

"Wait!" Gwynceffyl called. He motioned for Bryn to come and speak to him. "Are you certain you should do this?" he asked in a low voice. "Boudica can be unpredictable. From what you've told me, your training is incomplete. What if you fail to satisfy Boudica with your prophecies? She can be dangerous. I wouldn't want her anger directed at me."

"It doesn't matter," Bryn retorted. "I must go."

"You think this seeress is Sirona, don't you?" Cadwalon said. To

Gwynceffyl, he explained, "She was a companion of his youth and he's determined the two of them will handfast someday." He frowned at Bryn. "Perhaps you should think more about this before you enter the palace. Find out for certain if this seeress is Sirona."

"It must be her. There can't be but a few seers in all of Albion, let alone a young female one."

Cadwalon nodded. "If you're determined to do this, then I'm going with you. We'll say I'm your servant or bodyguard."

"I wouldn't mind having the company," Bryn said.

Gwynceffyl still looked worried. "If things go ill with you and Boudica, I can offer little help. Perhaps before you do this you should find another Learned One and have them accompany you."

"Do you know of any other Learned Ones in this camp?" Bryn asked.

Gwynceffyl frowned. "There was a Silure man named Kellach, but I haven't seen him since the beginning of the sunseason. I think he went off to convince more warriors to join us. But I also recall an old man among the Cornovi camp who performs sacrifices at every full moon."

Bryn turned to the queen's servant. "Let us find this man. The more Drui who gather together, the more power we'll have in calling down the gods and discerning their will."

* * *

As they walked through the warriors' camp, Bryn felt overwhelmed with emotion. Was he finally going to see Sirona? What would she think of him? Would she believe him worthy of her regard now that he was a full-fledged warrior? A twinge of anxiety stirred in his gut. If only he'd learned to drive a chariot better. It would be wonderful to have her watch as he raced down the trackway. How could she help but be impressed?

But he shouldn't be thinking of such things. At this moment, Sirona was very likely in danger. If she'd angered Boudica, there was no telling what the queen would do. It was said that Boudica was as harsh as any man, that she thought nothing of having slaves put to death if they displeased her. She'd banished a chieftain of the Trinovantes who opposed some of her plans, and on the way back to his home dun, he'd died in a very suspicious manner. Nay, the queen was no one to cross. Even her own warriors spoke of her with a hint of fear.

"You're looking very grim, my friend," Cadwalon muttered under his breath. "Are you having doubts about pretending to be a Learned One?"

Bryn shook his head. "Nay. I'm trying to think of a way to get Sirona out of this mess."

"You're absolutely certain the seeress is Sirona?"

"Aye,"

"I thought you said she was gifted with special abilities, almost a goddess herself. If that's true, why are you so afraid for her?"

"As a young girl she did a lot of witless things. I blamed Cruthin for most of it, but still... she didn't always show the best judgment."

"Especially when she favored him over you, eh?" Cadwalon grinned at him.

Bryn tried to smile back, but the sick feeling in his stomach wouldn't relent.

They found the old Drui among the Cornovi camp. He was white-haired and ancient, with a long flowing beard. When they told him the queen wanted someone to make a sacrifice and advise her on the future, he fixed them with rheumy blue eyes and said, "I will try, but the auguries are often very hard to read."

He gathered together his bag of sacred objects and they walked toward the palace complex. The slave led the way while Bryn, Cadwalon and the old Drui, called Ysganon, followed. Ysganon eyed Bryn shrewdly. "What's your part in this thing? You look like a warrior to me, not a Learned One."

Bryn gestured to his crys, bearing the three sacred colors, which he had put on before leaving the Iceni camp. "I trained in the grove for many years. But it's been a long time since I participated in a real ceremony."

Ysganon smiled faintly. "It's quite simple. We must discover what Boudica wants to hear and tell her that it will come to pass."

Cadwalon whispered to Bryn, "The old man sounds like trouble. It might be best if he didn't see the queen." He touched the knife at his belt.

"We mustn't offend the gods" Bryn whispered back. "Killing a Drui would certainly anger them."

"Whatever you think, my friend," Cadwalon muttered. "But if it comes down to him or us, I know who I'll choose."

They reached the gate of the fortress and were waved in, although Bryn sensed the sentry regarding him and Cadwalon with curiosity. They passed the busy workshops, the source of the weapons, shields and armor flooding the warrior camp, and finally reached the palace, a vast square structure. Entering, Bryn was astonished by what he saw. Gwynceffyl had said that Boudica still possessed much wealth, but he was still surprised at the ornate décor of the palace: Roman-style benches and stools, stone figures as large as a man, gilded lamps and fixtures, painted walls and patterned floors. Bryn had never seen such fine furnishings, and it angered him to compare the splendor here with the poverty of the warriors' camp, with their simple leather tents and shelters made of branches, their ragged-looking children and worn, weary wives.

They were escorted into a large, well-lit room. In the center of the chamber Queen Boudica reclined on a long bench padded with scarlet and gold cushions. She reminded Bryn a little of his mother, but with brighter red hair, blue eyes instead of brown and heavier features. But if Boudica wasn't as pleasing to look upon as Rhyell, she more than made up for it with the aura of power surrounding her. Few men Bryn had met were half as intimidating as this woman.

Also in the room were several older men who appeared to be the queen's advisors, as well as a number of slaves hovering around, waiting for the queen's command.

Their escort bowed low to Queen Boudica. "These men are Drui," he said. "They've agreed to perform a sacrifice and foretell the future for you."

As Boudica looked them over, Bryn felt a twinge of unease. The queen's gaze quickly passed over Ysganon and rested on him and Cadwalon. "Why do the two of you wear the mustaches of warriors?" she demanded.

"We trained as warriors in order to fight the Romans," Bryn answered. "But having spent long years in the grove in our youth, we still consider ourselves Drui."

Boudica nodded at this. Then she asked, "What do you need, a bullock or ram? And where do you want to spill its blood?"

Ysganon started to answer, but Bryn interrupted, "A white bullock is best. Have you such a beast among your herds?"

Boudica gestured for one of her advisors to come near and then spoke to him in a low voice. Bryn repressed a smile of satisfaction. White bullocks were rare. It might take days to locate one, even among all the herds of the Iceni.

"The animal need not be pure white," Ysganon said. "If the beast has several patches of white on its back, that will suffice."

"But the more clearly the animal is marked by the gods, the more powerful the ceremony of sacrifice," Bryn added.

Again, Boudica conferred with her council. Finally, she said, "We'll seek out an appropriate animal. In the meantime, you will remain here in the palace." She motioned to one of the slaves. "Take the Drui to a guest chamber and make certain they have water to wash with and something to eat."

"I see that you wish to enjoy the queen's hospitality for as long as possible," Ysganon said as they left the queen and followed the servant down a corridor. "I can't blame you for taking advantage of the situation. But beware, the longer the queen waits for the divination, the more impressive she will expect it to be. It won't be enough to simply tell her what she wants to hear; we'll have to appear to perform magic. Are you up to the task, young man? Do you know some tricks of sorcery to impress the queen?"

Bryn ignored the old Drui. He had to find Sirona and get her out of the palace. After taking her someplace safe, he and Cadwalon would join up with Boudica's army, disappearing among the mass of warriors.

They were conducted to a large chamber with straw-filled pallets on the floor. In the corner was a table with a plain bronze ewer and a bowl for washing.

"The queen obviously sees us more as servants than guests." Ysganon's gaze swept the room contemptuously. "She would never house a chieftain in such mean circumstances. I remember the days when Drui were received everywhere with the best the tribes had to offer. Chieftains sought our favor and treated us with respect. The champion's portion came to us, and at night we slept in the guest house, the finest dwelling in the dun. We were waited upon by slaves every moment and had beautiful young women to warm our beds."

"What happened?" Cadwalon asked, obviously intrigued by Ysganon's description of his former life. "Why have the Drui fallen out of favor?"

"The Romans," Ysganon said bitterly. "They hate us and persecute us, and they've convinced many chieftains that we're of little value. The Romans tell them that if they build temples and shrines, they can petition the gods directly. The Romans still use diviners and auguries, but they have no more status than what a skilled craftsman might have. Nay, it was a sad thing for our kind when the Romans came."

"Which is why we must drive them out of our lands," Cadwalon said. "We must kill as many of them as we can and force the rest to leave."

The old Drui shook his head. "The tribes will never come together to fight the enemy. They're too busy fighting among themselves."

"That's not true," Bryn argued. "Think of the huge army camp out there, made up of warriors from a half dozen tribes. And all of them determined to destroy the Romans."

"It's too late," Ysganon responded. "The Romans are everywhere, and their influence has poisoned us. Even if you could defeat the Romans and drive them off, some men would grumble, missing the luxuries the invaders have brought." Ysganon gestured. "Look at this woman, Queen Boudica. She lives like a Roman herself. Do you think she would be willing to give up all of this? And yet, that's the only way we can go back to being what we once were—a people in control of our own destiny."

As Bryn watched Ysganon go to the table and wash, he couldn't help thinking there was sense in the old man's words. What if they succeeded in driving the Romans out of Albion? Who would come to power? Would it be leaders like Boudica, men and women who cared more for their own circumstances and comfort than for the people who served them?

But Cadwalon clearly had a different reaction. "The Romans must be destroyed," he repeated. "There's no other answer. If they're not vanquished, then we, and everything we believe in, will perish."

Ysganon smiled. "Good. Good. That's exactly what we must tell Boudica when we read the auguries."

Bryn and Cadwalon took turns washing. A servant had brought them food—a pot of savory stew and some plump chewy mealcakes to dip into it. "Ahhhh," Ysganon sighed as he ate. "I've missed Roman bread. Like their wine, it's a delight that a man can easily become used to."

"So, you're as corrupted by Roman ways as anyone," Bryn remarked. He didn't have any food himself, having recently eaten the stew in the Iceni camp. For that matter, his stomach was churning too fiercely to even think of eating.

At Bryn's words, Ysganon nodded agreeably and went on chewing. Bryn paced around the room. As soon as he could, he must try to find Sirona.

After eating, Ysganon lay down on one of the pallets and began to snore loudly. Cadwalon finished the wine—which Bryn refused—and came to stand beside Bryn as he stared out the one small window, which showed a view of a large open area crisscrossed with stone pathways. Small trees were planted here and there, while in other areas, plants grew in neat lines.

Cadwalon said quietly, "I presume the demand for a white bullock was a ruse to buy time."

Bryn nodded. "We must find Sirona and leave this place as soon as possible.'

"How do you intend to locate her?"

"Once everyone retires for the night, I'll search the palace."

"How will you know where to look?"

"If she is alive at the whim of Julia, the queen's youngest daughter, she will probably know where Sirona is. I must find Julia's chamber."

"I'll go with you."

Bryn shook his head. "I think it's better if I do this alone. That way, if anything happens, you might still be able to help me escape. Once I've found Sirona, I'll come and get you and we'll find a way out of the palace."

"I hope your plan succeeds," Cadwalon said. "And I hope that

Sirona is worth all this trouble."

"Of course she is," Bryn said fiercely.

* * *

Bryn was amazed. It was late at night and almost everyone in the palace was asleep, yet lamps burned in all the corridors, a huge waste of fuel... but a boon to him. He'd easily seen the sentry, leaning to the side of a doorway, and guessed there must be a prisoner inside. His heart pounded in his chest as he approached the man, not so much from fear as the astounding realization that he might be only moments away from looking upon Sirona's beautiful face.

The sentry straightened as he saw Bryn. "What are you doing here?" he demanded.

"I'm a Drui," Bryn answered. "The queen sent for me. She wants me to discredit the seeress. I would like to speak to this young woman. Sirona—isn't that what she's called?"

"I don't know her name. But she's young, and fine to look upon. It seems a pity that someone so fair should be put to death."

"Is that what the queen has planned?" Bryn asked breathlessly.

The sentry shrugged. "Why else would she be imprisoned here?"

"I must see her." Bryn made his voice stern. "I must meet this woman who's made dire predictions against the queen."

The guard still blocked his way. "You don't look like a Drui."

Bryn gave him a faint, cold smile. "What will it take to convince you? Perhaps I should set a curse upon you. I curse you by the might of the heavens, the weight of the earth, the—"

"Stop!" the guard cried. He stepped aside. "Enter as you will. I want no trouble from the gods."

Bryn went inside. In the light coming through in from the hallway, he could make out a bedplace and someone lying upon it. He started toward the bed and nearly tripped on a straw pallet on the floor.

"Who's here?" a familiar voice called from the pallet.

Bryn's heart thudded in his chest. His mouth felt too dry to speak. "Sirona?" he whispered hoarsely.

Sirona got to her feet. As he glimpsed her face in the light from the doorway, Bryn thought she was every bit as lovely as he remembered, as rare and fine as a snowdrop blossom gleaming white and perfect among the first green foliage of spring.

She stared back at him. "Bryn?" He nodded, too stunned to speak. She let out her breath in a sigh. "Oh, Bryn. It's good to see you." She reached out and embraced him, burying her face in his crys. "I have felt so alone... for so long."

He held her in his arms, overwhelmed with tenderness. "You aren't alone anymore. I'll take you from this place. I'll keep you safe."

She raised her head and said sadly, "If you try to help me escape, we'll both be killed."

"Nay, I won't accept that!"

"Shhh." She put a hand to his mouth. "Don't wake Julia. There are guards everywhere, and Boudica has told them that if I attempt to leave, they should kill me. I don't doubt they'll obey."

"There must be some way out!" he whispered harshly.

"Aye, there will be. The Goddess will guide me safely away from here…when it's time."

"Why won't you let me help you now?"

"Shhh," she said again. "The Goddess has always shown me the way. She's rescued me from death many times. Why would she save my life in the past only to let me perish here?"

"Which Goddess do you speak of?"

"She has many faces: Arianrhod, Lady of the moon; Ceridwen, keeper of the cauldron; Modren, the great mother… "

"I don't need a lesson in the names of the deities!" Bryn whispered in aggravation. Then he implored, "Whoever it is that you put your trust in, consider that she might have sent *me* here to rescue you."

"Nay, the Goddess hasn't spoken yet, telling me what I must do."

Bryn let out a groan of frustration. Sirona hadn't changed. She was still maddeningly stubborn. "Listen. There's not much time. I've been brought here to discredit you. I pretended to be a Drui so I could get into the palace. I knew when I heard there was a seeress imprisoned here that it must be you. There are two other men with me. One is my friend. The other is determined to give the queen what she wants. He will foretell the opposite of whatever you've predicted. Then the queen will order you killed." His insides twisted with anguish at the words.

"If you're found here, you're the one who will be in danger," Sirona insisted. "I still have some protection because Julia has begged her mother to spare my life. Julia has tried very hard to convince her mother that she is better so that Boudica will feel beholden to me for helping her." Sirona looked toward the bedplace where a young woman lay sleeping. "She has a sweet spirit. I hope she will have a good life after this is over."

"I don't care about Boudica's daughter! I care only about you! Please. Come with me now. We'll sneak out of the palace. I'll tell them that we—Cadwalon and I—are taking you away to perform a special ceremony in the forest."

"They'll never believe you."

Bryn clenched his jaw. She was right. He would have to think of a better plan. For a moment, he considered overpowering the man outside the door, taking his sword and using it to fight his way out of the palace. Nay, that would be witless. There were guards and warriors everywhere. He would have to bide his time and hope Sirona remained safe for a little longer.

"Tell me what you told the queen," he said. "I need to know what you did to anger her so greatly."

"I told Boudica that I've seen a vision of a great battle where the Pretani were defeated. I warned her not to meet the Roman army with all her forces in the same place, that she must find some other means of defeating the enemy. Anything to avoid that terrible battle." She shuddered.

Bryn let out his breath in dismay. "The queen lives and breathes vengeance against the Romans. She will fight them any chance she gets. No wonder she's so angry. You've told her that if she throws all her forces against the Romans, she will lose."

"It's true." Sirona nodded emphatically. "If that battle takes place, it's the end for all of us. Our people will be destroyed, annihilated." She trembled in his arms.

Bryn felt a kind of icy dread himself. He fought against it. "Not all visions come true," he asserted. "You told me your mother said I would die in the first battle I fought in, but that clearly didn't come to pass."

"Aye. The future could be different. But only if that great battle doesn't take place."

"The queen's plan is to attack the Roman settlements here in the east. They're said to be poorly defended and very vulnerable."

"But if she does that, it will surely bring the Romans down upon us."

"That's the idea. But in the meantime, we'll have done much to damage their settlements. If we cause them enough difficulty, perhaps they'll give up and leave Albion."

"I doubt the Romans will be so easily discouraged," Sirona said. "If Boudica carries out these raids, the enemy will be very angry. They'll bring all their forces against us. I fear these raids will eventually lead to the battle in my vision." She sighed wearily. Bryn could see how discouraged and helpless she felt. He couldn't blame her. It must be awful being imprisoned here, wondering if she was going to die.

She touched his arm. "Promise me something, Bryn. Promise me that you won't fight in the battle I've seen. At least give me hope you'll survive. Leave this place. Go north, to the midnight lands. You'll have another chance to fight the Romans there."

"I won't run away from my destiny! Even if you tell me I'll die fighting the Romans, I must still do it." He was shaking with the force of his emotions. What did she think, that because he'd trained in the grove, he was a coward? He was a warrior. Death was not something he feared. Not as much as he feared failing the convictions of his heart.

"Oh, you are stubborn, Bryn," she said. "So much like your father. I only hope you don't come to the same end as he did."

"Nay, there's a difference. My father gave in to the enemy. I never will."

"Don't you know what happened to Tarbelinus? Haven't you heard, at least since you came here?"

Bryn grew breathless. "What do you mean? What's happened to Tarbelinus?"

Sirona sighed. "After two years of paying tribute to the Romans, Tarbelinus finally rebelled. He was defeated and taken away in chains. They say he died in Rome, or on the way there."

The ground beneath his feet seemed to shift. His father—dead? His father—led away in chains? "I should have been there," he moaned. "I should have gone back and tried to help him."

"If you'd been there, you would be dead also." Sirona put her hand on his arm. "It must be the will of the gods that you should live."

"Will of the gods—what nonsense!" He shook off her hand, the despair washing over him.

"Aye, the will of the gods that you should live to fight the Romans, to have vengeance for your father's death. But promise me, Bryn, promise you won't take part in the battle I've seen. There will be other chances for you to fight the Romans, I know it."

He hardly heard her words. The last few days he had felt so exhilarated, so full of hope. Now it had all turned to ashes. He hadn't gone back to Mordarach because he was angry with his father. And because of his stubborn pride, his selfishness, his father was dead. He thought of all the times he'd been furious with Tarbelinus. His father had loved him, tried to protect him. And he had repaid Tarbelinus's efforts with defiance and anger.

Sirona leaned near and embraced him, but his grief ruined the satisfaction of having her slender body so close. "Bryn," she said. "You mustn't blame yourself. You were spared for a purpose. The gods want you to live. You have some important destiny yet to fulfill." Her words echoed hollowly. He felt utterly wretched. Gently, she released him. "You must go now. The guard will wonder if you stay too long."

"I can't leave you here," he said in a broken whisper, "I can't fail you as well."

"You won't. Wait for the Goddess to guide you. She will tell you when it's time to come for me."

"What's this?" The sentry entered the room. His voice was sharp and suspicious. "Why is this taking so long?"

Sirona took a step away from Bryn. "Leave me, Drui. There's no more to be said between us."

Chapter 19

Bryn's thoughts were in turmoil as he retraced his steps to the guest chamber he shared with Cadwalon and Ysganon. His father was dead. Knowing that, he felt as if he should return to Mordarach. But that would mean missing this opportunity to fight the Romans and avenge his father's death. For that matter, the members of his tribe probably hated him, especially his mother. He hadn't been there when they needed him. How could he face them under these shameful circumstances? Before he went back, he must make the enemy pay for what they did to Tarbelinus.

Besides, there was Sirona to consider. He must get her out of the palace. Unlike her, he was unwilling to depend on the gods to keep her safe. He must take action himself.

When Bryn entered the bedchamber, Cadwalon was sitting on one of the benches, polishing his dagger, while Ysganon snored from a nearby pallet. "Did you find her?" Cadwalon asked Bryn.

"I found her." Bryn couldn't keep the distress from his voice.

Cadwalon raised his dark brows questioningly. "What's wrong?"

"What's *not* wrong? Sirona is imprisoned here and I can't find a way to get her out. And my father is dead, killed by Romans!"

Cadwalon rose to his feet. "Your father is dead? Sirona told you this?"

Bryn nodded, gritting his teeth in fury and regret. "Tarbelinus finally decided to rebel against the Romans. They defeated him and then took him captive. He died in Rome, or on the way there."

Cadwalon gazed at him sympathetically. "I would be pleased if I heard Cadwyl was dead. But clearly, you don't feel that way about the man who sired you."

"I didn't hate my father... although he sometimes angered me greatly. The thing we argued about most, besides my becoming a warrior, was the Romans. Yet in the end, he decided to fight them and his actions led to his death. I should have been there to aid him, or to die beside him, if that's what it came to." Saying the words, Bryn felt like weeping. Then the anger came and overpowered his grief.

"What purpose would your death serve?" Cadwalon asked. "Then you wouldn't be here to fight beside *me* when we defeat the Romans." He smiled broadly.

Bryn paced across the room. "I learned another troubling thing from Sirona. It seems she's had a vision of a great battle between our people and the Romans. In her vision, we are defeated."

Cadwalon shrugged. "I've never much believed in Seeings or predictions."

"But Sirona has a special connection to the gods. If she sees this thing—" Bryn's anxiety deepened.

"How many of her predictions have come true? Has she always been right?"

Bryn thought hard. Did he believe Sirona was a seeress because her visions had proven true? Or, was it because he loved her?

"I don't know if her vision will come true or not, but that doesn't change the fact we have to get her out of the palace. We've been brought here to discredit Sirona. Once that happens, Boudica will surely kill her." He shook his head. "But Sirona is being difficult. Even if I could think of a means of escape, I fear she'd refuse to leave. She believes the goddess still had a purpose for her here."

Cadwalon said, "From what you say, she's not big enough or strong enough to resist if we carried her away by force."

Bryn wondered if he had the resolve to drag Sirona away against her will. It might save her life, but she would never forgive him. Of course, if he didn't rescue her and she was killed, that would be worse. "I suppose that's what we must do," he said. "But first, we must have a plan."

* * *

Poor Bryn, Sirona thought as she lay on the pallet beside Julia's bed. If only she hadn't had to tell him about Tarbelinus. His response when he learned what had happened to his father had nearly broken her heart. Yet, despite everything, it had been wonderful to see him. What a strong, well-made warrior he had become. The sight of his proud, handsome face and broad, muscular form had made her want to collapse into his arms. To lean on him and forget all her troubles. But she couldn't allow herself to do that. There was something else she was supposed to accomplish here. Another piece of the pattern must be woven.

She felt the tears slip down her face as she wondered if she would ever see Bryn again. But she could not dwell on that. Her life was not her own. She'd known that ever since the wolf came and guided her on her journey north. It was her destiny to follow the will of the Goddess wherever it led her, even if it meant ignoring what was in her heart.

The thought provoked a deep throb of grief inside her. She clutched the goddess stone for comfort, but even that didn't entirely ease her pain. Shifting position on her pallet, she sought the oblivion of sleep.

She woke what seemed like only a short while later to find Sybilla,

Julia's sister, standing over her.

"I knew you were a healer," Sybilla said. "But I recently heard you trained as a Drui. Is that true?"

Sirona immediately grew wary. Sybilla reminded her of Boudica, radiating the same implacable will and dangerous energy as the queen. "I spent a number of years training in the grove," she answered.

"Good. I have need of one such as you. Come with me."

Sirona sat up. She could tell from the light filtering in through the window that it was morning. "But your mother said I shouldn't leave this room."

"The guards won't gainsay *me*," Sybilla said in a cold voice. "Now, come with me."

"Where's Julia?" Sirona asked as she noticed the bedplace was empty.

"I told her that our mother wished to speak to her. It will do her good to leave this room for a time."

Sirona got up, feeling uneasy. But she could think of no way to refuse Sybilla.

They left the bedchamber. As Sybilla had predicted, the guard didn't try to stop them. Sybilla took Sirona to the palace garden. In an area set off from the neatly cultivated plants, two workmen were building a small structure out of stone. Sybilla ordered them to go away and said, "When this is finished, it will be a temple. Every temple needs a priestess or priest. You could be the one who served here."

Sirona was startled. Boudica wanted only to be rid of her. Now her daughter was offering a place in the palace household. To give herself time to think, she asked, "Why build a temple here?"

Sybilla gave her a hostile look. "It's traditional to have a household temple close by. Besides, this is a special temple, dedicated for a special purpose."

"I would need to know what that purpose is. Especially if you wished me to serve as guardian of the place."

Sybilla began to pace. Her face was set in a grim mask. "They say you are a devotee of the Goddess, so you must know that one of the faces of the Goddess is death. She is also a protector, ruthlessly guarding her children and punishing those who would hurt them. This temple will to be dedicated to Andrasta, the deity who oversees war and vengeance."

Sirona glanced at the growing pile of stones that would form the temple. Blood would be shed here. She could smell it. The sickly sweet odor of death. And fear. The rites and rituals honoring Andrasta would involve the killing of some helpless creature as Sybilla called upon the Goddess to destroy her enemies.

"I'm sorry. I can't serve as your priestess." Sirona tried to sound regretful. "I worship a different aspect of the Goddess. I worship her as she represents birth and healing, the rhythmic passage of the seasons and the endless circle of life. It's true the Great Mother has a dark side, but I choose not to dwell upon it." She touched the amulet hanging between her breasts. "My Goddess is of the earth, of growing things and sunshine and healing. If She brings death, it is because it's the natural way of things, part of the timeless, ancient pattern."

"You're a fool!" Sybilla spat out. "Someday you'll suffer some horrible offense at the hands of men and then you'll understand. Then you'll also want vengeance. You'll yearn for someone to pay, to suffer!"

Sirona repressed a shudder at Sybilla's rage. And yet, how would she react if she had to endure what Julia and Sybilla had endured? Would she not also hate men, and Romans especially? Nay, that wasn't right. Those who pursued the dark side of the gods found only more darkness awaiting them.

"I'm sorry," she said again. "I don't think I'm the right person to perform the ceremonies you desire."

Sybilla glared at her. "I can't believe your stupidity, to refuse power when it's offered. You and my weak, whiny sister deserve each other!"

Sirona bowed her head, hoping Sybilla would leave her. Instead, Julia's sister continued to pace around the half-finished temple. "I don't need you," Sybilla ground out. "I'll find another way to get my vengeance. You'll see. Soon my mother will lead all the warriors gathered here into battle. They'll attack the settlement of Camulodunum and kill everyone. Not a soul will be spared. The women especially." Sybilla smiled coldly. "I will make sure they suffer as I have suffered."

Sirona was alarmed. She remembered her dream of the woman and her baby being brutally slaughtered. "That seems very cruel."

"You don't understand," Sybilla said. "They *must* be destroyed." She looked at Sirona, her blue eyes wild. "They've bred with the hated Romans. They must die and their half-Roman whelps also."

Was this some delusion of Sybilla's disordered mind? Or did Boudica truly intend that the vast army gathered outside the palace should kill everyone in the Roman settlements?

"Does your mother know about these things?" Sirona asked.

"Of course. It was her idea."

Sirona stood there, stunned and shocked as Sybilla strode away. Memories of past Seeings filled her mind. The woman being cut down by a Pretani warrior. The baby flying through the air. The glowing flames behind Boudica. The people screaming. The rank odor of roasting flesh. It seemed that her horrifying visions were about to come true. Sickened, she sank down to her knees next to a bed of herbs and closed her eyes.

"What is it? Are you having a vision?"

Weakly, she looked up. A boy of about ten or twelve winters stood a short distance away, watching her. Her gaze took in his plain crys and the burdens he carried. She guessed he must be a slave and was surprised he had the courage to speak to her. When she didn't answer his question, he persisted, "Tell me what you see," he said. "I want to know if you truly have the Sight."

She stood wearily, wishing he would go away.

"You must have seen something bad." The boy's dark eyes focused on her intently. "You look very pale."

"Aye, it was awful," she finally answered. "I have no desire to talk about it."

The boy took a step nearer. "That means you really are a seeress. If you were a fraud, you would tell everyone what you saw. You would want all to know about your powers."

Sirona sighed wearily. "Aye, I'm a seeress. It's a terrible gift."

The boy moved even closer. She could see the dusting of freckles on his nose and the glint of red in his brown hair. He looked Pretani, but with some kind of foreign blood mixed in. "I would make a bargain with you," he said in a low voice. "If you'll help me find my sister, I'll help you escape." He put down his burdens, a basket of bannocks and a steaming cauldron, and leaned close to whisper, "The queen plans to kill you. It will be something subtle, an accident. But you'll end up just as dead."

A tremor of fear traced down Sirona's spine. She frowned at the youth. "You want me to help you find your sister? How am I supposed to do that?"

"Maybe you could see her in a vision and tell me where she is."

Sirona shook her head. "The power isn't mine to command. I can't *will* visions to come to me."

The boy looked disappointed. Then his face brightened. "You could try. But first, we must get you away from here. I have a plan. Tonight there will be a ceremony in the garden. The three Drui Boudica has brought to the palace will sacrifice a bullock and predict the future. But they're frauds." His mouth twisted in disgust. "I've seen them. They have no more influence with the gods than I do. But they will tell Boudica what she wants to hear. Anyway," he continued, "while the queen is busy at the ceremony, I'll come to Julia's room and take you out of the palace."

"There are guards everywhere, with orders to kill me if I try to escape."

"Boudica will want everyone in the household to observe the ceremony. The only people who won't be in the garden are the slaves, and most of them think as I do. They would be pleased to see you escape. They want to see the queen thwarted."

Sirona nodded. This was the opportunity she'd been waiting for. Her instincts told her the Goddess had sent this youth to help her.

The boy looked around the garden, then back at her. "What do you say? Is it a bargain?"

She nodded. "If you help me escape, I'll try to do what you wish. Although I can't promise I'll be able to help find your sister."

He smiled suddenly, showing slightly crooked teeth. "I must get back to the stables. But I'll see you tonight."

He picked up his supplies and prepared to leave. "Wait," Sirona called. "What's your name?"

"I'm Rufus," he said. This time, his smile was bitter as he turned to look at her. "A stable boy… and Prasutagus's bastard."

* * *

There was a knock on the door. Bryn rushed to open it, thinking it must be Cadwalon. Outside was the slave who had come to Gwynceffyl's camp. "The queen says to tell you that the ceremony will be held tonight."

Bryn was alarmed. Only moments before, Cadwalon had gone to tell Sirona about their plan, which was to convince Boudica that they needed to leave the palace to seek out a white bullock. They would pretend Sirona was a slave boy sent along to lead the animal back to the palace. Cadwalon had gone to fetch Sirona while Bryn went to the queen. But if a bullock had already been found, their scheme would never work. "Have they found a white animal already?" Bryn demanded.

"The sacrificial animal is waiting in the garden."

Bryn repressed a groan. "Are you certain the animal is suitable? It must be all white or nearly white, or the sacrifice won't be as powerful."

"If the queen is satisfied, that's all that matters."

"But it's not even twilight yet," Bryn protested, desperate to find some reason to delay. "The ritual should be held after dark, under the light of the Hay Moon, which won't be full for several nights."

The slave looked at him as if he had lost his wits. "This is the queen's command. She expects you to obey."

Ysganon came up beside Bryn. "Tell the queen we'll be there soon. First, we must change into our ceremonial garments."

When the servant had left, Bryn paced across the room in agitation. "We can't leave until Cadwalon returns."

"Where has he gone?" Ysganon asked.

Bryn struggled to think of some way to convince Ysganon they must delay the ceremony. Nothing came to him.

Ysganon put on a clean crys. Then he looked at Bryn and said, "We must not keep the queen waiting."

* * *

Bryn stood in the garden beside Ysganon, his stomach churning. Clearly, he should have tried to get Sirona away the night before. Now it was too late.

He tried to calm himself and regain his composure. Glancing around the garden, his gaze fell upon the neat rows of plants and shrubbery, the gravel walkways and stone statues. He experienced a wave of disgust. Here was more evidence that Boudica lived like a Roman. The only reason she wanted to attack the enemy was that she was angry at them for throwing her out of her home and abusing her and her daughters. She cared little for her own people. Her purpose was simply to satisfy her own sense of vengeance. Even this ceremony was a mockery. Boudica didn't want to hear the will of the gods. She wanted only to hear that she would gain a great victory. If they foretold anything different, she would have them expelled from the palace or killed.

The thought reminded him of Sirona and his stomach lurched with fear. As he shifted his weight, he made up his mind. If Boudica killed Sirona, he would kill her.

"Stop fidgeting," Ysganon spoke beside him. "It's unseemly for a Drui to act like an impatient child."

Bryn sought to focus on something besides his inner turmoil. As he looked around, he saw something odd on the other side of the garden. There was a kind of half-built structure. In front of it were several dead hares, their fur caked with dried blood. What was this? he wondered. Some kind of sacrifice?

"The queen is coming," Ysganon whispered. "If you value your life, I would advise you to allow me to perform the ceremony as I see fit. I'll make certain to please her."

Bryn let out his breath in a sigh. What choice did he have?

A moment later, he caught a glimpse of the moon, rising above the roof of the palace. It was only a few nights from being full. He wondered if he would still be alive by then. As he concentrated on the three-quarter circle of light, a strange sense came over him. It was almost as if he could feel Arianrhod's presence, pure and serene and beautiful. Was this what Sirona meant when she spoke of the Goddess? *Please let Sirona be safe,* he silently implored the Lady of the moon. *Please.*

He clung to the thought as the queen entered the garden, followed by what appeared to be most of her household. Boudica wore a crimson mantle and a patterned gown of saffron and scarlet. With her vivid red hair, she reminded Bryn of a burning flame. The mantle was thrown over her shoulder, revealing her bare, well-muscled arms, gleaming white

202

against the bright colors of her garments. Around her right wrist was wrapped a gold armband with the ends shaped like the head and tail of a serpent. The jewelry was so cunningly fashioned it seemed as if a real snake was curled around her arm.

Immediately behind the queen walked her two daughters. Both had red hair, but there the similarity ended. One young woman's features mirrored the cold arrogance of Boudica. The other had a much softer, sweeter countenance. Bryn knew instantly which one must be Julia.

Boudica nodded to Ysganon and Bryn to indicate they should begin. Ysganon approached the bullock, raised his arms to the heavens and began to call down the gods. Bryn watched, cynically observing Ysganon's performance. The Drui was very convincing. His voice was powerful, his manner, confident and assured. He named the major deities and their attributes and then paused. "Now, we call upon the Triple Goddess," he intoned, eyes closed, arms raised. "She who presides over war, death and destruction. Morrigan, the raven of death. Andrasta, the invincible one. Brigantia, the goddess of victory. We ask Her blessing upon us, that she might strike down our enemies and destroy them."

A chill went down Bryn's spine. He'd never attended a ceremony where Morrigan, the phantom queen of death and destruction, was invoked. To name her was to call upon the darkest forces of the spiritual realm. Her power was terrible and indiscriminate. She *was* Death, and she carried off the spirits of the fallen, be they the enemy or your own people. To Bryn, it seemed like an ill omen. But Boudica was clearly pleased. He saw her smile and nod her head.

Ysganon removed his ceremonial knife from his satchel and held it up so it shimmered in the torchlight. He motioned to Bryn to come forward and hold the bullock.

The sacrifice continued. Bryn, his thoughts on Sirona, was only vaguely aware of the things going on around him: The bullock's low bellow. The way its head jerked when the knife went into its neck. The faintly sweet scent of blood, mingling with the odor of fresh dung. The animal slumping to the ground as its lifeforce drained away.

Ysganon was talking again, commanding Bryn to help turn the animal on its side so he could open the belly. Although Bryn had heard of the practice of divining the future from the appearance of the intestines of the sacrificial animal, the Tarisllwyth Learned Ones had never performed the ritual. It seemed odd to think the gods would speak by the means of a bullock's entrails. But he supposed Ysganon favored the practice because it gave him an opportunity to claim he knew the gods' will.

With the help of two slaves, they moved the carcass on its side and exposed the beast's belly. Ysganon rolled up his sleeves, and then used the ceremonial knife to slit the animal open. As the slimy entrails spilled onto the ground, they reminded Bryn of a swarm of snakes.

Ysganon crouched down and began to poke at the intestines with his staff. Then he slowly stood and faced the queen. His eyes were closed, his expression still and solemn. He opened his eyes. "The gods have spoken!" he cried out in a booming voice. He raised his staff. "We must march into battle as soon as possible. If we do this, then the gods will grant us victory. A great victory! They will strike down our enemies! The blood of the Romans will flow in rivers! Their bodies will cover the land! Their heads will lie in piles as an offering to Morrigan!"

Ysganon's gaze was wild and his face suffused with color. Bryn decided that this was one of the most skilled pretenders he had ever witnessed. He watched in amazement as the old Drui went rigid. His body jerked and twisted and he fell to the ground. His eyes were wide open now, staring straight ahead. Bryn waited with the rest of them, expecting Ysganon to get up and continue his tirade. But there was no movement in his face or body. After a time Bryn realized Ysganon was dead.

The realization shocked him. He glanced around. Some of the people gathered there also looked stunned. But Boudica couldn't have been more pleased. She gave a wild, triumphant laugh. "You heard him!" she exclaimed. "The gods are with us! They have spoken through this man, Ysganon, their servant! And to confirm the truth of his words, they have taken his spirit back with them to the Otherworld! We will triumph! We will prevail against our enemies! The streets of Camulodunum will run red with blood!"

Bryn's insides curdled with revulsion and fear. Something strange had happened here. It was almost as if the goddess of death had truly been invoked.

"You, Drui, come here."

Bryn realized Boudica was speaking to him. He walked to where the queen stood.

"You must carry news of this to my army," she said. "Tell them what has taken place here. They must hear that the gods have promised us victory. But, nay," she raised her hand abruptly. "*I* will tell them." She smiled. "Go to the warriors' camp and order them to assemble outside the gates before dawn. There I will speak to them and explain that our victory has been assured by the gods!"

She raised her arm in a gesture of triumph. As she did so, it seemed the snake bracelet came to life and hissed at Bryn.

"Come on." Someone touched his shoulder. He turned and saw Cadwalon. "We must do as the queen bids," he said.

* * *

204

As soon as they were out of earshot of Boudica and her daughters, Bryn asked Cadwalon in a frantic voice, "Where's Sirona? Is she safe?"

"She's gone."

"Gone?"

Cadwalon nodded. "I went to Julia's bedchamber. There was no one there. I saw a female servant in the hall outside and asked her where the seeress was. The woman gave me an odd look and then said she didn't know. I asked another servant, and they acted the same. I think Sirona has escaped."

"What makes you believe that?"

"Where else would she have gone?"

"Boudica might have...done something to her." Bryn winced as he said this.

"I don't think so. If the queen had her killed, then someone would know of it. Slaves and servants always gossip."

Was it possible Sirona had gotten away? Perhaps the Great Mother had helped her escape. But he couldn't take the matter on trust. He had to know for certain. "I must go back," he told Cadwalon. "I must find out what happened to Sirona."

His companion nodded. "I'll go to the warriors' camp and give them Boudica's message. Meet me at the Iceni gathering hall as soon as you can."

Bryn hurried back to the palace. As he neared the entrance, a man stepped into his pathway. "Are you Bryn of the Tarisllwyth?" the man asked.

"I am."

"I have a message for you: The seeress has left the palace."

Bryn shifted so he could see the man better. His face was weathered and old and he wore the plain crys of a slave. Bryn remained suspicious. "Why should I believe you?"

"I have no reason to lie."

"Where has she gone?"

"Is it not enough that she is safe?" The man turned and began to walk away. Bryn considered following him and then realized he was being foolish. Why would Sirona tell a slave where she was going? The fewer people who knew, the safer she would be. Sirona knew to travel far away from this place, somewhere Boudica couldn't find her.

He let out his breath and allowed the sense of relief to fill him. The Goddess had answered his petition. He would never doubt Her again.

Chapter 20

"Oh my! I think I'm going to be sick," Sirona groaned as she balanced in the chariot, gripping the side of the vehicle with all her might.

"Open your eyes," Rufus ordered. "And stop thinking you'll fall. Instead, consider how rapidly we're leaving the palace behind. By the time the queen knows we're gone, we'll be far, far away."

"I hope she doesn't punish Julia for my escape," Sirona said. "I worry Boudica will blame her."

"Julia was in the garden at the time, doing her mother's will. If anyone is punished, it will be the sentry. And it serves him right for being distracted from his post by a comely slave girl."

"What if Boudica punishes the slave girl?" Sirona asked, thinking of the thin, nervous young woman who had enticed the guard.

"I don't think the guard will be stupid enough to mention her," Rufus said. "If he has any sense, he'll think up a much better reason for why he left you unguarded. He might say you vanished. Already there's talk among the slaves that you have magical powers."

"If I had magical powers, I would find some other means of travel!"

"You'll grow used to it, I promise."

Sirona wondered if this was true. It had been a shock to realize they were going to escape in a chariot. After Rufus sneaked her out of the palace, he took her to the stables where the vehicle waited. He told her to crouch down in the base of the chariot next to the baskets and bags of supplies and then covered her up with a cowhide. At the gate he told the sentries he was taking the chariot to a warrior who'd been called back to his tribe. The guards waved them through and they set off down the bumpy trackway.

Crowded in with the supplies, Sirona endured the teeth-rattling, bone-jarring ride until Rufus decided they were far enough away from the palace that it was safe for her to stand up. But standing had other disadvantages. Although she was more comfortable, the sight of the scenery whipping past unnerved her. "How much farther?" she asked.

"If we can make it to the forest, we should be safe. We'll spend the night there."

"And then?"

"That's up to you, lady. You're the seeress."

Sirona tried to decide what to do. She'd traveled here to tell Boudica about her vision and attempt to change the future that way. That plan hadn't succeeded, but she couldn't give up. She must trust the Goddess to tell her what to do next.

Sirona shivered at the thought of her narrow escape, then abruptly realized Rufus was right. For a moment, she had forgotten she was riding in a chariot. Perhaps it was because it was darker here beyond the torchlights of the army camp and she wasn't so aware of the scenery spinning past. Squinting, she glimpsed trees ahead. Rufus reined in the horses and the vehicle slowed.

When they halted, he told her to get out while he drove the chariot deep into a thicket of hazel. Afterwards, he unharnessed the horses and rubbed them down, all the while speaking to them in a soft, crooning voice. He hobbled the team so they couldn't wander away. Then he and Sirona took the supplies out of the chariot.

"How did you come by all these things?" she asked as she observed rolled-up sheepskins, blankets, full beverage skins and bags of food.

"The slaves in the palace were eager to see you get away safely. From the cooks in the kitchen to the men in the stables, they all wanted to make certain you had what you needed."

"But why?" Sirona asked. "Is it because they despise Boudica and wish to thwart her?"

"In part. And then there's the fact that you helped Julia, the one member of the queen's household who's looked upon with fondness. Besides, you're a seeress."

"Aye, a seeress no one will listen to," Sirona said glumly.

"*I'll* listen." Rufus paused in unrolling a sheepskin. "Indeed, as soon as you're rested, I would ask you to use your powers to tell me how to find my sister."

Sirona grew uncomfortable. She'd never done anything like what Rufus wanted. "Why do you think I can help you?"

"Julia said that when you spoke, she could feel the power of gods flowing through you."

"I wish I could have said goodbye to her."

"She will have to be content to know that you're safe. Like everyone else, she understood you had to flee the palace. Boudica intended to kill you as soon as she found a way to discredit you. That was the purpose of the ceremony being held tonight."

Sirona thought of Bryn pretending to be a Drui. She hoped he was able to leave the palace before Boudica discovered he wasn't really a Learned One. That thought of Boudica confronting him chilled Sirona. But if she believed the Goddess was protecting her, she could hope the deity was also protecting Bryn.

Turning her attention back to the present, she realized Rufus was waiting for her to use her "powers" to help him. "Come sit next to me," she told him. "I'll try to help you discover where your sister is."

He scrambled to obey, sitting cross-legged opposite her on one of the sheepskins.

"First, you must tell me a little about how you came to be a slave in Boudica's household. Is true you are the son of her dead husband?"

"It's true. My mother was a slave, a Roman. She was beautiful. Prasutagus lusted after her and took her to his bed. But when my sister and I were born, he refused to recognize us as his offspring."

Sirona was surprised. Among her people, no man would reject a son, even if his mother was a slave.

"Though he wouldn't acknowledge us, Prasutagus made certain we were well treated," Rufus continued. "Our lives were tolerable. I helped run errands for the household and Dacia did weaving and sewing. But then Prasutagus took sick, and Boudica had my sister sent to the slavers' market in Londinium to be sold as a bedslave. She was barely twelve years old." Rufus voice hovered on the edge of tears. "I was sent to the stables. I suppose it's not so bad a life, since I love horses. But my sister… I miss her terribly. Before, although we worked in different parts of the palace, we slept in the same room and talked every night. We were close, as close as when we shared our mother's womb."

"You were twins?" Sirona asked in surprise. She knew from Nesta that when a woman carried two babies, often one or both wouldn't survive.

Rufus nodded. "Perhaps that's why I'm so small for my age. We were born early, but healthy enough."

"No wonder the bond between you is so strong," Sirona said.

"Now you understand why I must find out what happened to her." Rufus's voice was anguished. "I must try to rescue Dacia. For over a year, that's been my plan, to go to Londinium and search for her."

Sirona felt a twinge of warning at the thought of Rufus searching for his sister. Her instinctive response worried her. Was his sister dead? Was that why she experienced this sense of foreboding? She thought of Risa, Calpurnius's daughter, and how she'd felt her presence in the bedchamber. When she touched the necklace belonging to the young woman, she'd known she was dead. "Do you possess anything that belonged to your sister?" she asked. "A garment perhaps?"

Rufus went to the chariot and searched in one of the bundles. He returned holding a small bronze object. "It's one of my mother's earbobs," he said. "She gave one to each of us when before she was sent away. Although this one didn't belong to my sister, it represents the link between us."

Sirona took the earbob in her hand. Closing her eyes, she sought out the spirit of the slave girl named Dacia. A vision filled her mind. The young woman had large, dark eyes framed by thick black lashes and surrounded by some sort of paint that made them appear even darker. She reclined naked on a bench. Her full breasts thrust up enticingly and her legs were parted, revealing her sex. She smiled and gestured to the man, urging him nearer. He approached the bench, leaned down and put his mouth on hers. His hands moved over her body. She writhed and moaned, seemingly enjoying his touch. But as he stood to remove his clothing, she glanced at the table next to the bed where a small pile of coins lay. Her brief, faint smile said that she took her pleasure not from the man's body but from the silver he paid her.

Sirona opened her eyes, deeply unsettled by what she had seen. "What does your sister look like?" she asked Rufus.

"Like our mother. Dark hair, black eyes and dusky skin. I'm the one who resembles Prasutagus, for all the good it did me. Dacia is all Roman."

Sirona had no doubt the young woman in her vision was Dacia. She also felt certain Dacia didn't want to be rescued because she had chosen the life she was living. Even more compelling was her sense that if Rufus tried to search for his sister, he would end up in great danger.

As Sirona chewed her lower lip, trying to decide what to do, Rufus demanded, "What's wrong? Why don't you speak?" When she still didn't say anything, he exhaled sharply. "I have to know, even if it's something awful."

Sirona nodded. "I saw her. She's alive. And yet… there's no way you can search for her. She's been taken across the sea, back to Rome. But never fear. She isn't being mistreated. Indeed, she seems content with her life."

"Content? How can she be content? She's a bed slave!"

"Was your mother content with her life when your father was alive?"

Rufus stared back at her. "I… I suppose so," he finally answered, frowning.

"Well, that's the way of it with Dacia. She has found a situation that pleases her."

Rufus was silent for a time. Then he let out a deep sigh. "Now what do I do? I've planned for years to rescue Dacia. Now I have no purpose. No reason to live except to avenge myself against Boudica." He began to kick at the nearby vegetation. "She's the reason my sister was sent away.

I hate her! I want her to die! I should go back to the palace this night and kill her!"

The thought of Rufus taking on the huge warriors who guarded the queen filled Sirona dread. She couldn't let him throw his life away. "Listen to me," she pleaded. "If you try such a thing, you'll be killed, and that would be a terrible waste. You mustn't concern yourself with getting revenge against Boudica. If what I've seen in my vision is true, the queen will eventually lose everything that matters to her. She will suffer, and suffer greatly."

And so will hundreds of my countrymen, Sirona thought grimly.

Images of death filled her mind, memories of her Seeings. The one that distressed her most was her dream of the young mother being cut down and her baby brutally killed. Somehow she had to stop that part of it. It was one thing for warriors to die in battle, but much more dreadful for women and children to endure the same fate. Abruptly, she knew what she must do. She stood up. "Don't go back to the palace," she told Rufus. "I need you to drive the chariot and take me to Camulodunum."

"Camulodunum? Why do you want to go there?"

"Because I have to warn them what Boudica intends." Sirona wrapped her arms around her body as the sickening images filled her mind. "She will slaughter everyone living there. Everyone. Even the children. The babes in their cradles."

"I agree it would be good to see Boudica's plans ruined, but I thought you were on the side of the Pretani. If you warn the people of Camulodunum what Boudica intends, they'll send for the ninth legion, stationed at a fortress in the north. The Romans will sweep down and attack Boudica's forces. Even though her army is large, I'm not certain it's large enough to defeat the Romans. They are very disciplined, cunning fighters. When Prasutagus was alive and allied with them, the Romans used to visit the old palace. I was very impressed with their weaponry and their shrewd outlook. They don't lose their heads like the Pretani do. If Boudica's army were to meet the Roman army at Camulodunum, my wager would have to be on the Romans."

Sirona felt a stirring of alarm. This must be the battle of her vision. The ninth legion would come south and confront Boudica's army and defeat them. But what if a few things were changed? If events happened differently, the destiny of her people might be altered. What if instead of attacking Camulodunum, Boudica's army drove north to meet the Romans before the enemy knew what was happening? Or, even better, what if Boudica's army lay in wait to ambush the Romans?

She sucked in her breath. Finally she'd thought of a way to use her knowledge of the future prevent the disaster facing her people.

But how to make it happen? There was no point in her going back to the palace and trying to convince Boudica to change her plans. The queen would have her killed before she had a chance to open her mouth. She must convince someone else of her idea. *Bryn.* He was a warrior, although posing as a Drui. Boudica might listen to him.

"I need you to help me," she told Rufus excitedly. "I need you to go to the palace and fetch a man called Bryn ap Tarbelinus. He's pretending to be a Drui, although he is really more warrior than Learned One. I need you to find this man and bring him here."

"Now? Tonight?"

"Aye. There's no time to waste. I've thought of a way to save my people."

"What about Boudica?" Rufus asked. "What about making certain she is punished for what she did to Dacia?"

"Some things are more important than vengeance," Sirona said sternly. "Vengeance is concerned with things in the past. It's better to focus on the future." She could sense Rufus wasn't convinced, and she felt a sudden apprehension that he might try to kill Boudica while he was at the palace.

She grabbed his arm. "You must do this for me," she told him. "For me and the Goddess. If you believe I have power and a special connection to the gods, you have to listen to me. Find this man and bring him here. Don't become distracted or tarry while you're at the palace. You must make haste."

"I will do as you bid," Rufus said. "Although my hatred for Boudica burns fierce in my breast, I owe you for telling me my sister's fate. I will find this Bryn and bring him here."

* * *

Bryn lay on his bedroll outside the feast hall of the Iceni and tried to block out the sounds of revelry and celebration coming from within. Fools, he thought. The time to celebrate was *after* they had taken Camulodunum. Victory was not assured, not at all. If only they knew what an imposter Ysganon was. But then, it was probably better they didn't. A confident army had a better chance of prevailing than an apprehensive one. And for all he loathed the queen's gloating outlook, he couldn't help sharing a bit of their enthusiasm. It would be good to finally march into battle.

Although it was hard to tell when they would actually set out. Another example of Boudica's arrogance and poor planning. Tomorrow most of her army would have aching heads and muddled wits after staying up all night celebrating a victory that hadn't yet happened. At this rate, they wouldn't set out until the next day, or even the day after.

He plugged his ears with his fingers, but sleep still refused to come. He kept thinking about Sirona. The message she had escaped had eased some of his fears, but he was still worried for her. He hoped by now she was far, far away. Would he ever see her again? There was every chance he might die in the upcoming battle. Why hadn't he told her what she meant to him when he saw her in the palace?

Their meeting had been so rushed, so chaotic and confused. The news about his father had distressed him, and kept him from properly appreciating the joy of seeing Sirona and holding her in his arms. His worries for her safety had distracted him even more. Now he realized he might have missed his only opportunity to tell her he loved her. *Please, Great Mother, grant me the chance to be with Sirona once again in this life.*

He'd barely had the thought when he felt someone shaking him. Opening his eyes, he sat upright. Cadwalon stood over him, smiling drunkenly. "There's someone here to see you, Bryn," he slurred. "A slave boy. Says he has a message from Sirona."

Bryn was on his feet in seconds. He looked the boy up and down. His reddish hair and dark eyes made him look like some sort of Pretani-Roman mongrel. "What is it? Where's Sirona? Is she safe?"

"You're Bryn?"

"Aye."

"You're supposed to come with me." The boy started off.

"Wait," Bryn called. "Let me dress… and get my sword."

The boy stood by impatiently while Bryn pulled on his warrior's crys and got his weapon.

"Perhaps I should go with you," Cadwalon said.

"You wouldn't be much use in your current condition," Bryn said as he strapped on his swordbelt. "You look as if you've drunk a whole lake of wine."

"Nay, a river," Cadwalon drawled, grinning. He grew serious. "Maybe it's a trap. Have you thought of that? Maybe the queen has discovered Sirona is missing and thinks you're responsible."

Bryn glanced at the slave boy, shifting restlessly from one foot to the other. "You, there," he called to the boy. "Prove to me that your message comes from Sirona and not from the queen."

"The queen?" The boy's features contorted. "I would never do the queen's bidding, the evil sow!"

Bryn looked at Cadwalon, who shrugged. "All right," Cadwalon said. "But you must be careful."

"I will." To the slave boy, Bryn said, "Where are you taking me?"

"Sirona waits at the other end of the valley."

They set out, making their way through the noisy camp and past the paddocks where the horses shifted and nickered in the darkness. The moon shone high in the sky, reminding Bryn of his petition to Arianrhod. It was almost magical how quickly the goddess had responded to his plea. He was going to have another chance to speak to Sirona. His heart soared at the thought.

The boy trudged on ahead, his breathing faintly labored. It was a long walk. Along the way Bryn tried to get the slave boy to tell him more, but the youth refused.

When the reached the other end of the valley and entered the forest, Bryn felt a shiver of unease. The boy seemed harmless enough, but it was still eerie to follow a stranger into the darkened woods. They'd already gone farther than he had expected. Of course, Sirona had to hide somewhere the queen couldn't find her.

All at once, the boy—who'd said his name was Rufus—halted so abruptly that Bryn almost ran into him. "Wait here," the boy said.

Bryn did so, glancing around warily. He could see very little. Only small dappled patches of moonlight filtered down through the dense foliage. Then a familiar slender figure appeared and his heart soared in his chest. "Sirona," he breathed. "I'm so glad you sent for me. There's much I wish to say to you."

"And I to you. I've thought of a way to keep our people from being defeated." She sounded excited. "You must convince Boudica to plan an ambush. The ninth legion is north of here. Once they know of the threat to Camulodunum, they'll march south to the colonia's rescue. Boudica's forces must hide somewhere along their route and fall upon them while they're still unprepared to engage in battle. If you can kill enough of them before they reach Camulodunum, I believe the battle of my vision can be avoided!"

Bryn was stunned. Of all the things he'd expected to discuss with Sirona, Boudica's battle strategy was not one of them.

"Will you do this?" she demanded. "Will you try to convince Boudica to alter her plan to attack Camulodunum?"

"I don't know. And...I have questions. If we don't attack Camulodunum, why would the ninth legion come south?"

"They could hear a rumor that Camulodunum is in danger."

"It would take more than a rumor to make the Romans set a whole legion on the march. And if they only send part of their forces south, the ambush won't be effective. But it's a good idea," he added. "After we destroy Camulodunum, a part of the Pretani army could go north and lie in wait for the ninth."

"Destroy Camulodunum! So you are like the rest of them, eager to shed the blood of innocents? To slaughter helpless women and children?"

Sirona sounded furious. He couldn't imagine why she was so upset. "We must take the colonia in order to show the Romans it's not safe for their people to settle here," he told her patiently. "Doubtless, some who aren't warriors will die. It's the way of war. But remember, this isn't some skirmish between tribes over cattle or territory. This is a struggle to the death, to see who will survive and possess this island." It was the truth. They couldn't afford to be soft in their dealings with the Romans. "Did the enemy consider the welfare of the Tarisllwyth when they carried my father off in chains? Nay, they did not. Why then should I worry for their people?"

Sirona let out a moan. "If you could see the things I have seen in my visions, you might feel differently. Blood... slaughter... fire and destruction... "

Bryn tried to soften his voice. "Of course, it's hard for you to accept these things. You're a woman. Your nature is tender and compassionate. You're also a Learned One, accustomed to dealing in matters of knowledge and spirit, rather than the brutal realm of war."

Sirona made another sound of distress, and Bryn considered how poorly things were going. When he saw her a few days before, Sirona had clung to him. Now she was upset and distant. How could he reach her? He touched her arm. "Someday this will all be finished. Then you and I can go back to Mordarach and make a new beginning."

She shook off his hand. "What makes you think either of us will be alive by the end of the sunseason? I fear there are terrible things ahead, for both of us."

Her words filled him with dread. She was a seeress. If she feared the future, it must be awful indeed. That thought made him decide to risk everything. "If we're going to die, then I want you to know... " He hesitated, and then plunged on. "I want you to know that I love you and would do anything for you." He took a step nearer and pulled her into his arms. "Let's make a vow to be together, to handfast," he whispered against her hair.

Two heartbeats. Three. Four. Still she didn't answer. He began to lose hope, but at least she hadn't pulled away. He felt a tremor move down her body. "I can't promise you anything," she finally said. "The Goddess guides my destiny. I'm not free to follow my heart."

His spirits lifted. Her words implied she returned his affections, that if the Goddess allowed it, she would agree to be his wife.

She gently disengaged herself from his embrace. "Now, go to the palace and talk to the queen. Suggest this new strategy to her. Convince her that destroying the colonia of Camulodunum won't accomplish what she desires."

"I'll do my best," he said. "For you, I would do anything." He grabbed her hand and squeezed it.

* * *

After Bryn left, Sirona could still feel the warmth of his embrace like a mantle around her, banishing the sense of loneliness and loss she'd felt since leaving Mordarach. Did that mean she loved Bryn? She forced the thought from her mind. The future was still terribly uncertain. Whatever she felt for Bryn, she couldn't act on those feelings yet. She had too many responsibilities yet to fulfill.

Rufus appeared beside her. "Now what?" he asked.

"We wait to see what the queen decides," Sirona answered. "We might as well try to sleep. I don't expect Bryn to return until morning."

* * *

Bryn hurried back to the Iceni camp as fast as his legs could carry him. Once there, it took him a while to find Cadwalon, passed out near the hearth in the Iceni gathering hall.

"Where's Sirona?" Cadwalon asked groggily when Bryn roused him.

"Still in the forest. She wants me to go to the palace and speak to Boudica."

Cadwalon groaned and swiped a hand through his hair. "What does Sirona want with the queen?"

"She wants me to convince her to change her battle tactics."

"What?"

Bryn told him of Sirona's plan. "It's a clever notion," Cadwalon said when he finished. "But that doesn't mean Boudica will agree."

"She's not likely to listen to me. I've decided we should have Gwynceffyl bring up the idea of an ambush."

"Good idea," Cadwalon said. "Have you talked to him yet?"

"I want you to come with me."

Cadwalon groaned again and then got up.

They went to Iceni commander's tent and asked one of his men to wake him. Gwynceffyl appeared alert and clear-eyed as he joined them outside the tent.

"I'm sorry to disturb your sleep," Bryn said, "But this is important." He explained the idea of an ambush.

"Who thought of this?" Gwynceffyl asked.

Bryn hesitated. He wasn't sure it would be a good idea to say Sirona had suggested this plan. Motioning to Cadwalon, he said, "It was something we came up with together."

Gwynceffyl grunted and rubbed his whisker-stubbled jaw. "It might work… if Boudica will agree. But I doubt she will. She's already made up her mind. First, Camulodunum. Then south to raze Verulamium and Londinium. She intends to lay waste to all the coloniae of the sunrise lands."

"Why not wipe out a whole legion of Roman soldiers instead?" Bryn asked.

"I think she worries our losses would be too great if we confronted their army directly. She's trying to be cautious, to attack the easy targets."

"You think it will be easy to destroy Camulodunum and these other settlements?"

"Oh, aye," Gwynceffyl answered. "They scarce have any defenses or troops. We'll fall upon them and cut them to pieces."

Bryn thought of Sirona's distress over women and children dying in the attack. It did sound brutal. "If you could at least try to speak to Boudica," he implored.

"I will," Gwynceffyl responded. "In the morning."

Bryn repressed a groan of frustration. He hated waiting. But it probably wouldn't be a good idea to wake the queen. If she was irritated about being roused, she would be less likely to listen.

* * *

The warriors moved through the settlement, carrying burning brands. They set fire to the thatch on the roofs of the dwellings they passed. Flames lit the night sky and smoke filled the air. A figure ran out of one of the dwellings, a young boy. His clothing was on fire. He screamed as the flames seared his skin. A warrior passing by knocked him to the ground and killed him with one quick sword thrust.

Sirona woke, her body rigid and drenched with sweat. She waited for her pounding heart to slow and tried to relax her muscles. When the worst of the horror had passed, she got up and began to pace. The dream had been so real, so vivid. She could almost still smell the smoke.

She halted as she suddenly realized what the dream meant. Boudica wasn't going to give up her plan to destroy Camulodunum. There would be no ambush of the ninth legion. Killing Roman soldiers would never satisfy the queen's bloodlust.

A sense of resolution filled Sirona. She must do something to prevent the slaughter she'd seen in her dream. Somehow she must try to save at least some of the people of Camulodunum.

She went to where Rufus slept. Bending over, she shook his shoulder. "Rufus, we must leave."

He sat up and rubbed his eyes. "Leave? Where are we going?"

"I had another dream. About Camulodunum." She grimaced at the memory. "We have to go there. We have to try to change things."

"But what about your plan to have Boudica's army ambush the Romans instead of attacking the colonia?"

"Boudica will never agree."

"Did that man—Bryn—did he come back and say this?"

Thinking of Bryn, the familiar yearning welled up inside her. If she left now, she might never see him again. She fought the pain the thought evoked. She couldn't deal with any of that now.

"Nay, Bryn didn't come back. He didn't have to. I know Boudica will never listen. Her goal isn't merely to defeat the Romans, but to make certain their people suffer as she believes she has suffered. She's driven by the hatred in her own heart, rather than a determination to save her people."

"I believe you," Rufus said. "Besides, the cruel bitch has never listened to anyone."

Sirona nodded. "My dream was so clear, so compelling. I have no choice but to do this." She motioned to Rufus's bedroll. "I'll load the chariot while you get the team ready. We must make haste."

Rufus nodded and went to do as she bid. A short while later, they were on the road to Camulodunum.

* * *

Bryn paced outside the gate to the palace. It was well past dawn. When would Gwynceffyl ever return?

A moment, later the older man appeared.

"What did the queen say?" Bryn demanded.

Gwynceffyl motioned to indicate they should walk back toward the Iceni camp. "She said that our course of action was already decided."

Bryn stopped and turned toward the other man. "Did you suggest the ambush? Did you try to convince her?"

"I did what I could, but you've met the queen. You know how resolute and determined she is. We leave the day after tomorrow. First light."

Bryn felt his heart sink. His worst fears had been made real. Now he must go and tell Sirona he had failed.

Chapter 21

As the chariot raced toward Camulodunum, Sirona was haunted by images from her dreams—corpses of women with their breasts cut off, children and babies lying butchered in the dirt. What horrified her the most was the awareness that many of the victims were her own people. She'd seen blue eyes staring sightlessly, red and fair hair soaked with blood. Her determination intensified. This was the reason she'd been sent those visions. This was what the Goddess wanted her to do.

When they reached a river, they forded it by tying their supplies to the upper part of the chariot, then clinging to the sides as the horses swam across pulling the vehicle. Sirona wasn't afraid of water, but she was still relieved when they reached the other side.

They sat in the sun to let their clothes dry. All at once Rufus slumped forward and hung his head in his hands. She touched his shoulder and he let out a moan. "For so long I have survived by holding on to my dream of rescuing my sister. Now that's been taken from me, and I don't see what I have left to live for."

His despair tore at her heart. "Your sister wouldn't want you to give up. Whatever happened to her, you have your whole life ahead of you."

"But what should I do? Where should I go? I can't return to the palace."

"Perhaps after we leave Camulodunum you could journey to the sunset lands with me."

"Do you really think they would accept me—a slave?" Rufus asked bitterly.

"After all my tribe has been through, I don't think they would turn away a young, able-bodied man like you."

"Even if he is half Roman?"

Sirona knew a stirring of doubt. Although they might allow Rufus to live with them, the Tarisllwyth were not likely to accept him as a member of the tribe. It would depend upon what the head Drui decided. For that matter, if Fiach was still in control at Mordarach, she would not be welcome there herself.

But she must give Rufus some encouragement. "I'm confident that someone as clever as you and as skilled with horses will be able to find a place somewhere. You must trust the gods to lead you to your destiny."

"You think I'm clever?" Hope glimmered in Rufus's dark eyes.

"Aye. Very clever. Look how you planned our escape. I could never have managed on my own. And while I haven't been around horses before, it seems to me your knowledge of them is remarkable."

Rufus nodded. "Crispin, the stablemaster, says I have a special way with the beasts. But it's not magic or sorcery. I simply try to think like the animals. To remember they have spirits and minds like we do."

"In the grove we are taught that all the beasts have spirits," Sirona said. "When I was young, one of my companions was able to enter a wolf's mind and call the animal to him." She smiled ruefully, thinking of Cruthin's foolishness. "Of course, he nearly died when the wolf attacked. But that was Cruthin. He was never one to use common sense." Her smile faded. Cruthin might well be dead. At any rate, she was unlikely to ever see him again. And Bryn... would she ever have a chance to be with him?

She stood abruptly. "Perhaps we shouldn't speak of these things right now. There's much to do before we can consider the future."

"Such as?" Rufus also rose. "I don't even know why we are going to Camulodunum."

Sirona started toward the chariot and team. "Let's keep moving." She didn't want Rufus to realize she had no clear plan for when they arrived at the colonia. Although her faith in the Goddess was strong, she couldn't expect him to share it.

They resumed their journey. Soon after mid-day, they came upon a raised track paved with stone. "This is the Roman road that leads into the settlement," Rufus told her as he guided the team onto the smooth surface, where the iron wheels of the chariot rolled along easily. "The Romans build roads everywhere they settle."

Observing the piled up dirt and neat stonework, and calculating the work required to build it, Sirona was amazed. Thinking of a trackway like this extending all the way to the highlands, she began to see the enemy in a new light. Not only were the Romans clever and capable, but they appeared to have vast resources. Although there were many more of her people than the Romans, the Pretani would never be able to build anything like this. They would never agree to work together on such an endeavor, nor would they see the need for such a thing.

Yet as the chariot raced along, Sirona decided there were disadvantages to such a means of travel. When people walked somewhere on their own two feet, they were aware of everything around them, the grass and trees and growing things, the birds and animals. They had time to smell the scent of the blooming gorse, to hear the bees among honeysuckle and inhale the sweet scent of the flowers. This road was built of rocks only a handspan in thickness, but that layer of stone was enough to alter the connection between a person's spirit and the great forces around them.

She was still contemplating these things when she looked down the road and saw some men driving an ox-cart towards them. They quickly reached the travelers. The men wore checked and patterned garments and had long hair and beards in the Pretani style. Seeing how warily the travelers regarded them, Sirona asked, "Why are those men afraid of us?"

"They probably worry about being robbed. I'd wager there's wine in the wooden tuns and oil and guara in the tall jars. "

"What's guara?" Sirona asked, remembering Kellach mentioning it.

"It's a kind of fish paste the Romans use in cooking."

"But why would they think we mean them ill?"

"Chariots are seldom used except in war. When we get close to Camulodunum, it might be best if we hid the vehicle and traveled the rest of the way on foot. We would be far less conspicuous."

Soon after, Rufus slowed the chariot and drove it off the road. As they crossed an open field and headed for a stand of oak trees, Sirona was surprised by the roughness of the ride. It had been easy to get used traveling on the smooth surface of the roadway.

When they reached the oak grove, Sirona got out while Rufus guided the vehicle into the underbrush. He unharnessed the horses and led them deeper into the woods, where he would hobble them so they would remain in the same area.

While she waited for Rufus, Sirona's stomach churned with dread. They were about to enter the settlement of the enemy. She reminded herself of the Pretani traders they'd just seen. Obviously, those men had survived their visit to the colonia.

"Do Pretani traders regularly visit Camulodunum?" she asked Rufus when he returned.

"Of course. What did you think?"

"To me, the Romans are the enemy, and I would expect my people to avoid them. Years ago when I left the highlands and traveled north, my escort was attacked by Romans. They slaughtered the men sent to guard me and carried off everything of value, including the cart I was riding in and all my possessions. I only survived because I was off in the woods at the time. Since then, the Romans have seemed like monsters to me, savage beasts out of a child's nightmares."

"Perhaps in the wild territories of your homeland it's like that, but not in the sunrise lands. Here, Romans and Pretani mingle all the time." Rufus jerked his head in the direction of the colonia. "When we reach Camulodunum, you'll find almost as many Pretani living there as Romans. Such settlements are established when retired Roman soldiers are given land in a conquered territory. They build houses and marry local women. Their wealth attracts traders, merchants and craftsmen, some Roman, some of Pretani blood. Before you know it, a colonia of some size has sprung up."

"So, many of the people of Camulodunum are Pretani?"

Rufus nodded. "The women, certainly. And a good share of the merchants and craftsmen."

"And the queen knows this? She knows that if she destroys the colonia, many of those who will die will be her own people?"

"Of course," Rufus answered. "She probably visited Camulodunum several times when Prasutagus was alive."

"And what of the warriors who follow her? Do they know they will be killing their own race?"

Rufus shrugged. "I doubt any of them care. I told you, when a colonia is established, the retired Roman soldiers are given land, both within the colonia and outside the settlement boundaries. Where do you think that land comes from? There are many Iceni and Trinovante who have had their property taken over by the Romans. They're very bitter, and like Boudica, not particularly concerned with whether the people now occupying their lands are of Roman or Pretani blood. They simply want to destroy those who stole what once belonged to them."

Sirona felt a chill of horror. She wished she'd known this when she talked to Bryn. If he realized many of his own people were going to die, he might have fought harder to stop such a massacre. But what could he have done? Boudica would never listen, and if Bryn tried too hard to convince her, he might end up imprisoned or dead.

Bryn. She kept trying to push thoughts of him aside, but it was difficult. The idea she might not see him again filled her with a crippling sense of loss. Was this what Itzurra meant when she warned Sirona she would live her life in turmoil? That her flesh would be drawn to the things of the earth, while her spirit yearned for the stars? Her feelings for Bryn seemed to come from that part of her that belonged to the earth, while her duty to the Goddess called to her from the world beyond. No wonder she felt torn in two.

Yet, she couldn't change the fact that her life belonged to the Goddess. She must fulfill her destiny as a seeress and use her abilities to change the future of her people. Until she accomplished that, she wouldn't have repaid her debt to the Great Mother for saving her life, not once, but many times.

If only she could think of a plan. She needed to find a way to warn the people of Camulodunum. To get them to leave the colonia before Boudica's army arrived. But how?

When she recalled herself to awareness, she saw Rufus gazing at her. He gestured. "Before we enter the colonia, we should probably change our garments. We don't want to be taken for slaves. Do you have a plain colored gown? The Romans don't usually wear patterned garments. We'll blend in better if we dress like the people here."

Sirona thought a moment and remembered the linen gown Julia had given her to wear while her own garments were washed when she first arrived at the palace. She had forgotten to give the garment back to Julia. Now it seemed there was a purpose for her lapse in memory. "I have a bleached linen gown that Julia gave me."

"Put it on," Rufus said.

She went off in the bushes to do as he suggested. After she had changed clothing, she unbraided her hair and combed it out, thinking she would have to ask Rufus how to arrange it so she looked like the women of Camulodunum.

When she returned, Rufus stared at her. "In that white garment, you look like a priestess." He pointed to the goddess stone, which she now wore outside her gown. "What's that?"

"A gift from the Great Mother Goddess. Others have named it as a serpent's egg or a star stone."

"It makes you look even more impressive. People will think it's a magic amulet."

"In some ways, it is magic," Sirona said. "There are many things I have been able to do while wearing it that I suspect would not have been possible otherwise. Through it, I feel the voice of the Goddess guiding me." She remembered Plancina explaining her role in interceding with the gods. Of course, Sirona thought, if she spoke before the people of Camulodunum as a seeress, a representative of the Great Mother Goddess, her words would have much more impact.

She wondered what Rufus would think of her plan. "You asked me why we are going to Camulodunum. I believe I must warn the people here that their lives are in peril. I have decided to present myself as a seeress and a priestess of the Great Mother Goddess and prophesize the downfall of the colonia. I don't know if anyone will listen, but I have to try."

Rufus squinted in thought and finally nodded. "It might work. The Romans believe strongly in signs and auguries. They always consult their priests before a battle, so they will know when it's fortuitous to attack."

"What are auguries?"

"The pattern flying birds make in the sky, or the death throes of an animal sacrificed, or sometimes the appearance of the animal's intestines afterwards."

"I have heard of tribes who believe in such things. I didn't realize the Romans were like that."

"Perhaps the Romans learned such practices from your people. In many ways, the Romans are very cautious. They respect and honor the beliefs of most other races they encounter. They assume there's always a chance that a particular god possesses power, and they wouldn't want to offend any deity."

"How do you know so much about Roman beliefs?" Sirona asked.

"Their officers often came to Prasutagus's household to collect tribute and discuss policy. Sometimes I helped serve meals and waited on them. I was able to observe them quite closely. I know that many of them carried small clay or wooden figures of the gods among their possessions."

"So, you think the Romans might listen to what I have to say? What about the Pretani people living in the settlement? Will they listen to me? It's the women and children I'm most concerned about."

"If you arrive and announce that you're a priestess, aye, some Romans might listen. And it will be up to the men what the women and children do, whether they heed your warning and flee the city. Unfortunately, many of them won't be able to understand you. Not all Romans bother to learn the Pretani tongue. I will have to translate." He motioned to his own clothing. "Do you think I'm dressed appropriately to pass as the servant of a priestess?"

For the first time, Sirona noticed the fine crys and bracco he wore, fashioned of vivid red and yellow wool. "Where did you get those garments?" she asked.

"When I went to Londinium I planned to go as a chieftain's son, so I stole these garments and hid them in the stables."

"You look very imposing." She smiled at him.

Her smile faded as she recalled what was ahead. Dread filled her at the thought of speaking before a crowd of strangers, most of whom would be Roman. But she had no choice.

"I'm ready," she told Rufus. He hoisted a pack containing some of their supplies over his shoulder and they set out.

Following the road, they passed farmsteads built in the Roman style, with clay brick walls surrounding the rectangular structures. There were also cultivated fields and pastures. Sirona stopped to gaze at one of the extravagant dwellings. "I've always heard of the wealth of the Romans, but this is beyond imagining. It seems incredible to think of all the rooms in those dwellings, many filled with luxurious, expensive goods. My people value beauty, and our craftsmen fashion objects of extraordinary loveliness, but even the richest of the Pretani don't live like this."

"Some of them do now. Look at Boudica and her daughters. Before

Prasutagus died, their manner of living was the same as any other wealthy Roman family. And there are other Pretani chieftains who have done the same, at least here in the east."

Rufus's remarks worried her. The distinctions between her people and the Romans had already grown blurred and confused. Perhaps it was too late to prevent the eagle of Rome from triumphing over Albion. Even if they drove the Romans from their lands, the changes the enemy's influence had wrought would not be easily undone.

They passed another Roman villa, and Sirona felt the familiar tingling along her spine. As she stopped and stared at the dwelling, her nostrils were filled with the reek of smoke, and she saw flickering tongues of fire consuming the graceful wooden furniture inside the dwelling. The fire scorched the pictures painted on the walls and the elaborate pattern of tiny stones on the floors. Finally, it caught at the timber supports of the roofs. The blaze grew hotter and hotter, until even the tiles on the roof were blackened and scorched and began to collapse.

The scene changed back to the interior of one of the buildings. Corpses sprawled where they had been struck down. The flames licked over them, making them swell and turn black, and filling the air with the sickening stench of roasted flesh.

Sirona gagged and bent over, trying not to retch. Rufus clutched her arm. "What's wrong? What is it?"

"More visions. Ghastly visions." She took a deep breath and looked around. Everything was peaceful. The grass along the roadway swayed softly in the breeze. Brown and gold butterflies rose in a cloud from the fragrant stands of purple vetch and white privy. In the distance, the Roman style structures appeared sound and whole.

"What does it mean?" Rufus asked.

"That I mustn't give up. That I must try to prevent what suffering I can." She started forward.

The dwellings grew more numerous and closer together, although there was no ditch or earthworks, no wall or gate marking the settlement's borders. "How can they hope to defend themselves against attack?" Sirona asked. "With no ramparts or other defenses to slow them down, an enemy army could overrun this place with little effort."

"They obviously don't expect attack."

Sirona shook her head. The people of Camulodunum were even more vulnerable and helpless than she'd thought.

They continued to follow the road into the town and finally came upon a sprawling structure made of clay brick. "This must be one of the barracks," Rufus said. "The army headquarters should be nearby."

Yet they saw no soldiers, only a group of raggedly dressed children playing with a stuffed leather ball. The children stopped their game to stare, but their curiosity did not last long before they returned to their play. A woman came out of one of the doorways of the building with a pottery jar balanced on one shoulder and a toddler on her other hip. Sirona grew even more discomfited. This woman looked very much like the one in the dream she'd had before leaving the north. When she shuddered, Rufus asked, "What is it?"

"I think we're getting closer to where the main burning and killing will take place." She turned to look at him. "Where are the men? Who is charged with defending the settlement?"

"I thought we would find soldiers here, but they must have made the barracks into housing for the families of the merchants and craftsmen who serve the colonia."

Passing the barracks, they began to see newer, more lavish structures and more people, mostly roughly dressed slaves, many with blue eyes or fair coloring marking them as of Pretani blood. But there were also women dressed in rich, draped garments of the Roman style who also bore the coloring and features of Sirona's people.

The road ended at a large open area and they saw where everyone was headed. The open area was filled with lean-tos, carts and tables piled high with trade goods. "This must be the market," Rufus said. "There's another larger one outside the town, but this is probably where the women come every day to buy things for their households."

Sirona looked around with interest. She had never seen so many goods and foodstuffs in one place. There were fabrics and metalwork spread out on the tables; piles of leeks, cabbages and root vegetables; baskets of sloes and apricots, and other fruits and vegetables she was not familiar with. She also saw large wooden containers that Rufus said held wine, and pottery jars he told her would hold olive oil and guara.

"Where do all these things come from?" she asked him.

"We're not far from the sunrise sea. Many of these goods are brought across from the land the Romans call Gaul, then transported up the river to the colonia. There's also a large pottery and tile works outside the settlement. And many of the foodstuffs and other products are made in shops right here." He pointed to a table with baskets overflowing with steaming bannocks that filled the air with a warm, rich fragrance. "The bread was probably baked in that building behind the stall. And there are likely shops where you can have a pair of shoes made or a garment sewn. I'm sure they craft jewelry and tools and all kinds of other things."

"Would this be a good place to give my warning?"

"I don't think so. Most of those gathered here are women, slaves and craftsmen. It's the men you need to convince. This time of day, you will likely find them at the baths."

"The baths?"

"A building containing pools of water for people to bathe in. Although they do more than bathe. The men sit around and talk, sharing the important news of the colonia and the empire. We had a small bathhouse at Prasutagus's palace. I used to carry messages there."

Sirona recalled the room with the pool of water at Calpurnius's villa and imagined being inside such a place with a group of Roman men. She didn't think she could bear it.

"Come on," Rufus said. "The baths and other public buildings will be located in the center of the colonia."

"Do the Romans have a feast hall?" she asked. "A place where everyone goes to celebrate important events like the arrival of visitors?"

Rufus shook his head. "I've never heard of such a place."

"What about an area where sacrifices and other ceremonies are performed?"

"Those would take place in a temple. If there's an important temple here, it will probably be near the baths and other public buildings."

"We must go there."

Although her stomach seemed filled with small, swooping birds, she followed Rufus past more of the low buildings, then into another open area. Flanking it were the largest buildings she had ever seen. The only thing she could compare them to was the gathering hall on the sacred isle, except these buildings were completely enclosed, with gleaming white stone walls and red tile roofs.

"That's the temple." Rufus pointed to one of the buildings. The structure had stone supports on either side of the entrance, and in front, the bronze statue of a man on a horse. The man was holding aloft a sword in a triumphant gesture. Beneath the statue was a huge stone basin filled with water.

Sirona went to examine the statue more closely. She had seen figures like this one in Boudica's palace, but they were much smaller and the details not so fine. This man or god appeared real. Again, she was struck by the marvelous things the Romans could make. Magnificent buildings. Life-like forms of men made out of bronze. Beautiful paintings, designs and patterns, ornaments and jewelry. Such splendor. How were her people to prevail against invaders who possessed such wealth, who created such dramatic symbols of their power?

She looked at the base of the statue, where there were markings inscribed in the stone. There had been similar markings on some of the buildings in the marketplace. She pointed. "What do those mean?"

"That's Roman writing," Rufus answered. "It probably tells the name of the Emperor and lists some of his accomplishments, similar to what a bard would do when a chieftain appears before his tribe."

"How?" Sirona asked, mystified.

Rufus gestured. "The lines make sounds that make up words. If I could read, I could tell you exactly what it says."

"Lines and shapes that make words," Sirona said thoughtfully. A sense of awe went through her. Writing was a way to preserve words, so that they existed somewhere besides the mind of a Learned One. The Romans were clever, very clever. And their cleverness might be the undoing of her people.

As she had the thought, she felt tingling along her spine. Before her eyes, the statue began to sway on its stone platform. With a creaking sound, it fell forward and crashed to the ground. The body fell into the pool of water and the head of the bronze man broke off. A Pretani warrior came forward, picked up the head and held it aloft. The great temple behind the statue was now surrounded by other warriors, screaming and waving their weapons. Smoke poured out of the doorway of the temple, staining the white stone supports, and she could smell the awful odor of roasting flesh.

The vision gradually faded, and although her stomach heaved with distress, Sirona now knew exactly what she must do. She moved in front of the statue, then raised her arms and cried out, "Disaster! Disaster is on its way! The streets of the colonia will run red with blood! I have seen a vision of this statue tumbled to the ground and broken!" She gestured to the bronze figure. "Exactly as the people of Camulodunum will be broken!"

The few people in the area around the temple stopped whatever they were doing and turned to look at her. Sirona knew she must be careful to make her predictions vague. These people must not realize that the disaster she prophesied would come from Boudica's army. Otherwise they might send for the ninth legion to aid them. She didn't want to do anything to provoke the great battle of her vision.

Moving away from the statue, she pointed in the direction she believed was east. "Soon the waves of the sunrise sea will turn dark with blood. A great pall of smoke will blot out the sun. People will fall to the ground and die, struck down by some terrible force moving through the colonia!"

She paused to watch the people gathering around her. Many looked puzzled and she guessed they didn't understand what she was saying. She looked to Rufus, who nodded. He stepped forward and translated her words into the rhythmic, even tongue of the Romans. As he spoke, she was amazed by his poise. In his rich garments, his dark eyes bright with intensity, he looked every bit the chieftain's son.

More people had gathered… but not enough. Somehow her warning must reach the ears of the men in charge of this settlement. She must convince them that disaster loomed. To do that would take more than words. She must make them *see* the things she was talking about. Touching the amulet at her breast, she whispered, "Great Mother, lend me your power. Make the magic flow through me."

In her mind she saw the statue shuddering on its stone platform. She turned to face the real bronze figure and concentrated. Somehow she must make what was in her thoughts become real. Sweat broke out on her skin and her head began to throb, but as she watched, the statue began to shake. It didn't fall, but trembled on its stone support. She heard the people around her gasp and knew that they had seen the statue shift.

Taking a deep breath, she decided to try something else. *Let them see the blood,* she thought. The water in the pool below the statue began to churn and roil. It poured over the stone edges containing it and spilled out onto the stone walkway surrounding the pool. The liquid flowing out was not clear, but deep red. People screamed and stepped back. *Now,* Sirona thought. *Now is the time to speak again.*

"I am Sirona!" she shouted. "A servant of the Great Mother Goddess. She has given me the power to see the future, and I have seen what will happen here in Camulodunum. Blood. Death. Suffering. I urge you to flee, to take your families and run. Travel far, far away. Go north or west. Or if you have a boat, take it back across the sunset sea to the lands of the Belgae." She was careful not to suggest they travel south. The southern coloniae of Londinium and Verulamium were to be Boudica's next targets.

She paused and waited for Rufus to translate, then continued, "Flee quickly! There's not much time! Even now the hand of death hovers over us!" She raised her arms to the heavens and silently called upon the skygods, Beli and Llud, to aid her. The clouds churned and darkened. A flash of lightning lit what had only moments before been a clear blue sky.

Panic overtook the people around Sirona. They screamed and called the names of gods, some of whom Sirona recognized. Others turned and ran. Sirona felt triumph surge through her. She had done it. Her predictions had terrorized the people of Camulodunum and caused them to flee for their lives. At least some of them would escape before Boudica's army arrived.

She raised her arms once more to the heavens. "Hear me, all those who dwell in Camulodunum! Flee now, lest you perish in the flames that will engulf this place! Fire and smoke and death—all those things await you if you remain here! Hear me! Heed my warning! I am Sirona, servant of the Goddess." Her voice faded as she saw a huge, fleshy man approaching. His round face was flushed deep red, almost purple. His eyes were black as obsidian and full of fury. He pointed at her and shouted something in the Roman tongue. Sirona's heart seemed to lurch into her throat.

Chapter 22

Fear thrummed through Sirona as the man approached. She struggled for control, telling herself the Great Mother would not forsake her now. She must remain strong.

Rufus, standing next to her, whispered, "Make the statue shake again. Show him your power." There was an edge of desperation to his voice.

"I don't think I can," she whispered back. While she was prophesizing, the power had flowed through her, a kind of energy moving through her body, making her something more than muscle and tendon, skin and bone. Now it was gone. She felt small and empty and tired.

The huge man shouted something. "What's he saying?" Sirona asked Rufus.

"He's telling his guards to take you to the Senate house. You must not let them lay hands on you. Once he has you away from the crowd, he'll have you killed."

Two Roman soldiers with metal breastplates and plumed helmets appeared from behind the man. As they strode toward Sirona, she thought of Einion and Culhwch lying dead on the ground and was paralyzed with terror.

"Say something!" Rufus cried. "Make them understand you're a seeress!"

Sirona swallowed thickly. She raised her hand defensively and cried out, "Even if you kill me, Camulodunum is doomed! I have seen the future! I know what is to come!"

Although they could not have understood her words, something in her demeanor must have affected the soldiers, for they halted a few paces away.

The man who commanded them, the heavy, balding one, bellowed something. The soldiers again started forward. All at once, Rufus was in front of Sirona, shouting in the Roman tongue. He gestured to her, then to the statue. She could tell he was trying to explain who she was and what she had prophesied. He swept his arm around to encompass the crowd. His voice rose, as if he were asking them to remember what they had seen.

Despite her fear, Sirona experienced a sense of satisfaction. Rufus was acting like a chieftain's son. Boudica might have forced him into a life of servitude, but she had not succeeded in crushing his spirit.

Another man stepped out of the mass of people. He had close-cropped, iron-gray hair and a stern countenance. Coming to stand in front of her, he spoke to the heavy man in clear, ringing tones. Sirona scrutinized the two Romans. The one who had first accosted her wore a voluminous garment of bright white wool banded with gold. His thick fingers glinted with rings as he gestured, and his tone of voice suggested he expected immediate obedience. The other Roman was plainly-dressed in a short crys and a tight leather overgarment. Even though he carried no weapons and wore no helmet, his severely upright bearing and lean muscularity made her think he must have been a formidable warrior in his younger years.

Here were two kinds of power, she thought—wealth and the authority that comes with it, and the natural leadership of a warrior.

The thick-set man responded to the older man, his tone angry and contemptuous. The warrior answered back and gestured to the statue. Sirona turned and asked Rufus, "What are they saying?"

"The fat fellow, who is apparently a magistrate, is arguing that you should be taken from this place because you're upsetting the citizens of the colonia. The other man says that he saw for himself how you made the statue shake and the pool overflow with blood. He suggests you must be an oracle for the goddess Minerva and perhaps they should listen to what you have to say."

The two men continued to argue. Other richly garbed men came to join in. Many of the arrivals were fat, old or feeble-looking, but they were flanked by a group of soldiers who appeared every bit as formidable as the armed men who had first approached her. These fierce fighting men stood nearby, their postures suggesting they waited only for the magistrate's command to seize her and drag her away.

The magistrate made one final angry gesture and then approached. Fear rose like a bubble in her stomach. The man stopped an arm's length away. His black eyes bored into her, full of suspicion, anger... and something else, something that distressed her even more than his obvious hostility. She recalled Kellach looking at her that way, as if he was both repulsed and fascinated by her.

She held her breath as the man reached out for her goddess stone. Rufus immediately pushed his way in front of her, shouting something in the Roman tongue. The man gestured and the two soldiers grabbed Rufus. Sirona found her voice. "Leave him alone! He serves the Great Mother Goddess, as I do. If you harm him, you will have to face Her wrath!"

The gray-haired man spoke. Whatever he said seemed to disturb the magistrate, who took a step back. The gray-haired man drew near. "Priestess," he said in heavily accented Pretani, "If you can indeed see the future, you must know that you should leave this place. Your life hangs by a thread. I have told Cornelius Verecundus that if he touches you, your god will surely curse him, but he might overcome his dread at any moment."

Should she heed this man? Had she done enough to warn the people of Camulodunum? Sirona touched the amulet on her breast, hoping for a sign from the Goddess. Then she thought of Rufus. She had no doubt he would fight to the death to defend her. "Rufus," she said. "I think we should listen to this Roman." To the gray-haired man, she said, "Tell Cornelius Verecundus to release my companion, and we will leave immediately."

The gray-haired man spoke in his own tongue. Cornelius glared at him, then motioned angrily to the two soldiers holding Rufus. They released him, and Sirona and Rufus started to walk away. "Priestess, listen," the gray-haired man called. Sirona turned. There seemed to be some unspoken message in the man's light brown eyes. He jerked his head toward the statue. "Perhaps before you go, you could give us another sign of what is to come."

Clearly, he wanted her to display her power. Was it because he didn't think the people of the colonia were convinced of the threat they faced? Or was there some other message he sought to convey? She searched his golden brown eyes, trying to discern the meaning of his words. All at once, she realized he was afraid for her. He worried Cornelius would not allow her to leave the colonia alive.

She looked up at the statue. Her life might depend on her being able to make the bronze figure tremble and shake. Concentrating, she sought out the power of the Goddess. Her fingers went to the amulet. It grew warm in her hand. "Please, Great Mother, aid me," she whispered. "Arianrhod, who guides the stars through the sky and controls the tides of the sea, give me your power. Cyhiraeth, who rules the streams and rivers and whose awesome force can grind away mountains, lend me your might. Rhiannon, lady of the underworld, whose dark forces rule all our spirits, stand beside me."

She raised her arms, feeling the energy flow through her flesh like fire. Although there was intense pain, she gritted her teeth and kept her arms high. The statue began to shudder and shift on its stone base. Sirona imagined the forces she had evoked working on the statue: A great wind blowing. A rush of water bearing down. The earth beneath writhing and shaking.

The people around her screamed and cried out. She could sense them moving away. They feared her power, feared the force that flowed through her. The statue rocked back and forth, then tilted and fell backwards.

Sirona lowered her arms. She was breathing heavily and her whole body ached. It was a struggle to maintain consciousness. The area around the statue was full of people. They were screaming and trying to get away. Rufus grabbed her arm and drew her into the crowd. "Come on! Hurry!"

She heard the magistrate Cornelius shouting, trying to be heard above the din. But no one heeded him. The people were crazed with fear. They ran like a herd of stampeded cattle. The danger now was being trampled. Rufus dragged her away from the crowd and into a space between two buildings. "This way," he cried. "Come on!"

They ran and ran, darting down narrow passageways. Finally, Rufus paused for breath. He glanced around, as if trying to decide which way to go next. Sirona had no idea what to tell him. She felt like an empty grain husk that is swirled around and lands wherever the wind wills it.

They heard footsteps. The sound echoed, and they couldn't tell from which direction the noise was coming from. Rufus reached down and pulled a knife from a sheath fastened to his lower leg, underneath his bracco. He brandished the weapon, dark eyes glinting. Sirona's heart sank. It was a wicked looking blade, but still no match for an armed warrior.

They waited. One heartbeat. Two. They could hear the labored breathing of someone approaching. The man slowed as he entered the passageway, and Sirona felt a sharp pang of relief as she saw that their pursuer was the gray-haired man. He stopped when he saw them. "Come with me," he said. "I'll take you to a place of safety."

"Why should we trust you?" Rufus demanded. He held up the knife. "You are the enemy."

"Why am I the enemy?" the man asked. His eyes narrowed. "Where do you come from? Why are you here? And what is this danger you warn of?"

Sirona didn't know how to answer. This man would not be put off with vague predictions of an impending catastrophe. "Is it not enough that I have come to warn your people?"

"Warn them?" the man asked. "Are you certain you don't simply mean to terrify them with your sorcery?" He shook his head. "It's no wonder the magistrates seek to be rid of you. You're an insult to their power, an affront to their authority. If terrible things loom for the colonia, they should know of it and take action."

"Aye, they should," Sirona said. "They should send their families away from this place."

"Ah, their families," the Roman said. "They should get their families away, but not flee themselves? Is that what you are saying?"

"Nay. All should flee. The colonia is going to be destroyed. It's not safe to stay here." Even as she spoke, Sirona wondered if she was betraying the cause of her people.

"How will the colonia be destroyed?" the man persisted. "What will cause the fire and smoke, the blood and death you predict?"

"I can't say," Sirona repeated. "The Goddess sends me only glimpses, tiny hints of what is to come."

"Surely you must have seen the face of the enemy who will cause our downfall. But if you refuse to tell me more, I will accept it. Whatever gods you serve, they are certainly powerful. I have lived three score years upon this earth and traveled widely, from Carthage in the south and Germania in the north, and never have I see sorcery like what you performed in the temple square. Your powers are mighty indeed, especially for a woman. I thought you must serve Minerva, the warrior goddess, but now I am not so certain. Your concern for women and children suggests the goddess you honor might be Juno, queen of heaven and protectress of women and mothers."

"Perhaps Juno is another name for the goddess I serve," Sirona agreed. It was a relief to be discussing goddesses with this man rather than having him continue to question how Camulodunum would fall.

Rufus apparently felt differently, for he made a sound of exasperation and said, "I think you are both fools to be standing here, talking about gods and goddesses while our lives are in danger."

The Roman nodded. "That's why you must come with me. I will take you to a safe place. You can remain there until nightfall, then slip out of the colonia."

To Rufus, Sirona said, "I think we can trust this man."

"I will do whatever you say, priestess," Rufus responded. To the Roman, he warned, "Betray us, and she will curse you to the depths of the underworld."

The gray-haired man nodded.

The Roman led them past more dwellings. They saw a few women and children, who regarded them with little more than curiosity. Apparently word of Sirona's predictions had not reached this part of the colonia. Again, Sirona was struck by how few of the people looked Roman, although not all of them appeared to be Pretani either. Some had hair even lighter than her own, while others had dark brown skin.

As they walked, the Roman asked Sirona and Rufus's names. He said he was Gaius Martius Ventius, formerly of the ninth legion. He explained that when Paullinus Suetonius became governor of the island—which Gaius called Britain, rather than Albion—the Roman leader had decreed that all legionaries who had served twenty years or more must retire. Forced out of the legion, Gaius had decided to settle in Camulodunum.

"But now I question my choice," Gaius continued as they reached an area where the dwellings were larger and made of stone rather than timber or brick. "The people of this colonia have grown careless, and I fear we will pay for our indifference. We are surrounded by a people we have abused and humiliated but not truly vanquished, and that is a dangerous situation." He gave Sirona a searching look and she realized he suspected her predictions had to do with a Pretani attack.

"When they decided to raze the old fort's walls to make room for more dwellings," he continued, "I felt it was too soon. I am uneasy with the peace they have proclaimed here. This island is like a granary that catches fire. You fight the flames and think they are quenched, and yet they smolder in hidden corners, ready to burst forth with an even greater blaze when you have turned away."

Sirona felt more and more uncomfortable. This man guessed the truth. All she could do was hope he would not share his fears with the leaders of the colonia and cause them to send for aid.

As if he knew her thoughts, Gaius said, "If there were trouble here, the best we could hope for was that the ninth legion would march to our defense."

"Where are the rest of the legions?" Rufus asked. "I heard they were in the highlands."

Gaius gave them a shrewd look, as if considering what to say. He must have decided they could easily learn the location of the Roman forces from other sources, for he responded, "The twentieth and fourteenth legions are in the north. Suetonius has vowed to rid Britain of those cursed, bloodthirsty Drui once and for all."

Sirona's blood went cold. "What do you mean? What does this Suetonius intend to do?"

Gaius shrugged. "Round up the Drui and kill them, I suppose."

"Why does Suetonius hate the Learned Ones?" she asked. "We're naught but priests and poets, scholars and diviners."

"We?" Gaius gazed at her quizzically.

Sirona took a deep breath. She had already trusted this man with her life. "I trained for many years in the grove. As Learned Ones we are concerned with the realm of the spirits, with knowledge and truth, with reaching out to the gods and calling down their power."

"Ah, of course, your kind are all peace and gentleness, aren't they, except for practicing human sacrifice. Although it's difficult to imagine someone like you being involved in such bloody, gruesome rites, I know it's part of your people's beliefs." He nodded. "Once in Gaul, I saw a man burned to death in a wicker cage because he had broken some law of his tribe."

Sirona recalled the discussion she'd overheard on the sacred isle and the vision she'd had of the young woman being killed. The memory made her shudder.

"Suetonius is right to rid the island of the Drui," continued Gaius. "They have a formidable ability to influence the minds of their people. There are times when we have thought we've reached an agreement with a certain chieftain, only to have him send warriors in ambush against us. And when we finally subdue the chieftain, we usually discover it was some priest or Drui who convinced him to betray the arrangement.

"Nay, the Learned Ones aren't so concerned with the path of the stars in the heavens and the will of gods as to be unaware of the events affecting their tribes," Gaius continued. "They have been an active force in your people's struggle against us. It's even possible that some day they might succeed in getting several tribes to join together and attack us. If that happened, we would be in trouble. Your people greatly outnumber us." Gaius watched her expression as he said this and Sirona struggled not to reveal her thoughts.

"But mostly I doubt that even the Drui could unite your people," Gaius went on. "It's ever the same with barbarian tribes. Their chieftains and leaders fight among themselves instead of fighting us, their enemy. In nearly every land we have conquered, that's the reason we have dominated. And the Pretani are the worst I've seen at combining forces and working together. Each chieftain jealously guards his power and fights only for his own small domain. And then their territories fall, one by one."

Sirona thought of proud Tarbelinus being led away in chains. The image made her want to weep. "I don't see why your people had to come here," she said bitterly. "Don't you have enough land and wealth in your homeland?"

Gaius shrugged. "Why shouldn't we seek to increase our territories? Men have always sought to take what power they can. It's the way the world works."

The Roman spoke the truth, Sirona thought. There would always be chieftains who sought more power and territory and made war upon their neighbors.

They had reached a modest timber dwelling on the outskirts of the settlement. Gaius gestured for them to enter. Inside there were benches and tables and baskets, jars and chests on the floor. "I'll fetch my wife, Aamora," Gaius said. "She's probably in the garden."

While they waited for Gaius to return, Rufus sat on one of the benches while Sirona walked around the room, examining the furnishings. "This place does not seem quite Roman," she said.

"It appears Roman enough to me," Rufus answered. "See, they have the traditional mosaic of a guard dog at the entranceway, the walls are whitewashed, and they have a mural in the Roman fashion."

"Aye, but look at the mural. See the way the strands of wheat and the leaves of the vine curl around the image of the woman, and how her hair is braided. That design is more Pretani than Roman."

"But the woman depicted must surely be the Roman goddess Demeter, who represents harvest and plenty," Rufus argued.

"It looks like a mixture of the traditions of both peoples," Sirona said.

Gaius returned with a very young woman with reddish gold hair, blue eyes and a dusting of freckles across her narrow nose. Two small brown-eyed children peeped out from behind her. "This is my family," Gaius said, with more than a hint of pride in his voice. "My wife Aamora, and my son, Tiro and daughter, Helena."

Rufus bowed. Sirona smiled and nodded to Aamora. "It's a pleasure to meet you. Your husband has been of great help to us."

The woman nodded back but did not speak.

"Does she understand Pretani?" Rufus asked.

"Of course, although your accent might confuse her," Gaius responded. "She's from Gaul, where they speak a variation of your language." He motioned to Aamora. "Fetch food for our guests. The children can stay here with us."

Aamora darted off, reminding Sirona of a startled deer set to flight. "She's still shy and wary," Gaius said. "I think it's because she was abused before I purchased her. She never speaks of it, but sometimes I see a haunted look in her eyes."

"You *purchased* her?" Sirona exclaimed.

"Aye. I found her in the slavemarket of Londinium, skinny as a stick and covered with sores. I took her home thinking she could be trained to assist my old household servant, Messilina, but Aamora was too ill to do anything for quite a while. I ended up taking care of her myself. By the time she regained her strength, I'd grown quite fond of her and decided she'd make a better wife than a kitchen slave." He grinned sheepishly. "I suppose you think me an old fool, but she is lovely and sweet and a pleasure to come home to. Now that she has given me two fine children, I vow I am truly smitten." He nodded to Tiro and Helena, playing quietly in a corner of the room.

Aamora returned with a pottery bowl of water and some drying cloths. "I thought you might want to wash," she told Sirona. To her husband she added, "Messilina is bringing the food."

Sirona washed her face and hands, and an elderly female servant came in carrying a tray of bread, cheese and figs. Sitting on a bench next to the painting of the grain goddess, Sirona began to eat. Rufus sat beside her, chewing rapidly.

Gaius joined them. "As soon as you've finished eating, you must leave," he said.

Sirona nodded. "But before we go, you must promise me something."

"What is that?" Gaius asked.

"Promise me that you will take your family away from here. Otherwise, they will die."

Gaius didn't speak for a time, then he said, "I believe you are a true seeress, that you have really seen these things you speak of with such power. I will do as you say."

"Where will you take them?" Sirona asked.

"I have a good friend in Londinium."

Sirona shook her head vehemently. "Don't take them to Londinium, or to any of the Roman coloniae. If you value your family's lives, take them far to the south. In the land of the Atrebates they will be safe."

Gaius scrutinized her. "You believe the whole of the east is in danger?"

Sirona chewed her lower lip in thought. If this man guessed what was to come, he could warn the Roman leaders and set into motion the events that would lead to the great battle. She glanced at little Tiro and Helena, playing quietly in a corner of the room, and abruptly realized what she must do. She could not concern herself with battle strategy or war. The Goddess had sent her here to save lives.

"Aye, the whole of the east is in danger," she said. "You can't change what is to come. You must focus on your responsibility to your family and the other helpless women and children in the colonia. Try to get as many of them away from here as possible. Begin tonight. Round up supplies, and have Aamora tell her friends about the danger. Then, as soon as you can, leave this place. Travel south and don't stop until you are far away."

"How long will we have to stay in the south?" Gaius asked. She could tell he was still trying to understand what was to come.

Thinking about the great battle, Sirona felt a grim weight descend upon her. "Not long. I believe that before the snow season arrives, this part of Albion will once again be safe for your people." She faced Gaius resolutely. "But that does not mean you will defeat us. My people will never give up trying to win back our lands. Our spirits will not be broken, even if your army prevails against us."

"There is power in your words," Gaius said. "And I will heed them. You have come here against all reason to warn those whom you consider to be the enemy. Only someone driven by the will of the gods would do such a thing. I have one question left. What of you? Where will you go when you leave here?"

"I must return to my homeland in the sunset lands."

"Then I will give you some advice," Gaius said. "Travel south to Verulamium. A new road has been built leading directly from that colonia to the northwest. On horseback, a man can travel to the fort at Deva in four or five days. Until you reach Deva, you should encounter nothing more than small forts and supply bases."

"I thank you for your advice," Sirona said.

"And I, for yours." Gaius's stern face softened. He inclined his head to her and said, "May the strong sword arm of Minerva, the battle goddess of my people, be with you."

"And may the Great Mother Goddess protect you and your family," Sirona responded.

* * *

Leaving Gaius's home, Sirona and Rufus moved cautiously among the other dwellings, making their way to the edge of the colonia. All was quiet, and Sirona experienced an odd sense that everything that had happened there had been a strange dream. It hardly seemed possible that she had made the statue topple and turned the water in the pool to blood. But then she caught a glimpse of lamplight in the window of one of the dwellings and was reminded of the fire that would rage through this place when Boudica's army came. All of it was real, the strange events of this day and the horrible ones yet to come. She let out a sigh.

"Are you sorry you came here?" Rufus asked. "Do you feel you have failed?"

A wave of grief swept through Sirona. It distressed her to think she might not be able to prevent the great battle and the terrible loss of life that would result. But at least she'd warned Bryn. He would tell other warriors. Some of them might listen and avoid the dreadful confrontation. A few lives would be saved, and those individuals could make a difference in the future.

Sirona told herself she'd done all she could. Something positive would surely come of her efforts. To Rufus she said, "Based on my warning, some people, like Gaius and his family, will leave before

Boudica and her army attack. One of those children who escape might grow up to be a great leader or a powerful Drui, someone who will change the course of the future. The gods often work in small, subtle ways. We must trust that whatever I was meant to do here has been accomplished."

"What do the gods tell you to do now? Why do you think you must travel to the sunset lands?"

"As I had a sense that I should go to Camulodunum, I now feel I must return to my homeland. But you don't have to go with me. It's a long journey."

Rufus grew distraught. "If I left you, where would I go? Besides, you need me. Without the chariot, it would take you twice as long."

"I'm grateful for your aid, Rufus. But I may encounter much danger on this journey. I can't ask you to go with me unless it's truly what you want."

Rufus shrugged. "I have nothing better to do."

She smiled at him. "Thank you, Rufus. You've been a great help to me."

* * *

They spent the night in a grove of lime trees outside of Camulodunum. In the morning they set out for Verulamium. Several times they passed carts loaded with trading goods, and Rufus would call out a greeting in the Roman tongue to the men walking alongside the carts. The men usually shouted a greeting back, seemingly unconcerned by the sight of a war chariot on the roadway. It was as Gaius had said. The Romans here didn't see the Pretani as a threat. The tribes of this part of the island had long ago capitulated to the enemy, learning their language, adopting their way of life and interbreeding with them.

They spent the next night in a wood of beech and oak, and then started off again in the morning. By mid-day they neared Verulamium. Although they had encountered no threats so far, only traders and lone travelers, they decided to circle around the colonia and return to the road later.

Much of the countryside had been cleared for farming, so the going wasn't difficult, although it was not as fast as traveling on the paved roadway. They saw villas and farms with thatched or red-roofed buildings, cows and sheep, fields of golden grain, silvery green hay meadows and dark orchards. The sky was overcast and the hazy light made the dwelling places seem far away and almost unreal. Sirona could not overcome her awareness that this dreamy world of peace and plenty would soon be destroyed. Boudica's vast army would swarm over the land, burning and destroying. The fine stone structures and walls would be cast down and stained black by fire. The crops trampled into the dust. The livestock slaughtered.

They circled Verulamium. Like Camulodunum, this colonia had few fortifications and would be impossible to defend. Boudica's army would cut down these people as a scythe moves through a field of grain.

Sirona was greatly relieved when they finally reached the roadway Gaius had said led to the sunset lands. Now she could concentrate on reaching her own people and helping them, instead of enduring the helpless frustration of knowing she couldn't change what was going to happen in the east. As Rufus guided the chariot onto the stone-paved surface of the road, Sirona turned to look east one last time. As she recalled her parting with Bryn, her heart twisted inside her. She might never again see him again.

Chapter 23

The chariot carried Bryn forward, his dark green checked warcloak flapping behind him and the team's harness fittings jangling wildly. In the bottom of the vehicle were his spear and his shield, decorated with the white horse of the Iceni. Beside him and a little ahead, another four score of chariots raced over the grassy ground. Behind him marched the rest of Boudica's army, a huge mass of men, weapons bristling. They moved much more slowly than the chariots, but it seemed to Bryn that there was something even more formidable and terrifying in their advance. They were like a swarm of insects moving over the land, and like a plague of voracious locusts, once they had passed by, everything would be changed.

Intense emotions swirled through him. He should be thrilled to finally march into battle against the Romans, but his worries wouldn't allow him to enjoy the moment. Sirona had told him he must seek to alter Boudica's plans. He'd tried to do so and failed. And now he didn't know where Sirona was. It had been a shock to find her gone when he went to tell her that Boudica had rejected the idea of an ambush.

For the hundredth time, he searched his memory of his last conversation with her. Where would she go? To the sunrise lands? North to Brigante territory? He'd never been able to predict her behavior in the past; it seemed he was no better at it now.

With effort, he forced himself to put his concerns for Sirona aside. He was riding into battle. If he valued his own life, he must concentrate on the present.

It helped that it took much of his concentration to drive the chariot. Traveling cross-country rather than on a level trackway was very challenging. He had to pay attention to the terrain ahead and make certain there were no large rocks or scrub to overturn the vehicle.

The line of chariots crested a hill and below was a broad river valley. Along the silvery ribbon of the waterway several villas had been built. They looked much like the ones he and Cadwalon had passed in Coritani territory. Most of the settlements had stone walls, but they would be little defense against a great army like this one. He felt a stir of pity for the inhabitants. There would be women and children and slaves here, and they wouldn't be spared.

But chariots didn't stop at the villas. Instead, with Gwynceffyl in the lead, they surged toward the river, seeking out the lowest place to cross. Once there, they forded as they had been told to do, with the horses pulling the chariots across while the riders clung to the floating vehicles.

When he reached the other side, Bryn checked the team and examined the chariot. Then he tethered the horses to a tree, dried off as best he could and went to find Gwynceffyl.

"What now?" he asked the Iceni man when he had located him.

"Now we wait for the rest of the force. It might be a while. They're busy demolishing all the Roman dwellings on that side of the river. When all the warriors have forded the waterway, they'll plunder and burn the structures on this side."

Bryn grimaced. "At this rate, it will take another day to reach Camulodunum. By then, the people of the colonia will surely know of our approach."

"It won't matter," Gwynceffyl answered. "They don't have a chance against us."

"How can you be so certain?"

"Because the Romans have seen fit to withdraw their regular troops from places like Camulodunum. The only people left to defend the town are the former soldiers who've settled there. Since they razed the earthworks so more houses could be built, they wouldn't be able to defend the place even if they did have an army."

"No soldiers? No fortifications?" Bryn gazed at Gwynceffyl in dismay.

"Why do you think Boudica chose this strategy?" Gwynceffyl asked grimly.

Bryn's stomach twisted at the implication of the Iceni man's words. Sirona was right. If there were no soldiers at Camulodunum, most of those killed would be women and children, craftsmen and farmers. Already it was happening. A plume of smoke rose a distance down the valley. He couldn't help saying, "I'd hoped to do battle with armed combatants, not strike down the weak and helpless."

Gwynceffyl shrugged. "We must seize upon whatever means we can to prevail against our enemies. This isn't a heroic battle of champions such as the bards sing of, but a fight for survival."

Bryn told himself the Iceni leader was right. This was a desperate struggle to save his people. He must put aside his doubts and do what was necessary to drive the enemy from Pretani lands. He thought of his father being led away in chains. The image helped restore his determination. There must be some Roman men here. He would find them and kill them.

* * *

It was well past midday before the rest of the army had crossed the river and assembled to march. By then the valley reeked with the acrid odor of smoke from the burning settlements. The stench blocked out the fresh scent of the ocean they had been able to smell earlier. According to Gwynceffyl, Camulodunum was only a short distance from the eastern sea.

They started south, encountering more farmsteads and villas. Bryn urged his chariot past them. Ahead was a paved trackway leading into the colonia. He could see the sprawling settlement in the distance. Gwynceffyl was right. Many of the people of the colonia had built their homes outside the protection of the crumbling, ruined earthen embankments that had once served as fortifications.

Bryn halted his chariot, glad he must wait for the rest of the army to catch up. His stomach churned with anticipation and dread. He glanced up at the overcast sky and tried to decide how many more hours of daylight remained. It might be nearly dark by the time the rest of the fighting force arrived.

Many of the other chariots had halted in the same area, and one of the other drivers came to speak to Bryn. The warrior had masses of dark brown hair and a deep scar on the right side of his face. His filthy mantle and crys bore the yellow and green colors of the Catuvellauni tribe. "This looks like as good a place as any to leave our vehicles," he said.

"Leave them?" Bryn asked.

"Aye, it would be witless to drive them into the colonia. You can't fight from a chariot in an enclosed area."

"What if the enemy finds them?"

The man, who Bryn recalled was named Olwydd, grinned wolfishly. "We won't be leaving any of the enemy alive."

Olwydd's words chilled Bryn. Boudica's army was filled with men like this, men who had already lost everything—their families, their land and herds. All they possessed was the clothing they wore and their weapons. Even their chariots and horses belonged to Boudica. There was no reason for them to stay their hand against anyone who lived in the colonia. To them, all the people here were their enemies.

"Come, we must hobble our horses," Olwydd said. Bryn nodded. Grabbing the team's harness, he guided the horses into the brush.

* * *

"Isn't it always like this?" Olwydd grumbled as he and Bryn waited near the Roman roadway. "We hurry to assemble for battle, fire up our bloodlust, then wait around like tree stumps while the queen decides what we will do."

"I'm not thrilled at the prospect of following a woman into battle," said Corrio, another chariot driver. Like Olwydd, he was a tough-looking fellow, with so many freckles covering his weathered skin that they blurred into each other like the markings on a brindle hound. "But she's the one who drew all these men to her cause, and she has the wealth to equip us. And I can't complain about her strategy. This fine Roman colonia… " He gestured to the settlement ahead of them. "It will fall as easily as a rotten apple dropping from a tree. And the plunder… " He barred his blackened teeth in a hideous grin. "Those fools who took the time to loot the villas by the river were wasting their time. This is where the real treasure is. Gold. Jewels. Silk. Wine and spices. These people live like the emperor himself. We'll be hard put to carry it all. That's why I'm glad I drive a chariot rather than plodding along on foot. You'll be amazed at the booty I'll be able to cram into my vehicle."

"First things first," said Olwydd. "Before we carry off their treasure, we must kill these puling whoresons of Rome."

Bryn shifted his weight, uncomfortable at listening to the other warriors vent their bloodlust. To his relief, he saw Gwynceffyl striding toward them. "The queen is coming," the Iceni man announced. "It won't be long now."

In the distance, Bryn could see Boudica's crimson mantle like a splash of blood as she moved through the mass of warriors. She was speaking to the men as she passed. When she reached the area where the charioteers were gathered, Bryn saw that she was carrying a long staff. Impaled on the top was a round, hairy object—a human head, Roman by the looks of the cropped hair and beardless face.

Bryn felt a surge of contempt. He'd known warriors among the Dobunni to cut off the heads of their enemies, but Boudica hadn't killed this man, nor was she claiming his power and courage for herself. And she certainly wasn't treating the trophy head with dignity and respect. Boudica had taken a traditional symbol of Pretani belief and twisted it for her own purposes.

The queen passed by, exhorting them to let no living creature escape the attack of Camulodunum. Bryn turned away until the sound of her strident, angry words no longer filled his ears.

Then another, more welcome, voice sounded beside him. "Bryn, there you are. I thought I'd never find you."

He turned to greet Cadwalon. "If you weren't so uneasy with horses, you could have ridden beside me all this way."

Cadwalon tossed him a leather object.

"What's this?" Bryn asked.

"A Roman war crys. I found one for myself and thought you might find it useful to have one as well."

"You found these?" Bryn asked, examining the tight-fitting,

sleeveless garment.

Cadwalon's smile broadened. "Aye. The men they belonged to had no use for them any longer."

Bryn grunted.

"What's wrong?" Cadwalon asked. "For someone on the verge of a great victory over his enemies, you don't look very pleased."

Bryn drew near and lowered his voice. "They say we are to kill everyone."

"And what's wrong with that?"

"This is a settlement. There will be women and children. Old men."

Cadwalon shrugged. "What else can we do? We must send a message to Rome that it's not safe for their people to settle here."

Although Cadwalon's words almost convinced him, Bryn still felt uneasy. Perhaps he'd spent too many years in the grove and that was why it was so hard for him to simply obey orders. He'd been taught he must always consider what was right in the eyes of the gods. His teachers, especially Old Ogimos, had stressed the importance of listening to the voice of his inner spirit. Right now, that voice was warning him that what he was about to do was wrong.

A war horn sounded. Then another. A cry went up from the throng of warriors. Bryn glanced at the horizon, where the clouds had cleared to reveal a spectacular sunset. The waning sun was like a bronze brooch pinned against the deep blue mantle of the sky. "It will be dark before we reach the main portion of the colonia," he said.

"Once we set the place ablaze, there will be plenty of light," Cadwalon answered.

* * *

Sword drawn, shield in place, Bryn raced with the other men toward the colonia. Somehow, moments before the charge, he'd again lost track of Cadwalon. Other warriors were already pouring into the colonia through a dozen weak spots in the tumbled down earthworks, and some of the houses outside the ruined fortifications were ablaze.

He started down a trackway. To his right and left were long, low buildings made of mud bricks. He stopped and looked around for any defenders. Seeing none, his apprehension increased. Where were the fighting men? There must be some. Unless everyone had already fled the settlement.

Not knowing what else to do, he approached the nearest building and entered cautiously. A lamp on the wall still burned, but it appeared whoever lived there had left. Around the room were arrayed all the normal objects of everyday living. A brightly colored cloth decorated one wall, and there were a pottery dish and a basket of green apples on the table. He saw a loom in the corner, and near the hearth, a cradle. The sight made his blood run cold. Hurriedly, he left the dwelling.

Outside, he encountered another warrior who held out a burning brand. "Boudica wants everything set ablaze, so you'd best get busy."

Reluctantly, Bryn took the torch. The man darted off to the nearest building. He spent a few moments inside and then reappeared. Seeing Bryn, he called out, "You have to start the fires from within, where there are things that will burn." The man vanished down the passageway between two other structures.

Bryn started forward, still undecided what to do. Other men dashed past him, their forms silhouetted in the torchlight. He saw one man moving with great purpose, as if chasing something. Bryn followed and reached the man just as he cornered his prey. It was a wild-eyed woman, and the man had her trapped between two buildings. She jerked left, then right, trying to decide which way to run. The man laughed and unsheathed his sword. While Bryn watched, stunned, the warrior swung his sword and beheaded the woman. The warrior bent over the fallen body as if searching for something. Then he straightened and left, disappearing into the doorway of one of the nearby dwellings.

Bryn stared. Ten heartbeats had passed and a woman was dead. He walked over to where her head had fallen and looked down. His horror increased when he saw that she was Pretani. Her features and coloring made that clear.

He turned away, feeling sick. For a time he stood there, then again started forward. More houses. More warriors streaming by, setting fires. Some of them were weighed down with plunder, their arms laden with bundles he guessed must contain the riches Olwydd had spoken of.

He came upon another body, this one of an old man whose throat had been cut. The man stared up at Bryn with a look of surprise. His eyes were very blue. A little farther, Bryn saw a woman lying face down on the ground. Although it was hard to tell with all the blood, her hair looked light-colored. He noticed something lying nearby. At first he thought it was a bundle of valuables the woman had dropped, then he saw the tiny hand peeking out from beneath the linen wrap. He shuddered and cold sweat broke out on his skin. Where were the men who should be defending this place? Why had they left these poor unfortunates to look after themselves?

He started forward shakily, still queasy with revulsion. What was this place? Had he entered the realm of Arawn, the god of the underworld? All around him was the smell of blood and death, and the air was thick with smoke, like a noxious mist. He remembered Cruthin telling him about a dream he'd had of the place of the dead, his tale of being chased while rotting corpses pursued him. An awful dream, and yet this was worse. This was real.

He looked back the way he had come, wanting to run away, to find a river or stream and wash the stench of death away, then rub himself with green grass, fragrant with the scent of new life. But a sense of inevitability kept him moving. For some reason the gods had sent him here, set his feet upon this pathway. He must see where his destiny led him.

He decided he was nearing the center of the settlement. There were workshops and storage buildings, carts and barrels. Other warriors had already moved through the area, smashing whatever they could get their hands on, and the ground was littered with broken and ruined objects. Shattered pottery, spilled wine and oil, loaves of bread, scattered iron implements. A leatherworker's shop had been broken into and shoes and belts, ropes and hides were everywhere. Among the refuse lay the craftsman who had fashioned these things, his balding head oozing blood like dark red dye. His blunt fingers still gripped the awl he'd used to try to defend himself. Bryn consoled himself that the man at least looked Roman.

Nearby a warrior was attempting to shatter the wooden door of another shop with the blunt end of his sword. He shot Bryn a warning look as he drew near. "This one is mine," he said, baring his teeth like a dog. "Find another metalsmith to rob."

Bryn moved away. He wanted nothing from this place.

"Get to the temple," a warrior cried as he rushed past. "All the people have fled to the temple and taken refuge there."

"Where's the temple?" Bryn asked.

"This way."

Other warriors rushed by. Bryn followed. He could hear bits of their conversation.

"A disappointment... most of them gone..."

Another man answered, "It doesn't matter. They'll die soon enough."

He reached a place where there were massive buildings. Never before had Bryn seen such enormous structures. They loomed over this part of the settlement like the craggy peaks of the mountains in the sunset lands. In the open area between the buildings a large group of warriors had gathered. Torches had been placed all around and as Bryn approached he could see a statue of a man riding a horse. The statue was life-size and appeared to be made out of bronze.

The queen and her daughter Sybilla stood in front of the statue. "Behold," Boudica cried, raising her arms. She wore the crimson mantle and the gleaming gold snake jewelry Bryn remembered from the sacrifice. "This is Claudius, emperor of Rome!" Boudica cried. "The people here honor him as god. But this is how we honor him." She took up a great javelin with a curved metal tip and smashed it against the neck of the man on the horse. When the handle of the javelin shattered, she let out a muffled cry of rage.

Her frustration was echoed in a low, rumbling sound from the gathered warriors. As if of one mind, they rushed the statue. The bronze man-god immediately began to shake and sway and then, with a creaking sound, fell over. The crowd scrambled back as the figure toppled, as if they were shocked at how easily it had fallen. A warrior dashed forward and snatched up something, which turned out to be the head of Claudius, broken off from the body. As the man held the head aloft triumphantly, the rest of the warriors cheered, the sound echoing off the great buildings.

Even Bryn knew a stirring of pride. Aye, it was gratifying to see the head of the Roman emperor roll in the dirt. Claudius was responsible for the downfall of the Tarisllwyth and the death of his father. If only it weren't merely a statue, but the man himself. And if only there were some Roman soldiers here to also strike down.

Bryn's gaze was drawn to a stone structure directly behind the statue. Inside must be the survivors of the colonia. He expected Boudica to order her army to charge the place, but she didn't. Instead, she started telling the warriors to bring her the bodies of the dead. "Bring them here!" she screamed. "We'll make a pyre of their corpses and melt down this bronze monstrosity and use the metal to make weapons for ourselves!"

There was another cry of satisfaction. The gathering began to disperse. Bryn grabbed the crys of a man passing by. "What about the people inside the temple?"

"We'll kill them soon enough," the man answered. "If they refuse to come out and fight, we'll torch the place."

Bryn thought of Sirona's prediction, how her face had grown pale as she talked about the fire and the screams of the dying. She had foreseen all this.

He resheathed his sword. There would be no battle for Camulodunum. The colonia had fallen as easily as the statue of Claudius.

Glancing around, he tried to decide what to do. He recalled Sirona's plan for them to set an ambush for the ninth legion. At the time, he'd been concerned with how they could get the Romans in the right position to make an ambush possible. He glanced at the temple. Surely before they took refuge there, the leaders of Camulodunum had sent a messenger north to beg for aid.

His mood of despondency began to ease. He might still have a chance to kill Roman soldiers. All he had to do was convince some of these men to march north and lay in wait for the ninth legion as they attempted to come to the rescue of the colonia. He glanced around. Gwynceffyl was the man he needed. The Iceni leader could round up his men and explain this new strategy. Any true warrior would prefer attacking armed troops to killing helpless women and old men.

But where should he look for Gwynceffyl? Bryn had expected to find him here, among the rest of the warriors. Perhaps he and his men were still firing the buildings of the settlement. Bryn turned and started back through the colonia. The men he encountered were putting every structure they could find to the torch. None of them had seen Gwynceffyl.

Bryn continued to search. The smoke was choking now, and he had to hold his cloak over his mouth to breathe. At last, in the marketplace, he saw a familiar figure.

"Cadwalon!" he cried.

Cadwalon turned. His face was soot-stained and his blue eyes heavily bloodshot from the smoke. Seeing Bryn, he grinned broadly, his teeth a flash of white in his filthy face. "There you are. I wondered where you had got to."

"What are you doing? Still firing the buildings?" Bryn asked.

"It's better than butchering babies." Cadwalon made a face. "You were right. This is a slaughter. I haven't yet found anyone worth killing. But most of the other men aren't so particular. The Iceni and Trinovantes count all these settlers as their enemies."

"Then we must give them an opportunity to kill Roman soldiers instead." Cadwalon looked at him and Bryn continued, "Remember the idea Sirona had to ambush the ninth legion? We can still do that, if we leave now and get in place before the enemy marches south."

"You think the ninth is on their way here?" Cadwalon asked.

"They must be. Someone from the colonia will have sent word to them. These people wouldn't take refuge in the temple if they didn't believe someone would come to their aid."

"That's true," Cadwalon agreed. "But depending on when the message went out, the Romans might already be on the march."

"Which is why we must hurry. We must find Gwynceffyl and convince him to take his men away from here and give them an opportunity to do battle with Roman soldiers."

Cadwalon nodded. "I saw Gwynceffyl not long ago. He can't have gone far."

They searched the market for the Iceni leader, then finally gave up and made their way back to the temple. On the way, they encountered Gwynceffyl with a group of his men. He was as covered with soot as

Cadwalon. Pulling him aside, they explained their plan.

"It might work," Gwynceffyl said when they had finished. "If we can convince the queen."

"Surely now that she's satisfied her bloodlust, she will consider the idea," Cadwalon said. "Point out to her that we can kill a thousand settlers, but until we confront the Roman forces and defeat them, we have no chance of winning back the island."

"There's sense in what you say, but that doesn't mean the queen will listen."

Bryn thought of another idea. "I know Boudica provided the wealth to equip this army. But if you explained my plan to your men, wouldn't they choose to follow you and kill Romans rather than staying here with the queen and besieging the helpless people inside the temple?"

Gwynceffyl's bloodshot eyes narrowed. "You're suggesting I order my men to ignore the queen's wishes?"

"You're a seasoned warrior. Why shouldn't you make a tactical decision of this sort?"

"I'll think on it," Gwynceffyl said. "But first, let me talk to the queen. I think she's in the senate house." Gwynceffyl started off toward a building on the other side of the open area.

"So now we wait upon the queen's pleasure," Cadwalon said sourly.

"Or, we could start telling the warriors gathered here of our plan," Bryn suggested.

Cadwalon nodded. "Aye, we could do that."

The two of them split up and began moving through the crowd. Uncertain whether he dare approach men he didn't know and ask them to defy the queen's orders, Bryn looked for the other chariot drivers. He saw no sign of them and wondered if they had begun carrying booty back to their vehicles.

His search took him close to the fallen statue. It was a hideous scene. Spears topped with the heads of the fallen had been arranged in a circle around the ruined monument. Nearby was a substantial pile of bodies. In the torchlight Bryn could see that many of them were women, children or old people. He approached the pile, feeling sick. How could anyone feel good about this horrible slaughter?

"If you're looking to scavenge, you'll find much better spoils in the dwellings."

Bryn looked up as a man dumped the limp form of a girl of about ten winters onto the pile.

"I've already stripped that one of anything of value," the man said. "I'm sure most of the others have been picked clean as well. You could take their clothing, but it's hardly worth the effort when there's so much other treasure here. Besides, it will help them burn better."

Bryn glared at the man. "Is this all you came here for, to steal from these people?"

The man glowered back. "Why shouldn't we steal from them? They stole from us. They took our land and destroyed our farms and settlements! They ruined our livelihood!"

"Nay, these people didn't do that. *That* was the Romans. If you want to get revenge on your true enemy, your real oppressor, you should come with me. A part of Boudica's army is going north this very night to lay in wait for the ninth legion. As the enemy marches south to come to Camulodunum's defense, we'll ambush them."

The man frowned. "I've heard nothing of this. Are these new orders from the queen?"

Bryn opened his mouth to answer, but before he could do so, a woman's voice rang out harshly. "You! Drui! What are you doing here?"

Bryn looked around to see Sybilla, Boudica's daughter. Her clothes and hair were disheveled and her eyes wild. Bryn tensed. Sensing this woman's hostility, he realized he must answer her carefully. Should he tell her he was a warrior, as well as a Drui? But if he did that, she might think he had deliberately deceived the queen.

Sybilla didn't wait for his response, but started toward the pile of bodies. She kicked the pile with her foot. "Stinking whores!" Her voice rose in a hysterical screech. "I will make you suffer as I have suffered! I vowed to have my vengeance and so I shall!"

Sybilla whirled around, and Bryn took a step back, uncertain whether she would attack him in her frenzy. But she strode past him and grabbed one of the spears that ringed the pile of bodies. She shook the spear and the head on it went flying, landing near the ruined, headless statue. Carrying the spear, she approached the pile of bodies and began to poke at them until the corpse of a woman slid to the side. Then, very deliberately, she took the spear and thrust it between the legs of the dead woman, impaling the corpse. "How does it feel, Roman whore?" Sybilla cried. "How does it feel?"

She grabbed another of the spears. Bryn grimaced in disgust as she impaled another victim. Abruptly, Sybilla turned to him. "Give me your sword," she demanded. "Give it to me!"

He stared at her, wondering if her wits had fled. When she took a step toward him, he shook his head. "Nay, I'll not give up my sword."

Sybilla's eyes glinted with fury, but she moved away and approached the warrior Bryn had been talking to. Grabbing at the man's swordbelt, she ordered, "Give me your sword." The man appeared too stunned to resist. He let her wrest the weapon from its scabbard, then stood staring dumbly as Sybilla again approached the pile of bodies. She straddled the corpse she had previously impaled and awkwardly sliced off one of the woman's breasts.

The man whose sword she'd stolen grunted with distaste. Sybilla raised the sword again and took another swipe at the body. Then she dropped the sword, and leaning over the corpse, grabbed the bloody mass of the breast and attempted to thrust it into the victim's gaping mouth.

"By the might of Beli," Bryn swore. He met the gaze of the other warrior. "She's out of her wits."

The man nodded. "Aye, but she's the queen's daughter. And I can always find another sword."

Bryn watched with increasing revulsion as Sybilla continued her grisly attack on the dead. Then, all at once, something snapped inside him. His learning in the grove had taught him the importance of having respect for those who had left the world of the living. And some of these women were Pretani. They deserved better than this, regardless of whether they had lain with Roman men.

He started toward Sybilla. "Don't do this! These are your own people. Save your wrath for the enemy. Wouldn't you rather see Roman soldiers lying dead?"

Sybilla faced him, teeth bared. Her saffron-colored crys was spattered with blood, as were her face and arms. She reminded him of a ferocious she-cat defending its kill.

He took a step nearer. She was a slender woman and clearly exhausted from the effort of wielding the heavy sword. The weapon hung slackly from her hands. He reached out and grabbed her wrist, intending to wrest the sword from her. She writhed and twisted, screaming her outrage as he pried the weapon from her hand. As she dropped it, the powerful voice of the queen echoed off the nearby temple wall. "What's this? Who dares to lay hands on my daughter?"

In seconds, Boudica was there, a flash of swirling crimson and fire-bright hair. Bryn immediately released Sybilla. "I was afraid she would hurt herself," he said. "The sword was much too heavy for her."

Boudica's blue eyes met his, burning with outrage. "No man touches my daughter and lives."

Bryn tightened his grip on his own sword, preparing for the worst. He heard Boudica's shouted command, "Stop him!" and tried to lash out. A blurry shape filled his vision. There was a crack of thunder against his skull. Then everything went black.

Chapter 24

Bryn woke to dizzying pain. With each throb of his pulse, agony burst inside his skull. It was dark all around and the surface beneath him was hard and smooth. He searched his memory for any recollection of what had happened. Vaguely, he remembered coming to Camulodunum and being distressed by the slaughter. His next memory was of finding Cadwalon and telling him they must think of a way to leave this place and set up an ambush for the ninth legion. After that, there was nothing.

He touched his aching head, feeling the lump on the side of it. Either he'd been hit or he had fallen and struck his head. He tried to raise himself to a sitting position, but the movement made the pain worsen and aroused a violent nausea. Forced to lie down again, he let himself float back to oblivion.

The next time he roused he smelled smoke. Fear lent strength to his muscles and focused his wits. He tried to sit up and managed it this time, although he felt dizzy from the effort and his stomach churned dangerously. All at once he saw the orange-yellow glow of flames shining through an opening on the other side of the room. He struggled to his feet. The dizziness swallowed him and he went down again.

When he became aware once more, he realized the orange glow was even brighter and it was getting hot. He was in some kind of storage building full of pottery jars, wooden casks and piles of hides. His horrified gaze took in the straw packed around the jars. Once the flames reached it, the whole place would go up. He tried once more to get to his feet and doubled over with nausea. The smoke was growing thick. He couldn't breath. He coughed, tasting the acrid odor of death, and let out a moan. "Help me," he whispered. "Help me."

I believe the goddess will protect me.

Sirona's calm, trusting words filled his mind. He must ask the gods for help. He coughed again, then called out loudly, "Arianrhod, lady of the moon, goddess of the silver wheel of stars that guides our destiny, hear me now. Give me more years of life, that I might serve and honor you. Modren, great mother, come to my aid. Grant me more time in this realm, that I might fulfill my dream of being a true and valiant warrior. Ceridwen, keeper of the cauldron of wisdom, help me find a way out of this place."

The only response was the soft crackle and hiss of the flames, then someone shouted, "Bryn? Where are you?"

"Cadwalon, I'm here! I'm here!"

Cadwalon's anxious visage loomed over him. "Thank the gods," he muttered. "I feared you were dead."

Thank the gods, indeed, Bryn thought.

Cadwalon grabbed him by the arm. As his friend dragged him upright, the motion made the pain in Bryn's skull explode and waves of unconsciousness lapped over him. Dimly, he heard Cadwalon curse. "What have they done to you? Why can't you stand?"

"I was hit on the head," Bryn mumbled.

"I'll carry you if I have to. There's not much time. Already this side of the building is filled with smoke." Cadwalon dragged Bryn upright by his crys, then supported his weight against his own body. Bryn gritted his teeth and forced himself to remain conscious and move forward, although every step felt like a knife thrust through his temple.

In a haze of pain and smoke, they somehow made their way out. Even when they were quit of the burning structure, Cadwalon wouldn't rest. "We have to get away," he muttered in Bryn's ear. "If anyone sees us and tells the queen, we'll both be killed."

Splintered images and fragments of awareness danced before Bryn's eyes as Cadwalon pulled him along. Everywhere were bright flames, searing sparks, dizzying heat and choking black smoke. Once or twice he felt blackness looming up, but Cadwalon maintained his fierce hold, easing his grip only when Bryn bent over to vomit.

Finally, the air cleared and it grew darker. The night was no longer lit by flames, but only a smoldering glow and the stars and moon. Gazing down at the ground, Bryn saw they were following the paved road leading out of the settlement. The pain in his head had grown unbearable. The urge to lie down overwhelmed him. "Please," he begged Cadwalon. "Let me rest for a while."

"We can't stop yet."

"The chariot," Bryn croaked, his throat raw from the smoke. "We must get the chariot."

"Where is it?"

"In these woods. If you let me lie down and rest for a time, I can find it."

Cadwalon released his grip on Bryn and they both sank into the soft, dew-laden grass. After the stench of the smoke, the scent of damp vegetation was blessedly sweet. Bryn closed his eyes. He was faintly aware of Cadwalon shaking him and shouting, but the words blurred into meaningless sounds.

* * *

Bryn woke to find himself in a square, timber structure with no smokehole in the ceiling. Raising himself to a sitting position, he looked around. There was nothing in the room except the pallet he was laying on, a second pallet, a stool, a brazier like the one in the chamber in Boudica's palace, and a single wooden storage chest in the corner. He blinked in the daylight filtered in from one small window. Where was he? Had he been captured by Romans? Or was he dead and this some dwelling in the Otherworld?

As bits of memory returned, he discarded both notions. He recalled Cadwalon helping him walk and then the long ride in the bottom of the jostling chariot, where his head felt as it would explode with every bump they hit. His next recollection was of a woman leaning over him, her face serene and kind. She had pale hair, but it wasn't Sirona. He remembered that she made him drink water and broth.

She had done other things as well, bathing him and helping him use a pottery jar to relieve himself. He grimaced at the thought of being so helpless, then searched his mind for anything else he could recall.

There'd been another woman... young and red-haired. He remembered feeling panicked when he woke and saw her standing over him. At the time, he'd thought it was Sybilla, Boudica's daughter. Now he wasn't sure. Was it real or a dream?

He lay down again and closed his eyes. A vague headache still flickered behind his eyes. Trying to figure things out seemed to make it worse. He let his thoughts drift away for a time and then resumed his struggle to understand where he was. How long had he been unconscious? And where was Cadwalon?

Again, he raised himself to a sitting position. His muscles trembled with the effort, but he gritted his teeth and got to his feet. Using the blanket to cover himself, he staggered toward the door. Before he reached it, a woman entered, the same one he remembered caring for him. Her hair was pure white, although she wasn't old. She smiled at him and said, "So you have returned to us at last. Your friend will be very pleased."

"Cadwalon—where is he?"

"He'll be back soon," the woman answered. "Come, let me help you back to bed. You should eat before you try to get up."

She started to take his arm, but he jerked away. "I'm not going back to bed. I need to speak to Cadwalon. And where's my clothing?"

"I told you, Cadwalon will be here soon. As for your garments, I'll fetch them if you sit down." Grasping his arm firmly, she steered him over to a small stool. Once he was seated, she left the dwelling and returned in a moment with his crys, bracco and shoes. "Cadwalon has your other things." She handed him the garments. "Do you need help dressing?"

"Nay!" Bryn snapped, then immediately regretted his harsh tone. This woman had likely saved his life.

She turned her back while he dressed. It took a long while. His muscles felt shaky and weak. When he was finished, he said, "I'm sorry I lashed out at you, but I hate feeling helpless. Nor do I like being indebted to a woman whose name I don't even know."

"I'm Plancina, priestess of the Three Mothers."

"Are you a Learned One?"

She shook her head. "I come from the lands across the sunrise sea, which the Romans call Gaul. Only a few Learned Ones remain there." She regarded him thoughtfully and then said, "Since you refuse to return to bed, you might as well come with me to the temple. It isn't far." She took his arm again. He wanted to refuse her aid, but already his legs trembled from the effort of standing.

She led him out of the dwelling and along a well-worn pathway through the trees. Again, he asked, "Where's Cadwalon?"

"At the palace."

Bryn halted. "Boudica's palace?"

Plancina nodded. "Don't worry. The only member of the queen's family residing there is Julia, and she wouldn't harm your friend."

"I must go to him," Bryn said.

"First, you must eat," Plancina said firmly.

They reached a square stone structure. The workmanship and shape of the building reminded Bryn of the Romans, but there were other aspects, like the pattern of leaves around the doorway, which seemed Pretani. She led him to the back side of the structure where there was a spring. He saw offerings in the bottom of the pool at the base of the spring—jewelry, coins and other metal objects. Nearby, on a stone ledge, someone had left a basket. Plancina picked up the basket and looked inside. "Ah, bread and cheese. That will help restore your strength."

"Those offerings belong to the god of the spring," Bryn protested.

"As the caretaker of the spring, I have the right to decide what should be done with the gifts. And I choose to use the food to nourish myself and my guest."

"You're certain the god of the spring won't be angry?"

Plancina smiled. "Nay, the Three Mothers won't be angry. Nantsuelo, in particular, is a goddess of healing. She would want you to use the food to restore your strength."

Plancina indicated he should sit down on the grass beside the spring. When he was seated, she handed him a thick mealcake spread with soft white cheese. He ate it greedily. The fine texture of the bread reminded him of what he'd eaten in Boudica's palace.

"Where does this food come from?"

"Probably the palace. Some servant likely wished to ask a favor of the Three Mothers." She took a mealcake and ate, although more leisurely than Bryn.

"What do people petition the goddesses for?" he asked.

"Many things. The Three Mothers oversee healing, fertility, love, peace and prosperity. Most women seek help with these matters at one time or another in their lives."

"The people who make offerings here are women?"

"Usually, but not always. Those who plant crops and harvest the fruit of the earth are also dependent upon the female deities."

Bryn felt himself begin to relax. This woman reminded him of Sirona, and he felt he could trust her. Of course, it was probably witless to worry about such things. While he lay unconscious, his life had been in her hands.

"Have some more food." Plancina gestured to the basket.

"How long I have been here?"

"Five days."

Bryn was shocked.

"Cadwalon feared you would die, so he brought you here. He believed the waters of the sacred spring might heal you."

Bryn raised his gaze to Plancina's. "Is that what happened?"

Plancina shrugged. "I think it more likely that your body simply needed time to recover. Injuries to the head are very unpredictable. Sometimes the person dies. Other times they wake, yet are never the same. Sometimes, like you, they rouse and it's almost as if the injury didn't happen, except the person has lost some of their memories."

Bryn nodded. "I can't recall how I was injured or how I came to be here. Everything I do remember is blurry and confused. Did Cadwalon tell you what happened to me?"

Plancina nodded. "Although it might be better if Cadwalon explains things."

"You're certain he's safe?" Bryn demanded. "That no one at the palace will harm him?"

"Aye. He's safe, I vow it."

Bryn nodded, although his anxiety eased only a little. He put a hand to his throbbing head. It was pitiful to be this weak. For a moment, he closed his eyes. He opened them when he heard someone approaching.

Cadwalon entered the clearing by the spring. His face lit with pleasure at the sight of Bryn. "You're awake, thank the gods! I thought for a time you'd never rouse again." He crouched down beside Bryn. "But you mustn't exert yourself too much. I think that's what you did before and that's why you were senseless for so long."

"Tell me what happened," Bryn said. "All of it."

"Where should I begin? What do you remember?"

Bryn searched his thoughts. "The last thing I recall clearly is being in Camulodunum and talking to you and Gwynceffyl. After that, it's all confused and jumbled, like a pottery jar that's been broken into countless pieces."

"Apparently, you confronted Boudica's daughter Sybilla when she was in the act of mutilating the bodies of the slain. While you were trying to stop her, Boudica arrived and became enraged. I believe she would have had you killed immediately, except she thought you were Drui. She had you put into a storage building and then ordered her men to set it ablaze."

Bryn recalled the smoke and fire. "How did you find me?"

"Boudica has offended more than a few warriors with her high-handed manner. I asked around until I found one of those men and he told me where you'd been taken. By the time I reached the storage building, it was already on fire. You were very fortunate I found you when I did."

"Then what happened?" Bryn asked. "I vaguely recall walking back through the colonia. But after that..." He shook his head.

"After we left the colonia, I found the chariot and brought you here."

"You drove the chariot?" Bryn asked, incredulous.

Cadwalon shrugged. "I had no choice. You wouldn't rouse, and I knew that if we were discovered by the queen or the warriors of her household, we would be killed." Cadwalon's expression grew grim. "I don't like to recall that night. It was as if Boudica unleashed some evil force."

Bryn nodded. "I fear Ysganon did his job too well. He succeeded in conjuring the Triple Goddess of Death. Now She looms over us, a cackling hag glorying in our doom." He repressed a shudder. Even though he couldn't really remember what happened before he was injured, he felt a lingering sense of horror whenever he thought of Boudica or Sybilla. They represented the dark side of the Goddess, the raven of death. Sirona represented the bright and beautiful aspect, the radiant Lady of the moon.

"Still, all is not lost." Cadwalon clapped him on the shoulder. "Soon after we left Camulodunum, Gwynceffyl took a large force of men north and wiped out the ninth legion as they came to defend their settlements. At least two thousand Romans fell in the ambush. Only their cavalry escaped."

"That's wonderful!' Bryn exclaimed. Then he experienced the

familiar bitterness. "Except for the fact that I missed the battle." Would he ever get a chance to confront Roman soldiers in combat? "So, tell me, now where does Gwynceffyl lead his men?"

"Everyone is supposed to meet up at Camulodunum. Warriors from many other tribes are joining Boudica's army, eager to be part of the things now that they've had some success. By the time the force moves south to Londinium, Boudica's army will be huge."

Bryn recalled Sirona warning him of the fateful battle of her vision. If it were a true Seeing, then Gwynceffyl and the rest of the Pretani were headed straight to their doom. He got to his feet. "We have to find Gwynceffyl. We have to warn him about Sirona's vision."

Cadwalon's voice was gentle as he said, "I know Sirona is your childhood love and you believe she's gifted with magical abilities, but there's no reason to think we won't prevail against the enemy. If you will set aside your Drui learning, this nonsense of visions and the gods, you'll see that I'm right."

"It's not nonsense," Bryn said, growing angry. "What happened at Camulodunum will bring the full wrath of the Romans down upon us. Once they hear of the slaughter and mutilations, they'll gather all their forces together and retaliate."

"Let them retaliate!" Cadwalon exclaimed. "Even with all their legions, we'll outnumber them. Boudica's army swells every day. Most of the Trinovantes and Arebates have joined us, and even some the Catuvellauni."

"Numbers aren't everything in battle. Strategy counts for a great deal. And that's Boudica's weakness."

Cadwalon frowned at him. "The blow to your head must have affected you more than I realized. Never would I have thought to hear you express doubts about the battle prowess of your own people."

"I don't doubt the fighting ability of the Pretani," Bryn said. "It's the competency of the woman who leads them that I question. If it had been up to Boudica, the ambush of the ninth legion would never have occurred. Now she leads this great force to Londinium. What if the Romans await us there?"

"Then we will fight them and defeat them!"

Bryn shook his head. "Not if Sirona's vision is a true one."

"There's no reason to think it is."

Bryn felt his face flush. "The fact is, Boudica has no experience leading an army and she's driven by the need for revenge more than a desire for victory. Look at her target—Camulodunum and now Londinium. She's based her battle strategy on her desire to kill and destroy rather than tactical reasons. If the Pretani were led by someone other than Boudica, I might have more confidence. But the Iceni queen knows nothing of war, only of killing and burning the helpless."

"It's not Boudica who will be going against the Romans, but the Pretani army," Cadwalon retorted. "Now that several tribes have agreed to work together, we'll outnumber the enemy many times over. No army can prevail against such odds!"

Seeing the set of his friend's jaw, Bryn realized there was no point in arguing any longer. A sense of regret filled him. If Cadwalon wouldn't change his mind, eventually they must part company. But for now, there was no reason they couldn't travel together. "Let's make plans to leave tomorrow," he said.

Plancina spoke. "It would be better if you waited a few days. You're still very weak."

"I can't wait," Bryn said. "I must talk to Gwynceffyl as soon as possible. He's been like a father to me, taught me to drive a chariot and furnished me with a sword and shield. I must warn him what is to come." He looked at Cadwalon. "Even if he chooses not to listen."

Part 3
The Silver Wheel

Chapter 25

"Romans." Sirona motioned to the group of riders coming towards them down the roadway. Even from a distance, she could see the glint of their metal breastplates and helmets.

"We could drive off into the trees," suggested Rufus. "But since they've already spotted us, it might be better if we stayed on the roadway."

Sirona made a sound of agreement and tried to ignore the dread rising in her belly. This wasn't the first time they'd encountered Roman troops, having passed small groups of the enemy on several occasions since setting out from Verulanium two days before. But the Romans they'd encountered previously had been on foot and the chariot had swept by them so rapidly that Sirona hadn't been afraid. This time, the enemy soldiers were mounted.

As the group of riders drew near, Sirona could barely breathe. All she could think of was Einion and Culhwch lying on the ground, dead and bloody. She held on tightly to the side of the chariot as Rufus guided the vehicle onto the grass at the edge of the road to let the Romans pass. Soon the riders were near enough that Sirona could make out their shaven faces beneath their helmets. A moment later, the whole troop rushed by, hooves pounding.

Rufus gave a jubilant laugh. "By the Light! They didn't even see us! Your Goddess—whoever she is—has made us invisible!"

"Are you certain that's what it was?" Sirona asked. "Perhaps they simply ignored us."

"It wasn't that," he exclaimed. "Couldn't you tell? They didn't even look at us."

Sirona had also felt this, but she was still reluctant to accept the implication of Rufus's words. Was it true that the enemy couldn't see her? She'd been so afraid of confronting Roman soldiers. Yet she'd done so several times and survived.

Rufus drove the vehicle back onto the road and they continued traveling north. Soon they could smell water and marshland. A river came into view on the left of the roadway. The landscape grew more rugged, rising to high wooded bluffs on the far side of the river. Sirona gazed ahead to the place where the road and river met and felt the tell-tale tingling along her spine. She tensed, anticipating the vision.

All at once the scent of the river was blotted out by another smell. Death. Blood. Decay. Before her eyes, the grassy plain on the other side of the road became a scene of horror. Rotting corpses were piled everywhere. Pretani warriors, their patterned garments, fair skin and long hair stained dark with blood, lay where they had fallen. Bloated dead horses and crushed and splintered chariots sprawled beside them. At the far end of the battleground, she could make out overturned carts and more bodies. Many, many more bodies. More people had died here than had been in the army camp at Boudica's palace. Indeed, more people had perished here than she had ever seen in her life.

Sirona leaned against the side of the chariot and began to sob.

"Sirona, what is it?" Rufus called. "What's wrong?"

She shook her head, blinded by tears, speechless with anguish. Finally, she managed to call out, "Drive! Leave this place! Now!"

Rufus urged the horses on with guttural shouts. Sirona clutched the side of the chariot, grateful for the dizzying speed with which the vehicle could move. She willed the chariot to go even faster. As they fled, she felt the spirits of her countrymen around her, screaming their agony and despair.

She was barely aware as they passed the fort to the left of the road. They crossed a bridge and began to climb a hill. As they reached the other side, she caught her breath and rubbed at her tear-swollen eyes.

"What? What did you see?" Rufus demanded.

She shook her head, still unable to answer.

He slowed the horses to a trot. "What in the name of Minerva did you *see*?" he repeated. "You look as white as a nobleman's toga."

Sirona still felt so weak and empty she could barely speak. "This is where the battle will take place," she gasped. "My people are going to be crushed... destroyed. And there's nothing I can do to stop it." She felt overwhelmed with despair and fury. She wanted to rage against the gods, to curse them for what they had done to her. Why send her this powerful vision if the disaster she saw couldn't be turned aside? Why make her suffer twice, anticipating the downfall of her people and then enduring the reality of it as well?

Rufus touched her shoulder. "Don't give up. Remember what you told me. We can't always understand the purpose of the gods or see the pattern of our future taking shape. "

She nodded. Rufus's words rang true. Besides, she couldn't let Rufus be dragged down by her despondency. For his sake, she must try to have hope. She motioned abruptly. "Let's continue on. Perhaps in the sunset lands, things will be better."

A while later they reached a place where the Roman road split into two branches. Rufus halted the chariot. "Which way do you think we should go?" He motioned. "That way appears to continue north, probably to where the Romans have their main fort at Deva."

Sirona glanced at the broad, raised trackway ahead and a shiver of revulsion swept through her. After her sickening vision of the battlefield, she never wanted to look upon the enemy again. "Perhaps it's time we left the road."

"I don't know if that would be wise. Already, the terrain looks difficult and I suspect it will get worse as we head west. I don't know if I can manage the chariot on such rough ground."

Sirona thought of the rocky, hilly landscape of her homeland and glanced at Rufus, dreading his reaction to what she was about to say. "We might have to leave the chariot behind and set out on foot." A look of alarm crossed his young features. Knowing that much of his distress had to do with abandoning the horses, Sirona added, "Perhaps we can find a farmstead where we can leave the team and chariot, rather than turning the horses loose."

Rufus nodded. Then, all at once, his expression brightened. "For that matter, there's no reason we couldn't ride."

"Ride?" Sirona's stomach clenched. She was just getting used to the chariot.

Seeing her expression, Rufus said, "We could ride on one horse and lead the other behind us. We're both fairly light. I think it would work."

Sirona nodded reluctantly. His plan made sense, although the idea of sitting on the back of a horse still frightened her.

Rufus drove the chariot off the roadway into the underbrush. After he unhitched the horses, he and Sirona dragged the vehicle into a thicket of ash. When they had it well hidden, Sirona glanced at the darkening sky and said, "Perhaps we should camp here for the night."

Rufus nodded. "We could wait until tomorrow to try riding, especially since I must alter the horses' reins. But we must get farther away from the roadway." They retrieved their supplies and after fastening their packs to the backs of the horses, set off with Rufus leading both animals.

It was twilight when they found a clearing in the forest where the horses could graze. They spent the night there, wrapped in their cloaks under the sheltering branches of some oaks.

In the morning, Rufus shortened the horses' reins. Then he climbed on one of the animals' backs and reached down to pull Sirona up after him. She eyed the nervous, tail-swishing beast with trepidation. "It's all right," Rufus coaxed. "The mare will get used to us soon enough."

Clutching his hand, she scrambled up behind him and gripped his waist frantically as the horse began to move. She gave a shriek.

"Don't do that," Rufus warned her in a low voice. "You'll spook the mare."

Sirona clamped her mouth shut. Her heart was racing and she was beginning to sweat. All she could think about was sliding backwards off the horse and being trampled under its hooves.

Rufus told her to hold onto the horse with her legs, but not too tightly. Then he made some scarcely perceptible movement with his body and the horse started forward. Behind them, the other horse followed, its reins tied to Rufus's belt. Sirona clung to the belt as well, each step of the horse beneath her seeming to jar her whole body. "How did you learn to ride?" she asked. "It seems like the most unnatural thing anyone could possibly do."

"To me, it's exhilarating."

Sirona closed her eyes. Maybe if she couldn't see, she wouldn't feel so afraid.

"Relax," Rufus said. "Let your body merge with the horse's. If you hold yourself stiff, you'll be terribly sore by tonight." He laughed softly. "You've always reminded me of some sort of goddess, but it's certainly not Epona, lady of horses!"

She took a deep breath and tried to do as he suggested. Fortunately, the pathway through the trees narrowed and Rufus was forced to slow. By they time they reached open country, Sirona was a little more used to riding, although she continued to cling to Rufus. Then the land turned rocky and rough, and their pace grew plodding once more. Still, they were moving much faster than she and Rufus could walk. At this rate, they would reach her homeland in a few days.

They climbed a steep hill and then descended into a forested valley. "By Jupiter, this is harsh country," Rufus complained. "How can your people live here? I've seen little game and you could hardly grow crops in this place."

"See that?" Sirona pointed. "Some farmer is grazing his cattle among those hills. He probably also has a flock of sheep that his son is tending. Down in the valley, he will have wheat and barley planted. It's not an easy life, but my people have survived here for years. And before them, the Old Ones also eked out a living in the hills."

In contrast to Rufus's unease, Sirona felt a deep sense of satisfaction the farther west they traveled. Here among the wild hills and misty air, she could feel the ancient spirits all around. They lingered in the gray stones, waited silently on the hilltops, and gave voice to the gurgling murmur of the little runnels and streams that crisscrossed the tangle of bracken and fern in the ravines and hidden glens.

The horrifying visions of death and destruction gradually retreated from her thoughts. As she looked up and saw a gyrfalcon circling above them, hunting for prey, a feeling of contentment came over her. The wild mountain birds—the falcons and goshawks—surely they would rule this territory for years to come.

"It's not much farther now," said Sirona as they descended into a valley. Here and there, she recognized a stand of trees or a hill and was filled with a thrill of remembrance. Though this place might not be as lush and fertile as the sunrise lands, it was home.

She was eager to see the people of her tribe. Even the sight of Fiach or Dichu would please her, although she worried the high Drui would send her away. But surely he must realize that anyone who was willing to help counteract the influence of the Romans was of value to his people. If Fiach tried to banish her, she would make him listen to reason. After confronting Boudica, the idea of opposing Fiach didn't frighten her.

Besides, Tarbelinus was no longer there to enforce Fiach's will. A wave of sadness afflicted her, remembering the bold, proud chieftain. She wondered who had taken Tarbelinus's place. It should be Bryn. Perhaps some day it would be. If only he heeded her warning and avoided the catastrophic battle with the Romans. The thought that he might not listen agonized her. He was so headstrong and stubborn, like his father. She experienced another pang of grief. Although she was returning to the world of her childhood, everything had been irreparably altered. Nesta and Tarbelinus were in the Otherworld. Cruthin might be there as well.

As they reached the valley of the Tarisllwyth, she caught her first glimpse of the dun, now nothing more than a gathering of dwellings on top of the hill. It seemed strange there was no palisade wall, and a fierce determination overtook her. The Romans might prevail in the sunrise lands, but they wouldn't prevail here. Somehow she would stop them.

As they approached, she noticed how thick and tall the grass had grown around the settlement. Odd that they hadn't brought in the herds to graze, unless the Tarisllwyth cattle and sheep had been carried off by the Romans. If so, what were the people doing for food?

They followed the trackway up the hill and entered the settlement. Several of the roundhouses at the edge of the dun appeared abandoned, including the one Sirona had shared with Nesta. An old man came limping out of one of the dwellings. Sirona slid off the horse and hurried toward him. "Dergo! Dergo! It's so good to see you!"

He took a step back as she approached, looking uneasy. "Sirona, is that really you? They said you were dead."

She smiled at him. "I'm not dead. I promise."

Gradually his shock eased and he allowed her embrace him. Her eyes began to tear. She told herself she wouldn't weep. Drawing back, she said, "What's happened here? What have the Romans done to us?"

The leathercrafter shook his head. "They took Tarbelinus. Killed the warriors. Now, there's no one left but a few old men like me and the women and children."

"What about the herds?" Sirona asked.

"We have a flock of sheep that provides us with wool and some meat, but the Romans carried off most of the cattle. There are still some beasts scattered in the hills, probably half-wild by now. But no one here is fit enough to bring them back. There's not a youth over ten years nor a whole, uninjured man of less than forty winters remaining."

"What have you been eating?"

"Mealcakes, of all things. At first, Rhyell and the other women were able to exchange their jewelry for cartloads of grain. But now the jewelry is gone, and we've been trading other things to the Romans to get food." He grimaced. "If we didn't, we'd have surely starved by now. There's no one fit enough to hunt either." He gave a shuddering sigh. "Rhyell has held us together, kept everyone calm and urged all of us to continue on. After they put chains on Tarbelinus and led him off as if he were some wild beast, she made a vow that the Tarisllwyth would survive, that we wouldn't be destroyed by the Romans."

"Where is Rhyell?" she asked.

"In the feast hall, with the rest of the tribe. With our numbers so reduced, it made sense for everyone to gather there and share the hearth for cooking and light."

While Rufus saw to the horses, Sirona headed to the feast hall. Her heart was heavy as she entered the familiar timber structure. But at least the hall hadn't been destroyed.

A group of young children played in one corner of the hall. Around the hearth were gathered less than two score women and a handful of old men. The women were engaged in spinning and weaving while the men busied themselves with other crafts and handiwork. Sirona immediately noted how thin the people were and how ragged their garments. She guessed the cloth being made must now be traded to the Romans for food rather than kept for their own use.

No one took notice of her at first, but as she made her way toward the hearth, heads jerked up and startled glances met her gaze. "Sirona, it's Sirona," people whispered. Near the center of the gathering, Rhyell got to her feet, her eyes wide and amazed. There were streaks of white in her auburn hair and she was much thinner, but her brown eyes shone as fiercely as ever.

Sirona nodded to her. "No matter what you've heard, I wasn't killed by the Romans." She smiled weakly. "I can't tell you how good it is to once again look upon the faces of my people."

"Aye, what's left of us!" Rhyell's voice rang with bitterness. Then her face softened and she said, "Welcome, Sirona. It warms my heart to see you." She motioned to the others. "One of our own has returned, and we must celebrate. Anwyl, go to Rhyderch and tell him we're planning a feast in Sirona's honor. Gwendyth, come with me. The rest of you, clear away your work so there's room for us to sit down and eat." To Sirona, Rhyell said, "Let us go to my private chamber so we can talk."

Rhyell escorted Sirona to the bedchamber in the rear of the hall that the chieftain's wife had once shared with Tarbelinus. She told Gwendyth to fetch some water for washing. When the other woman had left, she went to a corner of the room and began to shove at the heavy chest located there.

"Can I help?" Sirona asked in bewilderment.

Rhyell sighed and swiped at her brow. "Aye, if you wish. There's a passageway underneath where I keep the grain and other foodstuffs. I must dole them out sparingly, lest we run out before we can find a way to purchase more."

Sirona helped her push the chest aside and open the door that led into the underground chamber beneath. Rhyell started to step into the opening. "Here, let me," Sirona offered. "I'm already dirty."

Rhyell nodded. "I'll hold the torch so you can see. Bring up two baskets of grain and a jar of oil. That should be enough for a decent meal. Oh, and see if there are any dried apples."

Sirona slid into the opening and found the things Rhyell had asked for. After Sirona had climbed back up, Rhyell replaced the wooden cover and pushed the chest back into place. She brushed off her hands and sat down wearily on a stool. "It's good that you know where the food is kept. Now that the other Learned Ones are gone, you are next in authority, in case anything happens to me."

Sirona felt pleased by Rhyell's calm acceptance of her presence, but alarmed by her remark about the Learned Ones. "Where are Fiach and the others? Did the Romans... kill them?"

Rhyell frowned. "Kill them? Nay. They struggled along with the rest of us this past year. Then, soon after Beltaine, a messenger came to say that all the Drui were gathering on the sacred isle. The Learned Ones left and we've not heard from them since."

Sirona felt a twinge of foreboding. She recalled Gaius's comment that the Roman commander meant to wipe out the Drui. If all of them were on the sacred isle, they would be an easy target for the enemy.

"Why did they go to the sacred isle?"

Rhyell shrugged. "Who knows? Perhaps they mean to call down the gods to aid us." She gave a snort of contempt. "Although it seems a bit late to petition the deities to save us."

Sirona's stomach clenched. If all the Learned Ones were killed, it would be worse than many warriors dying in the great battle. As long as there were children of her people left living, they might raise up a new generation of warriors. But if all the Drui were gone, the entire knowledge of her people would be lost.

She asked again, "You mean to say that every Learned One has gone to the sacred isle? What about those who aren't full Drui yet, like Math and Merin?"

"Oh, they're full Drui now and so they went. Everyone did. Even all Old Ogimos."

"Old Ogimos? He's still living? He seemed ancient when I left here years ago!"

"Aye, he lives. Fiach convinced him that they needed every member of the grove to be a part of this gathering."

Sirona sucked in her breath. This was a disaster. The Romans were determined to wipe out the Learned Ones. What if they discovered they were all in one place? She abruptly got to her feet. "I have to go to the sacred isle. I have to warn them."

Rhyell gaped at her. "Have you lost your wits, Sirona? They're the ones who banished you."

"With the help of your husband," Sirona retorted. "Tarbelinus could have stood against Fiach. Instead, he agreed to send me away."

Rhyell looked stricken. "That was because of Bryn. And it was a mistake. I see that now. I let my hatred of your mother blind me to your true nature." She sighed and the light went out of her eyes. "And because of my blindness, I've lost my son. Perhaps forever."

"That's not true. Bryn's alive. I saw him recently."

"You saw him?" Rhyell jumped to her feet. "Where? Was he well? Is he coming back here? I must go to him! I must explain... I must make him understand."

Sirona put a hand on the anguished woman's arm. "He's in the sunrise land."

"Why? What is he doing there?"

Sirona hesitated. How could she tell Rhyell what was happening in the east? Rhyell had just found out her son was alive. It seemed cruel to reveal the dangers Bryn faced. Sirona side-stepped Rhyell's question by saying, "Last time I spoke with him, he talked of coming back here."

Rhyell collapsed upon the stool, her face sagging with relief. "Oh, thank the gods." A moment later, she jumped up again. "How long ago did you see him?"

Sirona silently calculated. "Almost a fortnight."

"And you think he's on his way?"

"I hope so." Sirona felt a stab of guilt over her half-lie. Bryn *had* talked of returning to his homeland. Surely he would do so... if he didn't perish in the war raging in the east. Sirona winced at the thought.

Rhyell let out another sigh of relief. Then her gaze met Sirona's. "I've always feared Bryn was dead, since Banon predicted he would die if he ever became a warrior."

"I think Banon made up that Seeing. Although her prediction about Tarbelinus did come true. And, in a way, her one about Mordarach. The dun still stands, but it's hardly the same."

Rhyell shook her head. "All those years and no news. Nothing." All at once, her face flushed a deep ruddy hue. "I can't believe this. He's been alive all this time and not sent word to me. How dare he be so cruel? How dare he!" Her expression grew livid and she glared at Sirona. "If you saw him recently, why didn't you convince him to come back here with you?"

"Bryn still hopes to fight the Romans. But I made him promise to... to be careful" She couldn't bear to tell Rhyell about the battle she'd seen and the possibility Bryn might not listen and end up dying.

Rhyell began to pace, as if her emotions had shifted yet again. "My son's alive, and yet there is every possibility he might die in battle. I can't believe this! How can the gods curse me so? Isn't it enough that I've lost my husband, but I must also lose my son?"

"Calm yourself. You don't know that Bryn will die."

Rhyell's gaze seemed to pin Sirona in place. "Do you believe he will live? Have you seen a vision of him in the future?"

Cold dread clutched Sirona's heart. She'd made Bryn promise he would avoid the great battle, but would that be enough to deter him? Why hadn't she agreed to handfast with him and given him more of a reason to honor his vow?

But she dare not express her doubts to Rhyell. "Aye," she answered. "I believe Bryn will live many more years. I've seen no vision, but still.... I don't think the gods would have kept him alive this long only to have him perish in a cause I've warned him is hopeless."

Rhyell let out her breath in a weary exhalation. "I want to believe you, but it's so difficult. Look at us, the pathetic remnants of the Tarisllwyth. Less than three score women, children and old men are all that's left of our once prosperous tribe." Her face grew hard. "There would be more if it wasn't for that wretched Cruthin."

"Cruthin!" Sirona exclaimed. "What's this about Cruthin?"

Rhyell's mouth twisted. "Or should I say, 'the Shining One'? That's what they call him now. They say he can perform great magic. Alter the weather. Turn into an animal. Conjure the very stars out of the heavens." She motioned angrily. "I'm certain it's all lies, but people will cling to anything these days. Especially the young and desperate."

"What do you mean?" Sirona asked. Although delighted to learn Cruthin was alive, she was baffled by Rhyell's words.

"I mean that Cruthin, the clever fraud, has stolen all our young people. It's because of him we have no one to tend the herds. Because of him we must sell our cloth and pottery and metalwork to the Romans for scarcely enough food to keep us alive."

"Stolen the young people?" Sirona echoed. "What are you talking about?" And all along she'd assumed the missing youth of the tribe were dead, killed by the Romans.

Rhyell sniffed in disdain. "Cruthin fancies himself as some sort of chieftain. He's gathered around him all the youth of the tribes of the sunset lands—Ordovice, Silure, Tarisllwyth and Decangi, and set up a camp somewhere in the mountains. He claims to be forming a warband that will do battle against the Romans. But the only skirmish they've been involved in so far was an ambush of one of the enemy supply trains. Otherwise, all Cruthin's 'warband' does is hold ceremonies where he supposedly calls down the gods. I've heard these ceremonies are nothing more than drunken revels where the participants dance around wildly and crudely mate with each other." Rhyell's mouth twisted in scorn.

Cruthin was alive! And not all the young people of the Tarisllwyth had perished. Her tribe wasn't as diminished as she'd thought.

"Although you clearly resent what he's done, Cruthin's plan might be for the best," Sirona told Rhyell, "By gathering together these young people in the mountains, he might well be saving their lives. If he keeps them from attacking the Romans directly, then that's all to the good, for they would stand no chance against the enemy."

"They might survive… *if* he can find a way to feed them." Rhyell's voice was acid. "By next spring, I fear the rest of us will have perished of starvation."

"I wish I could stay here and help you," Sirona said. "But I must go to the sacred isle as quickly as possible. And to do that I'll need Rufus's help."

"Who's Rufus?"

"The slave who accompanied me here. But don't think poorly of him because he was a slave. His father was actually an Iceni chieftain. Besides, without his help, I'd never have been able to make my way back here."

Rhyell shook her head in puzzlement. "The Iceni are an eastern tribe. I thought you went north. But then… you did speak of Bryn being in the sunrise lands." She frowned in confusion.

"Perhaps I should tell you the whole tale from the beginning." Sirona glanced toward the doorway of the chamber, which was no longer covered by the white and black steerhide she remembered, but a mat of woven reeds. Rhyell had likely traded the door covering to the Romans for food. Many of the other luxury items Sirona remembered were now missing from the chieftain's chamber. "I have some time before I must leave. We'll need to eat, for certain. And the horses must rest before we set off again."

"Horses?"

"Aye." Sirona couldn't help smiling. "I've had many adventures since I left here."

Rhyell gestured for Sirona to seat herself on a stool and then sat down nearby. "Tell me all that's happened. We've had no news of the world beyond this valley all sunseason."

Sirona described to Rhyell her journey north over four years before. As she told how Einion and Culhwch were killed by the Romans, Rhyell asked, "How did *you* survive?"

"I believe the Great Mother was watching over me. She caused me to leave the cart before the Romans arrived. Otherwise, I'm certain I would have perished as well. Or, been captured and enslaved."

"I've never heard of a deity called the Great Mother." Rhyell's brown eyes probed Sirona. "But since you trained as a Learned One, I suppose you know about such things."

Sirona nodded before continuing her tale. She considered telling Rhyell about Itzurra and the wolf, but decided that part was too incredible to expect Rhyell to believe. Instead, she implied she'd made her way to Brigante territory by following the stars, as she'd been taught to do in the grove. "I was very fortunate," she continued. "The Drui of the first tribe I encountered was a woman I'd met on the sacred isle. She's a healer and offered me a place as her assistant. I stayed there until this spring."

"Why did you leave?" Rhyell asked.

"Another Learned One came to visit. You might remember him— Kellach, a handsome Silure man with dark red hair? He came here once." Rhyell shook her head, and Sirona continued, "He told me about Tarbelinus and the other things that had happened here in the west. He convinced me I was needed here, among my own people."

"If you thought you were needed, why didn't you arrive sooner? And if you traveled with this Kellach, where is he? And where did you acquire horses and a slave?"

"Kellach and I parted company on the way to Iceni territory. I've not seen him since." As she said this, Sirona wondered again what had happened to the Silure man. She'd worried she would encounter Kellach in the sunset lands, but strangely, there had been no sign of him.

"Why did you travel to Iceni territory instead of coming here?" Rhyell repeated.

"After convincing me to travel with him, Kellach changed his mind and insisted we go east. He told me about Boudica, queen of the Iceni, and how she planned to lead an uprising against the Romans. I felt it was important for me to meet this Boudica, to judge for myself whether she had the strength of character to prevail against the invaders."

"And does she?" Rhyell brown eyes shone expectantly.

Sirona hesitated. Knowing that tragedy was inevitable, she might as well prepare Rhyell for what was to come. She shook her head sadly. "I wish I could tell you that Boudica's army will prevail. But they won't."

"How do you know?"

Sirona sighed heavily. "Because I've seen it in a vision. Boudica and the army that follows her will not only be defeated, they will be destroyed."

Rhyell cried out. Then she glared at Sirona. "Just like your mother. Always predicting calamity and suffering!" She rose and moved to the other side of the chamber, her expression stiff.

Sirona also rose and went to her. "I'm not like my mother. I didn't tell you about my Seeing to poison your future or to manipulate you. I hope with all my heart that I'm wrong. I've beseeched all the gods I know to change things so that my vision doesn't come to pass. But... I feel that this is a true Seeing. Although I tried to alter the future, to turn my people from this pathway, I've been unable to do so."

"And so we will die," Rhyell said flatly. "The Pretani tribes will perish while the Romans prosper."

"Not all the Pretani will be killed. Some of our people will survive. Especially here, in the highlands. And in the north, where the Romans haven't yet ventured."

Rhyell turned away, and from the shuddering movement of her shoulders, Sirona realized how distraught she was. She went to the older woman and put her arms around her. "You mustn't give up. As long as some of us live, there's hope for the Pretani. Which is why I must leave soon and try to warn the Learned Ones. But I promise that when I've done so, I'll return and help you as best I can."

Rhyell faced her, her eyes red from weeping. Then she nodded and swiped at her cheeks. "Help me move the chest again. I want to bring up some more grain and oil from our stores, so you'll have some food to take with you."

"I don't want to deplete your supplies," said Sirona.

Rhyell smiled wanly. "You've given me a great gift by telling me that my son is alive. I must repay you. I'll worry about our foodstores another day."

Chapter 26

Bryn pulled the team to a halt and leaned wearily on the front of the chariot. "Are you certain we're headed in the right direction?"

"The old warrior who reported the ambush of the ninth said Londinium was about two days march from Camulodunum, directly to the southwest," Cadwalon said. "We should be near."

"Surely if such a large army had passed this way, there would be some sign."

"Aye. Boudica's army will stop at every Roman settlement, kill everyone, steal what they can carry and burn the rest."

"What about the livestock?" Bryn asked as he noticed a herd of sheep grazing peacefully in a meadow on the other side of a grainfields.

"They'll butcher and roast any of the animals they find. Feeding a huge army is no easy matter."

"Perhaps that's what has slowed them down."

"Or it could be they took another route from Camulodunum."

Bryn repressed a groan of frustration. He had pushed himself to the edge of his strength to reach Boudica's army and deliver his warning to Gwynceffyl. It appeared his efforts had been wasted. "What do we do now?" he asked. "Continue on to Londinium and wait for them?"

"Aye, we could. We know they'll arrive eventually."

Bryn sighed, and then clicked his tongue to the horses, urging them on.

A little farther, they saw a paved trackway up ahead. "This must be the road leading to Londinium," Bryn said. "I remember Gwynceffyl mentioning that the Romans like to link all their settlements with these 'rivers of stone'. But do we dare follow it and risk running into enemy soldiers?"

"If we see a large force coming, we can drive into the trees. And if there are only a few," Cadwalon touched his sword belt, "I wouldn't mind taking them on."

Bryn nodded. Despite his fatigue and aching head, he would be pleased to do battle with the Romans. It would be a fitting end to his years of companionship with Cadwalon. He was still dismayed that he couldn't convince his friend that Boudica's army was headed for disaster. If he couldn't convince Cadwalon, how could he possibly persuade

Gwynceffyl?

The thought gnawed at him as they traveled. A short while later, they saw another group of travelers coming towards them. Bryn and Cadwalon drew their swords. The handful of men looked Roman, but they were certainly not warriors. They walked beside two oxen-driven carts loaded with goods—amphora, wooden barrels, cloth bundles. Their dark eyes filled with fear at the sight of Bryn and Cadwalon, but they didn't draw weapons or otherwise prepare to defend themselves.

"Merchants, probably," Cadwalon muttered as the carts passed by. "We could cut them down and rob them of everything in a few heartbeats." He called out to the travelers, "You aren't so brave now, without your legions, are you, you stupid fools!"

This seemed to arouse the men's fear even more, and one of them began to strike the ox nearest him with a stick. It did no good as the beasts kept to their plodding pace.

"A pity we haven't room in the chariot for more goods," Bryn said. "But then it would be almost shameful to attack such men. They represent no challenge."

"Aye," Cadwalon agreed. "No challenge at all."

Bryn drove on. Ahead, he saw more travelers coming toward them. "What's this?" he wondered aloud. "Where are all these people going?"

They gradually made out what appeared to be a young Pretani woman—judging from her light hair—and two small children riding in a cart. Two foreign-looking slaves walked along beside the oxen that pulled the vehicle. Bryn pulled the chariot team to a halt and blocked the roadway. As the cart drew near, the woman's blue eyes grew wide with terror. She called out to the slaves in a foreign tongue and gestured frantically, as if urging them to turn around. Instead the two slaves froze in place. The oxen came to a halt a few paces away from the chariot.

Cadwalon got down from the vehicle and started toward the woman. "We mean you no harm," he called. "All we want is information. Do you speak Pretani?"

The woman nodded, her face contorted with fear.

Cadwalon softened his voice. "Where are you going?"

The woman's dread seemed to ease a little. She answered, "We're fleeing Londinium. The Britons are on their way. They will kill us and then mutilate our bodies." Her mouth worked. "My husband, Crassius, sent us out of the city." She pointed to Bryn and the chariot. "That's what I thought you were. British savages come to destroy us."

"We mean no harm to you or your family," Bryn called out. "But tell us about the Britons. Who brought you news that they mean to attack the city?"

"Everyone knows what happened at Camulodunum." She shuddered. "They mean to do the same to us."

"Is everyone leaving the colonia?" Bryn asked.

"Many are," the woman answered, "although there are plenty who won't abandon their shops and homes. And the poor people and slaves don't have the means to escape."

That was who had been slaughtered at Camulodunum, Bryn realized. The merchants and craftspeople who would not leave their wealth behind and the poor unfortunates who had nowhere to flee.

"Once word came that Suetonius was not going to send troops to defend the city, most people realized it was hopeless," the woman continued, her voice anguished. "My husband is a retired legionnaire, so he feels it's his duty to stay and fight. Even though… even though…" Her voice broke and she swallowed convulsively. Clearly, she believed he was going to die.

Bryn felt a stir of pity for this woman. Boudica and Sybilla would consider her one of the "whores of Rome" who deserved to suffer for their treachery in allying themselves with the enemy, but all he could see was a distraught and helpless young female. He wondered what circumstances had caused her to marry a Roman. Likely as not, her family had arranged the marriage. Why should she suffer for being a dutiful daughter?

And her children… Bryn gazed at the dark-eyed boys on either side of the woman. Both clutched at the skirts of her gown, and the younger of the two held one chubby hand to his mouth, sucking his thumb. Why would anyone want to slaughter these two infants? And yet, the truth was that someday they might grow up to be Roman soldiers who would kill and oppress his people.

He shook off the thought and called out, "Why has Suetonius decided not to send troops to defend the colonia?"

"The enemy army is too large," the woman answered. "There's no hope of defeating them."

"So, the Roman leader is afraid to fight?" Cadwalon asked. Bryn could hear the satisfaction in his voice.

"Nay. My husband says Suetonius means to engage the enemy, but not at Londinium."

"How many men does this Suetonius command?" Bryn asked.

"Two legions, and whatever other men are left alive from the ninth."

"Where are his legions now?" Bryn asked.

"Still in the north."

"And where does Suetonius plan to engage the Pretani forces?"

The woman shook her head. "I don't know. Please…" Her eyes

grew imploring. "Let me pass."

Bryn let out the reins and clicked his tongue to urge the team off the road. It took awhile for the woman to communicate to the terrified slaves that it was safe to go on, but eventually the oxen and cart moved by. As the rattling noise of the vehicle receded in the distance, Cadwalon climbed back in the chariot and said, "Surely the gods set the woman in our path. Now we know the Romans' strategy."

Bryn nodded. The Romans had abandoned the colonia to Boudica's army. That meant the fateful battle would not happen here. But it would still take place. He remembered the impassioned expression on Sirona's face as she told him about her Seeing, the desperation with which she made him promise he would not take part in any conflict involving a large number of Romans and Pretani.

He turned to Cadwalon. "Boudica's army is going to destroy Londinium, looting and burning and killing unchecked, until their battle fury is at its peak. This Roman leader, Suetonius, knows he can't defend colonia, so he leaves it to the ravening hordes. But when the final confrontation takes place, he'll make certain it's to the Romans' advantage." He shook his head. "I fear the outcome of that battle will be as Sirona as predicted. The Pretani will think they are invincible, even though they haven't yet engaged the enemy in any real conflict. They won't be prepared for true warfare." He met Cadwalon's gaze. "We must warn Gwynceffyl of these things."

"Or *I* could do so while you traveled to your homeland," Cadwalon offered. "I promise to repeat exactly what you have told me about the battle. Gwynceffyl will have an opportunity to consider withdrawing from this conflict if he fears it will lead to his death." A grim smile twitched his lips. "You know as well as I what he will say. He and I are bound to do this thing. There is no choice for us. We have no family waiting for us in the highlands, no lovely seeress to make us consider any choice but fighting the Romans. I vow it will not be so bad a death, at least if we can take a few of the enemy with us."

Bryn felt as if he were looking at Cadwalon across a great chasm. He'd always thought they were two of a kind. Now he understood how the years in the grove had changed him. His own pride and commitment to fighting the enemy were not enough to turn him from the path looming ahead. *You're not meant to die yet,* the voice inside said. *This is not your destiny.*

"I will warn Gwynceffyl," Cadwalon repeated. "Your duty lies elsewhere."

Bryn nodded. "I must return to Mordarach."

Cadwalon smiled, his deep blue eyes filled with sadness. "Farewell, my friend. May we meet again in the Otherworld."

The two men embraced, and then Bryn helped Cadwalon gather up some of the supplies and load them into a pack. He watched Cadwalon start down the road toward Londinium. Then Bryn climbed into the chariot and drove the vehicle off the paved surface and onto the grass. Now he must head west, west to the sunset lands.

* * *

It rained most of the way as Sirona and Rufus traveled across the mountains to the sacred isle, a soft, drizzling mist that obscured the view and made traveling difficult. Despite her oiled leather cape and heavy green checked mantle, Sirona was chilled and uncomfortable much of the journey. Even when they reached the foothills above the coast and the sun came out, her grim mood failed to improve. Rufus, who'd endured the discomforts of the journey in stoic silence, asked her what was wrong.

She shook her head, not wanting to put her fears into words. As she had the first time she visited the sacred isle, the closer she got, the more apprehensive she became. The place seemed to emanate death. She told herself it was her dread of the impending battle that caused her so much distress. She must press on, despite the disquiet that filled her every time she thought of arriving on the shores of Yys Mon.

They continued on through the forested hills leading down to the sea. When they reached the coast, Sirona breathed deeply of fresh ocean air and looked around. The settlement of the fisherfolk was as she remembered it. The fortress of the Segonti also remained, although it appeared abandoned. She saw no sign of any Romans. Despite that reassuring observation, her heartbeat quickened as she gazed across the stretch of gray water and glimpsed the blue-green mass of the sacred isle.

Rufus slid off the horse and helped her down.

"I'm relieved there are no Romans here," she said.

"You don't look relieved."

"I haven't seen any of the Learned Ones in four turns of the seasons, and when I left them, I was an outcast. How am I going to make them listen to me?"

"Rhyell listened," Rufus pointed out. "And she doesn't appear to be an easy person to influence. But she did all she could for us, providing us with food and other supplies, even giving us some of their precious grain for the horses."

"She adored the horses." Sirona smiled as she recalled Rufus's tale of going to check on the mares and finding Rhyell in the lean-to shelter, petting the animals and feeding them apples. "I think she would rather have provided grain for them than for us. Besides, she wants me to finish this thing quickly so that I can go back and fetch her son from the sunrise lands."

"Are you going to do so?" Rufus asked.

Sirona shook her head. "Bryn's fate is now in the hands of the gods."

"Do you think he'll live to return to Mordarach?"

"I hope so." Sirona's insides knotted with worry as she thought about the great battle of her vision and wondered if Bryn would perish there. *Please make him listen,* she silently implored the gods. *Please make him heed my warning.* To Rufus she said, "Surely if Bryn's end were coming soon, I'd have sensed it when he embraced me." Rufus gave her a sour look and she added, "Bryn and I grew up together. We're bound to be close, like you and your sister were."

"That man doesn't consider you his sister," Rufus grumbled.

Sirona had to agree. She recalled Bryn's offer to handfast with her, then quickly pushed aside the memory. The future was so uncertain. She dare not think about Bryn or her own feelings or she would end up paralyzed with anxiety. Instead, she must focus on her goal of warning the Learned Ones. "It's time to find the fisherfolk and ask them to take me across the straits."

"You're going without me?"

"I'm sorry, Rufus, but you must stay here and look after the horses."

"You can't go there alone! Who will look after *you*?"

Sirona tried to sound reassuring. "The Learned Ones are my own people. Why would they harm me?" She wished she felt as confident as she sounded. Still, she couldn't take Rufus along. If things went awry, he could do little to protect her. And she needed him to remain with the horses, so that when her task was finished, they would be able leave quickly.

"I don't like this," Rufus muttered. "Anything could happen. The boat could capsize. The Romans might already be on the island."

Sirona gently touched Rufus's arm. "Do you believe I'm blessed of the Goddess?"

The youth gazed at her intently and then nodded.

"You must trust that She will protect me. I've survived many dangers already. I might have been killed by the Romans years ago on my journey north, or been put to death by Boudica, or lost my life at Camulodunum, or been captured or killed by Romans on the way here. But none of those things happened. You must believe I will survive a little longer."

Rufus nodded, looking miserable.

As Sirona set out alone for the fisher village, she wondered at her own calm words. If she faced no danger on Yys Mon, why did she feel so apprehensive?

In the settlement, she encountered an old man with skin tanned to the texture of leather. He had one eye missing, but appeared sound otherwise. She greeted him with a smile and said, "I need someone to take me across to the sacred isle. I can pay in Roman coin."

The man regarded her with his good eye. "Are you certain you should go there? The men who gather on the isle are cruel and evil."

"You mean the Learned Ones? Or, are you speaking of the Romans?"

The man spat. "The Romans are evil, too. But they aren't here now. They left at the beginning of the sunseason."

"But they'll return. That's why I must go to the sacred isle, to warn the Drui that the Romans are coming."

"Why should you bother?" the man asked. "Let them die. They treat us like slaves, hoard the grain we grow. They care for no one but themselves."

"Not all Learned Ones are like that," Sirona answered. "Many are concerned for the welfare of their tribes. And they're my people. I trained in the grove for years. I have respect for their knowledge and traditions."

The man spat again. "Much of their knowledge they stole from us."

"Aye. I have heard the tale of what happened to the Old Ones when the Pretani came. But that's why I must go to the sacred isle. Because there's a new group of invaders, the Romans. And if they prevail and defeat the Pretani, the knowledge passed down for generations will be lost forever. Knowledge is a gift of the gods and must be protected, no matter who possesses it. Besides," she added, "I hope to prevent more bloodshed. War is wasteful and meaningless. To butcher animals for food, or even in sacrifice, makes sense to me. It's the natural way of things for one creature to die so that another might live. But men killing men seems stupid and futile."

"Ah, but war is also the natural way of things," the man said. "One people perishes so that another might thrive. If the Romans are stronger, they will prevail."

"But there's no need for all the Learned Ones to die. All those generations of learning, the wisdom passed down through the ages. What a terrible loss it would be."

The man shrugged. "Even so, life will go on. The seasons will change. Grass will grow thick and green in the places where the bodies once lay. The stars will still turn in the heavens."

His words deepened Sirona's discouragement. She didn't want to confront the things he spoke of. Her voice rose in anger. "If what you say is true, why bother taking your boat out to catch fish to feed yourself and your family? Why not lie down here and die? There is no future, no meaning for any of us!"

"Because of the will to live," the man responded. "It's in all of us. It drives us to survive, to struggle and fight. The gods made us that way. Imparted the urge to see the next day and the next." His expression softened. "I didn't say I wouldn't take you across. If you must go there, then so be it."

Sirona nodded, her eyes stinging with tears. She had to do this thing. It was her destiny.

After they were settled in the boat and had set out to sea, Sirona asked the man, who was named Growyn, where the Segonti had gone.

"They've all fled to the sacred isle. They think the Learned Ones there will be able to protect them."

She motioned back to the fisher village. "Have your people also left their homes?"

"Nay. They are all out fishing and gathering food. We don't fear the Romans. They won't bother with us." He glanced at her searchingly. "So, you're a Drui. I'm surprised. There aren't many women among them these days."

"Did there used to be?"

Growyn nodded. "When I first carried Learned Ones across the straits, there were at least a dozen females among them."

"What do you think happened? Why are there so few women now?"

"The Drui in power favor different gods and alter the rituals to fit their own beliefs. I also remember the days when we used to carry captives across who were to be sacrificed."

"Truly? That happened in your lifetime?"

"Aye. I was a boy then, riding along in my father's boat. But I remember the terror of the poor creatures. A fair number of them were Scoti prisoners who were captured in raids. But there were also Pretani who were being punished for some crime. They suffered the most. The Scoti had their own gods to pray to. But the criminals, they'd been told they'd offended the gods, and their blood must be spilled in order to appease them."

"Was that how they were sacrificed, by having their throats cut?"

"For the most part, although sometimes they died by the triple death—struck on the head, strangled and then drowned."

Hearing his description, Sirona felt sick. "I'm glad human sacrifice is no longer practiced."

"Don't be so certain," Growyn responded. "The Learned Ones I carried over not a fortnight past talked about a man whose spirit was offered to the gods in the territory of the Cornovi. He wasn't a prisoner or a criminal, but a chieftain."

"A chieftain?" Sirona exclaimed. "Why would they kill their own leader?"

"They believed his death would help them prevail against the Romans."

Sirona stared stonily at the gray waves lapping at the boat and fought the urge to tell the fisherman to turn back. But she had come this far. And even now, despite her fear, she knew there was a reason she must go to the sacred isle. Perhaps it had nothing to do with the Learned Ones. Perhaps, instead, it had to do with the sacred mound. Or with Cruthin.

She turned to Growyn. "Have you ever heard of a man called the 'Shining One'?"

Growyn gazed at her, his good eye narrowing. "Aye. He stayed among my people for a time."

So that was how Cruthin had survived after he escaped. "How long has it been since you saw him?"

The fisherman furrowed his brow in concentration. "A few years."

Sirona felt a sharp disappointment. For some reason, she'd thought she might encounter Cruthin on the sacred isle. But Rhyell had told her he was in the mountains somewhere.

As they neared the island, Sirona's tension increased. She told herself she wouldn't have to remain here long. Only as long as it took to find Fiach and the others and warn them what Gaius had told her.

When they reached the shoreline, she helped the fisherman drag the boat onto the beach. Then she handed him a Roman coin from her pack. "It might aid you, should the Romans come," she told him.

He thanked her, then added, "May the Goddess be with you."

"And with you."

Sirona watched the fisherman return to his boat, feeling very alone. She wanted to ask Growyn to stay and wait for her. But she had no idea how long her errand would take.

Chapter 27

Leaving the coast, Sirona followed the path through the forest to the gathering place. As she made her way through the ancient woods, she was assaulted with memories. She remembered Cruthin walking beside her, his steps light and swift. Bryn following behind, dragging half their supplies by himself. It seemed a lifetime ago, rather than a few years. Much had changed since then. And little of it seemed to be for the good. She felt a sense of despair as she thought of Camulodunum, the horror of the vision of the battlefield along the Roman road. So much darkness. So much death.

Her thoughts grew grim, and it was with great effort she forced herself to move forward rather than turning around and running back to the beach. *This is what you must do,* she told herself. *The Goddess has led you here.*

When she arrived in the clearing, she found the Learned Ones' gathering place had been transformed into a real settlement, with timber roundhouses near the huge open-walled structure. There were women and children everywhere, and only a few Drui.

A familiar looking red-haired man came out of a hut. He looked up at the sky, then glanced around and saw her. "Sirona!" he exclaimed.

"Math?"

He regarded her warily as she approached. "What are you doing here? I thought you were dead."

"Clearly, I'm not. I'm looking for Fiach."

"He won't be pleased to see you. After all, he banished you."

Sirona felt a twinge of irritation. "Well, he should be pleased. There aren't many of our kind left."

"True. There are but three score Learned Ones on the isle, which might be all that are left in Albion."

"Which is why Fiach should welcome me."

Math shrugged. "He blames you for the downfall of our people. When Tarbelinus was taken captive and led away, Fiach said it was your mother's fault. She cursed the chieftain years ago."

"I'm not my mother," Sirona answered coldly.

"You will have to take the matter up with Fiach."

"I will. When I find him. Please tell me where he is."

"He's probably in the gathering hall with the other high Drui."

Sirona started in that direction. Behind her, Math called out, "How is it Einion and Culhwch never returned, but you're still alive?"

"Clearly, the gods wanted me to live," she called over her shoulder.

An arrogant thing to say, but Math's attitude rankled.

Sirona made her way into the gathering hall. As she did so, she worried about what Math had told her. How could Fiach blame her for her mother's curse? It was unfair of him to hold her accountable for something that had happened when she was only a small child.

She found Fiach sitting with some men she recognized as the high Drui from other tribes, gathered around the hearth in the huge structure. Half-empty platters of food were scattered nearby and the Drui looked content. Fiach caught sight of her and got to his feet. His amber eyes widened in amazement, followed by a look of hostility. Then his expression grew bland and indifferent once more. Sirona repressed a shiver. This man was very shrewd and well able to manipulate everyone around him to serve his own ends.

"Sirona." Fiach's voice was smooth. "What a surprise. I was certain you'd perished. A victim of the vile Romans." He turned to the other Drui. "You recall Sirona? At the gathering years ago she was accused of blasphemy for leaving a sacred ceremony. As her punishment, she was sent north with an escort. The two warriors never returned. We assumed they'd all been killed by Romans."

Sirona sensed the other Drui regarding her with distaste. Already, Fiach sought to discredit her. "The gods chose to spare me," she said. "Obviously, they had another plan for my life."

"So," Fiach's voice was faintly mocking. "What have you been doing for the past four years? And why come join us now? Has some northern chieftain banished you from his bed as happened with your mother?"

Sirona felt her anger rise. "I shared no man's bed, but had my own place among the Cunogwerin as a healer's apprentice."

"But clearly, something happened to cause you to leave the north."

"Aye, a Learned One named Kellach came and convinced me I had a duty to come back and try to aid my people."

"Kellach? The Silure?"

Another man said, "I heard he was traveling all over Albion, urging chieftains to rise against the Romans."

"Where is Kellach now?" Fiach asked.

"I don't know. We parted company before reaching Iceni territory."

A third man spoke, "You went to Boudica's encampment? Is it true she's raised a vast army?"

"Aye. She's assembled a huge force, and they intend to attack the Roman settlements in the east."

The Drui looked at one another. The one who knew Kellach smiled. "Our petitions to the gods have finally been answered. At last, our people unite to fight the enemy."

Sirona bit her lip, resisting the urge to tell these men that Boudica's army was headed for disaster. But she'd learned her lesson. If telling the truth would make no difference, then it was better not to speak of it.

Fiach frowned. She suspected he was displeased she possessed so much information. "Is that why you've come?" he asked sharply. "To give us this news?"

Sirona took a deep breath. Now was the moment she'd dreaded. "Nay. I've come to warn you. While I was in the east, I learned that most of the Roman army is here, in the sunset lands. They plan to wipe out all the Drui."

"Where did you learn this information? Did it come to you in a vision?" Fiach's eyebrows rose mockingly.

She met his gaze with cool determination. "Nay. I was told this by a Roman, a retired legionnaire."

There was mumbling among the other Drui. A smirk twisted Fiach's hawk-like features. "Did this legionnaire tell you these things after you pleasured him?"

His words infuriated her so much she could hardly speak. Finally, she blurted out, "I've shared no Roman's bed!"

"How can we be certain of what you might do? You are your mother's daughter, after all."

"How dare you bring Banon into this? She died before I was old enough to speak!"

"It doesn't matter. Her blood flows in your veins."

Sirona tore her furious gaze away from Fiach and appealed to the other Drui. "Despite this man's dislike of me, I would advise you to listen to what I have to say. I've come here to warn you of the Romans. They intend to kill all of you. If you stay here, on the isle, you'll be trapped. If you go back to your tribes, there's hope you might survive."

The half dozen men looked at her. She saw fear in their gazes. But along with their dread was something else. Doubt and skepticism. An old man spoke from the back of the gathering. Sirona recognized him as Elidyr, the head Drui who'd led the ceremonies last time she was on the sacred isle. "You've given us the warning," he said in his strong, resonant voice. "Leave us now, and we'll discuss the matter."

Could it be happening once again, that no one would heed her? What a curse, to see the future and not be able to change it. But she faced the group of Drui with her head held high, and her voice was strong as she said, "I have no reason to come here and tell you these things except I believe there is value in all of you. You possess wisdom and knowledge that is important to our people. Because I fear that knowledge might be lost, I've come to warn you." With dignity, she left them.

On the way out of the shelter, she met Tadhg. He greeted her without hostility, and she decided to tell him about the Romans. "Many people are coming here, believing this is a place of refuge," she told him. "But if the Romans attack, you'll be trapped. I urge you to leave the island as soon as possible. You'll be much safer on the mainland."

"But how will the Romans get here?" Tadhg asked. "The fisherfolk won't bring them across."

Sirona wanted to scream at the bard for his ignorance. "They have boats, or the resources to build them. And horses. The straits are not so deep that it would be impossible for horses to swim across."

Tadhg's blue eyes narrowed. "How do you know so much about the Romans?"

"I've been traveling with a youth who used to be a Roman slave."

"A slave? Why would you spend time with such a person?"

"Because he offered to help me." Sirona gritted her teeth. All at once, she understood Bryn's endless frustration with those who trained in the grove. Instead of worrying about the Romans, Tadhg was concerned with the fact that her companion was a slave.

Tadhg appeared to be thinking things over. Even if she couldn't convince the high Drui, if she sowed seeds of doubt among the other Learned Ones, they might be able to force their leaders to take action. Next to Fiach, Tadhg had always been the boldest of the Tarisllwyth Learned Ones.

"Fiach and the high Drui say this situation is only temporary," Tadhg said. "That soon the Romans will be driven from our lands and all will be as it was before."

"How can they say that? *Who* is going to drive the Romans from our lands?"

"The gods, once we've regained their favor."

"If the gods were going to aid us, surely they would have done so by now. I find it odd they've allowed the Romans to overrun all of Albion, to kill many of our warriors, steal our livelihood and drive us from our lands, if they're going to save us in the end."

Tadhg made a dismissing gesture. "All those things happened because we weren't devout enough. We held back on our sacrifices, were stingy in our gifts. But that has changed. At the next ceremony we'll make the ultimate sacrifice and prove our devotion."

"What sort of sacrifice?" she asked, feeling the tension build inside her.

"One of our own. A Learned One will be chosen to go to the Otherworld to plead our cause with the gods."

Her worst fears had been realized. "How will they choose who will be sacrificed?"

"The gods will choose. A bannock with a burned portion will be placed in a leather bag and each Learned One will reach in and tear off a piece. The one who ends up with the burned portion will be the gods' chosen one."

"And all the Learned Ones have agreed to this, even knowing it might be they who will die?"

"I always thought you were lacking in piety, but this is proof. How can you worry over your own petty, worthless life when so much is at stake?"

Sirona closed her eyes in dejection. She might as well accept it. The Learned Ones wouldn't listen. Even as the Romans swarmed the sacred isle, they would deny the facts and witlessly put their faith in futile sacrifices. There was nothing more she could do.

Opening her eyes, she said to Tadhg, "I'm hungry. Is there somewhere I can get food?"

"If you go to the main hearth, the women will feed you." He pointed to a place on the other side of the gathering hall.

Sirona went to the area he had indicated and was given a freshly-made bannock. When she asked about something to drink, they motioned to table where a large pottery jar and some cups were laid out.

As she ate, she considered whether she should go back to the coast and try to find a fisherman to take her to the mainland. She regretted not asking Growyn to wait for her. But she'd hoped her former companions of the grove would be glad to see her. That they would show her some respect and listen to what she had to say. A wave of self-pity assaulted her, followed quickly by bitterness. She was well quit of these fools! Let them stay here and meet their deaths!

But even as she wallowed in her resentment, a part of her recoiled at the idea of all the Learned Ones being slaughtered. What if such a thing did come to pass? What if, by the time the Berry Moon rose in the sky, she and Bryn and Cruthin were the only ones left in Albion who knew any of the wisdom and learning of the grove? It made her wish she'd paid more attention all those years ago. She should have tried harder to absorb everything her teachers sought to teach her. Cruthin would recall more than she did. She must find him.

The Shining One. She wondered if Cruthin truly lived up to such his grand title. Had he learned to control the power she'd observed at the mound and circle of stones? All at once, a thought came to her. She wanted to go back to that place, to seek out the magic she'd once felt there. Why not? She was accomplishing nothing here, and it seemed unlikely she would be able to find anyone to take her back across the straits before nightfall.

She brushed the crumbs off her hands and took another drink of water. Then she looked around, trying to get her bearings so she could figure out which way to set out. Perhaps she should begin walking and hope the gods would lead her to her goal. She started across the clearing. A few steps later, someone called out in a frail, raspy voice, "Sirona!"

She turned and saw Old Ogimos coming out of one of the roundhouses. He was very stooped and thin now, his hair and beard completely white. As she hurried to him, hope rose within her once again. "Master Ogimos." She bowed respectfully, then gave in to her emotions and embraced him. As he hugged her back, she felt his bones like little sticks under his skin. And yet, when she released him, his blue eyes still appeared keen. Perhaps this man, though old and feeble, might serve as her ally.

"Ogimos," she said. "There's no time for me to tell you all that has happened these past years. But I have thought often of the things you taught me. You, of all the Drui, seem to me to possess true wisdom. I don't want that wisdom to be lost, and so I beg you now to listen to me."

"What is it, child?"

"The Romans are coming. They mean to kill all the Learned Ones. Promise me that you'll leave the isle." A thought came to Sirona. "Come with me now. We'll go to the beach and wait until morning. By then one of the fisherfolk will have returned and we can ask them to take us back to the mainland."

The old man looked at her with solemn blue eyes. "Perhaps what you say is true. I know Fiach fears you, and that can only be because he believes you have special abilities. But I can't leave my companions. If it's my fate to be killed by Romans, I won't flee from it."

Tears sprang to her eyes. "Please, Ogimos. Come with me. Save yourself."

He sighed. "I'm old, and won't live many more years. If it's my destiny to die here, then I accept it."

Sirona struggled to think of a way to sway him. "But the knowledge you possess—it would be a terrible thing if it were lost. What will happen to our people if there are no Drui, no Learned Ones to carry the beliefs and history and wisdom of the grove into the future?"

"Then perhaps it is time for those things to pass away, just as the knowledge of the Old Ones has been lost. The Romans will prevail, I'm certain. They understand war and wealth, power and politics, and those are the things that matter in this time. The Drui represent the past."

"How can you believe this?" Sirona cried. "How can you simply accept that this is the end and not try to change things? No matter what you say, no matter what you tell me, I won't give up!"

"Sirona? Is that Sirona?"

Sirona looked around to see Dichu coming toward her. The scrawny youth had become a stout, substantial man, although his fleshiness was primarily fat rather than muscle. His blue eyes inspected her as he drew near. "We thought you were dead," he said.

"Obviously, I'm not."

"But…what are you doing here?"

She opened her mouth to answer. The next moment she saw Fiach and the rest of the head Drui approaching. Fiach's fox-gold eyes gleamed with malevolence as he called out, "She's doing what she's always done, Dichu—causing trouble. But that will end soon enough. We'll see to that."

Chapter 28

Bryn woke out of a deep sleep. It was a dark, overcast night. He could hear the horses moving where they were tethered among the trees. *Someone or something was out there.* He got quickly to his feet. His sword was with the rest of his supplies in the nearby chariot, but he dare not take time to fetch it. Instead, he drew his knife from the sheath on his belt. With slow, cautious steps, he approached the horses. He could make out the shape of the animals... and another shape... a man. Nay, two men.

Bryn charged, knife drawn. He grabbed one man and threw him to the ground, then seized the other. With his arm around the man's neck, he pressed the knife against his throat. "Nay! Please!" the man cried. Bryn's every instinct was to kill, but at that moment, a shaft of moonlight shone down through the trees, revealing the other man. He was young and thin and clothed in the crude, ragged garments of a slave. His eyes focused on Bryn with abject terror. The man Bryn held in a death grip was also pathetically thin.

They're half starved to death. The thought moved Bryn to pity. He released the man and threw him down with one swift motion. Then, looming over both men, his knife still drawn, he demanded. "Who are you? What do you want?"

Neither answered for a time, then one of them said in a quavering voice. "We're slaves, from Londinium. Please. Let us go."

"Slaves? Who's your master?"

"A Roman named Novius Sabinus. We work in his stables." The man took a deep, gasping breath. "We only ran away because we heard the Britons were coming to slaughter us. Novius is a merchant. If he wants to stay and die, that's his choice, but we have no quarrel with the Britons."

"Where are you from?" Bryn asked, wondering at the man's foreign inflection.

"We were born in Londinium."

"But what tribe or race did your parents belong to?"

"A Teutone tribe called the Bructeri. At least, that's what our mother told us."

"You're brothers?"

"Aye."

"What do you want with the horses?"

"We were going to steal them so we could ride to the coast and then sell them for passage to Gaul."

Bryn gave a mirthless laugh. "You thought you could get away with that? Anyone can tell you are runaway slaves. They'd never believe the horses belonged to you. You'd be sold back into slavery by the first man you approached. Then he would take the animals for his own."

"You may be right," the first man said defiantly. "But we had to try. We thought this might be our chance to be free men."

"There's another problem with your plan," Bryn pointed out. "You're going the wrong way. The coast of the sunrise sea is in the other direction."

No one spoke for a time. Then the second man said, "Are you going to kill us? Or let us go?"

"Perhaps neither," Bryn said. His mind had been working, sorting through the things the slaves had told him. They said they worked in a stable and mentioned riding horses. It might be useful to take such men back to his homeland. "I'm traveling to the sunset lands. Many there have been killed by Romans. We need men such as you, who are familiar with horses and livestock. If I spare your lives, will you come with me and lend your skills to our tribe? You wouldn't be slaves, but free men. Except that you would be bound to me, as all men of a tribe are bound to their leader."

"Why would you do this?" the first man answered. "Why not kill us?"

"Because you have knowledge that's useful to me. Is it true you can ride on the back of a horse?"

"Some," the second man answered. "We weren't supposed to do so, but there are times when our master was away that we took the chance. Novius had several horses much larger than these, animals large and strong enough that even a man as big as you could ride them."

"I would like to find such horses," Bryn said, "But for now, come back to my camp. I will give you food and then bind your arms and feet so I can sleep peacefully."

"I thought you said we wouldn't be slaves," the one man said.

"You haven't proven yourselves trustworthy," Bryn answered. "Until you do, I will have to bind you at night so I can sleep without worrying you will try to harm me. During the day, I'll set you free."

He had the men get to their feet, and walking behind them, returned to the place where he had camped. After fetching some bannocks from his supply pack, he gave them to the men. He tossed them a waterskin to share and then sat down on the sheepskins that made up his bed. A sense of loneliness and longing went through him. Cadwalon should be here, so they could discuss the matter of the slaves. Cadwalon would argue that taking these men back to Mordarach was witless. In response, Bryn would explain that before he returned to the sunset lands, he wanted to find a stallion to breed to the mares that pulled the chariot. If he did such a thing, he would need the help of men who knew how to handle horses.

Imagining the conversation in his mind, Bryn's feeling of desolation intensified. For four years, Cadwalon had been his constant companion. Now it seemed likely he would never see him again.

He glanced up at the two slaves. They ate and drank rapidly, but still managed to whisper to each other between bites. Perhaps that was another reason he'd offered them a future at Mordarach. He wanted to have some company on the journey to his homeland.

Thinking again of Cadwalon, a pang of longing and grief pierced Bryn.

* * *

Bryn pulled the chariot to a halt, his gaze on the moving specks in the distance. He could see a group of riders, perhaps three or four of them. Romans.

He glanced at the two slaves walking behind the chariot. They were outnumbered, and he doubted Corrio and Balthar would be of much use in battle. Although he'd been surprised at how well they were able to keep up if he kept the horses to a walk. The slaves were not youths, as he'd thought at first, but grown men and surprisingly wiry and strong. With a little food, they'd gained strength rapidly. They were both very fair, with light yellow hair cropped close in the Roman style and blue eyes.

He turned his attention back to the approaching riders. Probably the wisest thing to do would be to stay on the roadway and hope the Romans passed by without stopping.

But the plan didn't satisfy him. Here was an opportunity to acquire more horses, horses big enough to ride.

He maneuvered the team so the chariot blocked the middle of the roadway, then turned and spoke sharply to Corrio and Balthar. "Change places with me and pretend you're driving. Quickly, now." When the two men had gotten into the chariot, he added hurriedly. "I'll wait in the woods. If the Romans stop to investigate, try to get at least two of them to dismount. I'll charge out of the trees and attack when the time is right."

"What if they seize us and make us go back to Londinium?" Balthar asked, his eyes wary.

"If you fear that end, then run away now," Bryn answered. "Otherwise, you can stay and aid me."

The two brothers looked at each other. Bryn didn't remain to see what they decided, but dashed into the woods. He found an old oak to hide behind, with a good view of the road. Sword drawn, he waited.

The Romans—there were four of them—were traveling swiftly, but they slowed as they neared the chariot. As Bryn had guessed they would, they stopped and spoke to Balthar and Corrio. He couldn't tell what the slaves answered, since they all spoke in the Roman tongue. But whatever they said, it seemed to capture the interest of the Romans. One of the enemy said something to his companions, and then dismounted. The Roman handed his horse's reins to one of the other men and started toward the chariot. When he reached it, he grabbed for Balthar. Corrio, obviously terrified for his brother, picked up Bryn's heavy leather pack and swung it at the Roman, striking him in the head. The man crumpled to the ground. Balthar, holding the reins of the chariot team, urged the horses into a trot at the same time another Roman leapt down from his horse to aid the fallen man. Bryn burst out of the trees.

Bryn struck the second Roman with his sword, nearly severing the man's neck, then ran toward the two mounted men. He saw their eyes widen behind their iron helmets. One of them shouted something, then spurred his horse and raced past the chariot and down the road. The other man drew his sword and urged his horse toward Bryn. The great glossy brown beast reared and Bryn struggled to get away from its flailing hooves. Even as he maneuvered in desperation, he knew a surge of excitement as he realized that a horse could be used as a weapon.

The animal's hooves struck the ground, barely missing Bryn. The horse danced for a moment, then reared again. Bryn spun away once more, avoiding certain death. Panting, he tried to decide what to do. His body urged him to flee. Perhaps if he did so, the man would ride away and leave them with the two horses. But then he saw the man turn the horse and start toward the other animals. Afraid that he would lose everything he'd won, Bryn charged the mounted Roman. At the same time, a knife whizzed through the air, imbedding itself in the Roman's neck. The man made a strangled sound and dropped the reins to clutch his neck. Bryn saw his chance and grabbed the trailing reins of the nervously prancing beast.

The horse whinnied and reared, causing the wounded man to slide off onto the ground. Bryn realized he was in more danger than ever. The horse was wildly agitated, jerking the reins. The animal reared once more, nearly dragging him off his feet. Bryn struggled to hold on. His shoulders ached as if his arms were being pulled from his body.

He told himself that two horses were enough and this one was not worth dying over. But he wanted this magnificent animal for his own. Looking into the horse's eyes, he spoke to it. "Be still. I won't hurt you.

I'm not an enemy, but a friend." He knew the horse couldn't understand his words. It was a Roman horse after all. But perhaps it could sense the feeling behind the words. Then he had an absurd thought, remembering Cruthin's experience with the wolf. He reached out with his thoughts, trying to touch the animal's spirit. He envisioned ripe apples lying on the ground. Piles of grain. Open meadows full of lush green grass. *Come to me. I will take you home to the sunset lands, where there are countless green pastures and glistening streams and you can run free among the hills.*

It was ridiculous, completely unreasonable, but the horse quieted. Its dark liquid eyes watched Bryn intently. Bryn edged nearer, moving up the reins until, finally, he reached the horse's head. It nickered and he smelled its hot, grassy breath. He stroked between its eyes, down its soft nose. It nickered again in response.

"Well done," someone said. He turned to see Balthar watching him with keen blue eyes.

Bryn patted the animal's neck. He knew he was smiling stupidly. He felt so exultant, so pleased with himself. Perhaps it was his Drui training, perhaps merely instinct, but somehow he had been able to speak to the horse and make it understand.

"Some men have a special relationship with Epona, the goddess of horses," Balthar said.

Abruptly, Bryn thought of Sirona. Where was she? When he reached the sunset lands, would he find her there? It was one thing to yield to the destiny the gods set out for him. Another to give up the dream that had sustained him for so many years. *Please let her be safe,* he silently implored. *Please.*

He turned back to the slave. Balthar was smiling. "Who threw the knife?" Bryn asked. Balthar pointed to his brother. Bryn nodded to Corrio. "Well done, yourself."

* * *

"Please listen to me!" Sirona shouted, trying to make her voice carry beyond the walls of the hut where she was imprisoned. "The Romans are coming! If you don't flee, they'll kill all of you!" She took a breath and listened. Surely some Learned One would hear and come to her aid.

She shifted position, trying to get comfortable, although it was impossible to do so with her wrists and ankles bound by leather thongs. The shelter where Fiach and the others had taken her was crudely fashioned of unstripped branches. If she could get a branch wedged underneath the thong binding her hands, she might be able to wear through the leather by rubbing it against the wood. She scrutinized the fresh boughs that made up her prison, trying to find one to use for such a purpose.

Before she could act on her plan, the hide door was shoved aside and Fiach loomed over her. She could see the hatred in his gold-brown eyes. "Like your mother, you would curse us even as you go to your death. Aye," Fiach added cruelly as he saw her fear. "You're going to die. Your spirit will be sent to the gods. If you wish to shout and scream, cry out to *them*. Ask *them* to save you."

"Don't do this," she begged. "I've done nothing to deserve death. I came here to warn you, not to curse you!"

Fiach's face tightened. "Elidyr says we must not waver in our belief that the gods will save us. Your words arouse doubts. You must be silenced."

"Please." She tried to speak calmly. "Let me go. I promise to leave without speaking to anyone."

A smile twitched Fiach's thin lips. "The damage is already done. Elidyr says the only thing that will remedy your blasphemy is for everyone to observe you willingly offering up your own life to the gods."

"I'll do no such thing!"

"Aye, you will." Fiach leaned near and she saw he held a beverage skin. She clamped her lips together, determined he would not make her swallow the contents of the skin. He grabbed her jaw. She squirmed and twisted, but the high Drui was stronger. He forced her lips apart and the bitter liquid filled her mouth. She tried to spit it out but some of it trickled down her throat. The battle between them raged until the skin was empty. He pushed her down and glared at her. "I'll come back in a while and see if you have drunk enough so satisfy Elidyr. If not, then, the two of us will force more down your throat. We will not be thwarted, Sirona. You'll pay for your arrogance. You'll pay for the damage your mother wrought. And for making a fool of me years ago."

Sirona coughed, her eyes watering. She tried to guess what was in the skin, what sort of herbs they'd used to poison her. So far, it hadn't affected her. Which meant she might have a little time to reach out for aid. Not with her voice but with her spirit.

She closed her eyes and focused her thoughts. *Help me! I'm a prisoner here. Come to my aid!* She sent the message out to anyone who might listen. The gods. The Old Ones. Lovarn. The wolf. Cruthin. Bryn. She envisioned herself inside the lean-to, standing above her body. Then repeated her cry for aid. Let it be a Seeing, for any who had the Sight, she thought.

The emotions and thoughts flowed out of her, like water in a river. Then, all at once, her spirit was outside her body. From a distance, she observed her still, pale form and knew a different kind of dread. Her body appeared empty of life, as if she were a husk, an empty shell. The longer her spirit was gone, the more helpless her physical form would become. With regret, she let her spirit return to her body. As she was sucked back into the solid weight of her flesh, she realized the energy of her spirit was also waning. She might have strength for only one more attempt to reach out for help. With that thought, she let herself slide down into darkness.

* * *

"Sirona. Sirona!" Someone was shaking her. She came to awareness gradually, her senses slowly returning. Sound came first. Then sight. It was almost twilight. She was standing in a clearing, surrounded by Drui. One of them stood on either side of her, holding her up. She tried to speak, but her mouth made only a dry croaking sound. With a renewed sense of horror, she realized how well the drug had worked. To anyone watching, she must appear awake and aware. Yet, she was unable to move or to cry out. She closed her eyes, wanting to give up, to tell them to finish. Kill her and be done with it.

A familiar voice spoke from nearby. "I never believed you belonged in the grove. But now, finally, you will do us some good. Your blood will appease the gods and all will be well."

She tried in vain to turn her head to see who spoke. The speaker moved into her line of vision. It was Dichu, his blue eyes full of disgust. He watched her from a few feet away, as if even now, drugged and helpless, she was a threat. Seeing him, hearing his cruel words, the anger surged through her. This man had no reason to hate her. She'd never done anything to him.

She wanted to argue, to strike back at him, but she couldn't speak. Then she recalled her vision of his death. She let the Seeing fill her mind and met Dichu's gaze, sending him her thoughts. Let him watch as the blows fell upon him. Observe his own body falling to the ground. His own eyes staring up sightlessly.

He drew in his breath in a hiss and started to back away from her. "Evil, evil…" he muttered. His eyes went wild and his body shook. Then he turned and ran, vanishing into the darkness.

She closed her eyes, exhausted by the effort of sending Dichu the vision. It was foolish to have wasted her strength for the purpose of frightening him. Her will was waning. She heard another familiar voice and opened her eyes. It was Old Ogimos, and he was arguing with Fiach. "Let her go," the ancient Drui said. "Sirona can't control her visions. She means us no harm."

"She's cursed, as her mother was!" Fiach cried.

"Sirona's nothing like Banon. She understands what it means to be a

Learned One. That's why she's trying to help us."

"I won't listen to this nonsense!" Fiach exclaimed. "She's dangerous! A threat to all we stand for!"

"You're wrong." Ogimos spoke in calm, reasonable tones. "The real threat is the Romans. They'll be the end of us."

"Shut up, old man!" Fiach's voice was an enraged hiss. There was another sound, a dull thud, like wood striking flesh, then another muffled thump.

"Should I move him?" someone asked.

"Nay, let him lie there!" Fiach snarled in response.

Her heart sank. Fiach had struck down Ogimos. He might have killed the old man. How cruel and senseless. But perhaps it didn't matter. Soon, they would all be dead. Being killed by Fiach was probably a gentler end than what the Romans would mete out.

Even so, tears rose in Sirona's eyes. She had cared for Ogimos and couldn't help mourning him. What a waste. All that knowledge, all that wisdom. Gone forever. How could the gods let this to happen?

Her tears fell silently. Then she heard Fiach speak once more. "I tell you, we can't wait for moonrise. We must do this thing now. Before she causes any more trouble."

"Aye," Elidyr answered. "We'll begin the ceremony." The high Drui of all the tribes moved into the center of the circle and began to call down the gods.

Sirona watched, sick with grief and anguish. Then her misery turned to rage. Pure fury flowed through her and filled her with a sense of power. She would try one more time to reach out and communicate her need, her desperation. This time she would not send her spirit as a mist, but something more formidable. The wind.

She concentrated, and as she had by the temple in Camulodunum, called out with her thoughts. *Arianrhod, Lady of the moon, she who guides the wheel of stars in the sky, she who sails the silver boat of destiny across the heavens, come to my aid. Lend me your power. Make me strong.*

She focused her fury and fear, her helplessness and dread. The energy built inside her and became a wild, violent force. She imagined a great storm sweeping off the ocean. The whirling air made the trees of the great oaks around them shudder and shake. In her mind she saw the gale blow across the rest of the isle, rippling the water of the lake of sacrifice and raising dust and debris around the mound and the circle of stones. It gusted through the harvested fields and tore at the thatched roofs of the houses and shelters dotting the island.

Her spirit surged upward and became one with the wind. She looked

down on the scene below and saw herself. Fiach and another Learned One
stood on either side of her, holding her upright. She appeared very pale
and weak, but her eyes were open. Nearby lay the still body of Old
Ogimos.

In the center of the circle, Elidyr stood with his arms outstretched,
calling down the gods. The sleeves of his crys billowed in the wind. His
booming voice was swept away by the tumult and a look of fear flashed
across his face. He lowered his arms and unfastened the ceremonial
satchel tied to his belt. Holding it open, he removed a large bannock. He
began to move around the circle, tearing off pieces of the bread and
handing them to each Drui in turn. When he reached her, he held up the
piece of bannock and shouted something. Although Sirona couldn't hear
his words above the wind, she guessed what he was saying. The burned
portion would go to her. She was the chosen one.

Elidyr forced the piece of bannock into her mouth. Fiach spoke
angrily to Elidyr, and then grabbed at the ceremonial satchel. Reaching
inside, he drew out the ceremonial knife.

Sirona watched from outside her body. Seeing the knife, the fear and
anger inside her seemed to explode. She released it, let it go, as if she
could fill the very heavens with her fury. There was a clap of thunder and
streaks of lightning lit up the sky. The wind intensified, raging through
the ceremonial grove. A branch crashed down from one of the great oaks.
Then another.

The people could barely stand against the force of the wind. A few
broke away from the circle and ran for the trees. More followed. Elidyr
and Fiach remained in the middle of the clearing, arguing, trying to shout
above the wind. Rain poured down, soaking them. Their garments clung
to their bodies. Their hair hung in dank strands. The other Drui supporting
Sirona abruptly let go. She saw her body fall to the ground. From her
spirit's vantage point, she watched Fiach approach, still clutching the
knife. He turned her prone body over and raised the knife.

Terror sent her spirit back to her body. She fell downward, into a
dizzying spiral. Images flashed before her eyes: Weapons glinting. The
moon a silver disk in a purple black sky. Rivers of blood. The sun an
orange sphere on the horizon. A babe lying on a stone altar. A knife
cutting into skin. A gush of blood that slowed to a trickle. Cold, empty,
ruined flesh, gleaming in the moonlight. Bodies falling into deep, dark
water. The dead floating beneath the surface of a moonlit mere. Bodies
rising up again, their faces pale and empty.

She tried to scream and could not. She tried again and this time
heard a choking, gurgling sound. For a moment, she wondered if it were
her dying breath. Then the world went black.

Chapter 29

Although her eyes were closed, Sirona gradually become aware of sounds and smells around her. The air, soft and warm against her skin. The scent of grass, flowers and rain-freshened earth. Nearby, a lark called, its song pure and achingly sweet. This must be the Otherworld, she thought. Perhaps it wasn't so bad to be dead.

Whispered voices intruded on her pleasant solitude. She tried to block out the buzz of voices, to return to the sense of peace she had experienced only moments before.

The sounds continued. With a sigh of aggravation, she opened her eyes. A group of the fisherfolk surrounded her. She wasn't in the Otherworld after all. Abruptly, she reached for her throat, searching for the wound that must be there. She felt a scratch running across her neck, but nothing else. Fiach's knife had scarcely broken the skin.

She sat up and laughed aloud, thinking how miraculous it was to be alive. The fisherfolk, who'd been regarding her with solemn, almost mournful expressions, smiled back at her. Her happiness and exhilaration intensified. Nearby were the mound and the circle of stones. How had they known to bring her here? But of course. This was a place of magic. All of it was magic. The storm. Her escape from death. Finding herself here, surrounded by the fisherfolk.

"You rescued me," she said. Then she laughed again.

Growyn stepped forward, nodding. "As I said, I don't trust the Learned Ones. After I left you on the isle, I went back to the village and got the rest of my people. We found you in the clearing. Unconscious, but alive. The Drui had all fled, all except the one who was injured."

"Injured? Who was injured?"

"The old man," Growyn answered. "We thought he was dead, but when we brought him here he revived."

Some of the fisherfolk moved aside so Sirona could see Ogimos propped up against a rock. He smiled at her. "It seems you were right, Sirona. Apparently, it's not my time to die yet."

Sirona let out another cry of joy. It was wonderful to be alive. And wonderful to know that Ogimos, the teacher she respected most, had also survived. "What about the rest of the Learned Ones?" she asked Growyn.

"They were so terrified by the storm, they didn't continue the sacrifice." A hint of amusement twitched his lips. "I didn't realize you had such power."

She smiled back at him. "Nor did I."

"It almost seemed you didn't need rescuing. Indeed, if it weren't for the Romans, we might have left you be."

"The Romans?" Sirona's voice rose in alarm. "The Romans are here?"

"Aye. They haven't yet crossed the straits, but they will. We must leave this place before the day is spent."

Sirona looked around. "Why did you bring me here? Why not take me back to the mainland?"

Growyn gestured to the circle of stones. "You needed healing. The effort of calling down the storm greatly depleted your strength. You've been here nearly a whole arc of the sun in the sky."

"No wonder it all seems so far away. Like a dream."

Growyn took her hand and helped her to her feet. "Now that you've roused, we must leave here." Two of the fisherfolk also helped Ogimos up, supporting the old man on either side. As they started out, Sirona quickly realized that Growyn was right. She was very weak. Every step was an effort. She couldn't travel much faster than Old Ogimos.

They passed by a farmstead and Sirona experienced a sense of wonder as she observed the flattened grass in the fields, the fallen branches and ruined buildings. The power of the storm had been ferocious. And she had summoned it. She had called upon the Goddess's vast power and She had responded. Sirona was stunned. Even compared to what she'd done at Camulodunum, this was true sorcery.

Her euphoria faded as the tingling began along her spine. She stopped and waited for the vision to come. All at once, she saw the beach, swarming with Romans. They were using boats to cross the straits, long flat boats made of wood, very unlike the round leather vessels the fisherfolk used. The warriors poured out of the boats as they landed. Other men appeared to have swum across. They rose out of the sea, dripping. Horses also struggled onto to the beach. The men caught the beasts and mounted.

"What is it?" Growyn said beside her.

"The Romans have arrived."

"We left our boats at an inlet to the west of the island. Come."

Growyn took her arm and they hurried on. Anxiety and guilt twisted Sirona's stomach. She halted once more. "I know that it's witless, but I feel I should try one last time to warn the Learned Ones. It will be a terrible slaughter."

"Come," Growyn urged. "Even your powers are not great enough to halt an entire army."

Reluctantly, she started walking again. It would be foolish to go back. She couldn't change things. Unless... She hesitated and turned to Growyn. "What if I tried to call down another storm? Perhaps that would scare the Romans away."

Growyn shook his head. "I don't believe you have the strength for it."

He was right, Sirona thought. Not only was her body weak, but her spirit felt frail and vulnerable, as if she were connected to her body by only a thin, gossamer thread. She shook her head. "If Fiach hadn't tried to kill me, I could have used my powers to call down the storm and halt the Romans."

Growyn's expression grew harsh. "Don't feel sorry for the Drui. They deserve whatever fate befalls them."

"I can't feel that way," Sirona said sadly. "I learned a great deal in the grove. Indeed, I think what I learned there is part of why I am able to wield the magic of the Old Ones."

She looked at Ogimos, who nodded. "Both peoples possess their own special gifts," he said. "It's your mixed blood that gives you such abilities. The power that flows through you comes from your ancient lineage, but it's your training in the grove that allows you to focus the power and use it wisely."

"What about Cruthin?" Sirona asked. "My grandmother always said he carried the blood of the Old Ones. And he also trained in the grove."

"Ah, Cruthin." Ogimos nodded. "I always sensed he was special. But so impatient. Always attempting things he wasn't ready for. His challenge is to learn some control and restraint, lest he destroy himself."

A thought formed in Sirona's mind. What if she and Cruthin combined their abilities? Together, they might be able to do amazing things.

"Come," Growyn urged. "I don't think the Romans will harm us, but I can't be certain."

They walked until they reached the beach. Once there, the tingling began again and another vision overwhelmed Sirona. She saw the gathering place. The Romans were everywhere, setting fire to the roundhouses and lean-tos. The large roofed shelter was ablaze, and the whole clearing filled with choking smoke. The area was littered with bodies. Her inner vision scanned the clearing, looking for people she knew. She saw Math's bright hair, surrounded by blood that was even deeper red. Nearby lay his twin brother, Merin. There was Dichu. He'd been struck down exactly as she'd seen in her vision. Farther on, she observed a stunned still face that looked like Cuill's and yet was far too pale, the eyes glassy and fixed. She recognized Elidyr's sparse gray hair, the mottled skin of his forehead, but the blood and brains that had seeped out of the gash in his skull didn't seem to be part of him. And Fiach. His tall, gaunt form lay crumpled on the ground. The cunning, gold-brown eyes that had always frightened her now gazed upwards at nothing.

She sank to her knees as grief rose up inside her. Many of those Drui she'd once respected and held in regard. In the end, they'd betrayed her, and yet they still didn't deserve to die so horribly.

She vomited and for a time was overcome with dizziness. Then, gradually, the horror began to ebb away. The fisherfolk helped her stretch out on the ground. The rich, ancient scent of earth and growing things soothed her. She told herself that where the dead lay, the grass would soon spring up greener and thicker than ever. Life would continue on. She thought of people's spirits, flowing from one life to the next, from one realm to the other. They were like water, like light. They moved in a circle, an endless circle, from one realm to the next and back again. From one life to another.

Still, the gnawing sense of loss wouldn't leave her. All that knowledge, generations of learning, lost in less than a day. But at least Ogimos was alive. And there must be others. Those too old or infirm to come to the sacred isle. Those who lived far away, like Dysri. She'd seen no women among the fallen Drui. Despite all the Learned Ones who'd died and all the warriors who would yet fall in the great battle, some of her people remained. She must find Cruthin. Together they had to find a way to save the Pretani.

With the aid of Growyn, she got to her feet. "Let's return to the mainland," she said.

* * *

"This is it?" Rufus asked as he and Sirona stared down into a valley where a dozen or so timber huts were arranged in a circle.

"It must be," answered Sirona. "This is where the fisherfolk said we would find the Shining One."

"The Shining One," Rufus scoffed. "What a silly name for a man. And he is only a man, after all."

Cruthin was a man, Sirona agreed, but a very special one. If Ogimos was right and her power came from combining the magic of the Old Ones and the learning of the grove, then Cruthin might well possess even greater abilities than she did. But she wasn't ready to say such things to Rufus. In fact, she hadn't told him what had happened on the sacred isle, other to explain that the fisherfolk had helped her and Ogimos escape from the Romans before they killed the rest of the Drui.

"Now that most of the other Learned Ones are dead, Cruthin is one of the few people in Albion who possess the knowledge of the grove," she told to Rufus.

"What about Ogimos?"

"He's very frail and has undergone quite an ordeal. I'm grateful the fisherfolk agreed to take care of him until he is strong enough to return to Mordarach. Besides," she added, "His knowledge is not the kind that's needed right now."

"I can believe that," Rufus said. "I've heard what the Drui study— lists of ancestors, the positions of the stars in the sky, stories and poems. What good does that sort of thing do anyone?"

"Understanding the way the sun and moon and stars move in the heavens is helpful for planting crops and finding your way on a journey from one place to another. And the old tales and legends explain the laws of the tribes, defining who we are and how we live. Although they might seem tedious and trivial to you, those things are important to my people."

Staring down at the settlement, Rufus said. "I know you believe you must speak to this Cruthin, but this place makes me uneasy. I'm not convinced you'll be safe here."

"Cruthin and I grew up together. He would never harm me."

"I'm going to make certain he doesn't!"

Sirona smiled at him. "Dear Rufus. You've been such a loyal friend. I would never have made it to the sunset lands by myself. And I certainly wouldn't have learned to ride a horse."

She patted the sleek neck of her mount. It had been Rufus's idea to teach her to ride. After the fisherfolk brought her and Ogimos back to the mainland, she'd found Rufus and told him of her plan to search for Cruthin. He suggested they could travel much faster if they each rode one of the horses. Although uneasy with the plan, she'd decided that if she could survive her ordeal at the hands of Fiach, she wouldn't worry about falling off a horse.

Rufus motioned to the valley below. "Do you want to go down there?"

Sirona nodded, although she couldn't help feeling a twinge of apprehension. How would Cruthin react at seeing her after all these years?

When they reached the settlement, they were met by a group of young men and women dressed in animal skins and roughly fashioned crys. One of the women, who had long, unbound hair the color of a fox's pelt, spoke. "So, you've come to join us. The Shining One will be very pleased."

"We would like to speak to the Shining One," Sirona said. "But first, we must tend the horses."

A gaunt young man with black hair and vivid blue eyes approached

Sirona's mount, eying the animal with interest. "We have no hay or grain. But there's a stream nearby and a meadow for grazing."

Rufus said, "I'll take care of the animals." He shot Sirona a glance that suggested if she should need him, he would be near. Sirona slid off the mare and handed the reins to Rufus, who remained mounted. He rode away, leading the mare.

"I'm Llewan," the black-haired man said.

"I'm Sirona. My companion is called Rufus."

"I remember you," one of the young people said.

After perusing his face and noting his reddish fair hair and tall stature, Sirona said, "Your name is Pryderi, isn't it?"

The youth nodded. "Tarawg, Eiryn and Amllawdd are also here."

Sirona smiled. "I'm not certain I would recognize them. You were but children when I left Mordarach."

"We must take her to the Shining One," interrupted the woman with red-gold hair.

"We will," Llewan answered. "But there's no reason she shouldn't have something to eat and drink first. She's our guest and should be treated with courtesy."

"I suppose you want me to fetch the food and drink?" the woman asked irritably.

"Aye, Madryn," Llewan answered.

Madryn walked off. To the rest of the young people, Llewan said, "It's discourteous to stand around gawking. Find something to do with yourselves until the evening meal."

After everyone else had left, Llewan guided Sirona to the hearth in the center of the settlement. "So, you're from the Tarisllwyth?" Llewen asked.

"Aye. The Shining One was also from my tribe. At least he lived with us for many years."

"The Shining One lived with you?" Llewan appeared startled. "I didn't know he had a tribe. I thought..." He shook his head.

"Did you think he simply appeared one day... perhaps dropped out of the sky?" Sirona smiled at the idea. "Nay, Cruthin—the Shining One— he's a man just like you. I knew him when he was a boy."

Llewan stared at her in awe. Then he said, "I'll go and see if he can have speech with you. If he's in a trance and off in the realm of the gods, you may have to wait."

Llewan left, and Madryn returned with a wooden bowl of stew and a leather skin. Sirona dipped her fingers in the stew and ate. The stew was awful, poorly seasoned and made with meat that tasted rancid. Fighting back her revulsion, she took another bite. It would be very discourteous to refuse what was offered.

Eager to be rid of the unpleasant taste of the stew, she reached for the skin. Unstoppering it, she took a cautious swallow. She'd expected water, or perhaps curmi. She was amazed to discover the skin contained wine. Delicious wine, as smooth and sweet as what she'd drunk at Gaius's home. She raised her gaze to Madryn. The young woman watched her, a sullen expression marring the beauty of her delicate, freckled face. "How did you come by Roman wine?" Sirona asked.

"It was a long time ago, before last snowseason. The Shining One told us that some Roman soldiers would be bringing a caravan of supplies through a certain mountain pass. We were able to set up an ambush and steal everything. The food didn't last long, but there was a great deal of wine. The Shining One ordered us to save it for ceremonies and special occasions, such as when we have visitors."

Sirona held out the skin. "Join me in a drink. It would please me if you did."

Madryn shook her head.

Sirona grew uncomfortable. This young woman seemed to dislike her, although she didn't know why. "Have you lived here long?" Sirona asked.

"We never stay in one place for more than a season."

"I meant, have you been part of this tribe for long?"

Madryn wrinkled her brow in thought. "It must have been nearly a year ago that I joined them. I hadn't yet started my moon times. The first time I bled, the Shining One had a ceremony for me. Five nights later we shared sex magic." She smiled, the expression lighting up her face. "It was wonderful."

Sex magic. Hearing the term brought Sirona's memories rushing back. Cruthin had also sought to share sex magic with her. There had been magic in what they shared, for certain, but the consequences had been disastrous. She couldn't forget that Cruthin had abandoned her. Although she might have been put to death, he hadn't cared.

Rufus returned and sat down next to her. "Our mounts are being cared for. I suspect the one youth who came to help me—Tarawg—will not leave them all night. I was exactly the same the first time I encountered horses."

Sirona handed him the half-finished bowl of stew. "I'm not very hungry, but I don't want it to go to waste." Rufus took the bowl and began to eat. He didn't seem to find anything distasteful about the food and consumed it rapidly. Sirona considered that as a slave, he'd probably endured far less palatable fare.

Llewan returned and said, "The Shining One will see you now."

Sirona rose and looked at Rufus. "I think I should meet with him alone."

A hint of resentment crossed the youth's face, but he nodded.

Llewan took her to a round timber dwelling, no larger or better built than any of the others. He paused outside the hide door and motioned for her to enter. She took a deep breath, then bent down and pushed aside the hide.

The interior was lit by a small oil lamp. She could see Cruthin clearly, sitting on a pile of skins. His chest was bare, and he appeared quite thin, his long, lithe torso reduced to sinewy muscle. But despite his leanness, there was nothing sickly about his appearance. His tanned skin was smooth and unblemished, his dark eyes clear. He had the beginnings of a beard, and that and his long, wavy hair only seemed to emphasis the intensity of his fine-boned face. Sirona was reminded of a wild animal, all haunting grace and fierce-eyed beauty. No wonder they called him the Shining One.

"Sirona." He smiled, and she saw his teeth were still sound. "I'd heard you were captured and killed by the Romans years ago."

"Obviously, I survived," she responded, her throat dry. "In fact, in the years since, I've endured many close encounters with death."

Cruthin nodded. Then he gestured and said, "Sit down. We have much to talk about."

She sank into the furs across from him. The whole hut had a dark, musky smell, again reminding her of an animal. She couldn't believe she was seeing Cruthin again. So much had happened, to both of them. She thought about how they had last parted. "How did you survive after you escaped on the sacred isle?"

"The Old Ones aided me," he answered. "Pellan's tribe. I stayed with them for a time, and then went up into the hills."

"Alone?"

A smile twitched his lips. "Aye, alone. I knew that to connect with the Goddess, I must go to Her by myself. I spent the rest of the sunseason in the mountains, trying to reach Her."

"When winter came, what did you do? No one could survive in the mountains alone during the snowscason."

"When it grew cold, I traveled north until I met a Decangi tribe. They urged me to stay. Their Drui had died and they had no one else who'd trained in the grove."

"You acted as their Learned One?"

"I made a more impressive high Drui than either Fiach or that fool Elidyr. The ceremonies I led will not soon be forgotten." He smiled again. "I made them feel the gods. They experienced the energy of the sky and the earth entering their bodies."

Sirona nodded. She would never forget the magic he had conjured at the mound and circle of stones on the sacred isle.

"I might have been content among the Decangi," Cruthin continued. "They honored and respected me, despite my youth. I had plenty of time to journey to the spiritworld and develop my knowledge. But then the Romans came." His mouth twisted in bitterness. "A whole troop of them overran the dun while most of the warriors were off hunting. They moved through the settlement taking whatever they wanted—tools, hides, wool, even a few of the younger women to serve as slaves. The Romans killed the youths guarding the herds and stole every beast they could.

"The next winter was one of terrible hunger. The very young and the old took sick and died. In the spring, those healthy men remaining decided to try to retrieve our cattle. They left and never came back. By then there were only a few of us. They turned to me as their leader. I wasn't trained as a warrior, but I had other abilities. I could go into a trance and leave my body. In that way, I was able to see things, to determine the movements of the Romans and where they kept their supplies. Using the knowledge I gained, we began to raid and attack the Romans as they moved from place to place.

"With the food we obtained we survived the next few winters. Stories about us spread among the sunset tribes and more young men and women came to join us. But the Romans built stout fortresses and garrisoned them with larger and larger numbers of soldiers. It became very difficult to steal the food we needed. They sent out parties to search for us, and we were forced to retreat farther and farther into the hills. This last year, we had to rely on hunting and fishing to survive." Cruthin's expression turned grim. "There must be some way to defeat the Romans. They are great warriors and very skilled at practical matters, but so crude and blind when it comes to things of the spiritual realm."

Sirona nodded. She thought as Cruthin did, that for all their power in this realm, the Romans were impoverished and weak when it came to the larger forces that controlled people's lives. That spiritual lack was the thing that made them vulnerable. But how to make use of it?

The frustration in Cruthin's eyes exactly mirrored her own, which made her realize how much he'd changed. He seemed genuinely grieved when he spoke of the Decangi's sufferings. He also seemed to feel responsible for this group of young people. It was a great step for someone who had once thought only to use those around him for his own ends.

Both she and Cruthin had been tempered and tested by the things they had experienced since leaving the grove. If the events on the sacred isle had not taken place, the two of them might never have left Mordarach. The things they had endured since had made them stronger, wiser and much more powerful. Her years in the north had taught her patience and offered her a time of contemplation and peace to develop her connection to the Goddess, while Cruthin had finally learned to care for something besides power and his pursuit of the mysteries. Now if they could only use what they learned to make a difference.

Seeing that Cruthin was gazing at her expectantly, Sirona said, "The task ahead of us won't be easy. And it's been made even more difficult by the fact there are so few of us left who possess any knowledge of the spiritual realm. The rest of the Learned Ones are dead, except for Old Ogimos."

Cruthin looked startled. "What happened to the rest of the Learned Ones?"

"The Romans killed them. All the Learned Ones had gathered on the sacred isle and the Romans came and cut them down."

"You're certain they're all dead?"

She nodded. "The few who didn't go to the gathering might have survived, but everyone else is gone." The familiar frustration returned. "I knew the Romans were going to attack the sacred isle. I went there to warn the Drui, but they wouldn't listen."

"Of course not," Cruthin scoffed. "They know everything."

Sirona nodded. "They tried to put me to death in a special sacrifice. But the Old Ones came and helped me escape. They also rescued Ogimos." She couldn't quite bring herself to tell him about calling down the storm. Despite his generally respectful attitude, she worried he wouldn't believe her.

Cruthin let out a rich-throated laugh. "You warned them, and they wouldn't listen. Serves them right, the pious, narrow-minded fools!"

She shook her head. "Most of the knowledge of our people died with them. All that learning, passed down from one generation to another. Now it's lost forever, trickling away like the blood from their wounds."

"Learning? Knowledge?" Cruthin cocked a dark brow. "What knowledge did they ever possess? Lists of our ancestors, laws and rituals, poems and stories, the history of our people? Those things don't matter. What matters is the magic, and they knew little of that. I vow almost everything important I've learned came either from the Old Ones or I've discovered on my own: the ability to become one with the gods' power, to go into a trance and leave my body, to shapeshift and make fire, to call down the power of the heavens—"

"You can do all those things?" She'd guessed at some of it, but shape-shifting? That sounded even more amazing than calling down a storm.

He met her gaze. "I'm still perfecting my use of the power. But I know these things can be done. I'm certain of it."

His words sent a thrill of excitement through her. Cruthin was even more gifted than she'd guessed. And yet, the arrogance with which he spoke of his abilities irritated her.

"You dismiss the learning of the grove as unimportant," she said, "but if you're honest, can you say that without such training, you would have ever pursued the magic? Our lessons in the grove opened your eyes and taught you to look beneath the surface of life. And Old Ogimos, especially, possesses real wisdom. It was because of him that I've come as far as I have in understanding my visions and what they mean. He taught us about matters of the spirit, as well as laws and rules and stories. He understands how things fit together—this world and the Otherworld and the gods."

"I always admired Old Ogimos," Cruthin agreed. "Although I could never understand why he didn't seek out the power he deserved. He should have been high Drui, not Fiach."

"That was his choice. He said often he didn't want the responsibility, that he preferred to teach in the grove and assist with ceremonies and have the rest of the time to himself. He refused to seek power for its own sake... as some people do," she added meaningfully.

"You think I'm power-mad?" Cruthin glared at her. "That I've brought all these young people here to so I could have my own tribe to lead? The fact is, I didn't seek them out. They all came to *me*. They found *me*." His dark eyes gleamed with fervor. "They see their world crumbling before them and they're desperate for hope. They want to believe they have a future. I offer them that."

"I agree you've helped them, and probably saved their lives by keeping them away from the Romans. But your influence over them seems excessive. They think you're some kind of god. Even I, who know something of your gifts, can't quite believe that." There, it was out. The real reason she felt so uncomfortable with Cruthin.

Cruthin smiled. "It sounds as if you're jealous of me. You wouldn't be the first. That's why Fiach ended up banishing me. And why Bryn always resented me."

"Bryn didn't resent you," Sirona protested. "It's only that—"

"Bryn *was* jealous of me," Cruthin interrupted. "Of what I shared with you. The stupid lovesick fool." His mouth quirked. "But now that I see you again, I think perhaps his obsession wasn't so ridiculous after all. You've grown into a beautiful woman, Sirona. That you're also gifted and powerful only makes you even more alluring."

His dark eyes fixed on her, making her heart race. She struggled against the breathless feelings his words aroused. Nay, she wouldn't let him distract her from her goal. "I've come to ask for your help," she said. "I think I've discovered of a way to defeat the Romans, or at least control their influence over our people."

Cruthin searched among the clutter around him until he found a beautiful gold and enamel cup and a beverage skin. He filled the cup and held it out to her, then found another cup and filled it for himself. "Tell me," he said. "Tell me what we must do."

She took the cup and drank. Then she said, "Remember that night at the mound on the sacred isle? How you called down the power of the gods so it shone around you like a brilliant light?" She took a deep breath. "Do you think you could do something like that again?"

Cruthin laughed. "Of course. That's the easiest of challenges. I do the same thing at almost every ceremony I take part in."

"If we could harness the energy you are able to call forth… Use it to change events in this realm…" She shook her head. "I'm not certain exactly what we must do. But I'm convinced you and I have lived our lives for this very purpose. The two of us combine the wisdom of the Drui and the magic of the Old Ones. There must be some way to use that joint power against our enemies."

Cruthin looked thoughtful. "It's an intriguing idea. Although I'm uncertain how to accomplish what you suggest. For several years I've been going into a trance so my spirit could journey far and wide to observe the enemy. But even when we know where the Romans are, my warband and I are limited by the size and strength of our forces. The last few times my spirit traveled, I didn't even tell my young warband what I'd seen. There are far too many of the enemy for us to risk taking them on."

"I agree," Sirona said. "And yet, there must some way to use our powers against the Romans."

Cruthin nodded again. "Perhaps I should go into a trance and seek the answer in the Otherworld."

Remembering her own experience of being outside her body, she said, "It's dangerous to travel to other realms. It would be very easy to go too far and not be able to return."

"What do you know of such things?"

His contemptuous tone irritated her. "I've also gone into a trance and left my body and sent my spirit on a journey."

He regarded her intently. "It's been a very long time since we last saw each other. Why don't you tell me everything that's happened since then?"

Where to begin? And how much to reveal? Should she tell him about the wolf leading her north? About Itzurra and the goddess stone? Somehow, at this moment, those things didn't seem important. Instead, she began her tale when she left the north with Kellach. She told Cruthin about her vision of the great battle and of her plan to warn Boudica. When she got to the part about Bryn, Cruthin grinned and said, "I'm pleased to know he finally found a way to pursue his true calling as a warrior."

"Aye," Sirona agreed. "Although I had to beg him not to take part in the great battle with the Romans. I only hope he heeds my words." Then she told Cruthin about how she had tried to warn the people of Camulodunum about the impending attack.

Cruthin frowned. "Why warn the enemy? Why not let them all die?"

"Many of the people in the colonia were Pretani. I can't say exactly why, but I knew I must try and save them. Afterwards, I became convinced there was someone dwelling there, a child perhaps, who the gods wanted to live. I did what I was called to do, then left and came west. After I reached Mordarach and learned all the Drui were on the sacred isle, I knew I must try to warn them of the Roman threat. My efforts saved Ogimos, which seems to me a worthwhile end. Then I realized I had to come here. That somehow you and I must find a way to defeat the Romans, at least in the highlands."

Tears filled her eyes as she thought about how much had already been lost. Every time she thought about the great battle with the Romans, she was afflicted with a gnawing sense of futility. But there was more to this struggle than one battle. She mustn't give up. Raising her gaze to meet Cruthin's, she said, "I believe we can change the future, you and I."

"What other gifts do you possess, besides your visions?"

"I can call down a storm. I did so on the sacred isle. The wind blew. The rain poured from the heavens. The sky was rent with lightning. It was a powerful enough display that all the Learned Ones ran away and Ogimos and I were able to escape."

"Go on," Cruthin said.

"When I was in Camulodunum, I was able to make the water in a pool turn to blood, the sky to roil with wind and lightning, and a statue fall to the ground."

Cruthin watched her, his dark gaze intent. Sirona began to feel unsettled. Did he accept her words as truth?

Cruthin put his cup aside, then reached across and removed the half-empty vessel she held in her hands. She could see the rosy glint of wine on his lips as he reached out and touched her face, stroking her cheek. "Ah, Sirona. Now I know why the Goddess sent you back to me."

She sat very still as his fingertips traced the line of her jaw, then trailed down her neck and under the fabric of her gown. With the gentlest of caresses, he touched her breast. Then he leaned near and kissed her. His breath was wine-sweet. The pressure of his tongue, sublime. And yet, a voice reminded her, this had nothing to do with her plans.

With effort, she pulled away.

"What's wrong?" he asked.

"I didn't come here for this."

He raised his brows. "Why did you come?"

"I've told you. We need to think of a plan to defeat the Romans."

He nodded, looking pained, then retrieved his cup and took a gulp of wine. When he spoke, his voice was emotionless. "You've told me many interesting things, Sirona. I wish to think upon them for a time. Alone." He made a dismissing gesture.

Startled and not a little irritated, she got to her feet.

* * *

Bryn gazed across the valley to the place where the dun of the Tarisllwyth used to stand. "Cursed Romans," he muttered. Despite knowing what had happened here, actually seeing his home so altered was agonizing.

Bryn glanced back at Balthar and Corrio. The two slaves rode the horses stolen from the Romans and led the two smaller animals that had made up the chariot team. They'd left the chariot behind, hiding it in the bushes some distance from where they had dragged the dead Romans off the road. Bryn worried the one who escaped might return with other soldiers, which was why he had insisted they abandon the chariot and set off cross country. Later, he decided the enemy must want all their troops for the battle against Boudica's forces. That conflict would probably take place soon. One day he might wake up and be one of the few left alive of all those who had gathered near Boudica's palace.

The thought filled him with guilt, and he wondered if he shouldn't have tried harder to warn Gwynceffyl and his men. Had he really done enough to keep his fellow warriors from disaster? But it was one thing for him to have faith in Sirona's vision, another to convince men who hadn't grown up with her and seen evidence of her abilities. It would have been nearly impossible for him to turn those men away from their goal of fighting the Romans. Nothing he could have done would have changed anything.

The grim thought made him wonder if the gods had decreed that this should be the end of the Pretani. Why the gods should forsake them, he didn't know, but it seemed they had. He would have to ask Sirona about these things when he saw her.

If he saw her. A dozen different calamities might have befallen her since he'd last beheld her lovely face. What if she was dead? Or imprisoned? Or suffering in some way? What if she needed him and he wasn't there?

His throat grew tight at the thought, and tighter still as they neared Mordarach. Instead of the stubble of harvested grain, the fields below the dun were filled with weeds, with only a few scraggly stalks of wheat and barley visible. And there was no sign of the tribe's cattle. Were they off in summer pastures far from the dun? Or, had they been driven off by the Romans? All at once, Bryn realized he must focus on what he could do to help his tribe.

As they made their way up the trackway to what was left of the hillfort, Bryn's tension increased. Everything seemed so quiet. There was no clang of metal from Gwgri's forge. No sound of children playing. No dogs barking to warn of their approach. And yet, he saw smoke rising into the sky. Someone had a fire going at least.

Reaching the place where the gate had once been, he dismounted and entered the settlement. There were plenty of roundhouses still standing, although many of them appeared uninhabited, their thatching half blown off, their doorways uncovered and open to the elements. The workshops also seemed abandoned. Bryn felt a renewal of his grief as he passed the smithy and saw no evidence of a fire. Like the hearth in the chieftain's hall, the forge's fire had never been allowed to go out. At least that was so while his father was chieftain here.

Poor Tarbelinus. Bryn felt the familiar ache of grief. Although he and his father had quarreled much of the time, and Tarbelinus had made his early life very difficult, that didn't mean he hadn't cared for his sire. Tarbelinus had been a good man and, for the most part, a good chieftain. He'd been wrong about the Romans and about his son, but he had held his tribe together and made certain they prospered for many years.

Bryn walked on stonily, heading toward the chieftain's hall. As the structure came into view, he quickened his steps. He entered the hall. The place was crowded with looms, women and children. The women talked as they worked, a steady buzz of feminine voices. There was a group of children weaving baskets near the doorway. One of them saw Bryn and stood. "Mama!" the child cried plaintively. Two dozen pairs of eyes—most of them familiar—focused on Bryn.

There was a shriek. "Bryn, Bryn, is it really you?" In the center of the hall, his mother got to her feet and started towards him. He was shocked by the streaks of white in her hair and the gauntness of her face. Indeed, everyone in the room appeared very thin. But his mother's careworn features were lit with a brilliant smile as she neared him. "Bryn, my darling. I knew you would come. I knew you would save us."

She embraced him fiercely, and he winced as he felt the bones of her body through her gown. His poor mother. He gently held her away from him so he could look at her. "I would have come home sooner, but I only learned about Tarbelinus a short while ago." In fact, it had been nearly a cycle of the moon. He felt another stab of guilt at the thought.

"It doesn't matter," Rhyell sobbed. She was weeping openly now, which unnerved him. He'd always seen his mother as strong and formidable. In some ways, he'd feared displeasing her much more than he'd ever worried about angering his father. "You're here now and all will be well," she sniffled.

The weight on his chest seemed to increase. These people, the pathetic remnants of his tribe, obviously expected him to save them. How was he to manage such a feat? If only he could find Sirona. He wet his lips and asked breathlessly, "Have you seen Sirona?"

"Aye. She was here not long ago." Rhyell wrinkled her forehead in thought. "She arrived a little after the Grain Moon reached fullness."

"She was here!" Bryn knew a surge of elation, then a stab of fear. "But where did she go? Why did she leave?"

"She went to warn the Learned Ones on the sacred isle that the Romans were coming."

Bryn's relief evaporated. "Why would she do such a thing?" He raked his hands through his hair. The Learned Ones would never listen to her. When she told them about the great battle and the defeat facing their people, the Drui would be infuriated. They might decide to punish her, to mete out some terrible judgment. He sucked in his breath. "By the gods, why did you let her go?" he demanded of his mother. "Why didn't you stop her?"

Rhyell gazed at him blankly. "How would I stop her? If she chooses to do these things, it's no business of mine. She's seeress, a Learned One. I wouldn't interfere in such matters. Oh, no. I learned my lesson with her mother."

Bryn wanted to ask Rhyell what she was talking about, but at this moment he was too worried about Sirona to bother with his mother's strange comment. "By Arianrhod, what do I do now?" he groaned. "She's put herself in danger once again—not only from the Romans, but also from the Learned Ones."

"Why should the Learned Ones harm her?"

"Because they're stupid fools! They nearly put Sirona to death years ago. Curse her! Why does she have to be so stubborn?"

"And why do you care for her so much?" Rhyell asked. "You should have heard her when she was here. She said she'd left you in the sunrise lands. Then, when I mentioned Cruthin, she grew excited. I tell you, son, although I admire and respect Sirona as a Learned One, I wonder if she's not every bit as cold and heartless as her mother was when it comes to men."

Bryn clenched his jaw. His mother was probably right. Sirona might never love him the way she did Cruthin. That thought was painful to contemplate, yet didn't alter the way he felt about her. "What about Cruthin?" he asked. "You mean to tell me he's still alive?"

"Aye. At least he was last sunseason. That's when Pryderi and the others went off to join his warband."

"Warband! Cruthin has a warband?"

Rhyell shrugged. "That's how people refer to his ragged group of youths, although as I understand it, they've had few engagements with the enemy. That's probably the only reason they're still alive."

"But Cruthin was never a warrior." Bryn shook his head. He'd come back to his homeland to find everything turned upside down.

"You asked me about Cruthin, so I told you," Rhyell said. "Now, I think it's time for you to introduce me to your companions." She motioned to the two fair-haired slaves waiting in the doorway of the hall. "Although our food stores are very low, I will try to find the means to prepare a meal for them."

Bryn turned and gestured for the two men to approach. "This is Corrio and Balthar. They are from…an eastern tribe." This didn't seem like a good time to break the news to his proud mother that he'd brought home two foreign slaves, not to serve them, but to work beside them as equals. He nodded to Rhyell. "This is my mother, Lady Rhyell, wife of Tarbelinus, the chieftain of the Tarisllwyth."

The two men bowed to Rhyell.

Rhyell regarded them with obvious apprehension. To Bryn, she whispered, "They don't look Pretani."

"I'll explain later," Bryn said. "For now, please treat them as you would any other guests."

Rhyell nodded and said heartily, "If you're friends of my son, you're welcome here. Now, I must excuse myself to see to preparing a meal to celebrate his safe return." She headed toward her private quarters at the back of the hall.

Bryn turned to Corrio and Balthar. "I don't want my mother to use up the food supplies of the tribe. We must go hunting and bring back some game."

He saw the doubt in the two men's eyes. Clearly, they had not hunted before. Bryn repressed a sigh. If only he'd been able to convince Cadwalon to come with him to Mordarach.

He started toward the door and was immediately surrounded by women and children. The other members of the tribe had held themselves back while he spoke with his mother. Now they drew near, murmuring greetings and touching him with cautious, gentle movements.

"Bryn, it's good to see you."

"It's wonderful to have you back."

"How strong and tall you've grown. You look like your father."

"Do you remember me? I'm Derwyn. I used to help care for you when you were little."

"Of course I remember you," Bryn told the elderly woman. "I remember all of you."

He felt abashed as he realized he'd almost walked away without greeting everyone. These were his people. He must take time to acknowledge them properly.

He spent the next few moments talking with the women, patting children on the heads, and generally catching up on what had happened in the lives of these members of his tribe. There was much that wasn't mentioned, such as all the people who were no longer with them. Indeed, Bryn began to wonder if there were any males left alive at Mordarach. As he finally left the hall, he saw an old man tottering toward him. "Gwrgi, it's good to see you!" he exclaimed.

The old man broke into a toothless grin. "Aye, and you as well, Bryn. What a fine brawny man you've become. So much like your father." Gwrgi's voice broke on the last word, and Bryn felt tears fill his own eyes.

"Thank you," Bryn said. "I hope I can be worthy of my sire and lead my people with courage and strength."

"Lead us?" Gwrgi responded in a quavering voice. He shook his head. "You must not even try. Save yourself. Leave this place. Go north. Somewhere the Romans won't find you. The blood you carry is precious. You mustn't let them kill you."

"I won't leave my kin and tribe and hide away from the Romans. If they kill me, so be it, but I can't abandon what's left of my heritage. Not for any reason. If I travel north, I'll take all of you with me."

Gwrgi sighed. "I would never survive such a journey. But perhaps you are right to take the rest of them from this place." He looked around sadly. "It's not the same these days. I've been too feeble to work metal for nearly three years. Now that Hyell is gone, my shop stands empty and quiet."

Bryn wanted to ask what had happened to Hyell, but he guessed the young man was dead. What a waste, he thought. Gwrgi had been a competent smith, but his apprentice, Hyell, was truly gifted, able to fashion weapons and jewelry that were almost magically beautiful.

"My companions and I are going hunting," Bryn said. "While we're gone, it would be helpful if you could look after the horses. He gestured to where Balthar and Corrio had left the animals, tethered to an abandoned storehouse. "Have a couple of the older children or the women fetch them water from the cistern. When we return we'll see about turning them out into the pasture below the dun."

"Ah, the horses." Gwrgi's mouth spread into a nearly toothless smile. "They look like fine beasts. Almost as fine as the ones the Romans rode when they came here and took your father away."

"Indeed, some of them are Roman horses," Bryn answered. "On the way here, we came upon some of the enemy. We killed them and took their animals."

Bryn recalled the incident with deep satisfaction, and then forced himself to concentrate on the task ahead. There was a quarter of the day's light remaining. With luck it would be enough time to find and kill some sort of game and bring it home to feed his poor, half-starved tribe.

He started toward the entrance of the dun, Corrio and Balthar following. On the way, he came upon the dwelling that used to belong to Nesta and Sirona. Although the thatching was battered by weather, the rest of the structure appeared solid and secure. He stopped a moment and gazed at the small roundhouse, the memories rushing back. He recalled all the times he'd come here. Nesta would greet him, her shrewd blue eyes making him uncomfortable. Often she would tell him that Sirona was gone, and then shoo him away as well. But sometimes he would find Sirona there, and she would come to the doorway, looking so small and perfect. Merely the sight of her was enough to make his chest grow tight.

Bryn let out his breath in a sigh. No matter what Rhyell told him, he couldn't stop loving Sirona.

He opened the door and looked inside. Bundles of herbs still hung along the walls, and other furnishings remained as they had been when Sirona and Nesta lived there—a rusty cauldron near the fire, some baskets and a big wooden chest pushed back against the far wall. He entered the dwelling and picked up a sheepskin lying by the hearth. Clouds of dust rose as he lifted it, and he realized how ridiculous it was for him to come here. Sirona was gone. He couldn't conjure her back simply by touching her things and yearning for her.

He left the hut abruptly. Outside, Corrio and Balthar were waiting for him. Bryn nodded to the other men. "Now, we go hunting."

As they started toward the gate, Bryn tried to decide what to do beyond the immediate task of finding food. His every instinct told him Sirona was in danger. He should go after her and try to protect her from the Drui. But how could he, under the circumstances? His mother would be devastated if he left again. These people needed him. He had a duty here. A duty as great as anything he owed Sirona. Besides, it might well be too late. If Sirona had left several days ago, she would have arrived at the sacred isle by now. Whatever dangers awaited her, she'd already faced. Either she had survived, or she hadn't.

His stomach twisted in dread. There was nothing he could do. Nothing except beseech the gods to continue to protect her.

When they reached the wildwood at the north end of the valley, Bryn pointed to a stand of ash trees and told the other two men, "This type of wood works well for hunting spears. I'm going to show you how to make one."

Chapter 30

Sirona walked briskly away from Cruthin's dwelling. His abrupt dismissal rankled. She thought he'd changed, but he was as cold and manipulative as ever. *I don't have to endure this! As soon as morning comes, I'll have Rufus fetch the horses and we'll leave! I won't even say goodbye!*

Taking a deep breath, she realized she could do no such a thing. She'd sought out Cruthin because the Goddess told her she must. Regardless of her own feelings, she couldn't leave yet. She must keep trying to discover what she was meant to do here.

Rufus approached. "Are you all right?"

"Of course." Her voice sounded sharp and unnatural, even to her own ears.

"Then why are you standing there with your hands clenched, scowling?"

Sirona didn't answer.

"We could go back to Mordarach," Rufus said. "You said Rhyell wanted you to stay, to be head Drui of the tribe."

"Perhaps I'm meant to do that eventually, but not yet."

Someone cleared their throat nearby. It was Llewan. "The hunters have returned," he said. "We'd like for you to join us for a meal. I promise the food will be much better than the awful stew Madryn gave you."

"Thank you," Sirona answered. "We'll come shortly."

"What's wrong?" Rufus asked again after Llewan had left. "What did Cruthin do to upset you?"

"It doesn't matter," Sirona said, her anger gradually easing. "I won't forsake my duty to the Goddess."

They walked back to the glowing hearth. Several young women were gathered there, cooking the food that had been foraged, which appeared to be two scrawny rabbits, several small trout and some roots and tubers.

Sirona sat down on a rock and asked questions of the women as they worked. Their explanations of how they came to be there were much as she anticipated. In almost every instance, their tribes had been overrun by the Romans and the chieftains forced to pay massive tribute. Many of the young men had decided they had no future among their own people. They'd heard of the Shining One and his daring raids upon the Romans and come to join him. The women had come along because they had either handfasted with the young men or expected to when they were old enough.

Living in the highlands was difficult, the women told Sirona. Since they could no longer steal from the Romans, they had to survive on game and fish, berries, roots and nuts. They moved their camp often, which forced them to build new dwellings. But at least they were free, not slaves of the Romans, one of them noted. Sirona saw that one of the women was far along with child. She couldn't help wondering if the babe was Cruthin's.

While they waited for the food, Llewan brought more wine. Sirona declined to have any, knowing she must keep her wits sharp to deal with Cruthin.

This meal was much better than the stew, although the portions were meager. Afterwards, Sirona decided to go down to the stream and wash. Rufus attempted to follow her, but she told him she wanted to be alone.

She made her way through the growth of alder and hazel and finally reached the small stream. Climbing down the rocky bank, she waded into the water. For a time she stood there, feeling the force of the rushing current against her ankles. One of the women had told her that farther down the valley there was a waterfall, which made her think of Cyhiraeth, the goddess of streams and running water. Nurturing and bountiful, Cyhiraeth also could be destructive, washing away trees, rocks and earth during the spring floods. Like all goddesses, she had two faces—bringing life, bringing death.

Sirona shivered, partly because the water was cold and partly because of her dark thoughts. She reminded herself how good it was to be back in the highlands, cradled in the verdant green embrace of this small, lovely valley. The brilliant stars shone above her, like innumerable blossoms of light scattered across the blue-purple meadow of the sky. The night air was cool against her skin, even though it was midsummer. She breathed in deeply, smelling water and stones and grass. Then, realizing her feet were going numb with cold, she bent down and began to wash.

She thought of the luxury of bathing in warm water while at Boudica's palace, and the rich, plentiful food she'd eaten. The comfort of sleeping on a soft, straw-filled pallet rather than the hard ground. Living like that was pleasant, but not truly satisfying. Beautiful things and agreeable surroundings didn't fill the void within her heart as this place did. Such things didn't feed her spirit. Only the gifts of the goddess did that: The warmth of the sun. The music of flowing water. The sweet breath of the wind. The lacy, green loveliness of a budding tree in spring. The perfumed radiance of a hawthorn bush in bloom. The beguiling curve of a hill. The splendor of all the creatures of this realm: the fleet, wary doe flashing through the trees, a hawk swooping through the sky, the bright blaze of a fox hunting in the meadow, the sleek, silent glint of trout feeding in a shallow stream. Those were the things that gave richness and meaning to life.

That was the essence and magic of her people, that they understood and honored the things of the Goddess's world and appreciated their connection to Her and to all life. It was that link to the gods that made her people what they were. If the Romans destroyed that, if they seduced her people into forsaking their bond with the earth and the sky and the deities who represented those things, then the Pretani would truly be defeated. It was not enough that her people survived, that in the future there were children who possessed Pretani blood and the fair skin and blue eyes typical of her race. What was crucial was that those children should understand their place in this realm and honor the things that were sacred.

What if the Romans ended up possessing these lands, but were unable to change the hearts and minds of the people who lived here? If the races of the highlands retained their beliefs and their way of living, despite the Romans? Would that not be a kind of victory? A victory perhaps more important than who prevailed in battle or who controlled the land. For how could the highlands ever belong to the Romans anyway? They didn't understand this place. They saw the land as a thing to be tamed and conquered, not as a living aspect of the Mother.

All at once it became clear to her. The Romans were of the physical realm. They had little understanding of the spiritual. And that was their weakness. A weakness that might be used against them. There was a way to harness the power, to use the force of the gods to defeat the Romans. It required magic, not warfare.

She recalled her very first vision of the people dancing on the hillside by the sea and the great light they called down from the heavens. There was power in that light, and even if it could not be used to defeat the Romans in battle, it could be used to defeat their influence on her people. She grew breathless with excitement, knowing she must find Cruthin and share these thoughts with him. His coldness would not deter her. She would go to him and make him understand. Between the two of them, they could do this thing.

She started walking back to the settlement. Her spirit felt lighter and freer than since the beginning of the sun season. At last she knew why she had been sent visions of the future.

When she reached the circle of huts, she went directly to Cruthin's dwelling. "Cruthin," she called. "I must speak with you." When he didn't answer, she pushed aside the hide door. She'd expected to find him in a trance. Instead, in the light from the lamp she saw two bodies entwined on the bedfurs. Embarrassment flooded her as she realized he was coupling with Madryn. "Cruthin," she said firmly. "I must speak to you. It's important."

He rolled off the young woman and pulled the bedfurs over his groin. "Leave us," he told Madryn.

Madryn sat up and thrust her lovely red-gold hair away from her face. She glared at Sirona. Then she slowly, leisurely, found her gown and pulled it over her slim, pale body. She fumbled near the bedplace and retrieved a bronze comb. As she began to smooth her long tresses, Sirona lost patience. She gestured. "Go. Go now."

Madryn left. Sirona sat down on the bedfurs, ignoring Cruthin's near nakedness. "I've thought of a way to defeat the Romans. It may not drive them from our lands, but it will protect what's important."

She explained her plan to find the circle of standing stones she'd seen in her first vision and hold a ceremony there. "If you could do what you did that night on the sacred isle, and call down the power of the stars and the moon and the night sky, I believe we could use the energy summoned to weave a kind of spell of protection over the highlands. It wouldn't keep the Romans from coming here, but it would keep their influence from destroying us."

She waited for him to respond. When he didn't, she went on, "I'm not certain where this place is, but I believe we can find it. It's by the sea, as I've said. There's a circle of standing stones there, most of them about knee-high. If we ask the Old Ones, they should know of it. Cruthin, will you help me?"

He cocked his head. "That depends," he said, half-smiling.

"Depends on what?" she asked.

"If we do this, you will have to have sex magic with me, in the center of the circle."

Her heart began to pound. "Why?"

"Because that's the only way to combine the energy between us. Together we will unleash the magic within both of us and create a force so powerful, it will accomplish what you desire and transform the realm of the highlands."

Sirona sat back, wondering if Cruthin was right. If the reason he'd been able to call down the silver wheel of light on the sacred isle was because their bodies had been joined, albeit briefly. The thought of sharing sex magic with Cruthin both intrigued and frightened her. Would he turn into Cernunnos this time? And if he did, would she be able to overcome her fear and finish the ceremony?

Finally, she said, "I will lie with you. But only because the Goddess tells me that I must do whatever is necessary to save my people."

"I care not why you do it, only that we capture what is between us."

The husky warmth of his voice unsettled her. She couldn't help but feel he was manipulating her. And yet, she had to do what the Goddess told her to do, and mating with Cruthin was part of it.

She sought to change the mood between them. "The important thing is to find the place to hold this ceremony," she said. "And to send out word to all the Old Ones that they must join us."

"How will we do this?"

"If I can summon a storm, then I should also be able to summon the Old Ones."

Cruthin nodded. "I will go into a trance and seek out this place by the sea." He gestured. "Go and find Llewan and tell him to bring me more wine."

"You use wine to induce a trance?"

"It aids me in going deeper into other realms."

"But it's dangerous to travel too far. What if someday you can't find your way back?"

"Perhaps I will find what I am searching for and will have no desire to return. Besides, there are always risks in using the power." He cocked a dark brow. "You know that, don't you?"

All at once, Sirona recalled the spirit-man Lovarn warning her about the dangers of using magic, the weaknesses that made a person vulnerable. What was her weakness? What dangers lay ahead of her?

She rose and left the hut. Outside, she encountered Rufus. He was carrying an oil lamp, and he held it up so he could see her face. "Are you all right?" he asked.

She smiled at him. "Aye, I'm well. Very well."

He regarded her critically, as if he didn't quite believe her. Then he said, "I've arranged for you to have a hut all to yourself. Can I take you there?"

"Aye."

Rufus led her to the hut and held aside the hide door so she could enter. Inside was her traveling pack, a pile of furs and sheepskins and, on a rock that served as a table, a bronze ewer and another of the finely wrought cups.

"I told them you were a great seeress," said Rufus. "The young man, Pryderi, who used to live with your tribe, confirmed that you'd trained in the grove. Everyone was very impressed. They agreed you should have this dwelling all to yourself."

"Thank you," Sirona responded. "Now if you will leave me, I would like to lie down and rest."

With obvious reluctance, Rufus started to go. A moment later, Sirona called, "Wait." Rufus turned to look at her. "In the morning," she said, "If I haven't woken by the time the sun has marked a quarter of its arc in the sky, come and rouse me." Rufus frowned at her. Then he nodded.

When he'd left, Sirona sank back on the bedfurs. She felt a little better knowing that there was someone in this realm to call her back if she traveled too far. That is, if she was even able to enter a trance. She glanced at the ewer and the cup. Cruthin used wine to help him begin the journey. Perhaps she should do the same.

She picked up the ewer and examined it. The object was obviously Roman. The workmanship was fine, the shape graceful. But she could not help thinking how different it would look if it had fashioned by a craftsman of her people. Hyell, for example. He would have seen some animal's form in the long neck of the container—a swan or heron—and made the creature part of the design.

But the Roman who created the ewer had been satisfied for the object to be nothing more than a vessel for storing liquid. He had used some curving patterns along the base, so it was not utterly plain, but still, it was merely a ewer. The Romans saw objects for what they were on the surface, while her people knew to look deeper, to see in all things a connection to the realm of the Mother, and to honor that connection. In everything they made, from the simplest basket or wooden bowl, to the elaborate jewelry and woven garments that represented the most accomplished of their creations, they revealed their understanding of these things.

This discovery filled her with even more enthusiasm for her plan. She'd begun to see the true difference between her people and the Romans. Not merely the surface things, but the deep, profound contrasts. The Romans were obsessed with land and conquest, material goods and physical comforts. They had little interest in the realm of the spirits. Rufus said they worshipped gods, but they did so in superficial ways. They built ornate temples and carried carved figures of their gods, as if by means of their talismans they could find a connection to the world of the spirits.

Their approach seemed foolish to her. To seek out the gods, one didn't need a building. You had only to go into the woods or stand on the crest of a hill, find a spring or other source of water. Indeed, the gods could be reached from almost anywhere. All that was required was quiet and an attitude of respect and reverence.

But perhaps it had become so difficult in the Romans' world to find those things that they'd forgotten how to reach out to the spiritual realm. From what she knew of them, the Romans lived in crowded settlements, surrounded by man-made objects and buildings. Those things and people might interfere with attaining the proper mood of contemplation and awareness that was necessary to connect with the gods. Because of that, they had to set aside special places for the purpose of worshiping their deities.

But how could they think to confine the great forces of the gods in small temples, or make tiny clay or wood representations and expect those crude objects to embody the vast forces swirling around them? Could the moon's light be captured in a pottery amphora? The wind be constrained within the walls of a building? Of course not.

The Romans were very clever in many ways. They could create amazing objects and buildings. They organized and trained their warriors to such levels of skill and discipline that they were almost unbeatable in battle. They had the power and ability to rule the world. But they were blind to the things that gave meaning to life. Someday that lack would destroy them. She knew it in her heart. But her people, if they could keep their spirits strong and remember their connection to the earth and the sky and the gods, they might survive and someday even prevail. For the things of the spirit would endure, even when all the glory and wealth of the Romans had vanished.

She poured some wine in the elaborate cup and drank it down. Immediately, her body warmed. Her thoughts seemed to become more acute. Then, as she lay down, they grew languorous and fuzzy. She closed her eyes and imagined her spirit leaving her body, floating upwards and looking down on herself. A sharp sense of melancholy pierced her. It was difficult to leave her flesh behind and not know if she would return. She felt fear, gazing down on the empty shell of herself, wondering what would happen to her. Then she forced herself to push the anxiety aside as her spirit began its journey.

She floated over the highlands, observing them by moonlight. Dark valleys, rocky, barren peaks, clouds of mist. Silent and still in the night. Only a few creatures came out in this midnight world. Owls glided low, searching for prey. Other hunters stalked soundlessly under cover of woods and darkness. This world was ruled by the night sky. Around her spirit the stars glinted and the Lady of the moon watched, serene and distant. For a time, Sirona was content to float in the magical realm of shadows and light, silver and black, purple, violet and gray. Then she forced herself to remember her purpose. She must seek out the Old Ones.

She searched valleys and hidden glens. Although she found evidence of her people—an abandoned hillfort as well as several settlements still in use—there was no sign of the Old Ones. And yet, she knew they were there. She must find some other means of reaching them.

She formed the image of herself lying in the hut far below, then sent out the message: *Come and help me!* She floated the thought on the night wind, sending it as a whisper out into the darkness. She imagined a great white owl, gliding over the land. Her words were contained in the pulse of its huge wings, her message flung out with each sweeping arc of feathers. Her voice drifted on the breeze, like pollen or seed pods wafting across the land. *Come and help me!*

She saw them waking in the night. Their dreams interrupted, they rose from their pallets and dressed in garments of leather and fur. Now she understood why she hadn't been able to find them. The Old Ones of the highlands lived in the very hills themselves, underground in dens, hidden from the world of her people.

She saw them grab their weapons and gather up supplies. The weapons surprised her. She was calling them to a ceremony, not to a war. But then she realized they would know better than she what was needed. If they saw fit to bring their small, sharp knives, marked with ancient symbols, to attach bows to their supply packs and carry quivers full of small arrows, fledged with hawk and kestrel feathers, over their shoulders, then there must be a reason for it. They brought other supplies as well, food wrapped in leaves and beverages carried in skins, leather pouches of herbs and mushrooms, feathers and stones and shells, all the adornments their people used. And gold. She caught the glint of it hidden beneath their garments. Jewelry and weapons made of the precious metal. Objects filled with power, with magic.

Satisfied that she had accomplished her mission, Sirona let her spirit float upwards. She knew she should go back, but it was so beautiful here. The stars seemed so close. The face of the Lady of the moon shone very near. It seemed Arianrhod smiled and beckoned. Ah, to float upon the moonlight, to dance in the swirling currents of the stars winking in the distance. To feel so light, so free, so utterly content—

"Sirona! Sirona! Wake up!" She heard a voice in the distance. Far away and faint. She told herself it wasn't real. This was real, this place of magic and light.

"Sirona!"

With irritation, she let herself float nearer to the earth, even if made her spirit ache with loss. The stars receded. The Lady of the moon turned her face away. She was falling. Falling.

She returned to her body with a burst of pain so fierce it made her cry out. Or perhaps part of her agony came from the fact that someone was shaking her violently. "Stop!" she gasped. "Stop!"

Instantly, her attacker released her. She lay there, eyes closed, her whole being steeped in misery and regret. She hadn't wanted to leave yet. The sheer unfairness of it made her want to weep.

"Sirona, please speak to me. Tell me you're all right!" Rufus. At this moment, she hated him. Once again, he shook her, although more gently this time. "Sirona, please!"

Her eyes snapped open and she regarded him with fury. "I'm well enough! Can't you leave me be?"

She saw his stricken face. His mouth worked silently. She let her breath out in a sigh, trying to release the anger that thrummed through her.

"I thought... I thought you were dead," he muttered. "I'm sorry."

She sighed again, feeling the tension and resentment trickle away. "It's all right," she answered. "I know you were trying to help me. And you did."

She felt unutterably weary. All she wanted to do was sleep. When she closed her eyes and began to slip away into the dreamworld, Rufus woke her once again. She was more patient this time, telling him she was all right, but she needed to rest. After she reassured him several more times, he finally her left her alone. She gave in to the deep lethargy and drifted off

* * *

When she woke, everything was dark and quiet. She sat up and ran her fingers through her tangled hair. Her mouth tasted horrible and her head ached. It felt as if she had drunk too much wine or mead, and yet she knew she'd imbibed only a cupful. Her body was achy and tired as well. *Water,* she thought, *I need water.*

She got up and left the hut. Outside, there was no sign of the moon or stars in the overcast sky. She walked a short distance from the hut, paused and looked around, trying to get her bearings. Eventually she spied the faint glow of the hearth in the distance. She moved toward it.

Around the dying fire, several of Cruthin's little band slept wrapped in their cloaks. Sirona saw Llewan and Madryn among the sleepers. Glancing at the young woman, Sirona knew a stir of pity. Madryn was clearly besotted with Cruthin, but he was using her, and the poor child didn't know the difference.

But she knew. Cruthin would mate with her, not because he desired or loved her, but because through her he sought access to the Goddess. Bryn had warned her a long time ago about Cruthin. How wise Bryn had been back then, and he barely a man at the time. She felt a deep pang of longing, wondering where Bryn was now. What if she never saw him again?

The thought filled her with grief. Bryn had always been there, but she hadn't appreciated him. The kind of love he offered was rare and precious. If the Goddess granted her the opportunity to see him again, she must tell him what he meant to her.

She released a long, drawn-out breath and shivered. Here in the highlands, she could almost feel autumn coming, even though it was barely past time for the celebration of Llewnasa. The festival marked the end of harvest and the beginning of preparations for winter. It was a rite celebrating the fruitfulness of the earth, thanking the sky gods, Beli and Llew, for their summer bounty. It was usually held during the fullness of the Grain Moon, but that time had already passed. Arianrhod's face was waning now as she shrank down into the thin crescent of the crone moon. Her power would not be as great as when she was waxing.

But Sirona knew they couldn't wait for the Berry Moon. The Romans were moving too quickly. The great battle would take place very soon. The troops who had overrun the sacred isle and killed all the Learned Ones were already on their way south to meet Boudica's forces.

Sirona felt the familiar wave of horror as she thought about the disaster to come. *Please, Bryn. Heed my warning. Come home to the sunset lands where you will be safe.*

Her thoughts made her too anxious and agitated to remain still. She moved silently around the hearth, and finally found what she was looking for, a pottery jar of water. She drank until her thirst was quenched. Putting down the jar, she started to move away. "Sirona?" someone called.

She turned and saw Rufus rise to a sitting position. "Go back to sleep," she said. "Everything is well. I'm merely restless from sleeping so long."

"Aye," he said. "You might be. Over a day you were in a trance. You wouldn't wake, except to mumble and groan and insist you were still tired."

A day? She supposed she shouldn't be surprised. On the sacred isle, after calling the storm, she had slept for almost that long. Spirit traveling was obviously exhausting. She wondered how Cruthin did it so frequently. The thought made her anxious. If anything happened to him, the ceremony could not take place.

She made her way to his hut, taking cautious steps in the darkness, recalling how his dwelling was set off a little way from the others. When she encountered the timber walls of his hut, she groped around until she found the doorway and pushed inside. "Cruthin," she called, "are you here?"

"Aye," he answered.

She sank down onto the floor of the hut. "I thought you might be in a trance."

"My search has been futile. I can't find the place we seek, the place where the ceremony must be held."

"Perhaps when they come, the Old Ones will be able to lead us there."

"You think they're coming, do you?" His voice was harsh with sarcasm.

"Aye, I know they are. I *saw* them."

He didn't respond, and she suspected he resented her success when he had failed.

"Perhaps it's easier for my spirit to travel in this realm," she said. "While you are skilled at visiting the Otherworld, a place I've never gone."

"Perhaps."

"We each have our own gifts. To perform this ceremony will require both of us. As female energy complements male power, my abilities will enhance yours. The magic we create together will be formidable."

He didn't answer for a time. Then he said, "Aye. You will play goddess to my god. The Lady of the Moon to the Lord of the Forest. The Great Mother to the Sky Father. The Queen of Summer to the King of the Land."

Sirona shivered. When Cruthin spoke of these things, she could feel the power rising between them.

"Come to me," he said. "Mate with me now. Let us be joined, male and female, darkness and light, sky and earth, fire and water."

"Should we not wait until the ceremony?"

"Nay, the time is now. Can you not feel it?"

She felt something, that was certain. But she worried it was only lust, the aching desire Cruthin seemed so skilled at arousing.

He reached out in the darkness and took her hand. "Come. Lie with me."

She trembled as he pulled her down against him. Was she strong enough to do this? Did she possess enough power to stand against his fierce energy? Fear fluttered inside her, like a moth in the darkness. *Great Mother*, she whispered silently. *Make me strong, make me bold and courageous.*

They moved with grace in the darkness, removing each other's garments, stroking and caressing. She reveled in his hard, lean form, muscle and sinew, smooth skin and coarse body hair. His smell, musky and wild. He savored her femaleness, exploring soft curves and smooth skin. Tasting her lips as if he drank nectar from a flower.

And it was as he said, male and female, fire and water, the sun and moon. The energy flowed between them, and they became another creature altogether. Sexless, featureless, but full of energy. A swirling wind. A raging river. The being they made together overwhelmed both of them, until their bodies, their spirits, even their thoughts were joined.

She felt the relentless, questing hunger of his spirit and knew he was aware of the aching yearning of her own. She dragged him back to earth, pulling him down into ancient rhythms and the endless wheel of the seasons. At the same time, he sought to carry her away from all that was solid and familiar, and transport her to worlds that were strange and magical and threatening. Everything in her realm had a pattern and a purpose, while his spiritworld was full of confusion and disorder, things unreal and unknown. Together they fell, spiraling into nothingness, and she clung to him, certain she would fall into an endless void if she ever let go.

But the landing was peaceful, despite her fears. She found herself once more in the earthly realm. He lay across her body, breathing heavily. She felt sticky and sore. The air of the hut was thick with a miasma of sweat and lust and the slightly sweet scent of his seed, spilling from between her legs. She knew a sense of wonder and also vague regret. At last she had mated with Cruthin and it had been every bit as magical as she expected. But it had nothing to do with love, or the yearnings of her heart. Cruthin was part of the pattern of her life, spun deeply into the weave of her destiny, but he wasn't her mate, the man she belonged with. Their joining was ancient and primal, a thing beyond this world. But she could not help longing to someday share her body as a woman, rather than a tool of the Goddess. To mate with a man who was merely a man. To satisfy the needs of her spirit, rather than her responsibility to the deities.

She thought of someday mating with Bryn, how right that would feel, how perfect. After briefly savoring the notion, she forced it aside. There was no way to know if she would ever see him again. And she still had much to do before she indulged her own longings. Besides, it was probably unseemly to think about Bryn when she had just lain with another man.

And it wasn't that she didn't care for Cruthin. Indeed, he was very dear to her. She reached to smooth his hair as he lay with his face pressed against her breast, and a wave of tenderness washed over her. She'd always thought him strong, but she feared he was really frail and vulnerable. Poised as he was on the edge between two worlds, he lacked her connection to the earth, to the world of sunlight and warmth and growing things. He spent too much time in his hut, lost in dreams. When she followed him into the Otherworld, she'd felt death. It was waiting for him there, and she worried it would not wait much longer.

The thought distressed her and she began to weep silently, overcome by her feelings. Cruthin shifted and muttered something, already asleep. She continued to stroke his hair, ignoring the weight of him and the discomforts of her body. She might never have another chance like this. For this time, she held him in her arms. For this short while, she could keep him safe.

Chapter 31

In the morning, when she left Cruthin's hut, she was greeted by Llewan. The look of apprehension on his face alarmed her. But then he said, "Some people have come for you," and she knew at once it was the Old Ones.

She found them waiting outside the settlement, like wild animals wary of entering a place that bore the scent of man. They appeared as they had in her trance, garbed in skins and hides and carrying their weapons.

She greeted them using the hand to the forehead gesture the Croenglas had taught her. "Welcome," she said. They made the same gesture back, their expressions solemn. "This is the settlement of the…" She hesitated for a moment, trying to think what to call these young people. "…the settlement of the Amddifallwyth, the tribe of orphans," she finished. She motioned to the youths huddled by the hearthplace, breaking their fast with berries and water. "They won't harm you."

A man of the Old Ones stepped forward. "We care not who they are. We come for you, lady. Because you called us."

She nodded. "I'll tell you what must be done. But, first, you must meet someone." She left them and went to Cruthin's hut. He was still sleeping. For a brief moment, she stood watching him, admiring his beauty and thinking about what they'd shared the night before. Then she leaned over and shook his him. "Cruthin."

He gave her a lazy, sensual smile as he woke. She felt an answering response inside her, but she ignored it. That part of what they shared was finished.

"You must dress and comb your hair," she told him. "The Old Ones have come."

He nodded and dug in the clutter around the bedfurs to find his bracco. He put them on and also his shoes. After draping a necklace of wolves' teeth around his neck, he pushed past her, out of the dwelling. She hurried to follow as he started toward the Old Ones.

By the time she reached him, Cruthin had already greeted them. They gathered around him, seemingly accepting him as one of their own. Perhaps he was. With his leather bracco, bare, tanned chest and long, dark hair—still wild and tangled from sleep—he might well have been one of the ancient race, although he was taller than any of them.

As she approached, Cruthin spoke. "Has Sirona told you about the ceremony? Has she explained our plan?"

The Old Ones' leader didn't answer, but simply looked at Sirona. "I haven't," she answered. "I thought they should meet you first, but, clearly, they already know you."

"Aye." Cruthin smiled. "They know me well."

The leader of the Old Ones said, "You wouldn't have called us here if the matter wasn't urgent. Tell us what we must do."

Everyone looked at Sirona. She said, "I have a plan to defeat the Romans and drive them from our lands. But it has nothing to do with warfare, but rather, magic. I want to weave a spell over the highlands to keep out the influence of the Romans. To make our people strong in their spirits, so that they can resist the temptations the invaders offer. To do this, we must hold a ceremony and call down the forces of the heavens. We must appeal to Arianrhod and Dyeus and the other gods of the sky to aid us, to lend us Their energy and make us powerful in our hearts and minds. To protect this land with Their magic."

She paused and met the gazes of the Old Ones gathered there. As their dark eyes watched her, serious and intent, she worried they would tell her that her plan was foolish, that there was no hope of doing such a thing. Two heartbeats passed. Three. Then their leader said, "We will help you."

Sirona released the breath she'd been holding. "The first matter is the location. I've seen this ceremony in a vision. In my Seeing there is a circle of standing stones on a hillside above the sea. Do you know this place?"

The Old Ones' leader nodded. "Aye, we do. It's north of here, along the coast, near where the great mountain river meets the sea."

"How long will it take to go there?"

"Two days of walking."

"Two days," Sirona said thoughtfully. "We'll have to bring supplies."

"Aye, or we can steal them from the Romans," Cruthin said. "I'll tell my followers to ready themselves to travel." Cruthin nodded to their guests. Then he headed to the hearth place where the young people gathered.

Standing alone with the Old Ones, Sirona grew uncomfortable. These people clearly honored her and felt bound to her, yet didn't quite accept her as one of their own. She excused herself. "I must prepare also," she told their leader.

When she reached the hut where her things were, she found Rufus waiting outside. His expression was accusing. "You weren't here when I came this morning."

"Nay. I was with Cruthin."

"All night?"

Sirona suppressed a smile at Rufus's outrage. "Don't worry," she assured him. "Everything is fine between us. In fact, we'll all be leaving soon to have a ceremony at a place by the sea." She entered the hut.

Rufus pushed in after her. "By the sea? There are Roman settlements everywhere along the northern coast."

"I've survived encounters with the Romans several times before," she said as she found her pack and started to gather up her clothing and other personal items.

"It's not merely the Romans," Rufus said. "I'll tell you, I don't trust this Cruthin... or Shining One, or whatever he's called. He strikes me as a man who cares only for himself. Did you know he has bedded nearly every woman here, and little Melangell carries his child?"

Sirona continued to gather up supplies. "She's probably very pleased with her circumstances. She knows her babe will have high status and protection among this group because of who its father is. Such knowledge would satisfy most women, especially in these uncertain times. My own mother shared the bed of the chieftain of the Tarisllwyth for over a year. If she could have borne him a child, she would have. Of course, if that had happened, my life would have been much different."

What would have happened if Banon had given birth to a child of Tarbelinus's blood? Sirona wondered suddenly. Would he have handfasted with Banon instead of Rhyell? If so, would Bryn have even been born? And what of her? If Banon hadn't been banished and died, what would her own life have been like? Would Banon have abandoned her to dote upon Tarbelinus's child?

Sirona felt a sense of amazement at all the circumstances that led her to this place. Their lives were like one vast piece of fabric, woven of thin strands of wool. If one thread was changed, the whole pattern was altered. And now with this ceremony, she hoped to alter many threads, to weave a new destiny for her people.

* * *

"What's the point of this ceremony?" Rufus asked as he and Sirona walked along a ridge above the river running north. When it began to rain a while ago, they had both taken their oiled leather capes out of their packs and put them on. Rufus led one of the horses, while a little way back in the procession, Tarawg guided the reins of the other mare. On the backs of the two animals were the meager supplies of the tribe, which as far as Sirona knew, didn't include food. All anyone had eaten this day were berries.

"The point of the ceremony is to defeat the Romans, not with weapons, but with magic." she answered. "That's all I can tell you. You'll have to wait and see for yourself."

They'd traveled far already this day, journeying two valleys away from where the tribe Sirona had christened the Amddifallwyth made their settlement. According to the Old Ones, now all they had to do was follow the river north. The site of the ceremony was almost due east of where the waterway joined the sea.

"But is there danger involved?" Rufus persisted. "I know you well enough to sense you're anxious about this ceremony."

Sirona smiled at him. "I worry whether it will work."

"And if it doesn't?"

"At least I will have tried."

"But are there risks? You haven't told me."

"Aye," Sirona said, swiping raindrops from her face. "But there are risks in all of life. It's dangerous to be born. To grow up and to fall in love and to dream dreams and desire a different life. But we do all those things anyway. Because we must. Because it is the nature of our kind to be that way."

"You speak in riddles," Rufus complained. "I'm only asking because I need to know what to do if something goes awry. I can't help thinking about when you went into a trance and I couldn't wake you. What if that happens again?"

A cold finger seemed to trace down Sirona's spine. She, too, feared the ceremony would take her spirit to a place from which she would not easily find her way back. "Just keep calling my name and trying to rouse me. That's what reached me last time."

"And there's this matter of a raid on the Romans to gather supplies. Oh, aye," he continued when Sirona gave him a sharp look. "I know about that. Cruthin says it will all be done under cover of night, that there will be no risk. But you know how easily things could go wrong and people could end up being killed or captured."

"Cruthin has great powers. Perhaps he truly can protect his followers from the enemy."

"But why take the chance at all?"

"Because we're all hungry, and it's much easier to steal food than to track game or search it out in other ways. And there's not much time. The ceremony must be held within the next few nights or it will be too late."

"Too late for what?"

Too late for my people. Too late to change the course of the future. "Right now there aren't many Romans in the sunset lands. Most of their army has traveled southeast to meet Boudica's forces. Now is the time to set our power against theirs."

"Do you know when the battle between the Romans and Boudica's army will take place?" Rufus asked in a subdued voice.

"Not exactly. But it's coming. With every breath I take, I feel the future racing towards us. Perhaps that's why I feel so anxious."

"It must be awful to see visions, to know the future."

"I used to think that, but now I'm not so certain. Because I see farther than most people, I'm able to catch a glimpse of the larger pattern that surrounds us. In some ways, that comforts me. I know this is not the only realm. Nor is this the only life I will know. My soul, as Old Ogimos always said, is imperishable. And the worlds of life and death are connected in ways that few of us understand."

"When you speak like that..." Rufus turned to look at her. "You seem so brave and fearless... like a goddess."

Sirona smiled, remembering the night before and Cruthin saying that their joining would be like the mating of the gods. Perhaps the power people thought of as belonging to the deities was really nothing more than the life force that was in all creatures. Perhaps they were all gods in some way.

She glanced ahead to where Cruthin walked at the front of the group. He hadn't donned a rain cape, and his hair and bare upper body were soaked with moisture. Although he carried a walking staff in one hand, he scarcely used it, and the pace he set wasn't dignified and regal like a head drui's, but graceful and quick as a boy's.

Sirona was immediately reminded of the time when they'd crossed the mountains on the way to the sacred isle. Her throat grew tight at the thought of how long ago that seemed. So much had happened. Except for Bryn, Cruthin and her, everyone else who had gone on that journey was now dead.

As she watched, the sun suddenly burst through the clouds. A shaft of light shone down on Cruthin, making his wet hair gleam black and turning his skin to polished bronze.

"I don't see why you feel you must do this," Rufus said, "Why risk your life when you don't even know if it will make a difference?"

"Because I must," Sirona answered. "I feel as if all my life has been spent preparing for this ceremony. The years in the grove, my journey north, my visions—all of those things have led me to this place."

That night they made camp a little way down the vale. Several of the young men were able to catch some trout from the river, and the women gathered berries. While the trout were cooking over a fire, a woman of the Old Ones approached. "We have flour for mealcakes." She held out a pottery jar that reminded Sirona of the one she'd seen in the mound where she'd met Itzurra.

The women cooked mealcakes, and then they shared the food among them, all the Old Ones and the Amddifallwyth gathered around the fire. Portions were small, but the chewy mealcakes made the meal much more satisfying. After eating, they all rolled up in their cloaks and saics, as the Old Ones called the animal skins they wore for outer garments. Everyone except Cruthin, who strode off into the darkness. Lying wrapped in her cloak, Sirona wondered if he intended to go into a trance.

She had difficulty sleeping. To relax herself, she touched the goddess stone. It lay between her breasts, warm as a living thing. Feeling its smooth surface comforted her. She could almost hear Itzurra's voice in the darkness. *All is well. Everything is happening according to the Goddess's plan.*

* * *

She woke as soon as it began to grow light in the east, and found that the Old Ones were already up. Cruthin's followers took longer to rouse, but soon they were all gathered around the cold hearthplace—everyone except Cruthin. There was discussion of whether to send someone to look for him. The leader of the Old Ones, who was called Druem, said, "We must leave now if we are to reach the place you seek by nightfall."

"We can't leave without Cruthin," said Llewan. The other Amddifallwyth nodded and murmured in agreement.

Sirona could sense the Old Ones' displeasure, and she feared the fragile alliance between the two groups could break apart. "Druem is right," she said. "We must set out now. Cruthin will find us."

Madryn stepped forward. Brushing her gleaming hair out of her face, she said, "I will stay behind and wait for Cruthin."

"Aye," echoed Melangell. "I will wait also." Several of the young men nodded and moved beside Madryn.

Sirona looked to Llewan, hoping he would support her. The young man frowned. He looked from Madryn to Sirona, then back again. Then he said, "The Shining One has made it clear that he honors and respects Sirona and these people from the hills. I think we should do as they ask."

"Respects her!" Madryn's voice was scornful. "He spent one night with her. That's all. Clearly, he tires of her already."

Sirona felt her face flush. Madryn's words made it seem she was no more to Cruthin than a bedpartner. She opened her mouth to explain, but before she could do so, Rufus confronted Madryn, his dark eyes flashing, "You must not speak that way about Sirona. Are you aware of the powers she possesses? She not only sees the future, but she can leave her body and travel to other places with her spirit. She knows great magic and has used it to escape being killed many times. But most of all, she's more fearless and courageous than any warrior I've ever known. She dares to do what is right, what the gods tell her to do." He paused for breath and then gestured to the Old Ones. "She called these people here to aid us. If *they* honor her wishes, then you must also."

No one spoke when Rufus had finished. Madryn glared at Sirona, but the rest of Cruthin's followers looked cowed and ashamed. "This man speaks the truth," Llewan said. "The Shining One would want us to listen to Sirona. If she says we should go on, then we will."

Sirona nodded. "Cruthin will find us after we arrive, I'm certain of it."

* * *

The river they were following broadened into a marshy wetland full of reeds and stands of willow and alder, faintly tinged with the gold of fall. The air was filled with gnats and midges, blue dragonflies and yellow swallowtail butterflies. Birds were everywhere—fishers, herons, swans and mallards. Sirona could smell the ocean and realized they were almost at the mouth of the river. Then, all at once, the Old Ones, who were in the lead, veered away from the waterway and onto a track hidden among the underbrush.

The narrow, overgrown path led them out of the valley and onto the grassy, rock-strewn hills above the river. There, on a broad, open plain above the sea, they found two stone circles. As soon she spotted the larger one, with its irregular stones glinting white against the gold-green expanse of the hillside, Sirona knew this was the place. Meeting Druem's dark gaze, she nodded. He nodded back. Then he gestured to his people. They started to walk away. Sirona called to them. "Wait! Will you not stay for the ceremony?"

"When everything is ready, we will return," Druem responded.

She looked around. Cruthin's followers had gathered around and were watching her. All except Madryn, who appeared sullen and hostile as usual. Sirona felt a twinge of unease. Since Cruthin hadn't yet appeared, they expected her to tell them what to do. "We'll have the ceremony here," she said. "When Cruth... the Shining One comes. In the meantime, we must prepare for the ceremony. Go about your tasks as usual."

Llewan came up to her, his thin features twisted into a frown. "Should we go down into the forest and hunt for game? Fish the river? Those things take time, and I thought you said we must hold this ceremony as soon as possible."

"You're right. There's little time for foraging. I know Cruthin intended for you to go to the Roman settlement and steal food from them." Llewan looked uneasy. She could tell he was afraid. "There will be few warriors there," she reassured him. "Almost all of them have gone south to meet Boudica's army. I will aid you. I will go into a trance and guide you there and back again safely."

The idea had come to her even as she was speaking. She'd presumed Cruthin would be the one to use magic to protect his band of followers, but since he wasn't here, it was up to her. "You must trust me," she told Llewan. "I wouldn't send you on this quest if it wasn't safe." She motioned. "I'll ask Rufus to go with you. He's familiar with the Romans and will be able to help."

Llewan went to tell the others about the plan. Sirona spoke to Rufus, who was unloading the horses. When she explained she wanted him to take part in the raid, he whirled to face her, his expression alarmed. "But I can't leave you. You'll be in a trance. Anything could happen."

"One of the women can stay with me. Never fear. All will be well."

* * *

Sirona found a rise of land and stretched out on the soft, fragrant grass. Within moments of closing her eyes, her spirit began its journey. Soon she could see the Roman settlement in her mind. The stout timber walls, built in a square. Inside, there were several large structures, living quarters for the soldiers and more lavish dwellings for the leaders. There was evidence of building everywhere. Holes dug in the ground. Piles of lumber and stone. But for now, there were too few men here to continue with construction. Along the walls were other buildings, which she guessed were storehouses. Inside would be baskets of grain, pottery jars full of oil, wooden tuns of wine. Plentiful food. But how to gain access to it?

Her spirit floated higher above the settlement and she saw the sentries in the watchtowers on either side of the gate. Only a small force had been left behind, but it still wouldn't be easy for Cruthin's tribe to get inside. They would have to use stealth and cunning. Wait for night and then create a distraction by the gate.

But there was no time for that. Cruthin's band had almost reached the fortress, and they needed to steal the food and return before sunset. She thought of trying to use her energy to create a spell of protection, so the Romans wouldn't see them. But she didn't know if she could do it. If she failed, some of Cruthin's small band of followers might die.

Her spirit drew back, floating on the currents swirling between the ocean and the highlands. The land and sea spread out before her, and she could see the great mountains in the distance, dark and wild, and below them, the beautiful green valleys that had once been filled with herds of cattle and sheep belonging to her people. A mist floated along one of the valleys. Seeing it, she knew what she must do. If she could call down a furious storm, she could surely conjure a mist.

Cyhiraeth, lady of water, aid me. Rise into the air and form a thick silvery haze to hide your people. Allow them to creep unseen and unnoticed into the fortress of the invaders.

Even as she evoked the goddess, a cloud of moisture began to form. It floated along the river valley and crept across the land, finally reaching the Romans' fortress. There it curled around the stout walls of the palisade like a sleek white beast. By the time Cruthin's warband arrived, the whole stronghold would be veiled in mist.

As the group of young people approached the fortress, Sirona sent out another message: *Rufus, you're the most experienced in dealing with the Romans. Tell them what to do. Lead them where they need to go.*

To hold the mist in place, Sirona knew she must merge her spirit with Cyhiraeth. She must become water in all its forms. Flowing down the fells as the snow melted, rushing between the rocks, foaming and churning in mountain rivers, crashing over waterfalls, then slowing to a soft rippling current as she wound her way through the marshes. Water. The gift of life. Nourishing liquid, filling the womb of a pregnant female. Rain, falling from the heavens, making the flowers and trees grow. Quenching the thirst of man and beast. Sirona felt herself become clear and glistening. She was the dew upon the grass. The sweet breath of Blodeuwedd, the goddess of summer. The vapor rising from a bog, shifting like a wraith in the night.

Her awareness joined with the goddess's. Her spirit reached the deepest depths of a mountain lake. She flowed among the ancient stones there, feeling the darkness, the silent depths of the earth and bedrock below. It was cold here, so very cold.

She drew away from the place, seeking the light. When she crested the surface of the lake, sunshine flowed over her. She felt the mist evaporating, vanishing in the sizzling heat. At that moment, she was thrust back into her body. She woke with a gasp. The sun was shining down on her and she was drenched in sweat.

She sat up and waited for her spirit to completely rejoin her body. Gradually her thoughts turned to Cruthin's band and their quest to steal supplies from the Romans. Had she held the mist in place long enough for them to succeed? She wouldn't know until they returned.

Exhausted, she lay down once more.

Chapter 32

She roused to the sight of Rufus standing over her, his expression jubilant. "Sirona, it was amazing! The mist was so thick, the Romans couldn't even see us. We were able to sneak into the fortress and steal several tuns of wine, six sacks of grain and several jars of oil. I know you must have sent the mist. Is there anything you cannot do?"

She smiled at him wryly. "I'm certain there is. And bear in mind that every time I use my magic, I seem to have to sleep for days afterwards."

"You can't sleep now. You must perform the ceremony. Was that not the whole purpose of coming here?"

"Is everything ready?"

"Aye. The women are making meal cakes, cooking them in oil. We also have some figs and dried meat. It will be a wonderful feast."

Rufus grabbed her hand and helped her up. She still felt weak and light-headed, as if her body and spirit were not yet connected. She also experienced a vague uneasiness at the thought of having to use her powers when her strength was so depleted. For a moment she considered whether they could wait another night to hold the ceremony. But Cruthin's followers were more than ready, and her own sense of urgency hadn't diminished. She would have to draw strength from the other participants, to absorb their life and energy into herself. And Cruthin would also add to her power. The magic the two of them possessed would have to be enough.

* * *

As she and Rufus approached the stone circle, Sirona saw that two fires had been built near the perimeter of the larger one. A few of the women were gathered around one of the fires, cooking, while the rest of the women and the men sat in a circle around the larger blaze. They shared several wineskins, and in the waning light, Sirona could see that the mood was merry. People's faces were flushed and their eyes were bright.

As Sirona approached the circle of young people, they all stood. Their expressions were awed and almost worshipful. "It was as you said," Llewan exclaimed. "The gods protected us on our raid, sending the mist to keep the Romans from seeing us. If you could do that so we could steal supplies, why not use your abilities to defeat them in battle? What if you sent the mist and trapped them in a ravine and we were able to fall upon them and kill them as they tried to escape?"

Sirona shook her head. "It might work once or twice. But even if you wiped out all the Romans in the highlands, their leaders would always send more troops."

Llewan frowned at her. She could see he was swaying slightly and wondered how much wine he'd imbibed. "Are you saying we must give up and accept the Romans as our conquerors?"

"Nay. I'm saying there are better ways to fight them... and better ways to use my abilities." She looked around at the three dozen young people gathered there. "The purpose of this ceremony is to draw down the power of the night sky to use against the Romans. We can't drive them from our lands, but we can greatly reduce their influence over us. We can prevent them from taking over our spirits and enslaving us."

"Is this the Shining One's plan as well?" Llewan asked.

"Aye. His power joined to mine will make defeat of the Romans possible."

"If he has agreed to this, why isn't he here?" It was Madryn who spoke.

"He will be here," Sirona said.

"When?"

"When the stars fill the heavens and the moon rises, Cruthin will come." She gestured to the sky, hoping her prediction came true. What if he was off in a trance somewhere and had forgotten their plan? What if he'd chosen to send his spirit on another sort of journey? Nay, she had to trust that the bond between them was strong enough to bring him back.

* * *

A short while later, the women who'd been cooking brought platters of steaming mealcakes. Along with the mealcakes, there was chewy dried meat, olives and dried green fruits that Rufus called figs. They all ate until they could eat no more, washing down the rich food with plenty of wine. As twilight fell and the moon rose, Sirona began to wonder if she would be able to stay awake long enough to hold the ceremony.

But then the Old Ones came, appearing silently out of the shadows. The Amddifallwyth offered them the rest of the food, which was plentiful. In exchange, the Old Ones had brought skins containing another sort of beverage. It was earthy and bitter-tasting compared to the wine. Sirona took a few sips to be polite and immediately realized how potent the strange liquid was. Her fatigue vanished. Energy seemed to flow through her, and her skin felt tingling and sensitive. Looking around she saw Cruthin's followers were similarly affected. Many of them had left the fire and were moving around restlessly. The men began to pull off their crys. Sirona also felt very warm, even though the night air had seemed cool only a short while before.

Tantalized by her response, Sirona took another swallow of the mysterious beverage. Within moments, she experienced more peculiar sensations. Her breathing came fast and harsh, and she was aware of her own heart beating, the blood pulsing through her veins. She looked up. The stars in the night sky above appeared very bright, so close she felt as if she could reach out and touch them. As she watched the half moon over the hills behind her, she thought she saw Arianrhod's face, the curve of her cheek, one solemn dark eye, her mouth forming a faint smile.

Sirona blinked and wrapped her arms around herself. Magic was all around, intense and powerful. A part of her was afraid. The things she was experiencing weren't real. She decided to move back toward the fire, wanting to be close to people, to ground her spirit in the tangible realm. She heard music from behind her. Turning, she saw two men of the Old Ones pounding a rhythmic beat on large drums made out of leather stretched across huge, hollowed-out tree stumps. Another Old One—a young woman—sat cross-legged, playing a large wooden harp. Nearby, three pipers joined in, keeping the melody. To Sirona's surprise, she saw the pipers included not only a young woman from the Old Ones, but also Llewan and a young man from Cruthin's band named Pwyll.

The music was irresistible, eerie, sweet and compelling. It seemed to enter Sirona's body and flow through her veins, as if her very blood had come alive. Around her, people began to dance, weaving back and forth in slow, graceful patterns, moving around the fire. Sirona longed to join them, but some part of her mind warned she must not enter the state of the mindless revelry they were experiencing. There was something she must do, some important reason she must keep her wits about her. It puzzled her that she could not remember what it was.

She started to move away from the people and the fire, hoping she would be able to recall her purpose. Rufus came to stand beside her. He'd shed his crys and his thin chest glistened with sweat. The pupils of his eyes were huge. "When will the ceremony begin?" he asked.

"Ceremony?" Sirona breathed the word.

"Aye. When will Cruthin come so you can call down the gods?"

Cruthin. The ceremony. Sirona was startled to realize she'd forgotten the reason for coming to this place. She closed her eyes, struggling to sort out her thoughts. Somehow, she had to regain control. There was magic in the air, great power. But if no one directed and guided the force, it would end up wasted.

She decided she must find Druem. As the leader of the Old Ones, maybe he could help her gather the people together to begin the ceremony. She opened her eyes and scanned the area around the perimeter of the fire, wondering where the other Old Ones had gone. Perhaps they were near the musicians.

Even as she took a step in that direction, she experienced a prickling sensation along her spine and a sudden wind swept across the summit. It swirled around the dancers, tearing at their hair and making the fire leap and scatter sparks. Sirona backed away to avoid the flying ashes. The wind seemed to have blown the clouds across the moon. Except for the area immediately around the fire, everything was dark.

The musicians stopped playing and she could hear people talking in anxious voices. Sirona felt a stirring of fear. Something was happening. Another force had arrived, a different kind of magic. It banished the mood of revelry and celebration, replacing the atmosphere of light, harmony and contentment with apprehension and dread. Darkness overcoming light. Cold, swirling air banishing the warmth of the fire. The lilting melody was replaced by the wild, restless voice of the wind.

Rufus grabbed her arm. "Look!" he cried.

A shaft of moonlight escaped the clouds, shining down on the circle of stones. In the center of the circle was a huge, dark shape. Sirona's breathless dread increased. Then she realized it was Cruthin standing there. The wolfskin mantle draped over his shoulders made him appear much larger than a normal man.

She watched him stretch his arms up to the sky. "Mother of the heavens, queen of the stars, be with us!" he cried.

At his words, the clouds shifted and the moon's silver light again shone down on the hilltop. Around her, people gasped in awe. Sirona felt the familiar tingling sweep over her body.

Arianrhod's light flowed over Cruthin's face, revealing every graceful line. He threw off the wolfskin mantle, and Sirona saw that he wore a small shimmering cape around his shoulders. The cape seemed to be made up of small pieces of gold linked together, almost like the scales of a fish. It sparkled as he moved, reflecting the moon's light in dazzling patterns all around. He began to sing, and the drummers and other musicians joined in as accompaniment, softly at first, then gaining volume as they became more certain of the cadence of the song. His voice was all that Sirona remembered, deep and stirring. The timbre of it tore at her heart, making her want to weep.

He called out to the great goddess, invoking her by all the traditional names—Arianrhod, Ceridwen, Rhiannon, Modren, Cyhiraeth, Blodeuwedd. It was almost like a love song, as if he enticed a woman. He sang of the Goddess's sweet breath moving over the land, of her body, lush and bountiful, of her beautiful moon face, serene and glowing, blessing her children with silver light. Light to guide their way. Light to fill their hearts.

His voice rose and fell. The people listened, silent, unmoving, frozen like the standing stones that surrounded Cruthin. Finally, he ended his song and lifted up his arms once more to the heavens. The music halted. The wind stopped. The world seemed breathless, waiting.

Sirona. Come to me. She heard the words in her head, though she was certain Cruthin hadn't spoken. She walked toward him, drawn to him as powerfully as ever. His face was beautiful in the moon's light, a stark, handsome mask. "Be my consort," he said as she neared him, speaking aloud this time, but so softly only she could hear him. "Take off your gown and join me in the sacred circle."

She knew a twinge of embarrassment, thinking of being naked before all these people. But she told herself there was nothing to be ashamed of. The female form was beautiful and powerful, the essence of the Goddess. She pulled her gown over her head and dropped it to the ground, then stepped into the circle next to Cruthin. He eyed the amulet hanging between her breasts. Then his gaze dropped to her loins. "I have something for you," he said. He reached up and removed a portion of the golden cape, then knelt down and fastened the shimmering piece around her hips, so it covered her groin.

His hands caressed her gently as he arranged the links of gold, then he looked up at her, smiling faintly. "From your womb shall come the future, a blending of the blood of the Old Ones and the Pretani. No other people shall be able to defeat the magic we create this night. The power we evoke will linger over this place for thousands of years. No one can come here and not be touched by this force. Those who don't understand it will eventually leave. No matter what the invaders do, to this land, to our people, we will heal, even as the land heals. Trees and grasses will cover the scars left behind by buildings and roads, and our spirits will renew themselves. The force that is within us will not die, but spread out through the world, to wherever our people travel. The power of the Goddess will reign in our hearts forever."

Cruthin rose, and the drummers resumed a low, pounding beat. As the harpist and pipers took it up, Cruthin began to dance. He twirled and dipped, his feet moving in a complex pattern. His eyes were closed, his head thrown back, his expression intent.

His movements grew faster and then became jerky and violent. He began to twirl around rapidly, crying out in a harsh voice. No words, only moans, screams, grunts. Raw sounds like an animal might make, and yet there was a rhythm to it, as if it were some strange new language. Or a very old one. Sirona had the sense she had experienced a moment like this in the past. That this rite was ancient.

Abruptly, Cruthin reached out and grabbed her hands, making her part of his dance. As he whirled her around, she saw that everyone gathered on the hillside was dancing in a circle outside the perimeter of the standing stones. Many of Cruthin's tribe and the Old Ones had shed their garments. The naked bodies of the Old Ones were painted with symbols, spirals and circles and arrow designs. She remembered her first vision and knew that it had come to pass.

A powerful energy swirled around them, invisible at first, then turning into light. Cruthin twirled faster, dragging her with him into the radiance. Everything was a blur. The light grew even brighter. Brighter and brighter. Abruptly, Cruthin released her. She grabbed for him but caught nothing but empty air. It was as if he had vanished. She groped with her hands, unable to see anything in the blaze of light, unable to find him.

Suddenly, the light was gone. She blinked. She was in another place. On a kind of shore. She could see waves in the distance. And yet, she wasn't sure it was water, but some other sparkling stuff. The sun was very low in the sky. But it was a deep red sphere, nothing like the sun she remembered. She started to turn, to look back toward the land, and all at once she was falling.

Sirona felt her spirit leave her body and float up into the sky, past the moon and toward the stars. She closed her eyes as their light blinded her. All at once she was falling, but she knew no fear. Her descent was slow and gradual. She opened her eyes and saw stars all around. Then she looked down.

A bolt of surprise shot through her as she saw her own body floating in the vastness of space. She observed the features of her face, relaxed into a mask of sleep, and the pallor of her limbs. A memory flashed through her, of being a child and running free in a flower strewn meadow. Even as she had the thought, her bodily self began to transform until she was a small girl with hair as fine as swan's down and round blue eyes. She relived the breathless excitement of being a child, when every day was full of wonder and newness, as well as disappointment and pain. She felt herself struggling to grow up, the desperate urge to become a woman.

But her form did not return to adulthood. Instead, it shrank further, to a tiny babe, wet and curled up, as if she was still in her mother's belly. Then, to her dread, the babe grew smaller and smaller. It became an odd mass, a soft, deformed sort of sea creature with a great staring black eye on the side of its head. It shrank further, until she could scarce see it. Dread overwhelmed her. She feared her physical essence would disappear altogether.

But a tiny particle of light remained and it blossomed and grew. Much more rapidly than it had shrunk, her body was reborn and developed, until she saw herself reach adulthood, then pass beyond. She watched her hair turn white, her skin shrivel, her body grow wizened and twisted until it curled once more into the shape of a babe in the womb.

Then, slowly, her flesh faded away, leaving only bones. Gradually even they became a cloud of white dust floating in the blackness. The dust seemed to glow, as if it were not dust at all, but points of light, stars in the heavens.

Sirona watched in amazement. This was her self, her whole life from beginning to end. How strange that she had come from light and would return to it. Strange and somehow comforting. She would never fear death again.

But then, what if she was dead already? She couldn't feel any attachment to her body, left behind on the hillside by the circle of stones. Using her thoughts, she sought her physical self. Looking down, she saw a glowing orb, and realized that this was the earth. She was surprised to understand that what she had imagined as a flat expanse of land and water was really a vast sphere. In the half-darkness of the heavens, the earth shone almost as bright as a full moon. She was still falling slowly, drifting downward into the realm of stars. Eventually, she would reach the earth. Perhaps then she would be reunited with her body.

* * *

Bryn gestured to the black dots moving through the green gold vegetation at the other end of the valley.

"How many do you think there are?" Corrio asked.

Bryn squinted. Today they weren't hunting game, but seeking out the missing Tarisllwyth cattle. "Maybe a score of cows with calves and a few yearlings. Enough to re-establish the herd. Although it's a pathetic amount compared to the vast number my people once possessed."

"How do we capture them?" Balthar asked.

"We simply drive the animals back to a pasture near the dun. If we're fortunate, the cows are still giving milk, which the women can use to make cheese. Then, later in the fall, we'll butcher the yearlings, all except one bull for breeding."

"How will we drive them back to the dun?" Corrio asked.

"We'll need help. I'll go and fetch some of the stronger women and the older children. By shouting and waving sticks, we should be able to get them moving. The more of us there are, the easier it will be to manage the beasts. A pity there are no dogs left at Mordarach. They're very useful for herding cattle. But the Romans have a passion for hunting hounds, and Rhyell told me she traded every dog at Mordarach for grain."

351

Corrio nodded. "It's strange there are no men here, except for the elderly and children. Did the Romans really slaughter all of them?"

Bryn thought of the place on the top of a nearby hill where the bones of his people were traditionally buried. If he went there, how many fresh graves would he find?

"My mother told me that as of last sunseason, there were several young men living here. But a little while later, they left to join a man called Cruthin. It seems he has assembled some sort of warband." Bryn tried to imagine his former companion leading a troop of warriors into battle. It seemed very odd. Cruthin knew next to nothing about fighting or weapons.

Thoughts of Cruthin immediately turned Bryn's mind to Sirona. Where was she? Was she safe? The familiar dread pierced him. Almost as he had the thought, he saw someone running towards them. The scrawny youth had reddish hair and huge dark eyes.

Recognition struck Bryn. *It was Rufus!*

Rufus halted before Bryn, his face flushed and dripping with sweat. He drew in a gasping breath, and then spoke. "You must come with me. Sirona needs you."

* * *

It's so beautiful, Sirona thought as her spirit neared the glistening sphere of the earth. It shone iridescent in the vastness of space, as rare and magical as the gleaming body of a blue-green dragonfly. Gradually, she drifted near enough to see the shape of the land and the sea, to observe how immense this world was. Albion was but a tiny scrap compared to the other huge masses of land. Surrounded by the sea, cradled by water on all sides, her homeland took shape before her, like a jewel in the setting of a brooch.

She floated down and down, until she could see the mountains of the sunset lands, stark mounds of rocky earth guarding emerald green valleys, the paler green of the foothills, and then the lowlands of the east, a mixture of trees and rich pastureland, a wild, teeming world.

Like a gyrfalcon, her spirit flew over this great realm. She sailed over the great mountain Yr Wyddfa, proud sentinel of the sunset lands. Then north to Brigante territory, the midnight lands of still lakes and dark forests, lonely moors and rocky coasts. And south to the rich pasturelands crossed with trackways. She saw a great circle of standing stones, and a white horse carved in the hillside above a rich valley.

Beyond the sunrise sea were more lands, strange places with foreign tribes, huge settlements, vast realms stretching on and on, all to the way to Rome and even farther. Whole worlds she knew nothing of. Peoples and animals, strange and fantastic.

She drew back, reluctant to envision these unknown places, feeling overwhelmed and lost. The earth was so huge, and yet it was but one tiny speck in the firmament of the heavens. All of the settlements of all the people in the world were like anthills scattered over an enormous valley. How could she, one frail human, hope to alter this immense pattern surrounding her?

She saw herself again as but a fleck of light among the endless heavens. It would take nothing to quench it, for her spirit to be swallowed by the darkness. As she had the thought, she felt herself falling. Not toward the earth, the bright green of her homeland, but into a void of emptiness. Her spirit seemed to shrivel and fade, and she sensed that off in the world of the living, her body was dying.

* * *

"How long has she been like this?" Bryn demanded as he stared at Sirona's pale, still face. She lay wrapped in blankets in a hastily erected hut of tree branches not twenty paces away from a circle of standing stones. The hillside where the stones were overlooked a huge, open bay.

"It's been three days—since the night of the ceremony," Rufus answered.

"Why didn't you bring her back to Mordarach?" Bryn asked.

"The Old Ones said we shouldn't move her from this place. That this was where her spirit would seek out her body."

Bryn grunted. On the journey to the coast—during which they'd both nearly ridden their mounts to death—Rufus had told him what had happened to Sirona, explaining the purpose of the ceremony and the events of that night. He'd also told Bryn about the tribe called the Old Ones and their part in the ceremony.

"Tell me again," Bryn said. "You say Cruthin vanished. What do you mean? Do you think he ran away while no one was watching, or do you suggest something else?"

"I mean, he vanished. Gone. One moment he was there and the next he was not."

"But if there was all this light around and everyone was dancing... You said yourself that the beverage the Old Ones brought made your wits disordered and confused." He fixed Rufus with a stern look. "Isn't it possible that Cruthin simply made it appear he had vanished?"

Rufus shook his head miserably. "I don't know why it matters. I don't care where Cruthin has gone. I never thought it was good for Sirona to be around him anyway. He manipulates people. Even as strong as she is, she gave into him."

Bryn sighed. "I can't help thinking that if we could find Cruthin, he might be able to help us get Sirona back."

"Back from *where*?" Rufus asked, his dark eyes wide with foreboding.

"The realm of the spirits, I suppose." Bryn gestured helplessly. "I know little enough of these matters."

"But Sirona said you trained in the grove. That you were a Learned One like her."

"Oh, aye, I spent many days in the grove of the Drui, but I didn't pay much attention to my teachers. For that matter, I don't recall them ever mentioning anything like this. It was Cruthin who always talked about his spirit leaving his body and traveling to other worlds."

Bryn reached out and touched Sirona's face. Her cheek felt cold. Despair grabbed his heart and squeezed. He took a deep breath, trying to decide what to do. Rufus had brought him here, hoping he could save Sirona. But how was he to help her? He turned to the slave boy. "Where are the Old Ones now?"

"I don't know. They must have gone back to their homes."

"And where is that?"

Rufus shook his head. "They live in underground dwellings, built into the hills. That's what Sirona told me, although I've never seen evidence of such places."

"We have to find them. They might be the only ones who can help us."

"I'm not certain even they can aid her. In the morning after the ceremony, when I tried to rouse Sirona and couldn't, I found the leader of the Old Ones waiting nearby on the hillside. I begged him to help me call Sirona back to life. He looked at me in that cold, emotionless way his people have and said it was up to the Goddess whether Sirona's spirit returned to this world."

"Curse the Old Ones! Curse all of them!" Bryn turned and pushed his way out of the shelter. He stood there for a time, shaking with the force of his emotions. His hands were clutched into fists and he longed to strike someone or something, to find some way to release the terrible frustration inside him. "I won't accept that she's gone," he said. "The Goddess can't have her. She's too young. She has too many years left to live. And I... I need her." He breathed the last words as tears filled his eyes.

Rufus came out and stood beside him. Bryn considered wiping the wetness from his cheeks, but refrained from doing so. Let this youth understand that it was no shame for a warrior to weep. He'd known more than a few brave men to sob openly over a fallen companion.

"You love her, don't you?"

"Aye," Bryn answered fiercely. "I would do anything for her."

"So would I," Rufus agreed. "But I sense your feelings run even deeper than mine. You grew up with her, shared all those years together. I understand how you feel about her, for when I lost my sister, I felt as if I would die of the pain."

Bryn nodded, his throat tight. If he looked back, it seemed his whole life had been entwined with Sirona's. Despite having spent nearly four years away from her, the moment he'd seen her in the Boudica's palace, his feelings for her had been as strong as ever. If only he'd known then what dangers she faced. That it wasn't the Romans or even the Learned Ones he had to worry about, but Sirona's connection to the gods and the realm of the Otherworld that threatened her life. How did he call Sirona back? How did he reach out for her when her spirit was so far away? He turned to go back into the shelter.

"What are you doing?" Rufus asked.

"I'm going to try to rouse her," he answered.

"Don't you think we've tried that!" the slave boy cried shrilly. "The first day, I shook her and called her name until I was hoarse. I might as well have been trying to raise the dea..." He clapped a hand over his mouth.

"But she's not dead," Bryn said. He clenched his jaw so tightly it ached, and told himself that it was true. As long as she still breathed and the blood flowed through her veins, there was hope.

He pushed into the shelter. Grabbing up Sirona, he cradled her limp form against his own body. She felt so small and fragile. It made him want to weep all over again. But even though her flesh was cool against his, it wasn't cold, and when he put his fingers to her throat, he felt a pulse, faint but steady. He took a deep breath and began to stroke her face. "Sirona," he whispered. "Come back to me. Come back to *us*. We need you. The whole world needs you. Your strong, brave spirit. Your generous heart.

"Rufus told me about the ceremony, about your plan to cast a spell over the sunset lands, to protect your people from the Romans. If you don't come back, you'll never know if you have succeeded. I believe you've worked great magic here, and that your powers are great enough to do miraculous things. But in order for the enchantment to work, we need you here, in the world of the living." He took another ravaged breath. "Sirona, you may speak to the gods and call down the moon, but you aren't a goddess. You're a woman. You belong to the earth. We need your spirit here, with us. Come back! Come back!"

* * *

Her spirit passed through waves of darkness, through a mist so dense she couldn't see. At last she reached the earth. But was it the earth, or some other place? She saw a boggy wasteland. A mist clung to the ground, swirling around her in eerie, gray shapes. She could see faces and bodies in the haze. Spirits, she thought. This must be the realm of the dead. Nothing was alive here.

She floated over hillocks of dead grass and twisted, dead tree trunks thrusting up out of pools of gloomy black water. Gazing down into the dark depths, she saw bodies in the murk, the forms and features of the people untouched by decay. Some of them grimaced, as if their features were frozen in a moment of suffering. Others appeared calm and peaceful. They hovered beneath the water, bloodless and pale.

She searched their faces until she saw the girl with the shorn hair who been sacrificed at the lake of the dead. The familiar pity and horror filled her. This was the realm of the dead whose spirits lingered among the living, those who could not cross over to the Other Side. A terrible place, full of grief and suffering… and anger.

She didn't want to stay here, and yet she feared she belonged to this realm. As long as her body stayed on the hillside by the standing stones, her spirit would never be free. A sense of despair came over her, and it was as if her spirit took tangible form. She could feel her limbs and the ground beneath her feet. The dark oozing earth was sucking her down. Down, down into the rank blackness of death. She started to run. She must keep moving. But there was nowhere to go. The bog was endless, stretching on forever. Still she ran, panic gripping her. Was there no escape? No way out of this place?

She saw someone ahead of her, a woman with dark gold hair. The woman was not running, but walking slowly and deliberately, her bare feet floating over the surface of the bog. The woman turned, and Sirona knew it was her mother. Banon's expression was so melancholy, it made Sirona's heart twist in her chest.

"Go back," Banon said. "Go back." She gestured in the direction Sirona had come from. "He calls for you. He loves you."

"Who?" Sirona whispered. In some vague part of her thoughts, she knew that her mother didn't mean Cruthin. Cruthin was gone. She'd seen him vanish, his form disappearing into the silver wheel of light.

"The one they call Bryn." Her mother frowned. She appeared impatient. "Go back. Before it's too late."

"How can I trust you?" Sirona asked, and then hated herself for saying the words.

But Banon only smiled, a sad, bitter smile. "I didn't love you enough to save you, but this man does. Search your heart. You know it's true." Then she reached out, her long, elegant fingers touching Sirona's arm. "Hurry. There's not much time." Her voice seemed infinitely gentle, and her face was so beautiful. No wonder all those men had loved her. Sirona didn't want to leave her mother. Hadn't she waited all her life for her mother to look at her like this, to gaze upon her with tenderness?

Abruptly, Banon's expression altered. Her expression was once again cruel and mocking, the way Sirona remembered from her Seeing. "Go," she said. "There's no place for you here. This world belongs to me."

Sirona stared at her mother, seeing the coldness in Banon's gray eyes, the selfish, grasping spirit beneath the exquisite features. Then the image wavered, and she saw a glimpse of the warmth once again. She realized her mother was trying to help her.

"Go," Banon whispered, and Sirona heard the longing beneath the word. Her mother was very lonely in this gloomy, desolate realm, and yet she cared enough for Sirona to send her away.

Sirona started off, and then turned to look at her mother one last time. "Some day you will have another chance," she said. "You will live another life."

Banon smiled sadly. "But I won't be beautiful in that life. And I'm not yet ready for that."

Sirona nodded and moved away. Now she understood a little of this realm. Those who came here had to learn something from their past lives before they could return to the world of the living. Banon had finally learned to love, but she was still too vain to give up her beauty. How many years would she dwell here? Sirona wondered. But, then, time meant nothing here. The past and the future all blended together. Some of the faces she saw in this place might belong to people as yet unborn.

She shivered at the thought and walked on. With each step, she grew more aware of her body. Her arms and legs, which had seemed frail and insubstantial, gradually gained form and substance. The bog slowly turned into a marshland, a world of greenery and life. The sweet scent of grass and leaves filled her nose. Copper and blue butterflies fluttered in the moist, warm air, and birdsong surrounded her. The pools of water receded and the ground became solid. The vegetation thickened. Clumps of alder and willow turned to hazel and elm and oak. She was in a forest, stepping carefully among the deadfall, fern and bracken and canebrake crunching underfoot. There was the sound of water, a faint, laughing melody. She started toward the sound and found the source. Moss and dainty white dewdrop flowers grew around the rocky edge of the little pool the bubbling spring had formed.

She knelt beside the pool and dipped her hand into the water and drank of the cool sweetness. Then, because she'd grown sweaty and hot on the walk there, she cupped more water into her hands and splashed it on her face. The coldness of the water shocked her. She gasped and wiped the excess wetness from her eyes. When she opened them, she saw Bryn's face, his rust brown eyes gazing upon her face with an expression of awe—and then, almost instantly—joy.

Chapter 33

"Oh, Bryn, you're alive!" Sirona cried. Sitting up, she saw she was in a hut built of branches with a grass floor. Abruptly, it all came back to her: The ceremony on the hillside. Cruthin's disappearance. Her journey to the spirit realm. She shook her head, trying to sort things out. Then she looked at Bryn. "How did you get here? How did you know where to find me?"

"Rufus came and got me."

"Where were you?"

"Mordarach. You told me to go there, and I did."

Sirona let out a sigh of relief. Bryn had listened to her. He hadn't perished. Then her thoughts returned to what she'd just experienced. "You won't believe where I've been," she said. "The things I've seen…"

Bryn spoke sharply. "You can't go back there. You nearly died."

She nodded. "Don't worry. The realm of the dead isn't an appealing place. And yet, I think the journey most people's spirits make is much different than the one I made. I think a part of me was searching for my mother, and so I went to the realm where her spirit dwells."

"Your mother?" Bryn frowned at her.

"Aye. I saw her. She told me to return to the world of the living. She said you loved me and so I must return to you." She reached to touch his face, the hard square shape of his jaw, the rough stubble of his chin, the coarse hair of his ruddy mustache. A warrior, with fierce brown eyes full of fire. And yet those eyes could look tender and melting, as they did now. "Kiss me, Bryn," she whispered.

The feel and taste of him was much different than that of Cruthin. Bryn was earth and sunshine, the warmth of the hearth fire and the heat of the sun, while Cruthin had been moonlight and mystery and darkness. Instead of lean muscles and a dancer's grace, this man felt strong and powerful. His mouth tasted sweet, his skin, salty with sweat. With his tawny hair and rippling muscles, he reminded her of a wildcat or panther. Fierce and sleek and deadly, and yet like Rhyell's pet cat, Myglyd, he could be content curled up by the fire. He would let her stroke and caress him and hold him close to her heart.

She did so now, and couldn't help smiling when he made a sound almost like a purr.

"Bryn?" They were interrupted when Rufus poked his head into the shelter. "Bryn, I…"

Sirona heard the youth's sudden exhalation. "It's all right, Rufus," she told him. "I'm back."

"But how…?"

Sirona smiled at Rufus. "I realized it wasn't my time yet to leave this realm."

"Thank the Goddess!" Rufus let out a whoop of delight. He withdrew from the shelter and they could hear him rapidly and ecstatically explaining things to someone outside. "She's back!" he cried. "She's back among us." In seconds, he thrust his face in again. "But what about the spell? Did it work? Do you know yet?"

Sirona shook her head. "There's no way to know. For now, I think it best that we return to Mordarach." She crawled out of the shelter and got to her feet. Bryn followed her. Everyone around them began to cheer.

All the Amddifallwyth were there. And on the perimeter of the gathering, the Old Ones waited, watchful and solemn as always, although Sirona thought she detected a glimmer of a smile on some of their faces. She took Bryn's hand and led him toward them. She felt him tense as he saw their weapons. "Don't worry," she whispered to him. "They won't harm us."

Druem moved to the front of the gathering. He made the hand-to-forehead gesture to Bryn, and then bowed to Sirona. "Lady," he said. "You've journeyed far, but we're pleased you're back among us."

"I'm pleased to be here. I want you to meet a man of my people, called Bryn. He's the one who called me back." Druem scrutinized Bryn, and she could tell the leader of the Old Ones was as uneasy with Bryn as he was with them. "This man is my mate," she told Druem. "I will bear his children, and he will keep them safe so they grow up strong and vigorous. He will lead my tribe and defend them against the Romans. From his blood, and mine, will spring a new generation, who will rule the sunset lands for years to come."

Druem didn't speak for a time. Then he said, "Aye, he will do all those things, but it won't be his blood that rules, but that of his rival's. Have you told him that? Is he willing to nurture and protect another man's child? Does he love you enough for that?"

Sirona suddenly felt cold. When she awoke and saw Bryn, the future had seemed wonderfully clear. But she'd forgotten about the night she mated with Cruthin. The ultimate purpose of sex was not a joining of spirits, but combining the male and female essence to create offspring, flesh and blood. Now Druem was telling her she carried Cruthin's child, and she knew it was so.

Bryn hadn't spoken or moved since Druem spoke the fateful words, and Sirona was afraid to look at him. Afraid to see jealousy and pain darkening his eyes. It seemed very harsh that he must face the truth like this, in front of everyone. What could she say to ease his resentment? Now that he knew she carried Cruthin's child, would Bryn turn away from her? Did he love her enough to make such a sacrifice?

His deep voice rang out beside her, "I'll raise as my own whatever child she bears. For she will bear my children also. She will be my consort and my wife. My queen. As powerful as Sirona is, she needs me. Without me, she can't found this dynasty you speak of. It matters not whose blood the child in her womb carries. He will be my son, and I will protect him with my life."

Sirona felt the tingling along her spine and for a moment, the scene on the hillside vanished. She saw a young woman walking along a northern coast, among the rocks and mist. The woman was sly and fey and beautiful like Cruthin, and when she smiled, Sirona knew that her first born would also carry some of Banon's traits. Then the mist grew thick and she saw no more.

She turned to look at Bryn. "I don't carry a boy child, but a girl."

Bryn gazed back at her, an expression of awe on his face.

Druem said, "Remember, the future is always more complicated than we imagine. Life is tangled and twisted, like the branches of a hazel tree, and sharp with thorns like a hawthorn bush. Sometimes it gives berries that are sweet and nourishing, and sometimes they are as poisonous as black bryony. It changes with every thought and action that you have. Even you, with your visions, can't really know what is to come." He raised his hand to his forehead. "Fare you well, Lady. Remember our promise to you and to the child you carry. If you need us, we will be there."

The Old Ones turned away and moved off across the ridge. When they reached the circle of standing stones, they seemed to vanish. "By Arianrhod!" Bryn exclaimed. "Who are they?"

"The Old Ones, the ancient race. A long time ago, one of their women mated with a god. Now magic flows in their blood."

Beside her, Bryn shuddered. "I know they honor you and have vowed to protect you, but still…" His voice trailed off.

"You'd rather not see them again?" Sirona finished for him.

"Aye."

"You probably won't, at least not that tribe. The ones who live along the coast, Pellan's people, they're much more comfortable with us. But the Old Ones of the hills are secretive and wary. You might live all your life in these lands and never encounter them."

"Which would suit me very well," Bryn said fervently. "Although I'm glad they aided you and have vowed to protect you in the future. For I know there are things I can't defend you from."

"But it was you who called me back from death," Sirona said, smiling. "Your love and loyalty that gave me the strength and will to escape the darkness of that realm."

He smiled back at her and then pulled her against his broad chest. "Ah, Sirona, I love you so much."

* * *

They ate more of the food stolen from the Romans for the ceremony and then set out for Mordarach. Sirona rode in front of Bryn on a massive Roman horse he told her he'd acquired on his way to his homeland. Cradled in his strong arms, she decided she liked riding. Along the way, Bryn told her everything that had happened since he left the sunrise lands. How he'd gone to Camulodunum with Boudica's army and his dismay at the slaughter. About being injured and Cadwalon rescuing him. How he'd finally parted company with Cadwalon and headed to the sunset lands, and on the way, encountered two runaway slaves, who'd helped him overpower a small group of Romans and steal their horses. He didn't mention anything about the great battle, although all of Sirona's instincts told her that it would happen soon.

They stopped for the night in a rugged valley and camped near a clear, cool stream that rushed along between the rocks and finally tumbled along a narrow gorge, forming a small waterfall. She and Bryn climbed down to gaze upon the glistening veil of water, surrounded by mist and moss and small dark pine trees. The air seemed incredibly fresh here, as if the split in the earth revealed the Mother's deepest, wildest spirit.

That night Sirona dreamed she returned to the circle of the stones upon the hillside and below, where the river met the sea, she saw a fortress. It looked neither Pretani nor Roman, but a mixture of both. A troop of warriors rode toward the fortress. They wore checked and patterned clothing and brooches whose curving lines reminded her of the ones Hyell had made. Their long braided hair and bold mustaches looked familiar as well. She woke with a sense of satisfaction, believing the spell she and Cruthin had woven over the highlands had accomplished what they'd hoped. Her vision of the sunset lands of the future had revealed a world far more Pretani than Roman.

When Bryn woke beside her, she told him this and he pulled her close and made love to her. Afterwards, with her body still throbbing from the aftermath of his thunderous passion, she realized his blood would also survive in the future. Perhaps not in the sunset lands, but elsewhere. In the midnight lands, or even in the land of the Scoti, across the western sea.

They continued their journey back to Mordarach and arrived before dusk. Everyone came out to meet them. Rhyell embraced Bryn as if she would never let go. Then, she released him and gathered Sirona in her arms, thanking her for bringing him back.

They assembled in the hall, where they ate the remainder of the grain and fruit stolen from the Romans. Bryn decreed that the next night they would celebrate properly. One of the steers they had herded back to Mordarach would be slaughtered, and they would have a feast like in the old days.

After eating, Sirona and Bryn retired to the private portion of the hall, which Rhyell insisted now belonged to them. Sirona stretched out on the large bedplace and looked around, observing the few luxuries Rhyell had refused to barter off to the Romans—the woven wall hangings in the tribal colors of blue and green, a carved wooden bench, a table with a pottery oil lamp, the reed mat that covered the earth floor, the rich furs—wildcat and bear—that cushioned the bedplace.

Compared to the extravagant furnishings she'd seen in Boudica's palace and Calpurnius's villa, these few items of comfort and beauty seemed paltry. Yet, this was the life Banon had coveted. Sirona's mother had longed to be mistress of this place, to possess the authority and status of being the wife and consort of the chieftain of the Tarisllwyth. Odd to think that Sirona had ended up in the very situation her mother had sought so passionately.

It gave her a kind of chill thinking about these things. Her mother had been foolish and never really understood the things that were important. Power and authority, comfort and luxury—those were not what made a person happy. What mattered were love and connection and a sense of belonging. Over time, the material objects in this room would rot and disintegrate, even as the buildings and possessions of the Romans would one day fall to dust. All that would be left was the land itself, and the memories and dreams and feelings that people carried in their hearts and passed on to their children.

That was what was truly important about the Learned Ones. They'd provided a means for carrying the essence of her people into the future. Somehow, she and Bryn and Ogimos and the few others who were left must continue on with that purpose. They must not let the spirit of the Pretani die. She thought of the babe growing inside her. Through her and Cruthin, the child would carry the blood of the Old Ones. But it wasn't enough. Their daughter must also be raised in the sacred tradition of the grove. To her must be passed on all the knowledge possessed by the Learned Ones still left living.

Bryn, who'd been moving restlessly around the room, came to the bedplace and stretched out next to her. "What are you thinking?" he asked.

"I'm thinking about the future."

"Aye," he answered. "I am also. We have the beginnings of a new herd of cattle, and enough horses to breed mounts for riding. Between Cruthin's followers and the former slaves who've joined us, there are enough men to rebuild the dun. Gwrgi has promised to teach someone— whoever has the most aptitude for it—how to forge iron and do basic metalwork, and there are others who know tanning and leatherwork. There are a few sheep in the territory east of here that didn't get carried off by the Romans. The people who herd them were my father's clients. I'll ask them for a tribute of raw wool, so that my mother and her women can keep busy at their looms."

"Your plans suggest that you intend to remain here at Mordarach."

He nodded, and then gazed at her questioningly. "Have you had any visions of the future of our tribe? Will we be safe?"

Sirona nodded. "For a time, at least. After they prevail against the Pretani in the great battle, the Romans will be busy in the south and east, rebuilding what Boudica's army destroyed. I don't think they'll bother us for several years. Which is a relief," she added, smiling. "I really don't want to do any more traveling, at least not until the next sunseason."

She placed her hand on her belly, which remained as flat as ever. Bryn put his hand over hers. "Aye, it will be good to stay in this place where we grew up." His brown eyes met hers, warm and intent. "We'll remain here until the babe is born, and perhaps another one is conceived."

Sirona laughed. "You have such plans for me. Carrying a child and giving birth and raising it for the first few years is no easy task, and already you talk of a second babe." Her smile faded. "Is that because you won't be content until I bear a child of your blood?"

Bryn leaned near, his brown eyes glowing. "Nay, I have you, which satisfies me as nothing else could. You are my future, everything I've dreamed of."

Chapter 34

Sirona sat in the grove under the shelter of the autumn gold oaks. Around her were Llewan and Talhern from Cruthin's band, as well young Eleri and Anwyl, who'd also expressed interest in training as Learned Ones. She'd just finished explaining the different aspects of the Goddess when Bryn appeared.

"We have visitors," he announced. "Rhyell is preparing a feast. Thank the gods that we've just finished the butchering and have several carcasses available."

"What sort of visitors?" Sirona asked.

"You'll find out soon enough," Bryn responded.

They all started down the pathway to the dun. Joining Bryn, Sirona said, "It's not like you to be so mysterious. Won't you tell me who these visitors are?" When Bryn didn't answer, she grew uneasy. "At least give me a hint of what to expect when we arrive at the dun," she pleaded.

"The visitors aren't people you know. And yet, I think you'll be happy to see them." He shot her a faint smile.

Sirona shook her head and sighed. "I should have some inkling of what awaits me, but I sense nothing. Indeed, I've scarcely had a vision or premonition since the ceremony by the circle of stones. I wonder sometimes if the Goddess's power has left me."

The dun loomed ahead of them. On one side, a stone wall rose to the height of a man's waist. Sirona quickened her pace as they climbed the trackway to the entrance of the dun. *Who were the visitors? What did it mean?* Surely if something awful awaited them, Bryn wouldn't appear so calm. But he might not realize the implications of whatever news the visitors had brought. Thinking such thoughts, she grew breathless and afraid. It worried her that she no longer had visions. And there was something else, something she hadn't told even Bryn. She'd recently sensed a change in the goddess stone. It no longer grew warm when she touched it. She felt more and more certain that the power had left her.

Perhaps it had to do with the babe growing in her belly. Her abilities might have already passed on to her daughter. The idea made her feel very vulnerable. How would she go on without the strong sense of purpose her visions had given her? How would she survive without the Goddess protecting her?

Of course, she had Bryn now. And hopefully, she wouldn't face such dire challenges as she had the past sunseason. If the power had left her, that must mean she no longer needed it. She must trust the Goddess's plan for her.

When they arrived at the feast hall, it was filled with people, including Cruthin's followers, the remaining Tarisllwyth and a group of foreign warriors. The visitors' crys and bracco were so muddy, it was impossible to see what tribal colors they wore. A moment later, Sirona realized it wasn't mud staining their garments, but blood. These men had come from a battle. *The great battle of her vision.*

She grew dizzy and her legs seemed to turn to water. Bryn grabbed her arm and guided her over to a stool by the hearth. The world around her blurred, then gradually returned to normal. When she could see again, her gaze fell upon a short, stocky dark-haired man seated across from her. He watched her with eyes the vivid blue of a kingfisher's feathers.

"Cadwalon ap Cadwyl of the Dobunni," Bryn said, "I present to you Sirona, queen of the Tarisllwyth."

The dark-haired man nodded gravely. "It's a pleasure to meet you, lady."

Sirona struggled to find her voice. "I'm pleased to meet you also. From what I've heard, you've been a great friend to Bryn. I thank you for helping him and looking after him these past years. He said that if not for you, he likely wouldn't be alive."

Cadwalon let out a hearty laugh. "I'm not sure that was always the way of it, but I'll take your thanks, all the same." His gaze met Sirona's, burning into her. "If I'd listened to you, lady, I might have saved myself some suffering." With his left hand, he lifted up his cloak to show his right arm bound against his chest with a strip of cloth. "My failure to heed your warning about the battle with the Romans has cost me dearly. I fear my fighting days are over."

Sirona went still. "It's happened, hasn't it?" she whispered.

Cadwalon nodded. "Only a few of us survived. I shouldn't begrudge the use of my arm when I still have my life... and the use of my legs to walk here."

As she thought about the terrible slaughter, the dizziness afflicted Sirona once again. She shook it off and said, "Tell me." She looked around the hall. "Tell all of us what happened on the plain by the river."

Cadwalon closed his eyes, his face a mask of grief. "We thought we couldn't lose. There were so many of us. By the time we left Londinium, men of every tribe in Albion had joined us. And not merely warriors, but women and children, riding in carts behind the main force." He shook his head. "Gwynceffyl and the others questioned the wisdom of allowing noncombatants to join us. But by then Boudica had no control anyway. She struggled to get the army to leave the southeast, what with all the other Roman settlements and villas ripe for the picking. But she'd grown tired of the slaughter of merchants and old men and their families. She lusted for the blood of Roman soldiers.

"And so, she moved among the army, firing up the warriors' battle lust with tales of Roman humiliations and atrocities. Telling them that if they were free men and not slaves, they must destroy the Roman forces once and for all. She insisted we march north to meet the legions. At the time, it seemed a reasonable plan." He shook his head again. "Even now, I can't understand what happened."

He paused for breath, and his face spasmed with emotion—grief and regret and anger all at once. "I've heard for years of the power and might of the Roman army, of their discipline and methodical way of fighting. I've mocked them for their lack of battle fervor. I thought their lack of passion for their cause would hurt them. But I was wrong."

He grimaced again. "They defeated us with cunning and skill. They fought with grim efficiency, while our forces milled about, disorganized and confused. There were so many of us that it put us at a disadvantage. Untrained men got in the way of those who had some battle experience. I was never able to reach the Roman line. Like all the other men who fought from chariots, I ended up trapped behind those who fell to the Roman javelins.

"And yet, the chariot saved my life. Once my arm was injured and I couldn't fight, I was able to crawl beneath the vehicle and use it for protection. When the Romans broke our ranks and moved among us, killing freely, I pretended to be dead. They passed by me without notice. I'm not proud of it, but I knew by then the battle was lost and I could see no point in dying like that. I waited until nightfall, and then got away by crawling over the fallen. I'll never forget the horror of it. The ground was thick with blood and bodies, warriors and those who had come to watch. The Romans knew what we'd done at Camulodunum and Londinium and they spared no one."

"What about Boudica?" Sirona asked. "What happened to her? Where was she when the fighting began? Did she wield a sword against the enemy?"

"Before the battle she stood on a cart at the back of the army and screamed out taunts and insults to the enemy and exhorted us to bravery. Then, in the heat of combat, I lost track of her. I heard later that when things went against her and she was surrounded by the enemy, she fell on her sword. At any rate, she is dead, as are so many others." Cadwalon gestured to the half dozen men behind him. "We're some of the few warriors left."

"How many Pretani do you think survived?" Sirona asked.

"I saw perhaps three score men." Cadwalon shrugged. "But there must be more. After the battle, everything was confused and disordered, and I was thinking mainly of getting far, far away. Then I came upon these other warriors." He gestured to the men with him. "I realized we would have a better chance of escaping if we banded together."

"But why did you decide to come here?" Sirona asked. "And how did you find your way?"

Cadwalon smiled. "Now that was an odd thing. At first we simply traveled toward the sunset, fleeing blindly. Then I decided to seek out my old friend." He looked at Bryn. "I knew that Mordarach was in the highlands, but I didn't know where. Then a strange thing happened. I fell ill with a fever from my wound, and I had a dream. I dreamed of a great silver wolf with dark eyes. In my dream, I chased the wolf, intending to kill it for its magnificent pelt. It ran and ran and I ran after it. I followed it to a hillfort. When I woke, I knew that the hillfort was Mordarach and I could remember the way I took there in my dream."

Sirona let out the breath she'd been holding. Lovarn. The spirit wolf. She hadn't known he was still influencing events around her.

"It seems clear that I was meant to come here," Cadwalon said. "Although I'm not certain for what purpose. Can you tell me, seeress?"

Sirona sat rigid. This man expected her to foretell his future. But she had no idea what was to come. The power had left her. Yet, she couldn't say that in front of all these people. They depended upon her, nearly worshiped her. Their faith in her abilities was part of what kept them going.

"Are you certain the wound is that serious?" she asked, hoping Cadwalon was wrong about his situation. "If it's only been a few days since the battle, it might be too soon to tell how much use you will regain of your arm."

Cadwalon shook his head. "The Roman's sword cut me open from shoulder to elbow. Cyan here," he gestured to one of his companions, "he sewed me up as best as he could, but the muscles were cut completely and will never function the way they once did. Unless you can do healing magic as well as prophesize the future, there's no hope I will ever fight again."

Sirona nodded. Healing had never been one of her gifts, and now that the power had left her, it seemed even more unlikely she could mend Cadwalon's arm.

"I can't return to my tribe," Cadwalon said, turning to Bryn. "My men would never follow a crippled man."

"Here at Mordarach, we have need of other skills besides those of a warrior," Bryn responded. "You'll always have a place at my hearth, if you wish it." He nodded to Cadwalon's companions. "And the rest of you as well."

Sirona breathed a sigh of relief. Bryn had saved her from having to reveal that she no longer had any sense of what the future held.

Cadwalon grabbed up a nearby drinking cup in his good hand and held it aloft. "Then let us celebrate. To the future of Mordarach, the Tarisllwyth and the rest of the Pretani. We may have lost the battle and many of our warriors, but we are far from defeated."

Sirona rose with the rest of them. Someone handed her a cup and she raised it high as the hall resounded with cheers and exclamations. "To the Pretani!" people cried. "We are not defeated! We will never be defeated!"

Sirona took a swallow of mead, her eyes tearing as the potent liquid burned down her throat. Her heart swelled with a dozen emotions. Pride in her people for their strong, valiant spirits. Joy that so many of them were gathered here. Sadness for those who were lost. Hope for the future. Regret that she had not been able to do more to change the destiny of her race. Amazement at all the things that had happened. Awe at the thought of the life growing within her. And—as she met Bryn's gaze—deep love and satisfaction to know she had found her mate.

She needed him more than ever, now that the power was gone and she was merely a woman. Someday the gods would speak to her again. It might be years, but someday she would feel the energy of Arianrhod, Rhiannon and Cyhiraeth moving through her body, bright as light, keen as the wind, powerful as flowing water. Until then she must savor the magic of this world. Enjoy the pleasures of flesh, rather than yearning for the enchanted realm of the stars. Live in the present, rather than dreaming dreams of the future. The silver wheel of the heavens had turned, bringing her to this moment. She would not waste it.

She took another swallow of mead, raised her cup and let out a jubilant cry.

Dear Readers,

The Silver Wheel is a work of fiction, but even if many aspects have come from my imagination, others are based in history.

The writings of Tacitus and Dios record the Roman version of the destruction of Camulodunum and Londinium by Boudica's forces and the disastrous battle (for the Celtic British) that came after. Both Tacitus and Dios mention signs and portents observed before the destruction of Camulodunum: the Statue of Victory, which would have been part of the provincial altar, fell face down. A vision was seen in the Thames of the devastated colony and the sea was said to take on the color of blood. I have used similar images in Sirona's dramatic prophecy for the colonia.

As Sirona feared, the attacks were truly massacres. Tacitus says "all left behind were butchered, the British took no prisoners, nor did they consider the money they could get for selling slaves, it was the sword, gibbet, fire and cross."

My depiction of Boudica as a villainess rather than a liberator of her people is unorthodox, but she did lead a large number of her countrymen to their deaths and bring about the end of Celtic Britain. If the confrontation between the well-disciplined Roman troops and the combined British military force led by Boudica had *not* taken place, it's possible the Romans might have been worn down by raids and skirmishes and eventually given up and left the island. To some extent, that's what happened in northern Britain, where the Romans finally tired of fighting and built Hadrian's Wall as an acknowledged border of their empire.

Having set out to write a book about what is essentially the end of Celtic culture in Britain, I knew I needed to find something positive and up-lifting, some kernel of hope beyond all the death and destruction. To do that, I had only to look around Britain today. While remnants of Roman buildings and other constructions remain, and aspects of their legal and administrative systems still influence British government (and all Western political entities), the Roman conquerors left virtually nothing else behind, not their language (except as it influenced the later invaders, the Anglo Saxons) nor any religious or cultural beliefs. Nearly 2000 years later, it is the Celtic spirit that remains strong in Britain. Their deep-seated belief in a magical, supernatural realm permeates countless folk legends and has evolved into literary expressions such as the King Arthur tales. It can be argued that the Western (and Christian) concepts of immortality, spiritual transformation and the idealized hero owe more to Celtic belief than any other source. And having visited the highlands of Wales, I can tell you that in this place, where Sirona and Cruthin set their spell of protection millennia ago, the Celtic spirit remains as strong as ever.

Happy reading,

Mary Gillgan

About The Author

Mary Gillgannon writes romance novels set in the dark ages, medieval and English Regency time periods and fantasy and historical novels with Celtic influences. Her print books have been published in Russia, China, the Netherlands and Germany. Raised in the Midwest, she now lives in Cheyenne, Wyoming where she works at the Laramie County Library.

She is married and has two grown children. When not working or writing she enjoys gardening, traveling and reading, of course!

She always enjoys hearing from readers. You can write her at P.O. Box 2052, Cheyenne, WY 82003, or contact her through her website: http://marygillgannon.com.

Made in the USA
Columbia, SC
09 August 2018